3-18(38)
12-19(40)

DUE

TRUE JUSTICE

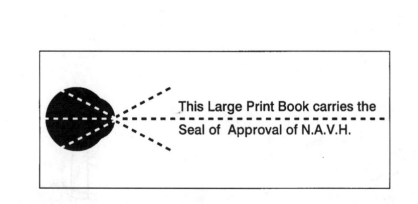

This Large Print Book carries the
Seal of Approval of N.A.V.H.

TRUE JUSTICE

ROBERT K. TANENBAUM

Thorndike Press • Thorndike, Maine

Published in 2001 by arrangement with
Pocket Books, a division of Simon & Schuster, Inc.

Thorndike Press Large Print Mystery Series.

The tree indicium is a trademark of Thorndike Press.

The text of this Large Print edition is unabridged.
Other aspects of the book may vary from the original edition.

Set in 16 pt. Plantin by Rick Gundberg.

Printed in the United States on permanent paper.

Library of Congress Cataloging-in-Publication Data

Tanenbaum, Robert.
    True justice / Robert K. Tanenbaum.
      p. cm.
    ISBN 0-7862-3032-0 (lg. print : hc : alk. paper)
    1. Karp, Butch (Fictitious character) — Fiction. 2. Ciampi, Marlene (Fictitious character) — Fiction. 3. Public prosecutors — Fiction. 4. New York (N.Y.) — Fiction. 5. Trials (Murder) — Fiction. 6. Married people — Fiction. 7. Women lawyers — Fiction. 8. Teenagers — Fiction. 9. Delaware — Fiction. 10. Large type books. I. Title.
PS3570.A52 T78 2001
813'.54—dc21
                                              00-048002

To those most special,
Rachael, Roger, Billy, and Patti
and
to the memory of my boss,
Frank S. Hogan

ACKNOWLEDGMENTS

Again, and yet again, all praise belongs to Michael Gruber, whose genius and scholarship flows throughout and who is primarily and solely responsible for the excellence of this manuscript and whose contribution cannot be overstated.

Special tribute to my early mentors at Berkeley, Professors Jesse Choper and Robert Cole, whose enthusiasm and passion for justice have always inspired me and who make Boalt the best.

Special thanks to three of the best DAs who ever served at the N.Y.D.A.O., Robert Lehner, Mel Glass, and John Keenan, all of whom instilled within me their passion for justice and the process to achieve it.

Also, heartfelt gratitude for my dear friend Richard A. Sprague, the finest trial lawyer in America, whose advice and wisdom have always resulted in True Justice.

1

A Salvadorean Chinese man wearing a red Hebrew National apron with a black-checked *kefiya* around his neck and a Yankees hat on his head — in short, a typical New Yorker — jaywalked across Tenth Avenue at Fifty-second Street, contemplating, like so many of his fellow citizens, a minor offense. He was a food vendor, the January dusk was closing in, and he wanted to dispose of the considerable trash that had collected on his cart after twelve hours of dispensing edible garbage. He was supposed to carry it back to the cart depot, but he was now about to deposit a fat plastic bag in one of the row of trash cans he knew was kept behind the pizza joint across the street. The commercial trash collectors of the city were still recovering from a week of snow and ice, though, and he discovered that the five cans in the alleyway off Fifty-second were full, with bulging black bags stacked around them. The man looked over his shoulder to see whether anyone was watching and lifted up one of the bags. His plan was to secrete his own modest contribution behind one of these stinking blimps. Instead, he froze, goggling, and stumbled backward, knocking over one of the trash cans. Someone else had obviously had the same idea, because a dead baby was lying on top of the trash bag he had uncovered. It was slaty-blue, faceup, the little face shriveled like an old vegetable. It was a boy, with the exaggerated genitals of the neonate, and its long, ropy umbilical cord dragged down into the shadows beneath the trash.

"What's happening?" said a voice in Spanish behind him. A kitchen worker in whites and a cheap black parka stood behind him. The vendor was speechless. The kitchen man said, "Hey, man, what're you doing, kicking over my . . . ," and then he saw the baby, too.

"Oh, shit!" said the kitchen man.

"Oh, shit, is right," said the vendor. He spoke both Spanish and Cantonese and was thus able to converse with nearly every low-level food-service worker in the city.

The kitchen man looked at him narrowly. "You didn't put that baby there, did you?"

"What're you, crazy? I just come here to stash my garbage from the wagon. That baby's been here awhile. Look, it's all blue and stiff."

"Poor little bastard! It's a boy, too," said

the kitchen man. "Hey, man, where're you going?"

The vendor had turned away and was starting back toward Fifty-second. He paused and said, "I got to get back to my wagon, man."

"Hey, but we got to call the cops."

"You got a green card, man?" asked the vendor.

"Yeah, I got a green card."

"Well, you call the cops, then," said the vendor, and walked off.

What followed had happened well over a thousand times in the previous year, and already twenty in the current one, the digestion of a dead human by the bureaucracy established for that purpose. The police arrived, two patrolmen, who secured the crime scene and took an initial report from the kitchen man. Then the crime scene unit arrived in its van and examined the dead baby and its surround for clues. The baby was lying on some paper toweling, and they bagged that. Then the patrol sergeant arrived, and an ambulance from Bellevue, and shortly after that two detectives from the unit assigned to Midtown South. These looked at the baby and the scene and asked questions and found the Chinese Salvadorean vendor and yelled at him a little. Then the ambo took the dead baby away to the morgue. The next morning, an

9

assistant medical examiner autopsied Baby Boy Doe Number One and discovered that it had died of exposure. Since exposing a baby to January weather in New York falls under the section of the homicide statute having to do with death resulting from a depraved indifference to human life, the death was ruled a homicide. The District Attorney's Office for the County of New York — that is, the isle of Manhattan — was duly notified, and thus it came, but only modestly, into the cognizance of the district attorney's chief assistant by means of a pair of lines on a computer printout. This printout was generated by the complaint bureau, an organization that was to the district attorney's office as the little ovoid plastic tube on the top is to the Cuisinart. The lines for Baby Boy Doe Number One indicated that this was a fresh case, that no arrests had been made on it. The chief assistant's name was Roger Karp, called Butch by everyone except his aged aunt Sophie.

Karp's eye moved on to the seventeen other people who had been killed in Manhattan since the beginning of the year. In ten of these, an arrest had been made, and these were naturally of greater interest to him. Karp had been doing this work for over twenty years. He had been a famous homicide prosecutor, and then the chief of the homicide bureau, and now he was the chief assistant district attorney, the operational head of the entire organization. He had not, he hoped, become callous, but he had a lot to do. The murder rate had risen rocketlike in recent years in pace with the citywide crack epidemic, and one more dead baby did not appear just then as pressing a matter as the legions of teenagers then roaming New York with heavy semiautomatic weapons. But he did not forget it, not entirely. Not forgetting the slain of Manhattan was one of his major talents.

That was the first dead baby. The second dead baby was found two days later, on January 12, by a track worker on the Broadway line, just south of the Ninety-sixth Street station. It was wrapped in newspapers and stuffed in a supermarket shopping bag. The complexion of the first dead baby suggested it was Hispanic, and this one was a girl and black. The track worker had called the cops immediately. A different team of detectives arrived, and another crime scene unit arrived, who collected and tagged the newspaper wrapping and the grocery bag. Service on the Broadway line was delayed for several hours, as a result of which the second dead baby created somewhat more of a media stir than the first one had. On autopsy, the second dead

11

baby proved to have been smothered, and thus after the usual grinding, Baby Girl Doe Number One also appeared as a homicide line on Karp's daily computer printout, along with the four other people who had been killed (all drug-related shootings) since the last time he had looked. Baby Girl Doe Number One attracted rather more of his attention than her predecessor. Karp was not a political creature — far from it. Still, Karp understood that the New York DA's office existed in a corrosive bath of media attention, and two murdered babies in a week was perhaps unusual even for the Big Apple. He paused and made a note to give his boss, DA Jack Keegan, a heads-up, so that he would be prepared for any questions should one of the city's many journalists choose to do a bleeding-heart piece.

That note proved, in the event, somewhat de trop, because on January 17, the third dead baby appeared. The third dead baby was different, and different for reasons peculiar to New York. On the late afternoon of that day, a young man named Raul Jimenez, a communications student at the Tisch School of New York University, was walking along 112th Street near Lexington Avenue. He was working on a school assignment, which was to make a three-minute video on "animals in the city." Jimenez had grown up in this neighborhood, had avoided, more or less, the drugs, gangs, and cops, and was now rising, but rising, he felt, with an edge. The other kids were going to do pigeons, puppies, and squirrels, he figured, while he was going to do bad dogs. It had lately become fashionable among the *guapos* on the street to keep large, nasty dogs, pit bulls or ridgebacks or rotties. Given the average life span of this class of person, and their average level of responsibility, many of their pets were abandoned, scavenging in garbage for food, menacing people, and usually ending up gassed in the pound or shot by the police. These feral dogs of Spanish Harlem were Jimenez's subject, and the location he now gingerly approached was a burnt-out building and an adjoining vacant rubble-field, where he knew the beasts congregated.

He heard a scrabbling sound and a growling from the rubble. Slipping through a gap in the ragged chain-link fence, he advanced cautiously, holding his Panasonic VHS camcorder up to his eye. Movement. Louder growling, a real dogfight, now. He came closer, correcting the focus. A white pit bull and an emaciated, mangy young Doberman were fighting over some garbage. The Dobe retreated, snarling. Perfect, thought Jimenez, good action, the contrast between the colors of the dogs, perfect. He used the zoom to close in on the pit bull, at what the dog was eating. Bile rose in his throat, but he kept the camera going. Suddenly the Doberman lunged and grabbed a piece. That was the beauty shot. The pit bull heaved harder and trotted away with its prize, leaving just a small piece for its rival, and vanished down into the weed-grown cellar of the former tenement. Jimenez sat down on the bricks and threw up his lunch. Later that day he brought the tape to his professor, who helped him negotiate the sale to NBC and the *Post*. The network used a doctored version of the tape that evening, with blur zones to water down the awfulness and also on advice from legal, but the *Post* gave it a full front page that evening: under the headline HORROR! a picture of two dogs, one black, one white, tearing apart a baby in the city of New York in the last decade of the twentieth century.

Karp was, as it happened, working late that day. His wife and daughter were out at his daughter's school for some event, and his seven-year-old twin boys were being taken out for pizzas by their nursemaid and her boy-friend. Karp was, in fact, a workaholic, but he thought he had it under control. Yes, he got to work at seven and worked weekends, but he dined with his family nearly every evening and saw his wife and children at least once each day. The job he had — managing a system that ate three hundred thousand serious crimes each year including three murders a day, with over four hundred assistant district attorneys — was frankly impossible to do; it would have consumed any three people. Nor was it one he particularly liked, although he had become fairly good at it. What Karp liked to do was try murder cases, and he was very good at that. With the recent increase in workload, Karp had acquired his own secretary, an Irish girl named Flynn, and a special assistant, a willing infant named Gilbert Murrow, and a nice many-windowed office in the DA's suite on the eighth floor of 100 Centre Street, the New York County courthouse.

Karp had never imagined himself as the sort of person who had special assistants, but he had swiftly become used to the pleasures thereof. Murrow was quiet, efficient, good-humored, and relatively free of the mental diseases to which special assistants were susceptible, such as megalomania and paranoia. He was fresh out of law school but had not taken the bar and was wondering whether, in fact, lawyering was really his thing after all, so this job suited both him and his boss. Murrow lived in a tiny cubicle outside Karp's office, summonable by a bellow.

Karp bellowed now. No answer. He punched the intercom button: "Flynn, where's Murrow?" No answer. He looked at his watch: five past six. They wouldn't have simply gone home without telling him, hence a mystery. Karp rose, stretched; a remarkable sight, this, for he was over six feet five inches tall, still reasonably lanky in his mid-forties. He walked out of his office, observed without surprise that Flynn was not at her desk, and proceeded to the DA's outer office, where he found that Mary Margaret O'Malley, the DA's secretary, was not at her desk either, which was rather more surprising. He recalled that the DA himself was busy upstate at some political do. There were sounds emanating from behind the paneled doors of the DA's office proper. Karp went in.

Murrow, Flynn, O'Malley, and a few other late-staying eighth-floor workers were grouped around the DA's huge TV. Karp noted with astonishment that O'Malley, a hefty woman with jaw and hair of iron, was dabbing at her eyes, although the rumor had it that O'Malley had shed her last tear on the occasion of JFK's assassination. A couple of anchors were on the screen, looking grave. Somebody's been shot, was Karp's immediate thought: the president, the DA . . .

"What's going on, O'Malley?" Karp asked.

"It's horrible, Butch," she said. "Unbelievable, in this day and age. I beeped him already, he should be calling any minute now."

Karp was about to ask again what was going on when the screen changed and flashed the startling *Post* front page: HORROR! Then, a talking head began talking about the decline of morality among the young and conflating the recent years of teenaged gunplay with the murder of babies: now the girls were getting into it, too, was the conclusion. Somebody flicked the remote at the screen, the channel changed to NBC, and Karp got to see the Jimenez tape, slowed down to provide more *news,* the Doberman tearing away a white blur that was clearly a baby's arm. Then the news moved on to other things, and the group stood around the noble office, gasping and murmuring.

Murrow said, to no one in particular, "This is going to be a firestorm. Unbelievable!" Karp felt the eyes of the room on him. He looked at Murrow and frowned unconsciously, both because of the remark and because of Murrow's dress, which was a hairy tweed sports jacket worn over a navy sleeveless sweater, a foulard bow tie, tan whipcord trousers, and shiny Weejuns loafers. This was not how Karp thought junior staff members should dress. (Murrow had shown up for work one day in a red brocade waistcoat with shiny buttons. Karp did not say anything to him about it, but had stared at him throughout that day as if observing a particularly gruesome traffic accident, and the item had not reappeared.) Karp himself was not interested in clothes and always wore the same outfit: a dark, pin-striped, single-breasted suit, of appropriate weight for the season, a white shirt, a tie with some infinitesimal dark pattern, and highly shined black shoes. Despite this civilized apparel, Karp often looked as though he should be unshaven and wearing crossed bandoliers. He had the roundheaded, flat-faced, high-cheekboned, quasi-oriental look of his maternal ancestors, a rapacious band of Odessa Jews, horse traders, petty criminals, and head-breakers. His eyes were gray, with peculiar yellow flecks, and were used to good effect in his famous laser stare. Around the office, Karp was considered cold, and something of a stiff, since he failed to find incompetence amusing. It made him grind his teeth and look fierce and stare unforgivingly. Among his few close friends and with his family, however, Karp was a different man, humorous, a dead-on mimic, boyish, occasionally goofy, a peaceable man actually, and quite even-tempered. It was not his fault that he looked like Ivan the Terrible's first cousin.

(His wife, on the other hand, looked like a Bernini angel, but she had a short fuse and occasionally shot people with a pistol in disagreements. Yet another thing that was not fair.) Meanwhile, Murrow, who did not understand this, writhed under the stare.

"I mean," said he, gulping, "the press is going to be all over this. It's not going to go away."

"And, what? Do you think we should be extrahard on infanticidal mothers because a dead baby got chewed up by dogs on the TV?"

"No, but . . . ," said Murrow, and he concluded weakly, stammering, "but, we have to do, or say, something. Don't we?"

"We do," said Karp. "In about two minutes, Mr. Keegan will be calling here, and he will order me to coordinate the office's response to that garbage. I want you to go down to Bill McHenry's shop and see what they're doing. We'll need a press statement from him tonight, and Mr. Keegan will want to be on one of the morning shows tomorrow, saying something suitably grave and meaningless. Get them to prepare some talking points for that. And, Murrow?" The young man was already preparing to dash. "Stir them up. Public affairs people, you know, they like to sit around in stained bathrobes, chatting to their pals on the phone and eating nougat. Not this time, okay? Let us have zeal."

"Got it. Zeal. No nougat."

Murrow vanished. Karp looked around and made shooing motions. "Go home, people, show's over." The room cleared of everyone but the two secretaries. Karp turned to his and said, "Flynn, why don't you call One PP and find Chief Torricelli for me. Tell him I'd like to discuss the dog problem in the city." Flynn nodded and departed. Karp rolled his eyes at O'Malley and stood like a lawn jockey, his hand out, palm upward. They waited. Almost immediately the phone chirruped. O'Malley picked up the extension on the side table near the TV. She said, "Mr. Keegan's office. . . . Yes, sir, he's right here," and slapped the receiver into Karp's waiting palm like the runner does in the four-forty relays.

"Jack."

"Jesus! What a mess!" said the DA. "I talked to the commissioner already. We've decided to issue a joint statement tonight. Did you . . . ?"

"As we speak. We should have a draft in about an hour. I'm looking for the chief of D, too."

"Good. You're handling it personally, the public affairs?"

"Personally," lied Karp.

20

"Okay, good. Any thoughts?"

"On the tape? Hell, Jack, right now it's an animal-control matter, not a DA thing at all. If we find it's an actual infanticide, i.e., the kid wasn't born dead or expired of natural causes, then we can start thinking about what to do. I assume you got my note on the other two?"

"Yeah, yeah, I did. Sweet Jesus, what ever happened to the basket left with the nuns?"

"What ever happened to switchblades and brass knuckles? Now they use machine pistols in gang fights. It's a changed world, Jack."

"I know it, and frankly, it stinks. Look, we're going to come under a shitload of pressure to crucify the poor godforsaken ladies responsible for these. That damned tape and that picture! The bleeding hearts and the string-'em-up crowd will be holding hands and yelling in chorus. This one's on you, boyo, by the way. Tight security, no leaks, and tell the cops that, too. I'm going to do some shifty moves until we get the mothers and see what's what."

"It could be the fathers, you know."

"Oh, it's always the mothers, this young. The fathers kill them when they're older. Look, I'm going to be tied up here for a while, and then figure I'll be by there around nine. We'll talk to the press about ten from Centre

Street. You're staying to follow up, I presume."

"Yeah, Marlene and Lucy are up at some shindig at Sacred Heart. I was going to stay late anyway. Lucky for me."

"Ha! Sacred Heart, huh? Is she armed?"

"Probably."

"Christ! Better start praying she doesn't shoot a nun. It'd be the end of a perfect day."

There were no obvious nuns in the ballroom of the Convent of the Sacred Heart this evening. The mesdames had never gone in much for elaborate habits, and now they had settled into dowdy outfits with big plain wooden crosses around their necks. In any case, most of the teachers at Sacred Heart were now laypeople. It was part of the new Church, clearly, and Marlene, of course, approved of all that on an intellectual level, but still, there was something dissatisfying about all that earnest wrestling with celibacy and abortion and homosexuality and liturgy. Marlene had never paid much attention to the specific moral dictates of the Church during her girlhood, but she had respected the magic and welcomed the forgiveness, which she had certainly required in inordinate measure. The first time Marlene had seen this room, she had been fourteen, a brilliant little barbarian

22

from Queens, and it had seemed to her the anteroom to paradise. She sipped her tepid coffee now and looked around at it. It was, famously, one of the most beautiful rooms in the city, high-ceilinged, floored with golden parquet, fitted with great Palladian windows and a noble fireplace, all perfectly proportioned and harmonious, as befitted the Renaissance palazzo from which it was copied. The space was an education in itself. Tonight it was full of alumnae and faculty, and rich people who might support the institution, circulating gently amid civilized conversation and soft music from a student string quartet. Marlene had not been a very good alumna in years past, but had resolved, upon her daughter's entry here, to improve, and she had.

She wandered down to the end of the room and studied her reflection in the great oval mirror above the fireplace. She was wearing her plum-colored Karl Lagerfeld suit, the most elegant outfit she owned. It fit perfectly, with the added benefit that the lush cut and heavy fabric quite concealed the thin nine-millimeter pistol on her left hip. On her lapel hung a sticker that read "Marlene Ciampi — '64." She'd had her hair done, too; it fell richly to her shoulders, a great faux-casual mass of crow-black curls, artfully designed to cast a heavy shadow over the right side of her face, where the eye was glass. She had already this evening met some of the girls she had gone to school with, and she wondered if she looked as good as the ones who looked good or more like the ones who did not and reflected yet again upon Camus's dictum that people over forty were responsible for their own face. She, with the help of various bad guys, certainly was. As she so mused, a voice behind her said:

Foeda est in coitu et brevis voluptas
Et taedet Veneris statim peractae.

Marlene spun around. Before her stood a plumpish woman of just her own height and age, with an unruly mass of red-gold hair frizzing out of her head, and a broad, big-toothed grin on her freckled face.

"Good God! It's Shanahan!" cried Marlene.

"Champ!" shrieked the woman, and they leaped into each other's arms.

"Wow, let me look at you," said Maureen Shanahan, pulling back and looking Marlene over. "Still gorgeous, curse you. What happened to you? You never come to these things."

"Do you?"

"I always come to these things. I'm very socially responsible, as you'll recall, except when I used to hang out with you. I figured you'd remember the Petronius."

"God, yes! We thought we were so clever finding it and offering it for our free translation, not realizing —"

"We were only the four thousandth nasty Sacred Heart girl to find that thing since the foundation. My God, I'm glad to see you! You won't believe this, but a week doesn't go by when I don't think of you."

"Maureen, that's crazy. Why didn't you call? I'm in the book. Or send a card? *You're* the orphan. I had no way to get in touch with you."

"I thought you hated me."

"What! Why would you think that?"

"Oh, you know, the last time we saw each other. Me and Ron . . ."

Marlene laughed. "Oh, God, that! The Odious Ron." She slapped her hand to her mouth. "Oh, Jesus, I'm sorry . . ."

"No, it's perfectly all right. The Odious Ron and I have parted ways. And you were absolutely right on about him. I put him through med school, produced two kids, and he dumped me for the usual beauteous intern. Pathetic and banal. The truth is . . . God, I don't know what the truth is. Ashamed? Embarrassed? Stupid? Ron was pretty good at cutting me off from my past life. Jesus, with you in particular it was hate at first sight."

"Likewise," said Marlene, and they laughed.

"Jeepers," said Shanahan, "I can't believe I'm standing here in the ballroom talking to Marlene Ciampi. What is it, eighteen, twenty years?"

"Or thereabouts, but who's counting? So what're you doing, Shans? You said you had kids?"

"Yeah, David and Shannon. David's a freshman at Georgetown law, Shannon's a senior, she's applying to colleges, if you can believe it. My baby. We live in Sherwood. It's just outside of Wilmington. You want to die of boredom? I have a walletful of pictures."

Marlene looked around the room, mock-furtive. "Do you think we could sneak out for a drink?"

Shanahan giggled. "I don't see why not. It never bothered us when we were juniors, and I doubt we'll get carded, although if we did, it would make my year."

"Great! We'll go to Hoyle's on Lex."

"Hoyle's is still there?"

"Oh, they couldn't close Hoyle's. Their French 75 is on the national register of historic treasures. Come with me, I have to go tell my daughter." Marlene clutched her friend's arm and together they left the ballroom and walked through the familiar halls to the Fifth Avenue lobby, where a table had been set up to welcome the alumnae and other supporters of the school. Behind the table were two sixteen-year-old girls, one a round-faced, pink-cheeked Chinese with small wire-frame glasses, a traditional bowl-cut hairdo, and a look of supernatural intelligence in her eyes. The other was a tall, thin, sallow girl with a punkish crew-cut and a hawk nose. Both girls were dressed in black jumpers with white collars showing.

Marlene said, "Girls, this is Maureen Shanahan, my best friend from high school. I haven't seen her in centuries and we're going to go out for a drink. Maureen, my daughter, Lucy Karp, and her friend Mary Ma."

Both girls rose and shook hands correctly. Shanahan looked at Lucy with some interest and was startled by the girl's return look, an unnaturally mature appraising gaze. Her eyes were startling, too: slightly aslant, large, and the color of Virginia tobacco. She looked nothing at all like her mother, except for the broad forehead and the heavy, straight eyebrows. It was not a girl-pretty face, but a memorable one, striking and severe, like that of a young saint rimmed with faded gold leaf on an icon.

Shanahan became aware she was staring and pulled her eyes away and started some chitchat with the two girls. Marlene was rummaging in her bag. "You'll need cab fare."

"We'll take the subway, Mom," said Lucy.

"Are you sure? It'll be late."

"Mom . . ."

This was said with such a tone of forbearance, as to a dotard, that Marlene shrugged and put her wallet away. She looked around. "Where's Caitlin?"

"She had a rehearsal tonight," said Lucy. "Her folks came, though." Several people arrived to ask for directions, and Lucy turned to help them. The women retrieved their coats (a black leather trench coat for Marlene, a quilted nylon, knee-length thing, lavender with a fur collar, for Shanahan) and took their leave of the girls. The evening was chill and damp; the lamps on Fifth wore misty halos. They walked east on 91st Street.

"She's beautiful, Marlene," said Shanahan.

"Hah! According to *her*, she's dog food. I've given up trying, and I refuse to accept any blame at all for that haircut. She worships Laurie Anderson. Of course, I explained to her that it's one thing if you have a little round face with tiny gamine features . . . but does she listen? I wash my hands."

"It's a stage. Who's Caitlin?"

"Caitlin Maxwell, the other side of the triangle. The cabal. She's a ballet dancer, apparently a budding star. An exquisite creature in the bargain. I think the other two have something of a crush. Rich as God, too, the dad is some sort of Wall Street tycoon." Marlene sighed. "You know, they're terrific kids, and all — by the way, Mary is also a little unusual, she does matrix algebra in her head, according to Lucy, not that I know what that means, but she's on full scholarship and MIT is already interested, but . . . sometimes I wish she would just hang out with regular kids."

"Kids have cliques. We did, if you recall."

"So I keep telling myself, and I would believe it if she was a normal kid, because as you'll also recall, I was something of a handful at that age, but Lucy is a little off the charts in a number of respects."

"So speaks every mother."

"Yeah, but in my case it happens to be true. It turns out she's a language prodigy."

"A what?"

"A language prodigy. Give her a dictionary and a grammar and seventy-two hours with a native speaker and she's essentially indistinguishable from someone who's spoken the language since birth. There's a whole laboratory over at Columbia P and S devoted to studying her brain."

"Really? But, Champ, that's marvelous! How many does she speak?"

"Oh, a dozen or so," said Marlene carelessly. "I can't keep track. And I suppose if I'd been a real nurturing mom, like, for example, the Mrs. Maxwell who's always being thrown in my face, I could have focused on her gift and got her past the thinking she was some kind of freak. But, given my chosen profession, she's had kind of a rough time of it, and I think she harbors resentment."

"You mean because you're a *lawyer?*"

Marlene looked sideways at her companion. "I'm not exactly a lawyer, Shans. Oh, right, you're not in the city anymore, so you wouldn't know."

"I wouldn't know? What, you're *famous?*"

"Infamous, actually. I run a security service for women who're being stalked. You know those vet ads where they say 'practice restricted to large animals'? Well, my practice is restricted to women in serious danger of getting killed. Keep walking, Shanahan, and don't goggle at me. Anyway, as a result of this, the loved ones sometimes get testy and go for me. Or Lucy. To make a long story short, she's been involved in a couple of shootings, she's been kidnapped twice, and I've had to shoot some bad guys, once right in front of Lucy. That doesn't count the clients who've decided to shoot the loved ones rather than be killed themselves."

"Wait a minute, you've actually *killed* people?"

"Only three. Here's Hoyle's. Still want to drink with me?"

"Are you kidding? Line 'em up! I'm shaking like a leaf."

Hoyle's was three steps down and about thirty feet long, dark and cozy, smelling of Manhattan saloon, with a long, shiny walnut bar, a banquette along one wall, ten round tables, and a tiny stage with a piano at one end. A young woman was playing "Paper Moon" with a lot of nice glissando as they entered and picked out a booth. The place was half full, mostly East Side singles and a few older couples. There were no Sacred Heart girls in evidence, nor were Shanahan and Marlene carded, nor did the waitress raise an eyebrow when, stifling giggles, they ordered French 75s.

Oiled by the confiding atmosphere of the boîte, and half-pints of low-end champagne spiked with shots of cognac, and her genuine delight in finding her old friend, Marlene found herself talking about her more memorable cases in some detail, which she rarely did, and the occasional celebrity-protection jobs she had taken under the auspices of

Osborne, a local security firm. She dropped some substantial names. It was nice having an appreciative audience; most of Marlene's near-and-dear did not approve of any of this.

Which prompted the obvious question. "What does your husband think of what you do?" asked Shanahan, after the tale of a particularly naughty caper. "Christ, I don't even know who you married. Or is he still around?"

"Oh, he's around all right. His name's Roger Karp. We call him Butch. He's the chief assistant district attorney for New York County."

Shanahan burst into laughter. "You're shooting people and running guns to women and you're married to the DA? Champ, only you! How do you carry it off?"

"Not very well, from time to time." Marlene gestured to the waitress for another round. "There's tension, of course. The way we work it is, he doesn't ask questions, and I try not to rub his face in it too much. But you can figure it hasn't done Lucy any good."

"Yeah, but at least you're still together. What's he like, Butch? God, nobody's a Butch anymore. Isn't it sort of a turn-of-the-century name?"

"Well, yeah, but he's sort of a turn-of-the-century guy. Very different from the guys I hung out with back then, by the way. You'll recall I went for crazy Irishmen with swimming-pool eyes and tight little bodies."

"Mick Finney."

Marlene cried out and covered her face. "Oh, Christ, how could you! Do you realize the mental energy I have devoted over the years to forgetting that jerk? And now I have to start all over again."

"I take it Karp is not a crazy little Irishman."

"An immense, serious Jew, since you ask. And the next obvious question is, why him, and so against my usual type." Marlene paused and drank deeply and was silent, staring at the piano player, who was doing "Spring Can Really Hang You Up the Most."

"And the answer?"

"Ah, the answer," said Marlene, smiling. "The answer is a mystery, like the Holy Trinity. As for the mere facts: We worked in the same office. He was a star; I admired, but nothing particularly groin-involved. His wife ditched him. We were at an office party and he got drunk. He can't drink at all. I helped him get home. The next thing I knew — and believe me, Shans, I didn't plan this and I didn't particularly want it — the next thing we were in the shower together, and the rest is history. Oh, yeah, I got blown up by a bomb and he got shot and kidnapped, and I got kidnapped, too, and we helped each other out, which tended to bring us a little closer than we would have been ordinarily. And I got pregnant with Lucy, and so we got married. Not a trip to the moon on gossamer wings, but something . . . I don't know, I didn't expect, not for me. We fight like crazy, but we're still together. He's a remarkable man. You'll meet him, you'll see for yourself."

"Marlene, this is stupefying stuff. Blown up? Kidnapped?"

"But enough of me," said Marlene with a laugh.

"Tell me about groin-involved?"

"No, really, what about *you?* You severed the Odious, and what? You're practicing down there?"

"Yeah, criminal law, mostly court-appointed counsel, you know, the usual hopeless mopes." Maureen laughed. "Yes, right, old softy Shanahan."

"I remember the sick pigeon."

"Yeah, I brought it in from the cold and it died in my locker. The story of my life. In any case, I have recently achieved, for once, a fair level of racy notoriety, and I was reasonably full of myself, but compared to you, I feel like I'm doing wills and conveyances in Gumboro."

"A fair level . . . ?"

"Yeah, I'm defending Sarah Goldfarb. . . . What? You don't recognize the name? Oh, God, now I'm totally crushed. Marlene, it was on national TV, it was in *Time*, it was in *Newsweek* . . ."

Marlene was shaking her head. "I'm sorry, Shans, I can't place her."

"A couple of teenagers went to a motel, the girl had a baby, the baby ended up in the Dumpster —"

"Oh, God, *that* one!"

"*Thank* you!"

"Wow, Shans, that's pretty high-profile. I *am* impressed. How did you happen to land it?"

"Oh, another long boring story. After they were arrested, someone at Mr. Goldfarb's work recommended a lawyer, a guy named Slotkin, and at the same time, the boy's parents hired their own lawyer, this Loreno character —"

"Phil Loreno?"

"Yeah, do you know him?"

"Slightly. Butch knows him fairly well. He used to be with the DA. Go on."

"Okay, the incident occurred last November. The kids have been in jail since then, because the state charged them with capital murder."

"Capital *murder?* For infanticide? That's loony!"

"Tell me about it! It's a classic case of prosecutorial overkill. The state's attorney has been bloviating to the local press practically since the arrest, and the attorney general's appeared on a national talk show. The AG's a woman, I guess she wants to demonstrate the girls can be tough, too, or maybe she wants to be governor. In any case, to start off they had a joint defense agreement, Slotkin and Loreno, but meanwhile my kid is still in jail, and the Goldfarbs are getting nervous. Their guy doesn't seem to be doing anything, he's letting Loreno take the lead. The boy did the actual dumping, of course, so he's under the gun and maybe getting set to play a little hardball. I happened to know the girl's aunt, also a lawyer, but corporate, and she called me and asked me to talk to the parents. I did, I got the story as far as they knew it, I saw Slotkin, who didn't know his ass from a hole in the ground in a case like this, I saw Sarah, and I said I'd take the case."

"I assume from this the kid is simpatico?"

"*Muy simpática.* Honestly, Champ, a puppy who wandered out in front of a truck. Bright, sweet, helpless — born yesterday."

"Not like us," said Marlene.

"No, not like us, but the last time I looked, poor judgment wasn't a hanging offense."

"How did the baby die?"

36

"Good question, and one the state never bothered to ask very seriously. The autopsy was a total botch. From what it looks like now, the poor thing never lived. Sarah was eclamptic and in convulsions during delivery. The boy said the baby was blue and never moved, didn't cry, didn't seem to be breathing, so the stupe bagged it and tossed it in the Dumpster. All he had to do was call 911 and yell for help."

"Why didn't he?"

"Oh, well, therein hangs the tale. All of this, the whole sad mess, came about because Sarah Goldfarb didn't want to tell her mommy she was knocked up."

"Don't tell me! She was hoping it would go away by itself."

"That, too. Her story is, she didn't know she was that pregnant. She had a medical exam a few months before and the doc didn't find any pregnancy, even though in fact she was six months gone by then, and also she was spotting, and she figured, 'Oh, my period, hallelujah!' So when she went into that motel, she thought she was at the most sixteen weeks gone. She thought she was having a miscarriage."

"Shans, excuse me, but that's somewhat hard to believe. She was full term and she didn't know? Nobody noticed?"

"Champ, I got photos — she never showed during her pregnancy. And I got a sheaf of clippings like this" — Shanahan held up her hand, the fingers stretched as if to grasp a Manhattan phone book — "about girls delivering babies no one knew they were carrying. They sit on the toilet, they think it was something they ate, and then splash, wah! wah! It makes you want to cry. And this kid, Sarah — all right, from a middle-class family, educated and all, but emotionally? I don't know: seven years old, eight? You have to see it to believe it. The kid was preeclamptic and suffering for months and wouldn't go to a doctor because she always went to the doctor with Mommy, and even if she went herself, she figured her mom would somehow find out and she was more afraid of her mom finding out than she was about maybe dying."

Marlene drained her glass and was motioning for a third when her friend said, "Whoa! I got to be at Penn Station in forty minutes. If I have another, I'll end up in Disneyland."

"Don't be silly! We'll get shit-faced and you can stay over at our place. We'll scandalize the children."

"Honestly, I wish I could, but I have pleadings in the morning and this judge is a bear. Another time, huh?"

A hurried exchange of addresses and phone

numbers, hugs and kisses, and then Marlene watched her friend depart in a cab. She stood there on Lexington for a while watching the cab disappear into the traffic. Then she walked slowly west on 91st to where her car, an elderly orange Volvo DL, was parked. Marlene had a sticker on her window announcing that she was a retired NYPD officer, a gift from one of her numerous pals on the job, which protected her from being ticketed for any but the most flagrant parking violations. The school, she saw, was dark and deserted now.

A deep grunt sounded from the backseat, and she felt hot, damp breath on her neck at she settled into the driver's seat. In her rearview she met the red eyes of an immense black Neapolitan mastiff.

She started the car and said, "Yes, I was longer than I planned, Sweety, but I met my old best friend from high school." Growl, low. "Oh, *you're* my best friend now, Sweets, but that was then. It was extremely pleasant. It made me feel like a real person, a respectable Sacred Heart alumna. It struck me that nearly all of my most intimate recent pals are people who have for various reasons killed other people. Birds of a feather, right? But I'm tired, Sweets. Of the life. I think I want a different life."

2

"How was I?" asked the district attorney.

"You were good," said Karp. "The line about a public tragedy, not a public menace, was very nice. It set the right tone."

The DA shook his head doubtfully. It was a noble one, covered with shining white hair and supplied with a hard jaw, eagle beak, authoritative jowls, and fine, considering blue eyes, a politician's head, although Jack Keegan was not merely a politician. Karp and he understood each other: Keegan would fight the political wars, and Karp would run the office more or less as he saw fit, up to the point where some decision of his, or some event ostensibly under his control, compromised Keegan's vast political ambitions. In that case Karp would get the boot. It is the sort of relationship not at all uncommon in American politics, with no hard feelings on either side, and it suited Karp well. What he couldn't abide was political *meddling* in the work of the DA, and this Keegan normally avoided.

"Yeah, well, it was a good script," Keegan said, "but I'm not sure it's going to satisfy the

40

jackals, this time. I swear to God, we had seven cops all killed at once a couple years back, and the outcry wasn't anything near as bad as this. The talking heads are stacked up like damn oranges in a bin. Social collapse . . . and I got to take it seriously, or seem to."

"It was that film," said Karp. "If it's not on TV, it's not really real. Normally, I'm a big First Amendment guy, but I'm starting to have second thoughts about prior restraint."

Keegan grunted, leaned back in his great judge's chair, and twiddled the big Bering cigar he never smoked. "What did Torricelli have to say for himself?" he asked.

"Ah, well, the chief of detectives had some good news. The police have arrested the two dogs."

Keegan barked, a loud laughlike sound. "Jesus! Well, good, the city sleeps safe tonight. What else?"

"He's put more resources into the two homicide zones involved. They'll work the informants, see who turned up not pregnant anymore but with no baby. It shouldn't take long."

"Any ideas on how to handle them when they do come in?"

"Infanticides? Hell, Jack, over in Europe they don't even give them jail time. Infanticide is considered a prima facie instance of se-

41

vere emotional upset. Mother kills baby — it's a tragedy, just like we said. What the hell can the law *do* to a mother that's worse than her baby dying, assuming the mother's in her right mind. If she's *not* in her right mind, on the other hand, there's no crime."

"QED. Still, this ain't Europe, boyo. Also, after the way we came down on Racic and Leary, we're starting to have a rep as being pals with baby killers."

Karp started to bristle, controlled it. It was part of Keegan's way of relating, to get Karp hot, if he could. It was an old prosecutorial trick. "Racic and Leary have nothing to do with all this. They firebombed an abortion clinic and killed an employee and we went for the top count at trial and we put them away for it."

"A lot of our fine voters think they were heroes. They think we should have cut them some slack." Meaning, you should have.

Karp cocked his head and forced a smile to his face. "What am I hearing, Jack? Are we starting to second-guess Racic-Leary? We're going to come down heavy on a trio of sad-sack women because . . . what, we want to illustrate the difference between pre- and postnatal abortion? There may be something wrong with my brain, but I can't quite grasp either the legal or moral issue."

Keegan looked off into the middle distance, placed the cigar in his mouth, waggled it, removed it. "We travel in different circles, Butch. There's a low burn going on about this abortion thing, and I don't mean the nutcases like those two. I mean decent people. It's like lava underground. It wants to boil out. It wants to boil out at *women*. I'm just reflecting, now, giving you the political background."

"I appreciate that, Jack," said Karp, not appreciating it in the least, trying to keep the stiffness out of his voice.

"Autopsy done on the third kid?" asked Keegan, switching subjects.

Karp nodded.

"How did he die?"

"Apparently, he was buried alive in a shallow grave. The dogs dug him out."

Keegan placed his cigar carefully back on his desk. "Oh, that's marvelous. Just *marvelous!* Does the press know?"

"Not yet. The cops are keeping it close for now."

"Oh, rest assured, they'll have it. Morgue attendants spend their vacations in the Bahamas on what the goddamn papers slip them for stuff like this. My God, I wouldn't be that girl for anything in the world. They'll lynch her."

"Not on my watch they won't, boss."

"Oh, yeah? I tell you what, boyo. You slap this girl's wrist, and when the cardinal archbishop gets on the horn, I'll let *you* reason with him about the sanctity of human life."

Some few minutes later, Karp found Murrow in his cubby engaged in the sort of operational scut work Karp used to do himself.

"How was His Excellency?" Murrow asked.

"Mr. Keegan was pleased with the way the morning show went."

"Great. So, what's up today?"

"Infanticide. When you can find time from your vital tasks, I want you to hit the library and look into the legal history of infanticide, in New York and generally. Cases, theory, history, the works."

Murrow made a note in a tiny leatherbound book he kept in his breast pocket. Karp admired this habit; he himself wrote notes almost exclusively on Chinese laundry tickets and on credit-card receipts.

"When do you need this by?"

"Oh, take your time — no rush. Next couple of days is okay."

Murrow glanced at his towering in-basket and grinned. "No problem, chief. I'll cut down on working on the novel during office hours."

"Do that," said Karp. "You know, you actually do have a way with words. I assume the talking points this morning were yours. They seemed a little too high-quality to be the usual PA product."

"Let me shuffle my feet and hang my head in becoming modesty. It's funny how no one in public affairs can write simple expository English."

"Yes, a puzzle," said Karp. "Anyway, Jack thought the talking points were good. I took all the credit, of course."

"Of course. I'm grateful for the few crumbs that drop from your lips. What are we going to do about these cases, do you think?"

"Oh, I expect they'll all cop out, to anything short of murder deuce. No Legal Aid in their right mind is going to want to go to trial in the current atmosphere. The Horror, and so on."

"But will they let you do that? Given the political situation, I mean."

"My boy," said Karp, "the discretion of a prosecutor with respect to what charges to bring is very nearly absolute. So there's no *they* involved."

"I thought the legislature was peripherally involved in that determination. I mean, defining felonies and all that. Or maybe I missed something in law school."

"Oh, *law school.* After you're around here

awhile, I think you'll find that law school doesn't have much to do with an actual DA's office. It's sort of like the difference between a parade with a marching band and a war. As for the legislature, they propose, but we dispose."

"Meaning?"

"Well, basically, the system, not just this office, but every large prosecutorial organization, is *essentially* corrupt. It's so easy to pass laws, pols love to pass laws. It's what they do. They pick the flavor of the month. Drugs? Lock 'em all up. Child abuse? Lock 'em up. Graffiti? Car-jacking? Same thing. And of course, almost all of it focused on poor, dumb people, but I won't even get into that aspect of the system. The problem is, it's a lot harder to spend money than pass laws. So the jails get crowded with mopes who got busted for selling dime bags, and you have to let the rapists out early. Spend serious money for drug treatment? Forget about it! Look, everyone knows twenty percent of the criminals produce eighty percent of the crime. Half our job is getting those guys off the streets, but we're — and I mean the whole system, courts, us, Legal Aid, probation — we're so overloaded that we can't *actually* do what we're supposed to do. So we perform an imitation of justice. You've been to a calendar court? Twelve seconds to make a decision involving someone's life and liberty. So that's corrosive. It's corrupting, because moving the system along becomes the prime value, not making sure that the laws are carried out. Get it?"

"Yes, sir. What's the other half?"

"Come again?"

"You said putting away the real bad guys was half the job . . . ?"

"Oh, yeah. The other half is protecting the people against us. You laugh, but it's serious. In a civil society, no human being should have the kind of discretionary power that a DA has, not Jack Keegan, not me, and I won't even mention the average twenty-five-year-old fresh out of law school, like you, for example, not without some check on it. Well, you say, there's the grand jury, but as we all know, the grand jury is a joke."

"Indict a ham sandwich, et cetera."

"Exactly, and the corruption you get from power is an order of magnitude more serious than the kind you get from what I was talking about, the necessity for pretense. Because it's personal. The world is patting you on the back for putting scumbags away, and you think you're quite a fine fellow, and you want more of it. It's intoxicating. You stop thinking about the defendant as a citizen with rights and start thinking he's *just* a scumbag, a chip you're going to cash in, and pretty soon you're looking the other way on perjury and tainted evidence, and making crappy deals with lying snitches, and then you start going after people who piss you off generally, newsmen maybe, or political enemies . . . what, you don't think it happens?"

Murrow adjusted his face from its disbelieving stare. "Okay, say that's a worst case. But in reality it must be vanishingly rare."

"No? How would you know it's rare? You think innocent people aren't hounded and broken and sent to jail? You think prosecutors don't play politics?" Karp grinned. "They don't teach this in law school, do they?"

"No, they don't. I don't see how they could, really. Instead of idealists you'd get all sorts of undesirable and unprincipled people entering the profession."

"That would be bad," said Karp, laughing.

"So what's the solution? Inevitable corruption and collapse and the end of the world as we know it?"

"Not while I'm in charge," said Karp.

"The philosopher king?"

"The philosopher chief assistant DA, although it lacks a certain ring."

"And *quis custodiet ipsos custodes?*"

"Oh, that's why we keep hiring fine, upstanding, idealistic youths such as yourself,

48

Murrow, certainly not because you're of any real use." They laughed. "The serious answer? Absent effective legal or practical constraints, the only solution is cultural — leadership, the enforcement of unwritten standards, the sense that people who don't play nice won't have any friends, sanctions for the worst offenders."

"That doesn't seem to work with the cops, if what you hear about the blue wall is true."

"No, that just *makes* my point. Police culture is extremely stable and it's what really runs the cops, not the thousand pages of chickenshit in the *Patrol Guide*. It says you can't rat on a brother officer, but you have to risk your life for him. It says you can pound on people up to a certain point, but you can't just shoot people you don't like. And so on. Illegal? Sure, and they've been trying to change it for years and it's still there. But that's *their* problem. Our problem is — put it this way: How do you stay decent in a system that's essentially corrupt?"

Here Karp paused and stared at nothing for so long that Murrow said, "And the envelope, please . . ."

Karp shrugged, grinned. Ever since Murrow had come on board he had indulged himself in these spasms of agonized philosophizing. The kid was the only person in the building who had to listen and could understand what he was saying and wouldn't talk to anyone else about it. "The answer is, I don't know. I review maybe one-tenth of one percent of the cases that go through this office. Admittedly they're the big-ticket items, and everyone knows I'm going to be studying them, and I still find boners, petty scams. I try to get the bureau chiefs to do the same. Maybe that's all you can do, show the flag from time to time."

"So gradually things will improve."

"No," said Karp sourly. "Things will get worse. But we'll fight it all the way down."

Marlene Ciampi, a *custos* whom her husband considered in need of considerable guarding herself, was at that moment engaged in one of the more boring and routine functions of her peculiar life. This involved picking women up from places where they were hiding from their estranged significant others, and driving them, together with their minor children, to a particular location, dropping the children off there, and driving the women back; then, after the husband had picked up the kids, performed fatherhood to the extent permitted by the court, and returned the kid to the neutral corner, she picked up the mom, drove to the neutral corner, and reversed the process. Marlene typically hired people to do this for her, usually moonlighting or retired cops, or people she had trained herself. The dads and moms were assessed a modest amount for this service.

Today, one of the regular guard/drivers was out sick, no one else was available, and so Marlene had driven a woman named Lily Kosabian and her seven-year-old daughter, Tamara, to the East Village Women's Shelter, on Avenue B. This institution was not the typical neutral corner. It was a storefront tenement, with the former glass windows replaced by heavy steel sheeting. It had a steel door, strapped and bolted in a manner that would not have embarrassed a nuclear submarine, and on the door was a sign, protected by thick safety glass, which read:

EAST VILLAGE
WOMEN'S SHELTER
Ring the Bell — We Are Always Open
If you are seeking shelter, you are welcome
If you are looking for trouble,
we have that too

The clientele of the EVWS consisted entirely of women, and their children, who were under credible threat of being murdered by their male loved ones. There are many shelters for battered women in the metropolitan area, but they are typically anonymous and do not therefore have signs of this type on their doors, because they hope that the estranged parties do not pay visits. The management here, a Mexican-American woman named Mattie Duran, on the contrary rather hoped for such visits, so that she could meet them with deadly violence, thus permanently eliminating the need for shelter and freeing up another bed. This was the only form of social work offered by the EVWS.

Behind the forbidding door was a short corridor and another forbidding door, this one equipped with a wire-glass porthole. Behind that was a small anteroom, in which Marlene waited, chatting with Vonda, part-time guard-receptionist and sometime attendee at City College. Vonda had a Mossberg twelve-gauge under her steel desk, a matching attitude, and took some knowing. Marlene had been associated with the shelter for years now and had penetrated this reserve. Marlene also had the cachet of having shot a substantial number of guys, once in a manner that had saved Vonda's life, so they were able to have a nice discussion about Vonda's studies. Marlene was just getting started on the place of the Second World War in twentieth-century historiography when a thin, dark,

52

well-groomed woman with a pretty, dark, child entered. The little girl took a hard candy from a jar Vonda kept on her desk, and the guard buzzed Marlene and them out through the inner door. In the corridor, Tamara skipped away from her mother and placed her little hand in Marlene's. For some reason she had formed an attachment and seemed to look forward to her contact with Marlene rather more than she did to the court-ordered visits with her father. Marlene imagined it was the glass eye. Once, during a pickup, the child had been distraught, and Marlene had amused her by exhibiting the wonders of this object.

"Can I sit in the front with you, Marlene?" she asked.

"Sure, honey," said Marlene distractedly. "Just wait here with your mommy for a second while I get the car."

Marlene closed the front door behind her and went out and did that, double-parking the Volvo at the entrance. She checked the street to make sure that Dad was not lurking, that his car, a red Celica, was nowhere in evidence. Clear. Leaving the engine running, she returned to the door and knocked. The door swung open and Tamara dashed out. She ran to the Volvo and tugged at the handle of the passenger-side door. It was such a little thing:

Marlene had forgotten to snap open the door catch. She now went out into the street, opened the driver's door, leaned across the front seat, and did so. Lily Kosabian came out of the shelter and walked toward the car.

At that moment, the rear door of a white Taurus parked two cars east popped open and the estranged dad, Julius Kosabian, rolled out from where he had been crouched in the rear footwell. He walked up to his ex-wife and shot her twice in the chest. Then he shot her again where she lay. This last shot proved to be the undoing of his plan, because it gave Marlene time to pull out of her awkward position, draw her pistol, and aim across the top of her car. Mr. Kosabian now pointed his gun at his daughter's head and then immediately sat down on the pavement, groaning, his pistol clanging away at some distance from his hand, because in those few desperate seconds Marlene had shot him four times.

Karp was attending a trial when he got the news. He tried to spend some time in a courtroom every day. Even as little as half an hour standing huge in the right-hand rear corner of the room, where whoever was at the People's table could see him when they rose to face the jury, made it clear that the all-seeing eye was upon them. This was the official reason. The real reason was that Karp loved trials, for the same reason he loved basketball, a reason primarily esthetic, both events being what Bill Russell, the great Celtics center, called "a combination of war and art." Oddly, such passion is almost unknown among lawyers, even among prosecuting attorneys. Nine out of ten lawyers believe that a trial is a failure, a breakdown of reasonable negotiations between reasonable people. A large proportion of lawyers go through entire well-paid careers without ever standing before a live jury. Also, trials are frightening, especially to people who haven't done a lot of trial work. You have to stand up there in real time and think on your feet; you have to do this under the nearly absolute control of a judge, whose prime qualification for the office is being a pal of some politician; you have to present a perhaps complex story to twelve people who are sitting there because they were too dumb to escape jury duty; and, scariest of all, you could *lose* — in open court, in front of God, the public, and your mother. To Karp, however, being a lawyer without trying cases was like being a matador in a bullring without the bull: you might have the music, the fancy costume, the pretty footwork, and the artistic cape-waving, but ultimately the thing was boring and pointless. This attitude was considered somewhat eccentric, even within the New York DA's office, a notably trial-oriented organization.

This particular trial, unfortunately, promised few real delights. *People v. Purcell* was yet another in the seemingly infinite series of what the cops call scumbag-on-scumbag murders. Leandro Purcell, the defendant, was, like nearly 60 percent of the people arrested for murder in New York, a black man, and like somewhat over 45 percent, he was under twenty (nineteen, in fact), and like virtually all of them he was poor, ill-educated, and angry. His lawyer was a Legal Aid six years older than he was, named Weissman. Weissman was a decent fellow, but he had not spent much time on this case. He had forty-five others in his caseload and had tried his best to get his client to agree to a plea bargain, which was how he disposed of all but a tiny fraction of his cases. The state had offered, in return for a plea of guilty to first-degree manslaughter, a sentence of eight and a half years. Weissman had explained that this meant that with good behavior, and no decrease in prison crowding, Purcell might walk out on parole after only twenty-six months in Dannemora, and that if the state was forced to try him, they would try him on the top count, second-degree murder, and that if he lost, he would go in for at least fifteen years, and maybe as many as twenty-five with a life sentence.

But Purcell had refused the deal. His counterargument was that Weissman was a smart Jew lawyer and would get him off; that he had things to do and wasn't going to no prison; that the victim (his cousin Ernest McGaffery, aged seventeen) had it coming because he had ripped him off on a drug deal; and that he, Purcell, had acted under the extreme emotional distress of being betrayed by a member of his own family, and therefore it couldn't be murder anyway. Weissman understood that his client was one of the many young men having difficulty making the transition from the juvenile justice system (in which he had been a frequent player) to the adult one. He had done six months in Spofford, the juvie jail, and five in Riker's awaiting trial, and as he had the foresight of an armadillo, the idea of being seriously punished for periods vastly longer than these micro-jolts had no reality to him. In his dull mind it was a mere phantasm, like a job, or a father.

Since Purcell had shot McGaffery five times on a street corner in front of several witnesses, including the victim's mother and a parole officer who happened to be wandering by, and had the murder weapon in his possession at the time of arrest, the trial was something of a joke. Weissman knew it was a joke; the judge, frowning and irritable behind his high presidium, knew it was a joke; Mimi Vasquez, appearing for the People and just getting her opening statement under way, knew it was a joke. Those who thought it was not a joke included the jury, four black, six white, one Hispanic, one Asian, four men, eight women, seven over sixty-five, five under, and all high-school-educated people from the middle-lower economic reaches of the economy; Purcell himself, who was pleased to find himself the center of more attention than he had ever had before (except when actually firing his nine-millimeter Colt); and the framers of the U.S. Constitution, who required a jury trial for any accused felon who wanted one.

Vasquez stood and faced the jury and began her opening. She was a neat, small, dark woman with a wide mouth, from which sprang a surprisingly deep voice. Her glossy, black hair was piled behind her head in a bun held by tortoiseshell combs. She was wearing an oufit as close as a professional woman could get to what Karp was wearing, a navy suit, severely tailored, a white shirt with a dark paisley scarf at the collar, stockings, and low-heeled pumps. Vasquez was a great admirer of Karp's.

He thought she was an up-and-coming kid, one of the homicide bureau's six female prosecutors. Karp was the main reason for there being any at all, since the chief of that bureau, Roland Hrcany, was, besides being one of Karp's friends, a famous male supremacist. Karp had to admit that there was some truth in the argument that women were not as successful at winning trials as men were. He attributed this not to some supposed absence of killer instinct (as Hrcany did) but to the unaccountable dislike some female jurors took to female prosecutors. Karp thought this problem (assuming it was real) could be overcome by a considered strategy of grooming and personal presentation. He had worked with Vasquez on it and she was showing right now that the work had borne fruit. First of all, no flamboyance. The image was severe, professional, serious, intense. A man could get away with acting up, a woman could not. Unfair? Of course, but there it was: no scarlet nail polish, no vivid makeup, no fussy hairstyles, no revealing clothes. Act older. And the voice, that was another unfair advantage. Low, rich tones connoted authority; light, high ones, immaturity, triviality. A woman could be a second Learned Hand, but if she delivered argument in a voice like Goldie Hawn's, she wouldn't win any cases. Here Vasquez had a natural advantage, that terrific contralto. Another advantage: an easy, honest, working-class style. The image was of someone destined by class and ethnicity to be a doughnut-shop waitress, who had made good, was getting over, but was she putting on any airs? No, she was not. Classy, but down-to-earth.

Karp listened as she described for the jury what she would attempt to prove beyond a reasonable doubt, to a moral certainty: that the victim had died in the County of New York, that his death had been due to the agency of the defendant, and that the defendant had intended to kill him. These facts were sufficient to demand a finding of murder in the second degree. She then gave what amounted to a table of contents of the evidence she was about to present. The medical examiner would testify as to the cause of death — the seven bullet wounds, two of which passed in and out of the deceased. The police would describe the murder scene. The detective would describe how the defendant was identified as a suspect, how his apartment was searched, how the gun was found in the freezer compartment of the refrigerator therein. The police laboratory technician would describe how they had determined that this was the gun that killed the victim. Vasquez then described the eyewitnesses and told the jury what they would hear from them: that the defendant was angry at the victim, that he had threatened to kill him, that at a certain time and place he had killed him and guiltily fled. She closed with a reminder of the nature of the murder charge and an assurance that the case she would present so matched the charge that the jury would have no rational alternative to a finding of guilty as charged. Karp had an ATM slip on which he had made some light notes, although the presentation was pretty close to what he would have done himself. No surprise there. He checked his watch. Forty-two minutes, about right for this sort of case. He was curious about how Weissman was going to respond to this powerful barrage, but the Legal Aid had just begun to extemporize on the presumption of innocence and how things were not always what they seemed when Karp felt a tap on his sleeve.

It was Flynn, offering a yellow phone slip. "You need to call your wife. An emergency."

Karp grabbed her arm and ushered her out of the courtroom.

"What did she say? Are the kids all right?"

"I wrote down what she said, sir, if you would read it. And might I have my arm back?"

Karp realized that he was squeezing the young woman's biceps hard enough to crush a soup can. He let go and read the slip. In quotation marks, in Flynn's neat European hand, he read, "I am okay and so are the kids. One of my clients was shot dead and I returned fire, wounding the perp. I'm at the Fifth Precinct. No charges contemplated at present."

"What did you do then?" asked Detective Baer.

Marlene said, "I pulled back off the car seat and stood up. I saw Mr. Kosabian point his pistol at his wife and fire again, once."

"He already shot her how many times?"

"I heard two shots," said Marlene carefully. This was the third go-around, and Marlene hoped it would be the last. She was tired and hungry. She had thrown up, as she always did when she shot someone, and she had puke on her shoe and on one cuff of her slacks. But she was willing to repeat her story as many times as they wanted to hear it. It was part of the process. Unlike people in films, Marlene did not complain that she had answered all these questions already.

Baer was a square-headed man with a pouchy face and a graying crew cut, whom Marlene did not know. But he, of course, knew about her.

"Okay, then what?"

"He turned and started to point his gun at Tamara, his daughter. I drew my gun and shot him."

"Just like that? You didn't yell out for him to drop his gun or anything?"

"No, I just shot him. In my judgment he would not have responded to a demand like that."

"In your judgment." An eyebrow lifted.

She ignored the tone. "Yes. I have a lot of experience in these matters and my judgment is based on it. Men who kill their families in broad daylight usually aren't planning to leave for Venezuela. He was going to kill the girl and then shoot himself."

"So you shot him. Four times."

"I fired until he went down."

"And then what?"

"I secured his weapon. I took Tamara back into the shelter building. I told the guard there what had happened and told her to call 911 and to take care of the kid. Then I ran outside to see if I could do anything for her mother. She wasn't breathing. I tried to give her CPR. Then the paramedics got there, and the police."

Marlene looked at her hands. She washed them in the police station, but there were dark stains on the sleeves and chest of her sweater. Marlene moved her mind away from what it had felt like as she tried to compress Lily Kosabian's chest. Her hands had sunk in deeply. It was like washing undies in warm water in a hotel sink. Across the scarred table, Baer was writing. In a corner of the interview room a female police officer leaned against the wall. She regarded Marlene with as much sympathy as she thought she could afford to show, with Baer there. Marlene had found that cops tended to be of sharply differing opinions about occasions when her work ended in violence. A good many of them thought she performed a useful service when she took out a guy gunning for a woman. Domestic altercations are among the most dangerous events in a typical cop's working life, especially the kind featuring armed altercators, and some police officers thought she was doing some cop a potentially lifesaving favor. A rather higher proportion, however, considered her at best a dangerous vigilante and at worst something just this side of a contract killer, and Baer was clearly of this persuasion. He finished writing, rose, and walked out of the room without a word.

Marlene looked at her reflection in the long mirror that is a standard fixture of police interview rooms. They are made of one-way glass, and Marlene imagined that most of the inhabitants of the Fifth Precinct had found an

64

excuse to wander by and have a look. She imagined also that the riding ADA would have been among that number; the kid (and they were all kids in that business) might already have heard the facts of the case and have come to a judgment. She expected that she had not been far wrong when she had optimistically told her husband's secretary that no charges were contemplated. The story she had told all three times, which was substantially true as far as the forensic events went, would not support a criminal complaint, even had she not been the wife of the chief assistant DA.

The forensic events were not uppermost in her mind, however. No, her head rang and her body trembled with the real story, which was, stupid Marlene lets herself drift for a scant minute, doesn't have the door open, forgets the drill she had taught her employees (car door open, guard standing against building, hand on weapon, keeping street under observation as client runs across sidewalk and into vehicle), doesn't even think that the shithead could have borrowed or rented another car, didn't have the dog on post and guarding, but who could have thought it? The guy was a taxpayer, he ran an auto glass joint, never any felony trouble, not until now. Marlene, markswoman that she was, had not killed the man, but he would not be using his arms for some time. So, guilt galore, corrosive and wrenching. Even after a lifetime as a semilapsed Catholic, Marlene was still not habituated to this kind of guilt, nor was she spared the understanding of why it was particularly bad in the present case. For the truth was that Marlene had not liked Lily Kosabian or her kid. It was nothing major, except that the woman thought that it was part of Marlene's job to offer sympathy on the long ride to and from Queens, and Lily never shut up about her hard life and what a bastard the husband was, in front of Tamara, naturally, and of course the husband was doing the same thing when he had the girl, and Marlene was in the middle of it. The woman never shut up, and the kid, as one might expect from parents like this pair, was confused and hurt and demanding in a particularly annoying, insinuating way. Can I sit in the front seat, Marlene? A little thing, compounding the careless error about the door lock, but the woman was dead as a result, and that would play out forever in Tamara's nightmare until maybe she picked one just like Dad and got killed, too.

"Excuse me?" said the policewoman.

Marlene looked up, startled. She had forgotten the cop was there and she stared at her.

"You said something," the cop explained. "Something about wanting out?"

"Did I?" said Marlene, embarrassed. Now I'm muttering in public, she thought. What I need is a shopping cart, some plastic bags, and four coats.

"You said, 'I want out. I have to get out of this.' Something like that."

"Oh, you know . . . just wondering how long this is going to take," said Marlene, dissembling.

"I could check with the lieutenant," the woman offered.

"If you would." Marlene managed a false smile and the cop returned a genuine one. When she was gone, Marlene stared fixedly at her reflection in the one-way glass, not caring whether anyone was looking at her from the other side. I'm past forty, she thought. I have no career, except this absurd one, the little Dutch girl with her thumb in the dike, and never enough thumb to hold back the black torrents, the endless sea of sexual catastrophe, the obsessive men, the stupid women, the ruined children. No, I didn't mean what I said, just now, I meant I want *out*. I want out of this life. This is over for me.

3

Marlene was in the tub when Karp got home, where he figured she would be. He greeted his sons, heard about their school day, heard about where they had been taken after school, had some words with Posie, the nanny, about this, left the kids watching cartoons, and ladled himself out some lamb stew from a pot that was simmering on the range. He thumbed through a *Sports Illustrated* while he ate and washed dinner down with a glass of jug red. Drinking wine with meals had once been as alien to Karp as facial tattoos, but seventeen years of marriage to Marlene had converted him, at least in the evenings. The first sip still gave him a faint start, however, as if he were drinking soured juice, and he was far from an oenophile, but he felt foolish watching his wife drink alone when she drank, which was often. Karp did not like feeling the puritan, though he certainly had that tendency. He thought, puritanically, that it should be resisted.

After stowing the dishes in the washer and the stewpot in the refrigerator, he changed his clothes for chinos and a T-shirt and knocked discreetly on the door of the bathing parlor. He received an affirmative noise from behind the door and entered. The great black tub was the last remnant of Marlene's rough single-girl loft existence, truncated by her marriage and by Karp's employment at a downtown tortmeister some years back. Karp had earned an obscene amount of money at this, and the couple had swept Marlene's improvised carpentry, plumbing, and electrical work away and replaced it with the sort of appointments featured in slick home-design magazines: actual walls, satiny oaken floors, marble countertops, track lighting, the Vulcan stove, the Sub-Zero fridge. But the tub survived. It was a five-hundred-gallon, hard-rubber electroplating tub left over from the galvanized-wire mill that had occupied the loft when Marlene had first moved in, circa 1970, when only artists had lived in what became SoHo. She had rigged a heater and an ozone filter on it, and she sat in it now, in steaming water, lit by six candles stuck in an old brass candelabra. The bathing parlor was the only room in the house that still retained a trace of premarriage Marlene, and she fled to it and stayed in it whenever she thought her life had taken some wrong turn. The air was moist and smelled of roses, and burning wax and ozone.

Karp sat down on a rickety cane-seated chair and regarded his wife lounging at the tub's far end, her face a pale oval above the black water, noting the bottle of Beaujolais standing on the tub's broad rim, noting the level of the liquid within. She, noting his noting, frowned and said, "Yes, I'm getting drunk."

"You had a rough day. Want to talk about it?"

"Not particularly. I told the story so many times it doesn't seem all that real anymore. The short version is: hubby slays estranged wife in front of shelter while big-time feminist bodyguard stands by with thumb up ass."

"The news said you saved the little girl's life."

"Oh, *fuck* the news!" She poured wine into the tumbler she held above the water's surface and took a deep drink. "Are the TV trucks still outside?"

"Yeah, a couple. And the freelancers. They looked pretty cold and wet."

"They want to know why the woman died. They want to know how I *feel*."

"How *do* you feel?"

He saw her shoulders move slightly, making ripples. "Numb, mostly." She sighed. "Nevermore," she said, and held her hand up, palm out. "From where the sun now stands, I fight no more forever."

"Meaning what?"

"Meaning I'm giving up the gun. Let them all murder each other. Or let the fanatics do the work."

He looked closely at her face. It was stiff and bleak and had the blurry look it took on when she drank. "You're serious?"

"Dead serious. It's been almost ten years, now, and whether I wanted to continue the work or not, I obviously can't do it anymore. I got that woman killed because I wasn't focused. Why? Because the truth be told, that work isn't me, not to the core. I compare myself with women like Mattie Duran or even Sym McCabe, and I can see the difference. It's what they live for. They're fanatics. I'm not, and you know, I used to look down my nose at them, my phony, aristocratic whatchamacallit . . . delicacy, diffidence, like perfection came down from God, like my shooting. I could shoot without having to learn how, a natural, so, a natural at the work, but no. It was just waiting to happen. And that stupid woman is dead, and I can't even feel anything."

She started to cry then, silently, the worst kind for her. Her face scrunched up into a gargoyle mask and got red, and fat tears dripped down into the bathwater, plunk plonk. Karp stood, took off his T-shirt, and hung it on one of the brass hooks on the wall. Then he took off the rest of his clothes and got into the tub. He held his wife while she had a long, shaking cry. She was weightless in the water, but she shook and thrashed like a dying tarpon and he had to hold on tightly. He didn't say anything, not even "There, there." It was familiar ground, for it happened to a greater or lesser extent whenever Marlene shot someone. It was not what he would have chosen; he doubted that guys married to Bloomingdale's buyers did much of this. On the other hand, had she not gone through this kind of hell after committing violence, he couldn't have lived with her for a day.

After a time she stopped shaking and re-laxed in his arms, taking deep, even breaths.

"Are you back?" he asked.

"More or less. And how was *your* day, dear?"

"The usual. Locked up a few more pa-thetic, dangerous black kids. Worked on stop-ping the menace of infanticide. Were you serious about giving it up, or was that just the liquor talking?"

"I was serious." She writhed around so she was sitting on his lap. Her body felt silky from the bath salts, and her skin smelled of roses and the wine. "I've been thinking about it since I left the cops this evening. Harry and Osborne can take over the celebrity protection with no trouble. Sym and Mattie can run the other stuff, if they want. People don't like it . . . what can I say? They won't invite me to the Feminazi Ball."

"Well, I'd be a hypocrite if I said I was sorry. Actually, this makes me really happy."

She wriggled a little to obtain better contact in the significant zones. "Yes, I can feel you're getting happy."

Karp looked meaningfully at the door. "What about the kids?"

"They're fine. That's why we have skilled child care on the premises." She pressed her mouth against his. This was the other part of the après-shoot period: first the hysterical weeping and then fuck-my-brains-out.

In the breathing space that followed, Karp said, "Our skilled child care is wearing a head scarf and an ankle-length *schmatte*. She took the kids to some kind of Islamic center today."

"Why shouldn't she? They live in our beautiful mosaic. And, face it, Islam is probably better for her than dope and rock and roll and ratso guys she picks up in clubs. Besides, she's in love with Walid, and he treats her like a pearl and I think it's sweet."

"He's a terrorist, Marlene."

"He's an ex-nonterrorist baker, as you very well know."

"Humph. And where's Lucy?"

"She's sleeping over at Caitlin's."

"On a school night?"

"Yes, she gets to sleep over on a school night every time her mother shoots someone. It's a warm family ritual. Are you going to be Dad all evening, darling, or are you going to wield that kosher salami in a suitable fashion?"

"Hey, men have feelings, too, you know," Karp pouted. "This is pretty emotionally upsetting for me, if you want to know. I'm sitting in court, trying to concentrate, and my secretary waltzes in with a message that my wife's been involved in another violent felony, underline *another*, and then we have our nervous breakdown, and I'm there with emotional support, and then I get told that we're going to abandon that career and go on to something else. My little world is shattered, shattered! And now you want sex? What am I to you, just a piece of meat?"

Marlene looked at him admiringly. "That was very good. Joan Crawford in *Mildred Pierce*."

"I was trying for Bette Davis in *Now, Voyager*. But, gosh, Marlene! Give me a minute, here!"

74

"Sorry, can't wait. I'll just have to use my famous bubble treatment."

"Oh, no!" wailed Karp. "Not the famous bubble treatment!"

Marlene took several deep breaths, plunged her head under the surface of the water, and applied it.

Only one such was required, and subsequently they splashed about like a pair of rubber duckies on yohimbine. Karp usually let all extraneous thoughts flee during these occasions, but now two kept rising unbidden: that Marlene had quit a profession in which lethal projectiles were likely to whiz about the heads of his loved ones was good, great, in fact, but clearly another one would be necessary for her, and he could not help wondering what it would be. The other thought was one that never quite left his mind, which was that his sweetheart and life's companion, brilliant, fascinating, warm, and delicious as she was after seventeen years of marriage, was still and had always been about half a bubble off center. So . . . what next?

Lucy Karp found out about what had befallen her mother while eating dinner at the home of her friend Caitlin Maxwell. The Maxwells occupied the two lower floors of a brownstone on Seventy-sixth Street off Fifth

Avenue, an establishment that Lucy thought as luxurious as could be desired by anyone, but Mr. Maxwell had just purchased the entire building, paying $8.5 million for it. Lucy thought this was a lot of money to pay for a house, even a very nice one, but Mr. Maxwell said he had lowballed the estate of the previous owner because the place needed a lot of work. This work was going on now, virtually around the clock, on the upper three stories while the family languished in what Mrs. Maxwell always referred to as the dump, as in "My God, I'll be glad to get out of this dump!"

There was a dining room in the dump, and the Maxwells usually dined in it, but tonight they were dining in the family room, the two adults sitting in comfortable chairs and the three youngsters, Caitlin, Lucy, and Caitlin's brother, Brian, sitting on the floor. The family room was the only room in the house that contained what Lucy thought of as regular furniture: chairs you could sit comfortably in, tables you could place objects upon, shelves with books you could pull out and read. The remainder of the apartment was furnished with antiques and objets d'art, over which Mrs. Maxwell watched with an assiduity that would not have disgraced the custodians of the Louvre.

At this decidedly informal meal, everyone but Mrs. Maxwell was eating spicy fried chicken and french fries and tossed salad, each dinner nicely arranged on a plate and brought out on its own tray by Vida, the Maxwells' present cook, the last, according to Caitlin, of a considerable series. Mrs. Maxwell was eating a shrimp salad and warm asparagus. The adults were drinking wine and the others San Pellegrino water with a wedge of lime stuck on the glass. Lucy, who knew a good deal about food preparation, thought that Vida was doing a terrific job, but the Maxwells did not seem to think so. Often they would direct her to do something differently — "Vida, you should cut the ends off the lime wedges before you put them on the glasses" — but in a nice tone. When she wasn't looking, they would roll their eyes at each other and smile ruefully. Caitlin had told Lucy that when the house was ready, they would be expanding the staff. There would be a full-time live-in maid, a driver-handyman, and a cook then, and the cook would not be Vida. The Maxwells hoped to hire a European cook, preferably a Swiss.

They were in the family room for dinner because work on the upper stories had shaken dust down from the plaster in the dining room and Mrs. Maxwell considered it unsafe, because of the lead that might be in the old paint. Mrs. Maxwell was very health-conscious. She was a tall, thin woman with beautifully cut pale blond hair, a pale, small mouth, and slightly protruding pale blue eyes. These often held a worried expression, as if something was not quite right and she was trying hard to think what it was. She had a great deal of energy, exhibited in sudden and rapid movements, and the snapping out of rapid orders to her children and servants, orders, however, that were typically couched in the form of steely suggestions ("Wouldn't you be happier with a warmer coat, Caitlin?") to which the answer no was not ever appropriate, nor ever tendered.

Lucy thought Mrs. Maxwell a little peculiar, but liked her anyway. She was extremely nice to Lucy and to Mary Ma, querying them about themselves and their families. Caitlin did not have a lot of time for friends, and Mrs. Maxwell thought that friends were an essential part of growing up and was more than willing to slot these into her daughter's schedule. She also didn't mind that they were exotic, a Chinese and the peculiar-looking little prodigy with the strange family background. She intended that her daughter shoot to the very top of the ballet world, and experience with odd people would stand her in good stead. So Mrs. Maxwell was generous with the girls, taking them on regular expeditions to those of New York's expensive cultural marvels she thought suitable, with elegant restaurant meals to follow.

They should have gone out to a restaurant tonight, and they would have, had she not been too exhausted by her day to argue with her husband, who wanted to stay home and watch some financial news show on television. Mrs. Maxwell thought it was impossibly lower middle class to dine while watching television. She had, however, decided to accept this solecism with good grace, as being a kind of amusing slumming, and something she could make up a good story about, featuring the primitive conditions the Maxwells had borne while their house was being repaired.

Now she felt observed and looked up from her plate and across the room. Lucy Karp was staring at her with those spooky tan eyes. Mrs. Maxwell smiled politely, dabbed hurriedly at her mouth with her linen napkin in case a bit of something was there to attract that stare (and didn't they teach children not to stare anymore? They did not, and both of them in a convent school that might be expected to devote more attention to deportment), and pulled her eyes away, back to the show they were all ostensibly watching.

On-screen, two men and the moderator were discussing the prime rate, in detail, and Mr. Maxwell was expostulating at them as if they were playing some exciting sport. (*No, it's not M2, you moron, it's the Eurodollar mess!*) Mrs. Maxwell had little interest in her husband's affairs. It really was enough work running this household and raising two children, one requiring an enormous amount of organization and the other . . . the other an extremely lovely child, who was going through a difficult stage. She let her eye fall on Brian, taking in with pleasure his astounding physical beauty: the hair of truest gold, worn long and curling — *hyacinthine,* the word was; the huge blue eyes, long-lashed; the pink, clear skin; the exquisite rosebud mouth. Unfortunately, the exquisite rosebud mouth had a long french fry in it, and the child was wiggling the potato strip so that it popped against his nose. His eyes held the usual blank, or, as Mrs. Maxwell preferred to regard it, dreamy expression. His rolling gaze found her and she hissed at him not to play with his food. He grinned and pulled the fry into his mouth, grinned again, popped the brown tip out a few times, and swallowed. Shortly, he was doing the same again, secure in the knowledge that she would not make a scene with company present.

The company had observed this interaction and filed it away in the mental dossier she was keeping on the family Maxwell. She was interviewing it for the position of surrogate and supplementary family, which had recently become open. Lucy Karp had been partially raised, from infancy, by a Chinese-American family named Chen. It was there that her astounding language gifts had first become manifest, as she sucked in Cantonese along with her noodles. Unfortunately, the liaison with the Chens had been broken some years previously, over an affair of warring tongs. The early experience had left her, however, with the habit of dwelling in more than one family, of extending a friendship with a girl by exploring that girl's relations. This is not a common taste among teenagers, who ordinarily prefer to imagine their pals arising from the ether, fully formed.

Lucy was different. Lucy was conscious of a deficit of mothering from her own mother and wished to judge just how great a departure this was from the mean. Compared, for example, to Mrs. Chen, Marlene was barely a mother at all. Mrs. Chen lived for her children. Lucy, a good enough minifeminist, did not think she wanted quite that intensity, but she would have liked to have been loved with a little more dedication than she typically was.

One thing Lucy liked about the Maxwells was just that: Mrs. Maxwell was *extremely* involved in her children's affairs. The story of her campaign to get Caitlin into the New York Ballet School was a family legend, much retold. The coming campaign to get Caitlin into the Juilliard program was already being discussed. Lucy had been surprised to learn the extent to which politics determined whom the public saw dancing on the stage. There were, as Mrs. Maxwell had often explained, thousands of competent young dancers in New York and dozens of absolutely first-rate ones. Each season ten twelve-year-olds were accepted to work with Mr. Rodenski and Madame Vernova at the city's premier ballet school. And you had to requalify every year. Three years at the school, three at the corps de ballet at the New York City Ballet, then two years as prima with a small but good out-of-town company, then the triumphant return to New York. Or, with luck, a girl might catch Rodenski's eye as a student, as so many girls before had caught Balanchine's eye, and then perhaps the ultimate glory at seventeen. At every stage of this progress, quite remarkable amounts of effort had to be expended: parties given, favors done, benefits organized, buttocks kissed, rivals scuppered. Although, of course, as Mrs. Maxwell was always careful to point out, the campaign, though necessary, was not sufficient, nor even the main thing. Talent was; talent and a capacity for hard work.

And Caitlin certainly had the talent and the capacity. Lucy looked down at her friend, who was stretched out on her belly watching the TV, or pretending to. She was wearing what she had worn to school, a fawn silk polo shirt, a green wool kilt, and tights of pale new-leaf green. The legs thus clad were, of course, enormously muscular, and they were never still, not for an instant, but always in motion, the bunched masses heaving under the thin fabric as she crossed the legs, stretched them, brought them up to the small of her back, snapped them down to go up on the toes. Looking at those legs and comparing them to her own overlong broomsticks, Lucy felt a mixture of admiration and, truth to tell, a faint queasiness, because the muscle masses on Caitlin's legs were not arranged where they ever were on a normal person. These legs had literally been deformed to perform the highly specialized functions required of classical dancers, a deformation, Lucy knew, that was the instantiation in flesh of tens of thousands of hours of concentrated effort, mixed with excruciations severe enough, had they not been voluntary, to attract the interest of

Amnesty International.

This was enough to awe Lucy, whose admiration for, and resistance to, hard, repetitive work were approximately equal and large. Lucy's own gift came, she understood, directly from God, postpaid, and all she had to do was figure out how to use it. She was therefore a despair to her parents, Trojans both, and her mother especially bewailed the sad fact that her daughter was perfectly fluent and no more than semiliterate in fourteen languages, English included.

The program broke for a commercial. Mr. Maxwell asked his daughter if she understood the concept of prime rate. The answer being neutral, he explained it, in some detail. He commonly asked questions of this sort. Lucy had often observed his desire that his family understand exactly what it was that he did for a living, whether they wished to or not. Mr. Maxwell, C. Ralston Maxwell, was a lawyer, like Lucy's father, but not the same sort of lawyer, which was why he was hard put to explain to his family what he actually did at work. (Lucy knew perfectly well what her father did and had known since the age of four.) Mr. Maxwell, or Rally as he was known, was a partner at a law firm on Broad Street that specialized in corporate mergers. When Behemoth wished to mate with Gargantua, Rally

Maxwell was there to bless the congress, and to insure that the great greasy organs slid into their appropriate receptacles, whether Gargantua was willing or not, or rather especially if it was not, if the deal was a rape. For this he was paid approximately thirty times what Lucy's father earned for representing the People.

Mr. Maxwell was in his early forties; his skin bore the tan of costly winter beaches, and his face the marks of power long exercised in perfect confidence. He had a broad, somewhat bulging forehead adorned by a Nixonian widow's peak, whose thinning dead grass–colored hair was bulked by weavings and plugs. Below were nearly invisible eyebrows and gray eyes; Mr. Maxwell's habit of tensing the muscles of his orbits to make these eyes more piercing had accumulated over the years a fine net of radial lines. He was disappointed in his nose, which resembled a new potato and which he thought too small for his face. Women should have small noses, Mr. Maxwell believed, while men were allowed the license of noble cutwaters (although not hooked ones, of course), and he regretted his genes not having taken advantage of this. His mouth was the usual Anglo-Saxon lipless line, and his chin was an aggressive pink hemisphere, with a cleft in it. Not bad looking was his assessment of himself, but not pretty, no, that was neither required nor desired. Mr. Maxwell thought he was tough-looking; "tough," in fact, was one of his favorite accolades, along with "decent" and "sharp." He was wearing his usual leisure-time outfit, carefully faded jeans, lizard-skin cowboy boots, and a collarless blue denim shirt, all from one of the designer boutiques on Madison. In Lucy's home, everyone went barefoot much of the time, but shoes were the rule at the Maxwells. She thought it a bit odd that Mr. Maxwell wore high-heeled boots while relaxing, but Caitlin had told her that it was because he was a little shorter than Mrs. Maxwell.

Mr. Maxwell put his tray aside, rose, commanded that the TV should be left on the current channel because he wanted to catch the news, and went off in the direction of the downstairs toilet, one of the apartment's five. After Mr. Maxwell left, Mrs. Maxwell nagged at Brian about a call she had received from his school. Brian wasn't paying attention, the headmaster had said. Brian was failing math and near failing English. He hadn't handed in assignments. Mrs. Maxwell wanted to know how could you fail *English?* They were running out of schools in New York — he had flunked out of three already. She wanted to know if Brian knew what would happen if Dad heard about this. Brian would be in military school before he could tie his shoes. Did Brian want her to tell him? Brian shook his head slowly. He caught Lucy's eye and gave her a bashful, inappropriate smile.

"Brian, look at me!" said Mrs. Maxwell. "I'm not going to say anything this time, but I want to see some improvement, okay?"

"Okay, Mother," said Brian, not looking at her, looking at Lucy instead. She thought he looked like someone with a sly secret.

Mrs. Maxwell was not pleased. To heaven she addressed her gaze and said, "Oh, why do I bother? This is absolutely too exhausting!"

"What's exhausting, dear?" said Mr. Maxwell, returning to the room. He sat in his chair. "Decorator got you down again?" As he said this, he looked at Lucy and gave a little wink.

Mrs. Maxwell picked up the cue. "Oh, the man is impossible. He dragged me to this silly fabric place all the way downtown, I mean it was the sort of neighborhood they stab people in, and the swatches the man had weren't even close to what I wanted for the bedroom. Peach, I said, but *burnt* peach. He's a decorator, you'd think he'd know what burnt peach is, but no, these were practically *tangerine* if you can believe it."

"Fire him and get someone else," Mr. Maxwell shot back. "There's no shortage of twee little faggots in New York."

"Rally!" said Mrs. Maxwell. Brian giggled.

"Get a peach and burn it next time, so he'll know." Mr. Maxwell winked at Lucy again. Lucy wondered what the Maxwells were like when they didn't have an audience for their various dramas. Another entry in the file.

On the TV, they had finished selling Pringles and Lincolns, and with a flourish of arrogant logos the news came on, two spiffies, male and female, and the male said, "Good evening. Tonight's top stories: a brutal murder in front of a women's shelter on the Lower East Side; another terrorist attack shocks Israel; the mayor says he's not to blame for the collapse of the school roof last week that injured thirty-one; and the president announces a new program to curb teenage pregnancies. Carol?"

The female newscaster arranged a grave expression on her semi-artificial face and began to talk about what had happened in front of the East Village Women's Shelter that afternoon. They switched to tape. The front of the building, the bloodstains, a frightened child being tucked into a police car, and then there was Mom, being hustled along to a blue-and-white by a large brown patrolwoman. Lucy felt, in succession, blank terror, relief, rage, and the most intense embarrassment.

"Lucy!" cried Mrs. Maxwell. "Isn't that your mother?"

Mr. Maxwell, who knew of his daughter's friend's parentage only that the father was high up in the New York DA, and instinctively ready to contradict his wife, said, "Don't be silly, Jeanne! How could it be her mother? They're *arresting* her."

But Caitlin said, "No! It is! Lucy's mom's a bodyguard. It *is* her, isn't it, Luce?"

Lucy felt her face getting red. "Yes, it's her." She stood up and said, in her formal voice, "Mrs. Maxwell, may I use your phone? I should call home."

"Of course, dear. You can use the one in the kitchen hallway."

All the Maxwells were staring at her, as at a freak. As she left the room, she heard Brian say, "Lucy's mom *killed* a guy? Wow, that's cool!" and Mrs. Maxwell respond, "Oh, Brian, *please!*"

Lucy pressed the buttons for Marlene's secret private line, heard the message, and at the beep said, "Mom, it's Lucy. Pick up if you're there." A short wait.

"Lucy?"

"Yeah. I heard about it on the news. I guess you're not in jail."

"No, it's not a crime to let someone you're protecting get killed. And I didn't kill the perp, so . . . are you still at Caitlin's?"

"Yeah. They invited me for dinner. What should I do?"

"Why don't you hang out there for a while, if it's okay with them. It's a madhouse here, with the press outside."

"Maybe I should stay over."

A little pause. "Sure. Did they invite you?"

"Uh-huh." Lucy disliked lying to her parents, but this one was fairly white, and she and Caitlin had actually discussed asking permission. She said good-bye and hung up.

As she turned away from the phone, there was Vida, with a pile of trays. Lucy backed the few steps into the kitchen to let her by. The kitchen was messy with meal prep, though extremely clean, and quite large for an apartment kitchen. It was, of course, equipped with top-of-the-line commercial gear, virtually the only thing the Karps and the Maxwells had in common. Vida put the pile down on the drainboard and sighed. She leaned for a moment on her knuckles with her head hanging, looking exhausted, then pulled energy from somewhere and began to unload the dirty dishes from the trays. She noticed Lucy standing there, watching her, waited to be asked to do something, then looked away and continued with her work.

Lucy said, "I really liked that chicken. When I make fried chicken, it's always black on the bottom or raw in the middle. How do you get it to stay crispy, with those little bubbles on the crust?"

Vida goggled at her, a not uncommon reaction to Lucy's speech when it was, as now, unexpectedly in the native tongue of the listener, and perfectly fluent.

"You're a *Mexican?*" asked Vida.

"No, I was born here. But I learned to speak Spanish from a *chicana.*"

"That's amazing, truly. A gift from God."

"I agree." Lucy looked around the kitchen. "You have a lot of work," she said, for want of something better. She was, like most Americans, including the Maxwells, uneasy with servants.

"Yes, well, it's not so bad. I don't like the ones that scream at you as if you were a child, and Mrs. Maxwell is always very polite. Listen, since you asked, the chicken: you have to use a very hot pan, use iron, only iron for the pan, and then you put ice cubes in the batter — the batter has to be cold, and use nothing but lard to cook it in. Also you rub the skin with chili powder before the batter. Do you cook yourself?"

"Yes, quite a bit. I like it. My mother is a

good cook and my uncle is a chef."

"Amazing. I thought American girls only knew how to open a package. You will forgive me if I start on this; my husband will be here for me in an hour. We have to go to our other job."

"You have another job?"

"Oh, yes. We both work night shift at Entenmann's."

"Aya, that's a lot of work."

Vida smiled and shrugged. "Yes, but it's good to work. Work is a blessing. The worst is when there's no work, like in Salvador." The woman began to load the dishwasher. Obviously dismissed, Lucy went back to the family room, which now lacked a family, although the TV was still flashing colorfully on mute. Lucy wandered down a hall, through the formal dining room with its long mahogany table and white silk chairs, and the sideboard with the heirloom silver. Much of this silver, according to Caitlin, had recently been bought at auction, but a few pieces were actually heirlooms, from Mrs. Maxwell's side of the family. The family connections of Mr. Maxwell were not much discussed. Mr. Maxwell had, one would think, appeared at Princeton from out of a mist, fully formed. He had, however, married into an adequately *Mayflower*-ed family and had adopted it as his own. Caitlin thought there were Jews not too far back in the paternal line, but this was something she had broached only to Lucy, she being déclassé enough not to be shocked and reliable enough not to let it drop. Lucy thought the whole thing was weird and time-warpish — I mean, who gave a rat's ass nowadays? — but apparently in the circles in which the Maxwells traveled, it was still notable.

She paused at the door to the living room, which lacked stanchions and velvet ropes, but was otherwise as much like a room in a museum as could be wished. All the furniture was Louis XV, gold leaf and silk upholstery striped green and white. At a flat table of this style sat Mrs. Maxwell, poring over swatch books, and making notes with a sterling pencil in a cloth-covered notebook. She looked up and saw Lucy.

"Oh, you poor child, how distressed you must seem! How did you find your mother?" she said in French, which she often spoke to Lucy, badly; occasionally her idiomatic reach exceeded her grasp and she gave voice to odd sentiments, as now.

Besides the humorous aspects, Lucy actually enjoyed speaking French with Mrs. Maxwell. It recalled for her the man who had taught her the language, a much-loved Vietnamese gentleman of unfortunate reputation who now lived away from the city, while at the same time the natural formality of the language (at least in the schoolgirl phraseology that they used together) reduced the slight unease she felt with the woman. Talking to Mrs. Maxwell in English was like talking to a guidance counselor of the what-are-you-going-to-do-with-your-life variety.

Lucy said, "My mother is well, thank you, Madame. Except, she tells me that the press is surrounding our home in the most vehement and hostile fashion. Therefore, she asks that you allow me to spend the night here. She is desolated, of course, but this disaster requires unusual measures."

"Oh, think little of it, my dear child, think little of it," cried Mrs. Maxwell. "I will have been delighted to negotiate you a bed, in your moment of inerasable sadness." She put her swatches aside, stood, and grasped Lucy by the hand. "Come, let us approach the invited room."

The Maxwells' guest room was a small chamber containing a spindle bed in walnut, covered with an elaborately flounced counterpane, a Federal three-drawer bureau (cherry, with brass fittings), and a stiff little love seat, covered in pink silk and outfitted with faded needleworked cushions. There was a flowered carpet on the floor and on the walls a

Currier & Ives original print of ice-skating throngs, and two small, bad oil portraits of anonymous elderly folk in mobcap and periwig. The room smelled of furniture polish and flowered sachet.

Mrs. Maxwell left Lucy in another burst of her unusual French, to return perhaps to her swatches. Lucy went through the bathroom to Caitlin's room, which connected. Caitlin was lying on the bed, on the phone. Lucy sat on a rush-seated rocker and leafed through a book of photographs of the Bolshoi in action.

"Who was that?" she asked when Caitlin got off the phone.

"Oh, some guy," Caitlin responded carelessly. "What's up with your mom?"

"She's okay. The mope isn't dead for a change. I asked your mom if I could stay over because there's wall-to-wall TV crews outside our place. My mom doesn't like me to get my picture on the tube."

"She doesn't? Why not?" Amazed surprise here, like not desiring salvation would be among the hard-shell Baptists.

"She's not too popular in some places, and I'm a target," said Lucy, and saw her friend's eyes widen and refused to elaborate on the statement, a little payback for that "some guy."

"Anyway, could I borrow something to sleep

in?" Lucy asked, and, after some rummaging in the walk-in closet, was given an elaborate rucked, ruffled, and lace-embroidered confection of the sort sold to rich loving dads for their little princesses. Much eye-rolling and giggles here.

They hung out in Caitlin's room for the next few hours, chatting about the usual subjects interesting to girls of that age, a froth of social comments and pop culture, and trying out for one another poses they had picked up from the adult world. Brian came by and was cruelly chased off by his sister. Lucy felt a pang of sympathy (and guilt: she had done the same often enough to her younger brothers) because it seemed to her that no one in the overachieving Maxwell family had any time for little Brian.

The girls did their English and French homework, Lucy helping somewhat because Caitlin, truth to tell, was half a step slow in the academic department, allowing Lucy that speck of contempt without which the soup of intimacy is intolerable. They left their math homework for the period before classes the next day, when Mary Ma would guide them swiftly through it.

Afterward, moving past the joking and arch comments, Caitlin opened her heart a crack. She had been selected for the important role of the Lilac Fairy in the junior company's winter production of *Sleeping Beauty*, her first serious solo part, and she was terrified. The whole of the New York dance world would be in the audience, and it was a chance to shine or fail. Caitlin was transformed when she talked in this way, quite different from the chattering and rather spoiled teenager of a few minutes ago, and Lucy understood that this was the core of what tied her to Caitlin, and the two of them to Mary: the three girls had each been touched by something Other, which had marked them and changed them and separated them from nearly all the rest of their peers and their families. Sometimes Lucy imagined the genies Language, Dance, and Number sitting up on a cloud and poking their chosen ones with sharp sticks. And occasionally dropping one of the divine sweetmeats that canceled out for a time the misery of isolation. She therefore listened carefully, although she couldn't really understand what her friend was saying about the difficulty of a particular series of steps in her new part. The jargon was French, which she knew perfectly well, but it was hard to visualize why one set of steps was harder than another. It was all hard enough, to Lucy's imagination; just the thought of supporting one's entire weight on point and leaping up in the air and landing on the toes made her faintly nauseated.

She had, however, seen her friend dance. Caitlin had what dancers called *ballon*, which is the ability to float in the air for a preternaturally long time and descend like a wisp of eiderdown, and the first time Lucy had seen it at a recital, she understood instantly that it was from God, like her own genius at language or Mary's ability to extract the cube root of a six-digit number on the fly, and holy. Lucy was still extraordinarily devout, and this was, sadly, one thing that she could not share fully with her friends, neither of whom were interested enough in religion even to be proper atheists.

Caitlin doused the lights and lit a scented candle and they sat together on her white four-poster bed and spoke cozily in the dimness, about dancing and about Chinese poetry, scrolls of which Lucy knew by heart, which Caitlin in her turn didn't really understand either but listened to carefully, for friendship.

In the guest room later Lucy knelt and said her prayers, first carefully locking the door so that no one might come in and be embarrassed by piety. She fell asleep thinking about her mother, for whom she had just strenuously prayed. And awoke, with dim dawn shining through the frilly white curtains, aware that a figure was standing against the white door, silently watching her.

Her heart bounced briefly and then settled when she understood who it was.

"Brian," she said hoarsely. "Brian, what are you doing in my room?"

"Nothing."

"You're not supposed to go into people's bedrooms. What time is it?"

Brian looked at the large and complex digital watch on his wrist. He was wearing a blue plaid bathrobe, from which skinny, naked legs descended. "Six-twelve A.M."

"Oh, Lord, I'll never get back to sleep. How long have you been standing there?"

"Since five twenty-five A.M."

"Just standing there in the dark?"

"I was watching you sleep. I can see good in the dark."

"You find this amusing?"

He shrugged and grinned. "You think I'm weird, huh?"

She sat up in the bed and looked at him, right into his eyes, in a way that he did not recall being looked at before. Usually when people looked into his eyes, his family or his teachers, he had to drop his eyes down. It was like a contest he was doomed to lose. But there was neither challenge nor annoyance in these. She said, "Actually, no. I think you're a regular eleven-year-old kid in a very weird family."

He took this in. A shaft of sun came through the window and lit up the top of his head, making its gold into a halo. She thought, He really is the most gorgeous kid, and what good does it do him, the poor little guy? Around here, that's just the base coat.

He asked, "Do you want to see my comic books?"

She sighed. "Well, Brian, I'm a little old for comics, but thanks any—"

"No! Not comics like you buy in the store. Comics I made up myself. Brian Comics."

"Oh. In that case, yes, but first let me pee."

4

As Karp had predicted, the police had all three of the Monster Moms, as the tabloid press called them, in custody by the end of January. The first to go down was the Monster Mom of Subway Baby, who turned out to be Demairis Jenner, a fourteen-year-old of African-American parentage. Demairis had apparently had her baby at home, under the impression it was a stomachache she had picked up from eating a slushie too quickly. She had stuffed the baby in her clothes closet and covered it with newspapers and dirty laundry for a day, and then, when it continued to make noises, she became concerned that her granny, with whom she lived, would find it. She therefore wrapped the infant in newspaper, placed it in a shopping bag, and tossed it off the open platform between the cars on the Broadway line. The cops found her because the grocery bag she had used contained a receipt that led to a fish store on 110th Street, where Demairis's grandmother was employed. The rest was easy. Demairis had fetal alcohol syndrome and an intelligence quotient of 78.

Two days after this coup, the Monster Mom of the Garbage Baby was arrested. Lourdes (or Lola) Bustamente was sixteen, a Puerto Rican. Her baby, she claimed, was the result of a rape she had never reported to anyone. Unlike Demairis, she had known she was pregnant, but had been able to cover it up, all the while hoping it would go away by itself. She just wanted to have a regular life, she told the police. This included going to dances, including one at a salsa joint on the second floor of the building at 52nd and Tenth. She had delivered the baby in a toilet stall, hacked through the cord with a nail scissors, expelled the placenta, and then simply tossed both unwanted items out the bathroom window, where they had fallen deep into the pile of plastic trash bags lying in the alley below. A friend of Ms. Bustamente's had turned her in, in exchange for a deal for a brother in trouble with the law.

The *Post* printed TWO DOWN! The decline-of-morality editorials had tapered off just a little with the discovery of the identities of the first two Monster Moms. Demairis was clearly a person hit by a truck. Lola Bustamente was a cold little number, all right, but even so, you couldn't get much irate-editorial mileage out of a rape victim of sixteen. Everyone therefore awaited with sick fascination the discovery of the Monster Mom who had cruelly buried alive the Dog Baby.

Among these, and waiting with special interest, was Roland Hrcany, the chief of the homicide bureau of the New York DA. He said as much to his friend and (from his point of view) longtime rival Butch Karp as they walked together down a courthouse hallway.

"I want it to be a twenty-eight-year-old civil liberties lawyer. I'll buy you a dinner at Lutèce if it's a twenty-eight-year-old civil liberties lawyer. Or —" Here he named a prominent member of the city council, a noisy critic of the police and the courts. "If it's her, I'll buy you a Caddy to drive to the dinner in."

Karp said, "Roland, I think women of that type know about abortions."

Roland laughed. "Hey, a guy can dream. Listen, I know you think I'm a big Nazi . . ."

"Not at all. A somewhat small Nazi, maybe."

"Fuck you, too. No, you know what I mean. The last time we had a serious case in this building, I mean with a middle-class white guy in the box and a decent lawyer, you know, get the combative juices going — hell, I don't know when it was."

He did, of course. Karp gave Hrcany a look. The man was eight inches shorter, but built like a truck, a serious weight lifter. He carried a heavy-featured, quasi-Neanderthal head on his seventeen-inch neck, decorated with straight blond hair swept straight back over his collar. He looked like a dull, brutal thug, but was actually smart and a first-class prosecutor. But brutal, yes. Hrcany and Karp had started in the DA's office on the same day, and the one other thing they had in common was that they had actually both been shot in the line of duty, an exceeding rarity for prosecutors in the United States. Being shot had made Karp even more serious than was his natural bent; it had made Roland angrier.

"You know very well when it was, Roland," said Karp. "It was when Waley whipped me in *Rohbling.*"

"Oh, yeah," said Roland, grinning. "How soon we forget." He gave a jaunty wave and turned into a courtroom. Karp continued on, thinking dark thoughts about *Rohbling* and its eponymous star, a wealthy young white man whose unfortunate weakness was the ritualized murder of elderly black women. Karp had handled the case personally, although he had been homicide bureau chief and did not have the time, really, to concentrate on a megatrial. But he had persisted in this, although warned by Keegan not to do it, and gone up against the legendary defense counsel Lionel T. Waley, and lost, his first and only loss after over one hundred victories in homicide cases. Rohbling was still confined in a mental institution, but he could walk out any day as "cured."

The case and its outcome and various things that had happened during the trial had combined to get Karp kicked upstairs to his present position. Given his gargantuan administrative responsibilities as chief assistant DA, Karp often felt that he might never try a homicide case for the People again, a possibility that, whenever it came into his mind, throbbed there like the pain from a sick molar. He forced his thoughts back to the Monster Moms. Roland was right about the defendants there. It was the dirty secret of all big-city public prosecutors. Almost every case was a slam dunk against midget defenders: the accused were usually dumb kids, the defense lawyers somewhat smarter kids, ill-prepared and harassed. Karp thought of his conversation with little Murrow; that was another thing that corrupted the prosecution, the paltriness of the typical defense. It made them sloppy; worse, it made them *feel* sloppy, mere social sanitation guys going through arcane legal motions to warehouse losers. This is why all serious prosecutors long for the great white defendant. Karp also recalled the assignment he had given the lad, back when the babies first turned up. Not that it would be worth much now. Demairis and Lola would probably be handled by the juvie court, and unless the Dog Baby's mom turned out to be the sort of person Hrcany hoped for, it was unlikely that a scholarly review of the law in re infanticide would be of much value.

Nor was it, as it turned out. The Dog Baby's mom turned herself in at the Twenty-fifth Precinct on the following day, accompanied by the Dog Baby's dad. Her name was Mary Jane Kopne, and his was Martin Donaugh. Unlike the other two Monster Moms, Ms. Kopne was a white woman and an adult. She had delivered the baby in secret in the room at the adult shelter where she lived, and they had managed to keep it secret during the infant's four days of life. They were afraid that it would be taken away from them. They were also afraid that its cries would draw notice from the other residents, and so they stuffed its little mouth with tissues and taped it shut when they weren't with it. When it stopped moving, they knew it had died and were sad. Mr. Donaugh knew of a vacant lot near where he worked, and they went there at night and dug a grave and said a prayer over it and even placed a chunk of concrete as a headstone. They would have written an inscription on it, but neither of them knew how to write. They had called their baby Penny, and they were sorry and hoped that people wouldn't be mad at them. No one at the cops had the heart to tell them that they had buried it alive.

"Roland, you know I'm not a big advocate of the death penalty," said Karp to Hrcany when these events had become known at the courthouse, "but it's going to give me a lot of pleasure to see you tear up Mary Jane Kopne in court and send her down for the big one."

They were in Karp's office, his *palatial* office as it was invariably called by his associates, and Hrcany was sitting on the leather couch, looking disgruntled, with his legs stretched out before him and his hands thrust deep in his pockets. Karp was in an armchair on the other side of the low teakwood coffee table. Hrcany snorted and said, "Oh, yeah, she's a cinch for the death penalty, right? And they'll promise her a lollipop if she holds still for the needle. Oh, *fuck!*"

"My sentiments," said Karp, "but in any case the Monster Moms now recede into the mists as far as we're concerned."

"Do they? I'll give you the Dog and the Subway. Jenner is a lamebrain juvie and Mary Jane is non compos, but I don't think we should let Ms. Bustamente off the hook so easy."

"You don't? Roland, she was raped."

"Yeah, and we only got her word on that, one, and two, it doesn't excuse tossing a live baby into the garbage out a two-story window. It shows depraved indifference."

"Wait, you're thinking about a murder indictment for this?" asked Karp, genuinely surprised.

"Thinking, yeah, why not? I'd be willing to go for second-degree murder as the top count. I'm not saying I would rule out a plea down to manslaughter one, but if not, I'd be willing to go to trial on the top count. And we'd win, too."

"She's sixteen, Roland."

"Almost seventeen, which is old enough to know you're not supposed to throw a baby out a window."

"Try her as an adult, you're thinking?"

"Damn straight! And another thing — I know you think the political end is horseshit, but it's there. The DA is a political animal whether you like it or not, and if we pass on three baby killings, *three* for Christ's sake, he's going to look like shit. He knows that, even if you don't."

Karp looked mildly at the bureau chief and made a noncommittal gesture. He refused to get into these fights with Roland anymore (they had on one occasion actually come to blows), but that did not seem to stem the other man's lust for combat. So Roland was forced into playing both combatants. Looked at from a certain angle, it was even amusing.

"Okay, you know we can't touch the other two. So the lovely Lola's in the crosshairs. She consciously and intentionally killed a human being and she's going down for it. No family court, no juvenile offender wrist-slapper. End of story."

"Well, okay, Roland, that's your decision. Jack will be happy."

"I'm not doing it to make Jack happy, damn it! It's the right thing to do."

"And how convenient that it's also politically popular. Lucky Roland!"

"Oh, fuck you! Look, this office stands for something, right? You do the crime, you do the time, that's what we're supposed to be about. And the decisions we make in an area where we got lots of discretion, that sends a message about what the people think is a serious crime. Prostitution? Slap on the wrist, right? Moral? Pross isn't a biggie. So we have lots of whores. Kidnap a kid? Watch out, because we're going to put you *under* the jail. Kidnap is pretty rare. That's how it works."

"Roland, I know how it works. I've been

here for the same amount of time as you have. What's your point?"

"My *point* is that killing a baby is not going to be a gimme on my watch."

Karp wrinkled his brow in a mime of heavy concentration. "Ah, let me see if I follow you here, Roland. If we don't come down hard on Lola, you think it would, um, *encourage* mothers to murder their newborns? That there might be a *rash* of infanticides?"

"We already *got* a rash of infanticides. For crying out loud, how many the fuck more do you want? What, *three* isn't a rash enough for you? How about eleven? How about forty-two?"

Roland's eyes were blazing and his face was moving down the spectrum from pink to brick. In the sweetest tones he could manage, Karp said, "Roland, I'm not questioning your judgment here. It's a bureau decision; you know I'd never second-guess you. I was just interested in your reasons for throwing the book at this kid."

"Well, those are them," said Roland, still a little huffy. "Why? You think they aren't good ones?"

"Good ones?" mused Karp. "Hey, what could be better than discouraging mothers from murdering their newborns? It's a slam dunk."

Roland stood up. "You know, I can't stand it when you adopt that fucking superior moral tone. When the fuck did you get to be such a bleeding heart?"

Karp smiled and said, in an effort to lighten it up, "Come on, Roland, I'm still tough. Not as tough as you maybe —"

"Oh, fuck that shit! You want to be a crusader for mercy, go get a job with Legal Aid. Meanwhile, the law is the law."

"Thank you, Inspector Javert," said Karp without thinking, and regretted it immediately, because Roland stormed out, slamming the door so hard it knocked a pile of papers down from a nearby bookshelf. Karp stooped and gathered them up and felt the familiar deadness when his artificial left knee took the strain. Karp was, of course, happy with the prosthesis, since without it he would have been a pain-riddled crip, but he also appreciated the reminder it provided of the fallibility of humans. The right one, made by God, was clearly a superior product, unlike the law, which was a sort of prosthesis that society had invented to substitute for justice, another product of the divine. Thinking thoughts along this line, Karp buzzed his special assistant and asked him to find out who was handling the defense of Lourdes Bustamente.

★ ★ ★

Marlene had spent the week disassembling her life of the past decade. It happened with surprising ease, an ease perhaps also a little disappointing; we all like to think ourselves indispensable. The first person she told about her decision was Sym McCabe, her assistant, whose chief reaction was to look at the large white-board on which were written the bodyguarding assignments of the little firm. They were in Sym's cramped room within the office Bello & Ciampi rented in a second-floor loft on Walker Street.

McCabe said, "Give me a week, ten days, we can cover it. I got some pretty good prospects, moonlighting cops most of them."

This was perhaps overcool. With some effort Marlene kept her jaw from dropping. She had found Sym McCabe as a seventeen-year-old street person, a part-time whore and a budding junkie. Marlene had started by giving her errands and shelter and had chased off the pimp who was trying to add McCabe to his stable. The young woman had the sense to see that Marlene was the first really good thing that had ever happened to her and had run with it. With Marlene's help, she had cleaned up her act, learned how to dress, type, spell, and do simple bookkeeping. More recently, she had received a degree in criminal justice administration from Manhattan Community College. She had also turned into a ferocious and skillful bodyguard and private investigator. Unlike Marlene, Sym McCabe did not care much for men. She had not shot any of them yet, but Marlene thought that when she eventually did, it would be about as annoying to her as breaking a nail.

Maybe Sym had not understood her. Marlene added, "I don't just mean temporarily, Sym. I mean for good."

"Out completely?"

Marlene looked at her former protegée carefully. She saw a thin, cocoa woman with a scrubbed, stiff face and cropped hair, dressed in a heavy cotton, knit, long-sleeved pullover in faded green, dark slacks, and a Colt Officer's .45 ACP with the alloy frame in a shoulder rig. Was that apprehension in her eye, or avidity?

"Well, I have an equity interest in the firm and I'll keep that," said Marlene carefully. "And I'd like to continue to be of counsel. I can still do the legal work, orders of protection and like that. What I meant is, I'm giving up the gun."

Sym nodded. "Yeah, I got that." Then she asked, more hesitantly, "So . . . who's like going to be in charge of this operation?"

"Well, Osborne will have something to say

113

about that, but Harry knows you, and I'll recommend you as strongly as I can."

McCabe nodded again, as if this were her due, and her face became blandly masked. Behind it, Marlene could practically see the gears whirling. After that, there was some business to discuss, details of finance and personnel, and then Marlene left to go see Harry Bello at Osborne, with some depression of spirit. She had not expected hysterical tears exactly, but some expression of regret might have been tasteful.

Osborne Security International, as it was now called, occupied three floors of a banal and anonymous smoked-glass office high-rise on Third Avenue off 63rd. It had grown a good deal in the years Marlene had been associated with it, cashing in on the world having become a less predictable, more dangerous place. Its main business was corporate-executive security, but it also did PI work and had a small but thriving celebrity-protection branch, of which Marlene was a substantial twig. The firm also lent informal support to Marlene's quixotic stalked-women operation, which was largely pro bono.

Harry Bello was a serious man, a solidly built ex–NYPD detective in his early sixties, with a sad Italian cop face bearing dark coffee-colored stains under the eyes. When

114

Marlene had first met him a decade ago, he had been a drunk, a detective without portfolio in an obscure Queens precinct, burning time toward either pension or suicide (something of a toss-up, back then). Somehow, he had fastened upon Marlene as upon a cork-ring in dark waters, and upon Lucy, too (whose godfather he had become), and after a number of interesting and dangerous years working with Marlene, he had reinvented himself in the good old American way, as a nondrinking, fairly classy security executive. He was Osborne's chief of investigations and Marlene's baby-sitter.

Marlene told him her story and put in the promised good word about Sym McCabe. Harry listened without speaking, both to what she said and, like the cop he was, to the meaningful spaces between her sentences. Before becoming a drunk he had been one of the best detectives in the NYPD, and this often showed.

After she wound down, he said, "Okay, it happens. You don't want to shoot people anymore. That's not a problem. As a matter of fact, now that it's out, all I got to say is, What took you so long?"

"Harry, but if you say 'I told you so,' I'm walking out."

Harry ignored this. "So . . . any plans?"

"Not yet. It didn't seem real to me until I started actually talking to people, making arrangements. In fact, it just got really real this minute, talking to you. Why? Did you have something in mind?"

Bello made an expansive gesture, with hands and arms. "Hey, you can write your own ticket at Osborne. You want to run the celebrities operation? We could set that up easy. You want to travel? We'll send you anywhere. We keep a suite at the Grand Cayman Sonesta. Go down there for a couple of weeks, catch the sun. You can give speeches . . ." He saw her face darken. "Don't knock it, Marlene. You want to retire from the world-saving business a little, do yourself some good for a change."

"Is that what you're doing, Harry?" She gestured at the large, many-windowed, well-appointed office.

He frowned, seemed about to retort, and then relaxed, sighing. "Yeah, Marlene, I do all right. I figure I paid my dues. The war, and then twenty-five years on the job, chasing scumbags down alleys, going through doors where you want to pee in your pants because there could be a jerk with a shotgun on the other side, going into rooms where people've been dead for a week in the summer."

"Harry, I didn't . . ."

116

"I got a hundred and twenty people under me, Marlene. I do a good job for the clients who hire us, and I make sure that there's no horseshit, which as you know is not all that easy, the kind of people who come around wanting to be a PI."

"Harry, for God's sake you don't have to defend your life to me. Stop it!" She chewed on a nail, staring off out the window. Bello gave her time, like a good cop, and after a while she said, "I guess . . . I guess I don't want to jump into anything else right now, you know? I feel derailed. Maybe I should spend some time with the family, think about things."

"Now, *that's* a good idea. Be an Italian momma for a while. Drive them all crazy."

She laughed. "I might just do that. And so, you'll make sure Sym doesn't get in trouble?"

"I can't promise that, but I'll keep an eye open. You know, the Marlene Ciampi Memorial Former Lowlife Association."

"I didn't know it existed."

"Hey, we have regular meetings." Then Bello got up and went around his desk and offered her his handkerchief and hugged her gently until she stopped crying.

"Her name is Jessica Siegel," said Murrow,

coming into Karp's office at the tail end of the day.

Karp wrinkled his brow and flipped through his mental Rolodex. It was no longer as current as it had been when he ran a trial bureau, and his face showed that this card was missing.

"She's new in felony trials, I understand," Murrow offered. "Not a bad rep, though. Out of Penn."

"Graduated last Thursday?"

"Last Monday, maybe. No, but she's fairly experienced for a Legal Aid. She had two years in Nassau County before coming to the city. Smart, ambitious, though a short person. Works like a dog; like me, she has no life."

Karp allowed himself an appreciative, thin smile. Murrow had clearly and characteristically gone beyond searching out a mere name.

"So we expect a spirited defense?"

"Yes, if . . . I mean, I guess we're going to prosecute this girl to the fullest extent, et cetera." Murrow paused. "I couldn't help overhearing. Mr. Hrcany was in full spate."

"Full is the only spate Mr. Hrcany knows," said Karp. "How are you coming on that infanticide stuff?"

"I'm writing it up now, just the legal précis, and some fun facts. Unless you want a lot more, you can have it tomorrow morning. I

118

don't mind working all night, sir."

"Murrow, is that an impish grin I see on your face?"

"Not impish exactly, sir. I was trying for a sarcastic leer."

"A grave demeanor is worth more to a lawyer than an apt precedent," intoned Karp.

"Who said that?"

"I did, just now. Why don't you give me the gist of what you found?"

"Gladly. The gist is, there does not appear to exist within the state criminal statutes any clear distinction of the crime of infanticide. *Infanticide* isn't even a term of legal significance in New York statutory language, and other states follow. The major interest in infants seems to be in determining when a fetus becomes one. Once an infant, there's no distinction made between a neonate and a three-year-old. Case law in child-abuse prosecutions for second-degree murders almost always refers to paragraph two of 125.25, the depraved-indifference standard. Which makes sense, of course."

"Yes, it gets you past intent. If you decide to go after the defendant for a top count of murder two, you don't want them arguing I loved my kid and didn't mean to kill her. So the burden is to show the injuries sustained were the result of depraved indifference. Go on."

"This absence contrasts with the criminal law in Western Europe. The British Infanticide Act, for example, says that if a mother kills an infant within twenty-four hours of the birth, there's an automatic presumption of mental illness, and the top count can only be manslaughter or less. Often it's less. The drill there, and in the rest of Western Europe, is for the woman to plead guilty to manslaughter or some designated lesser and be hospitalized for psychiatric treatment. There hasn't been a prison sentence for infanticide in Britain in over fifty years."

"That's interesting," said Karp. "What else have you got?"

"Well, on the legal side, not much. There's a good deal of variation in sentencing, of course, depending on the circumstances. The older the child, typically, the worse it is for the accused. Over the last five years, in this state, most prosecutors have been willing to accept a plea to manslaughter second degree for women who kill neonates. The average prison time is something like twenty-eight months. Obviously, that averages in sentencing for wildly different crimes. Obviously, a teenager who smothers a baby while trying to keep it a secret from mom is going to get a better deal than an older woman who tosses the newborn in an oven and turns on the gas or cuts it up and tries to flush it down the toilet."

"Yeah, I remember that case," said Karp. "Tossing out the window comes somewhere in between, I would say."

"As in Lola Bustamente. I take it she's what this is all about?"

"Sort of. I'm trying to figure out why I'm disturbed about what Roland is doing and about the public attitude toward these cases. I mean, as you point out, there's no ambiguity in the law, and I'm an agent of the law. Plus I've also always, as you know, had a real resistance to mental illness exculpation, except where the illness is long-standing and debilitating and unambiguous, the classic guy who cuts up the landlady because he thought she was a big salami. But . . . it makes me uneasy, and since I have a bright special assistant with ample leisure, I can indulge my uneasiness. I excuse it because this case is going to a jury and a jury reflects local culture, so it's part of my job to understand how an American, a *Manhattan* jury is going to look at this case. My fellow citizens."

Karp leaned back in his big leather chair and laced his hands behind his head. "So educate me, Murrow. Why is British law different from ours? Why do they give infanticides a pass to the funny farm?"

Murrow took a moment to flip through

pages of closely written notes. "Okay, way back, clearly, it wasn't that way at all. In fact, the Act of 1624 imposed a unique presumption of guilt on stillbirths. These were presumed to be infanticides unless the mother could come up with a witness to testify that the baby was born dead. At the same time, on the other hand, unwanted infants were being murdered like flies. They had so-called smothering nurses who did the job for the price of a drink. And these were almost never prosecuted. For some reason, they just didn't want the mom to do it immediately after the birth. In the next century, you had the dropped baby. Mom got drunk on cheap gin and dropped the babe on its head, the Hogarth scene, it's famous. Also no big deal for the law. Death by misadventure, next case. The nineteenth century comes, the picture changes. The classic case was the country maid, seduced by the local squire, in despair doing away with the baby. A lot of sympathy there, everybody was getting fucked by the squire, so, essentially we have jury nullification: between 1839 and 1906, no woman was convicted of infanticide in Britain. Typically, they got hit with the lesser charge of concealment of birth, and the sentence then depended on where they stashed the kid. Down the well was bad, by the side of a road or on the church steps was better. The notion was, if she left the kid in plain view, no murder was contemplated. Moving right along, midcentury, forensic techniques improve a little, but mainly docs instead of nobs are getting appointed as coroners, which means that they're not passing murders off as stillbirths so easy anymore — that was the big loophole the juries were using to get the women off — it's not murder, it's stillbirth, hence merely concealment. They get to punish a little without sending them to the gallows. So when you got women being threatened more credibly with actual hanging, you had the response of hyped up sentimentalizing of the fate of the betrayed women, *Adam Bede*, Hetty Sorrel . . ."

"These are cases? Bede and Sorrel?" asked Karp.

Murrow gave him a surprised look. "No, they're characters in a novel by George Eliot. Hetty gets pregnant by a deceiver, hides her baby, which dies, and she's tried and convicted, but pardoned by the queen. An example of public attitudes running in front of the law, which was turning harsher, with the Infant Life Protection act of 1872, which was really designed to get so-called baby farmers, a kind of murdering midwife. They actually convicted and hanged a bunch of those. In the

1890s, the women's rights movement took up the cause of unmarried mothers and advanced the notion that childbearing was intimate, private, no concern of the *men* who were writing the laws, and, not beside the point, who were also impregnating and abandoning the women, who were being forced to kill their infants as a result. Out of this idea we get the movements for the free availability of contraception, one; the privacy principle behind *Roe v. Wade*, two; and finally, in Britain, at least, the Infanticide Act."

"But not here; numbers one and two, but not number three here," said Karp. "Why not?"

"Speculation? Religion's a big one. The other industrial nations are all much more secular than we are. None of them have a religious right that amounts to anything politically. Then the sociological changes, no more Ozzie and Harriet. Women getting independence, it frightens a lot of people, men *and* women. So abortion is a lightning rod for that. This infanticide business is just the abortion story writ large. The same people who can't hang abortion docs anymore are dying to hang someone, and here she is. Can I ask you a question?"

"Shoot."

"Why is Hrcany going after this girl? Why

not a sweep under the rug with a man two and forget it?"

Karp thought about this a little before he answered. "Well, you'll recall me saying all that about the nearly absolute discretion of a prosecutor as to what cases to bring and what charges to apply, and here's an example. I kind of doubt that Roland has any strong feelings pro or con on abortion or infanticide, and you know, in the homicide business, although we don't like to mention it, the character of the victim is important. We're supposed to act on behalf of the People, capital *P*, but we don't know the People. We do know the vic's parents, their family, their friends. So, if one anonymous piss-bum kills another anonymous piss-bum, we are not going to get as excited as if some mugger kills a taxpayer. Oddly enough, however, we *will* get excited if a taxpayer kills the piss-bum, like those prep school kids a few years back who used to burn up street people for fun. We came down hard on them, I guess to remind ourselves that every living person enjoys equal protection of the law, which we feel obliged to do at least once a year. The various compromises and ambiguities of this work tend to clog up the sinuses, and you need to do something stark and legalistic occasionally, like sticking one of those inhalers up your nose and snorting.

125

'Harsh is the law, but it is certain.' "

"Did you say that, too?"

"No, Giambattista Vico did. Anyway, maybe this is Roland's snort. A defenseless baby, and he's going all the way for it. That, and it doesn't hurt him politically, either, but don't quote me." Karp smiled sadly. "I can see that your youthful idealism is crumbling like a clod under the spring rains."

"Yes, I'm struggling to hold back the tears. Do you want me to pass this infanticide stuff on to Mr. Hrcany?"

Karp chuckled. "Oh, only if you think it'd be fun to see him turn red and tear it up into little pieces. No, get it organized and file it; it might come in useful if we're ever asked to comment on legislation. And thanks; it looks like you did a good, thorough job."

"You're welcome, boss," said Murrow, suppressing the urge to beam. He racked his papers and got ready to leave, but paused. "It's funny. I can imagine killing someone in the heat of passion, or for gain or from hate or stupidity, but I can't imagine killing a baby by throwing it out the window in the middle of winter."

"If Yale Law wanted you to have an imagination, it would have issued you one with your diploma. You don't want an imagination in this business, kid. Roland hasn't got one, and I got along without one for years."

"But you have one now, or you wouldn't have got me to do this stuff."

"Actually, my wife's the one with imagination. I caught it from her, like a dose of herpes. And speaking of disgusting organisms, do you know anyone down in the trenches over at Legal Aid?"

"As a matter of fact, I do. I was housemates with one of the vipers the last year of law school."

"Really. How could you stand it?"

"It was hard. Sometimes, and I shudder to recall it, lacy underthings were left hanging from the towel racks. Why do you ask?"

"Because I would like to be put next to Jessica Siegel at some large, noisy, anonymous social occasion. I would like to be introduced and left alone for a short time. Do you think you could arrange such an occurrence?"

Murrow inscribed something in his tiny leather book. "I'll get on it. May I ask why?"

"You can, but I don't know if I can give you a straight answer. Years back, when I was just starting out in homicide, I used to talk over cases with Tom Pagano, who was director of Legal Aid for about a hundred years."

"Is that kosher?"

"Sure, why not? Look, we're all competitive as hell, but what we do isn't actually a sport. It's not the Jets and the Cowboys working up secret plays to outsmart each other. I mean, the whole purpose here is to come up with a solution to some social disaster that suits the purposes of society within the constitutional constraints. So, yeah, I used to go to Tom and we'd talk about what was the right thing to do in a particular case. He had a lot of accumulated wisdom about this business, and we could clear up a hundred cases in an afternoon. The current guy . . ." Karp wrinkled his nose and waved his hand loosely as if it had touched something unpleasant.

"Freeland," said Murrow.

"Yes, Milton is not the same sort of fellow at all. Milton thinks we're all part of a conspiracy to crush the lower orders on behalf of the ruling class."

"Gosh, aren't we?"

"Yes, but only on the three days before Rosh Hashanah. My point is, it occurs to me that it would be a social good if someone from this office had a conversation with someone from that office on the subject of this sort of case. We've had three, and it's unlikely that those will be the last. That someone won't be Roland, and it can't be Freeland. So that leaves me and the lovely and talented Ms. Siegel. So make it happen, Murrow."

5

Marlene discharged the remainder of her bodyguarding duties during the ensuing week, signed a set of papers that would enable Sym McCabe to act as the principal of Bello & Ciampi, and retired from the world of violence, or at least violence at first hand. One morning that week she walked for the first time in a long while out onto the cobbled street in front of her loft unarmed, except for the two-hundred-pound attack-trained dog loping along unleashed at her side. She was wearing green Wellington boots, black jeans, a black rubber slicker that came down to her knees, and a large gray tweed cap, of the sort cabbies used to wear in New York before they took up turbans, but peak backwards, hiding her unkempt hair. It was raining a cold, steady city rain, not hard enough to force pedestrians to run for shelter, nor light enough to be romantic, just serious water falling straight down from a sunless sky, with the intensity of the output of a low-pressure showerhead.

Time was the problem, Marlene knew, unstructured time, time without urgency and the threat of violence, without the vile serum of violence itself, delivered or presented. Marlene understood at some level that she was an addict; disguise it how she might with the rouge of helping, of protecting the innocent, of street justice, still the raddled face of the stone junkie showed through. A decade ago, she had tried to quit cold turkey, leaving her job as the bureau chief of the rape section of the DA's office and following her husband to a job he had taken in Washington. She recalled it as the worst period of her life and within a couple of months had contrived to obtain a position in which, for no pay at all, she was able to set herself up as a target for a band of efficient and dreadful criminals. And upon returning to the city, she had immediately (although burdened with two more children) set up the business she had just abandoned.

But I have a lot to do, she argued with herself. I have two small children in second grade, I have a complex adolescent daughter, I have a house to take care of, and a husband. I haven't read a decent book since 1972. I have a dog. She expressed these thoughts to the dog as they went in and out of shops and walked along Grand Street among the remains of Little Italy.

"Sweety," she continued, "if I were going crazy, actually crazy, you'd let me know, wouldn't you? I mean my family would be really polite, or maybe they're used to me, or maybe I've *driven* them crazy over the years, so it's a *folie à deux,* or *à quatre,* but you must have some primal instinct about it, I mean, you would growl and whine, wouldn't you? Would I *smell* right if I were nuts? Although, you know, a woman walking down the street talking to a dog, most people would think that a supermarket cart full of bulging black plastic bags would be just the right fashion accessory."

The dog was used to this and ignored it, choosing instead to inspect various decayed objects dropped along the curb.

"But on second thought, probably not. We still worship God, and if He's not crazy, I don't know what crazy is. So, what? Am I doomed, like the woman in *The Yellow Wallpaper*? Actually, my downfall will be grocery shopping, not picking at the walls."

Here she gestured with the heavy string bag she was carrying. "Did I need to buy fourteen different kinds of cheese? I went into Alleva to pick up some bread and half-and-half and I walk out with a cheese platter for thirty. The boys eat nothing but jack, 'regular' cheese as they charmingly call it, and Butch is hardly more adventurous; Lucy gnaws on Asiago at the rate of about an ounce a week, probably to mortify her flesh, and now Posie won't eat anything that's not blessed by a mullah. You're probably going to eat up three-quarters of it, aren't you? The world's most precious dog food. Kibbles? Don't be absurd! Bel Paese, and none of your low-end Wisconsin trash either."

Waiting on the curb for a break in the traffic on Lafayette, Marlene became aware that she was being stared at by a pair of tourists, artily dressed ladies only a few years older than she was, probably in from Westchester or Jersey for a little SoHo excitement and shopping. She knew they were tourists because no native would have looked twice at a woman talking to a dog, real or imaginary.

"Yes, I'm talking to my dog," she snarled. "You mind?"

They gawked.

"Lucky for you I don't carry a gun anymore," she added, at which point they pretended they hadn't heard and moved hurriedly away. Marlene crossed the wide street, muttering, splashing straight through a wide puddle. "Rich bitches!" she commented in a tone that made the dog look up questioningly. Is there someone to eat?

"Probably looking for something blue to go

132

with the love seat. Yes, Sweety, I know, I'm just wasting time. Butch works a twelve-hour shift, the boys are in school until three now, Lucy deigns to come home once or twice a week to check her mail, no, I'm being unfair, it's a fine family and Butch is so ridiculously happy when he walks in at night and I'm home and there's a hot dinner all ready, the Cro-Magnon!"

Thinking now of dinner (and the truth was, Marlene loved to cook and was good at it), Marlene crossed Grand, dropped the dog into a down-stay under the awning, and went into Sorrentino Brothers. Marlene now shopped for groceries every day and noticed that the only other women in the shops she frequented were twenty-five years older than she was and stout. She thought about wearing her hair in a bun and getting a black dress and a cameo pin. Once inside she robotically followed routine. She had Bruno cut her eight loin pork chops, each an inch and a half thick. She discussed his lower back pain for the usual four minutes, received and stashed the white-wrapped package, and went down the anise-scented aisles to the produce department, where she picked up three yellow peppers, two pounds of ripe egg tomatoes, and a pound of porcini mushrooms. There was a lot of other stuff she wanted, but there would clearly be other days, lots and lots of them. She then spent three minutes talking kids and dogs with Mrs. Guidi at the cash register.

She left the store and the dog rose, stretching and yawning, and fell into step beside her. "Busy day, Sweets," she remarked to the dog. "Got to keep moving. But maybe there's just time for a quick snort. How about it?"

She crossed the street again and went into Russo's, the dog following. When Marlene had first moved into her loft, in the early seventies, there had been half a dozen places like Russo's in Little Italy, Italian working-class saloons with tile floors and dark bars that did most of their business in anisette and red wine and drafts. Now this was the only one left, the rest having been trendied out of existence by the aggressive expansion of SoHo. She had always tried to stop in once a week or so, to help keep the place in business, but now she came by nearly every day. Inside, she took a deep breath of the true saloon perfume, damp and beery, that you never for some reason got in the chrome and ferny lounges. There were only three other customers this early, all elderly Italian men in shirts buttoned up to the collar and wearing flat caps, two together at a small square table and one by the wall alone, all drinking wine. Marlene stood for a moment and dripped on the floor, which was made of tiny hexagonal tiles, white interspersed with black. The front window had been painted opaque red, and most of the light came from the bottle shelves behind the bar, and the little dim lamps over the five booths and illuminated beer signs. On one wall was a large framed photograph of the Bay of Naples, unglassed and flyspecked, faded to unnatural pink and dun and ocher. On the other wall, over the booths, were framed and signed photographs of fighters, the famous ones — the Rockies Marciano and Graziano, and Jake LaMotta — and neighborhood pugs from the days when Italian kids still fought in the ring. There were also signed shots of local people looking drunk and happy, and one of Eddie Arcaro on Citation. A dusty mirror hung behind the bar.

A new guy stood there, fooling with the beer taps, a jowly fellow in his late twenties with a lot of shaggy, dark hair, smoothed slick on his head and curling up out of the gap in his body shirt. Marlene sat at the bar and the dog sat next to her on the floor.

The bartender came over and looked down and saw the dog and said, "You can't bring that animal in here."

Marlene said, "Yes, I can. He's a Seeing Eye dog."

The man narrowed his eyes. "Lady, you ain't blind."

Marlene pulled a swizzle stick out of a jar and tapped its little knob against her glass eye. It made a surprisingly loud sound. "I'm only half-blind, so he doesn't have to be a very good Seeing Eye dog. Where's Gino?"

"He went out for something."

"Okay, when he gets back, he'll tell you it's cool. Give me a glass of the house red and my friend will have a Bud Light. He uses a peanut bowl."

The bartender now had a tight, humorless grin. "Hey, lady, why don't you take your act somewhere else, huh? I've got stuff to do, and I don't got time to serve no beer to no dog." They were at the glaring stage now.

Fortunately, at that moment, the door kicked open and Gino the manager came in clutching to his chest a heavy corrugated carton full of shiny pipes and black tubing. He was a hefty man with a fat nose and gut and a full head of wavy, dark hair going white on the sides. He dropped the carton on the bar and greeted Marlene with a "Hey, how's it going, Mar?" but having been in the bar business for forty years and possessing a keen feel for a tense situation, he also added, "Jerry taking care of you there, and the pooch?" Silence, here. "Jerry, this's Marlene Ciampi, she's in

136

the neighborhood. Marlene, I'll be with you in a second, just let me set Jerry up with this new keg tap in the cellar." Gino took Jerry by the arm and led him to the steps that led downstairs. When they were alone, Gino asked, "What's going on up there? You got any idea who that is?"

Jerry shrugged. "Hey, I didn't know she was a friend of yours, okay? I thought she was some kook. She wanted a beer for that fucking dog."

"Hey, *stronzo,* she wants to buy a fucking Schlitz for a fucking anteater, you give it to her. I asked you, do you know who she *is?*"

The question was asked in a tone that in certain strata of the Italian-American community allows of only one response. Jerry paled and said, "Oh, fuck me! You mean she's *connected?*"

Gino grinned wickedly. "Nah, she don't have to be. She fucking eats wise guys. A few years back, they sent a couple big-time mechanics in from the coast to whack her out and she blew them off. Cut off one of them's pecker is what I heard. So she's someone you never ever want to fuck with, and besides that, she's a nice person. A word to the wise, right, Jerry?"

Jerry clumped down the cellar stairs without another word. Gino went back up to the bar and poured out a glass of good Barbera and drew enough Bud from the tap to fill a shallow nut bowl. Marlene put the bowl down for the dog and drank half her glass. The dog lapped enthusiastically below.

Gino said, smiling, "He likes the beer, eh?"

Marlene said, "Yes. He's off duty today." Gino crouched down below the bar and shouted instructions to the kid in the cellar. There were clankings and hissings. Marlene drank and studied herself drinking in the clouded mirror. It made her look like one of the absinthe bibbers Toulouse-Lautrec had painted, hair a wild tangle, skin green under the eyes, and lips almost black. It gave her a perverse pleasure to see herself that way, and she offered a ghastly smile to the reflection. And then, through some trick of association she remembered looking at herself in the oval mirror in the ballroom at Sacred Heart and meeting Shanahan that night. The poor woman had been hard put to control her envy, Marlene recalled, and recalled wondering what was so enviable about her life. Her former life. Oh, right, the fabled romance of violence, the American religion. Just watch the movies. Somehow, Marlene had never come up with a good one-liner after shooting someone or breaking his face with a pipe wrench. Usually, she was concentrating on not vomiting all over her shoes. And she further recalled — and the recollection stung — being just a tiny bit patronizing to Shans, the country-mouse lawyer. Who could, of course, now patronize her, Marlene, busy housewife and budding alcoholic. Maybe she should call Delaware and offer the opportunity.

Gino came back out from under, saw Marlene's empty glass, and asked, "Another round?"

"Sure. Why not?" Cut out one addiction and another rises in its place.

Gino poured out the thick, strong, almost black wine. "Another for the pooch?"

"No, he'll pass. He doesn't have the head for it, and he's a mean drunk."

Karp slouched on the green leather sofa in the homicide bureau chief's office, doodling little concentric circles on his yellow pad and listening with half an ear to the kid standing at the end of the table talk about the murder case he proposed to try. The kid (aged twenty-seven) was named David Pincus and the case was *People v. Buford.* The People were versus Buford because he had shot his common-law wife six times, thus causing her unlawful death in the County of New York. All thirty-two homicide ADAs, including Karp, were in the room, seated along both sides of the long oak table and in chairs along the walls, and Roland Hrcany was at the head of the table looking as if he had just eaten a small furry animal raw and wished another, which was his usual mien at these meetings.

Karp tried to attend as many homicide bureau trial meetings as he could manage because he thought that properly prepared trials were the most important part of the DA operation, and because murder trials were the most important kind of trial. Hrcany tolerated his presence because it was a demonstration (to Karp, first of all) of who was really in charge of the most important function of the entire office (Hrcany) and for another, more subtle reason. Karp and Roland were just of an age, and that age was now the oldest age in the room; they were the last survivors of what now seemed to be the golden era of criminal prosecution in New York, the late sixties and early seventies, before the deluge of crime made plea bargaining and other trimming dodges the most common way of disposing of cases. They agreed on few things, but one of them was that there was hardly a law school in the country that taught any of its students how to manage a criminal case, much less how to try a murder. So besides running a bureau and a prosecuting office, they also ran a little law school, of which the present meeting was the most intense and significant seminar.

Karp looked around the room. The twenty-four men and seven women were all in their late twenties to mid-thirties, the prime age range for an exhausting and relatively low-paying job. Most of these people would not stay here for a full career. They would sharpen their trial skills to a fine edge and then sell them for some interesting multiple of their current salary. A few would go into politics; they were all intensely competitive, and virtually all of them had played team sports in school. The intellectual level, Karp had to admit, was not uniformly high. But it should have been a little higher than this guy was showing.

"Pincus," said Karp, suddenly focusing his attention on the presenter, "why did he kill her?"

Pincus, a muscular, pale man, with thinning light brown hair and the regular and rather vague facial features of a plastic He-Man toy, stopped openmouthed. It was not a question he had expected.

"Um, sorry, I don't understand. I didn't . . . I mean, what does his motivation have to do with it?"

Good comeback, Karp thought. One of the points often covered in these meetings was the fallacy of the favorite saw of the fictional prosecutor, "motive, means, and opportunity." It was an analysis never performed in real life, in real cases, which were entirely concerned with preparing a set of unbreakable connections between a defendant and the circumstances of a crime — motive had nothing to do with the prosecution's case, although the apparent lack of one was something defense lawyers tended to dwell upon if they could.

"I don't mean his deeper motivation, Pincus. I mean why do *you* think he killed her?"

Pincus seemed relieved and answered, "Oh, she used to raid his stash. They were both crackheads, but he was a pretty fair-sized dealer. Going down, like they all do, but she was downer than him at the time. He was always beating on her. The night before the killing, one of his homies let him know that the word was out she was looking for someone to do him, so he went up there and whacked her instead. A simple case." Pincus smiled expectantly.

Karp smiled, too, and glanced at Hrcany, who also smiled and asked, "So, Pincus, how do you intend to present these interesting facts? I notice you didn't cover them in your opening."

"Well, no. I didn't think it paid to bring it

142

up. I figured let the defense do it, if they think it's exculpatory, but meanwhile we let it lie and come back at them during cross and in the summation."

Karp waited several beats and then asked, pacing his words for emphasis, "You didn't think it *paid* to bring it up?" His smile had gone, but Roland's smile had now broadened into a grin like the last thing a herring sees. His blue eyes glinted happily at Karp. They were going to double-team this sucker in the old-fashioned way they had both been double-teamed themselves back before the Flood by the kind of old bulls who used to dominate homicide prosecution in the bureau.

"Yeah, Pincus, that's good," said Hrcany. "Tell us about what *pays* in a homicide prosecution. No, wait, first tell us, why we do trials."

Pincus knew he was in trouble now, but he was game, or he wouldn't have been in the room to begin with. He swallowed, cleared his throat, and said, "To demonstrate that the accused is guilty of the charges beyond a reasonable doubt, to a moral certainty."

The schoolbook answer. He waited. Karp said, "Very good. And we do that by assembling evidence, correct?"

"Right. That associates the defendant with the crime."

Hrcany said, "But what about evidence that doesn't associate the defendant with the crime? We . . . what? We *hope* the defense flubs it?"

Pincus said, "Well, yeah. We come back on cross and show it's not really that exculpatory."

"Oh, Pincus," said Karp, "oh, Pincus! Pincus, let's go back. What *precisely* is your job? What is the job of this office? In trials, I mean."

"To represent the People in court," said Pincus. "And to win convictions."

"By outsmarting the defense, right?" offered Hrcany. "We select the evidence that does our case good and we leave the stuff that doesn't to the defense."

"Right," said Karp. "Both sides have access to the same evidence because of discovery rules. We pick the stuff that's good for us, and they pick what's good for them, and may the best case win. Is that what you're saying?"

Pincus looked at both tormentors. He sensed a trap but didn't quite know the way out of it. "Well, yeah. Obviously, we think our case is better than theirs or we wouldn't have gone to —"

Roland interrupted this obviousness with a loud and disgusting Bronx cheer.

Karp said, "Wrong! Booooo! Booo, Pincus,

shame on you!" Karp turned to Roland. "Roland, what is it? We're not speaking English? They have wax in their ears? What? This guy's got a year in criminal courts, two in felony bureau, and a year and a half here and we still haven't knocked this nonsense out of his head. Look!" Karp now focused his yellow gaze on Pincus, who had turned bright pink. "Let me say this yet again. We are *not* in the same business as the defense. We have a different function. It's not like two guys playing tennis or pool or poker. The art and skill in preparing a case are in organization and in presentation of the evidence, *not* in selecting it. The very *last* thing you want to do is leave the presentation of exculpatory evidence to the defense. You *want* the jury to hear exculpatory evidence from *your* mouth first. You're saying to them, yeah, I know about that, I've studied it, and for this or that reason it does *not* constitute reasonable doubt."

"But . . ."

Oh, he's not going to, thought Karp, he can't possibly. "But, what, Pincus?" he asked with disarming gentleness.

"But what if the defense doesn't bring it up? Why should you shoot yourself in the foot to begin with?"

Hrcany roared and produced an even juicier raspberry.

"No!" shouted Karp. "You *still* don't get it. It doesn't *matter* what the defense does. *Fuck* the defense! You have a positive, affirmative duty to present every relevant fact in the case. *Every* fact. And if, in your mind, the exculpatory material *does* rise to the level of reasonable doubt, what do you do?" Silence. "Pincus? What do you do?"

Pincus was sweating now, chewing his lip. "You . . . you don't go to trial?"

Both Karp and Hrcany began to clap, slow and heavy, one, two, three, four.

"Thank you, Pincus!" said Hrcany.

"God bless you, Pincus!" said Karp.

And they both cracked up, and after a stunned moment, everyone else in the room began to laugh, even, last of all, Pincus.

"I hear Vasquez put Purcell down for the top count," said Karp sometime later, when he and Hrcany were alone.

"Yeah, but that was a grounder," said Hrcany. "I'm going to give her Bustamente, see how she does when the heat's on."

"Good! A good choice."

"Yeah, she's a bright girl. Nice little ass on her, too."

"I'll be sure to mention that remark when she brings you up on sexual harassment charges."

"Oh, horseshit! I don't have to hustle ADAs to get laid."

"I'm sure you don't, Roland, but trotting out your famous string of conquests is not going to be an affirmative defense in a harassment case."

"Wait a minute: Did she come to *you* on this?" Hrcany's facial veins were starting to bulge, signaling, like the idiot lights on a car, an incipient overheating.

"No, and she wouldn't. She probably thinks you're an asshole, personally, but she's a city kid and she has a pretty high tolerance for that kind of shit. Guys on her block have been giving her grief since she was fourteen. But sooner or later you're going to run up against somebody who *won't* take it, and then you're going to be in serious trouble."

"I am *not* a harasser," said Hrcany vehemently. "Do you believe that it would ever fucking *occur* to me to offer an advantage for sexual favors or screw up some girl's career because she wouldn't put out?"

"No, as a matter of fact, I don't. But that's not the point here. You give little squeezes. You tell off-color jokes. You make suggestive remarks about their bodies. You freely use the word *cunt* to indicate individuals in the criminal justice system who don't come up to your standards, you —"

"What've you been, hanging out in the ladies' room? Where do you get this crap?"

Karp sighed. "It's my job, Roland. I'm supposed to keep track of stuff like this. I've mentioned it to you before, and I'm mentioning it
again now because —"

"Oh, shit! I can't stand this! You got a definite charge, fucking bring it, and I'll respond.
Meanwhile, this all sounds like a goddamn
witch-hunt."

"It *is* a witch-hunt, Roland. This is my
point. Look at me. Am I a racist?"

Hrcany did look at him, somewhat startled.
"Fuck, no! In fact, you're the original —"
Hrcany stopped and held his fingers mock-
prissily to his lips. "Oh, heavens! I almost said
a bad word, begins with *n* and ends with *lover.*"

Karp rolled his eyes. "Yes, that, but *I* lost
my job — the job you now have, not irrele-
vantly, by the way — because I shoved a re-
porter and he fell down and cracked his skull,
and it was caught on camera, and what it
looked like was a great big white guy pushing
a small black man to the ground, plus I somehow failed to convict a white kid who killed
half a dozen black grandmothers, ergo racist
son-of-a-bitch Butch Karp. Unfair? Get used
to it, or get out of public life. I won't mention
this again, Roland, but a word to the wise,
okay?"

"Okay, you made your fucking point," said Hrcany grumpily. He picked up a two-handled steel-coil exercise device, one of several he always had scattered around his office, and began to twist it strenuously, making the fabric over his biceps creak like a mainsail before a stiff breeze.

"Good. Changing the subject, any indication that Bustamente's lawyer is going to plead her?"

"No, not so far," and then, more truculently, "and if she doesn't, we're prepared to go the distance on murder two, depraved indifference *and* intent."

"You're arguing intent, too?"

"Of course, intent. She threw the baby out the window, for Christ's sake. They're going to argue that what? The kid just shot out of her c— oh, sorry, her *vaginal orifice* and flew like a bird out the window of the ladies' can?"

"Well, Roland, you know best," said Karp mildly. "But, sometimes a jury doesn't like it when you pile it on too high. Try to put the last orange on top of the stack and sometimes you end up with no stack at all. What we *don't* want, and I believe I can speak for Jack here, is going after this kid like she was a Mafia hit man and having to pick up a lot of squashed oranges off the floor."

"They won't go to trial," said Roland,

grunting around his twisted steel.

"Really? You're offering man one, fifteen years. That's a minimum five-year jolt. Pretty steep."

"She killed a human being, and she's got no serious defense. We can nail her for murder two and ask for twenty-five, with no max-out. Looking at that, she'll roll on it. Tell Jack not to worry. No, *I'll* tell him."

"I'm sure it'll make his day."

"I'll tell you what would make *my* day. If we once got a good clean case like those two dumb college kids in Delaware. White, middle class, no horseshit about deprived childhoods or mental deficiency. They had the kid, tossed it in a Dumpster, and drove away. A slam dunk."

"I think you need to move out of town to catch those, Roland," said Karp. "Funny you mentioning that one — it turns out that Marlene went to high school with the girl's lawyer in that case. She was telling me she ran into her the other night."

"Who, that girl Shanahan? *Was* the lawyer, you mean."

"She quit?"

"Canned by the judge. Some garbage about violating a gag order. It was on the news this morning. If I were the male chauvinist I am unjustly accused of being, I would make a

150

comment about how difficult it is for women to keep their fucking mouths shut, but I will not."

Karp rose from the couch. "Speaking of orifices, I have to get back to mine. Thanks for the laughs."

Hrcany chuckled. "Yeah, fucking Pincus. Actually, he's better in court than he sounded."

"I hope so." Karp paused at the door. "Roland, is it just me, or is there something a little *off* with these kids we're getting?"

"Hey, what can you do? Standards are dropping. These kids have never had their butts kicked like we did. Also, of course, there's your women's lib and the miscegenation of the races . . ."

"Roland, you're fucking doomed," said Karp, and closed the door.

When Karp returned to his office, Miss Flynn grabbed him and, with an energy surprising in one so slight, redirected him out the door and toward an event requiring his attendance.

"Forget yer foot if it wa'n't tied to yer leg" was Flynn's lilting comment, in a voice she imagined was an undertone, but which Karp heard very well. He made no remark, however, because he knew he deserved it. Karp was still not, after four years on this job, quite adjusted to having his time scheduled by others for events that he would not have chosen to attend, but had to. The district attorney's is a political office, and although Jack Keegan was conscientious and hardworking, opportunities to press the flesh of the DA's many constituents multiplied faster than available hours, so that Karp often found himself in the ballrooms of hotels and upstairs in restaurants, selecting dried-out canapés and lifting a glass of watery booze in service of some important, but not important enough for the DA himself, clambake.

This one was celebrating the retirement of Judge Timothy X. Monahan, a long-awaited event, actually, as Judge Monahan had not been an ornament of the bench for many years past; since he had been grandfathered by the current mandatory retirement rules, he had continued to serve (in a manner of speaking) well into his eighties. There was a considerable turnout at his racket, Karp observed, more than might have been predicted by his purely jurisprudential rep, for he was the last surviving judicial appointment of Governor Franklin D. Roosevelt, and many people wanted to be able to say that they had been there for it.

The venue was Sharkey's, on Baxter Street,

a saloon of the type familiar in courthouse districts nationwide, dispensing large drinks and chunks of costly proteins (though not quite at the volume of years past) in an environment featuring dark wood, red carpeting, brass rails, framed *Spy* cartoons, luncheon specials called The Judge, The Barrister, and The Verdict, and deferential waiters in black bow ties and long white aprons. Sharkey's had an upstairs room, fitted out like a movie version of a London club: oriental-style carpets; comfortable club chairs in studded red leather, arranged around low mahogany tables; a small bar, faced with the same red leather; fake beams on the ceiling, from which depended many-branched, brass candelabra. The walls were covered in bookshelves that had real books in them, of the sort bought by the yard from decorating firms.

Karp entered this room and immediately spotted Murrow hovering near the doorway. He seemed to be waiting for someone, who turned out to be Karp himself.

"You got wet," Murrow observed.

Karp was dabbing at his face and head with a handkerchief. He had not taken the official car for the three-block walk from the courthouse, and the chill rain was still falling heavily.

"Murrow, why don't we wear hats anymore? New York has a terrible climate and we get forty inches of rain a year, but no one wears a hat, and when they do, they look ridiculous. You see guys in navy pinstripes with ski hats on their heads."

"I think it's in memory of JFK. He didn't wear a hat. Or it's because boys don't wear hats and we all want to be boys. Why don't you get a snap-brim, gray fedora and revive the fashion?"

"I might do that. You'll have to buy a perky porkpie and sit it on the back of your head and say 'Swell!' and 'Gee, boss' a lot."

"Gee, boss, guess who's here?"

"Timothy X. Monahan, that'd be my first guess."

"Jessica Siegel. You mentioned . . ."

"Yes, and you arranged for Judge Monahan to retire so as to create an event where the two of us could plausibly have an unofficial ex parte conversation. That's really impressive, Murrow."

"Gee, boss . . ."

"Convey me, Murrow."

He did, to a corner arrangement of chairs around a table. Two women were seated there in conversation. One was ocher-brown, thin and elegant in a gray suit, with a neat cap of varnished hair. The other was short and verging on plump, but with the fine-featured, intense face of a taller, slimmer woman. She was wearing a dark suit and a white shirt with a long-pointed collar and an actual striped silk tie, although loosely tied to preserve femininity, and large, round, black-rimmed spectacles. Her hair was pulled back from a wide brow and fixed into a small, bobbing tail at the back. The two women felt the loom of the two men and stopped their conversation. The brown woman looked up, flashed an amazing array of bright tooth and pink gum, and exclaimed, "Hi, Mookie!"

Mookie (as Karp now had to think of him, with some distaste) made the introductions and invited himself and his boss to sit down. The brown woman proved to be the law school roommate, Deena Mitchell, now a Legal Aid lawyer. Karp thought of lacy underthings in the bathroom and suppressed the image; he had not had roommates of this type in law school. The absurd nickname was amusingly explained, conversation flowed, Murrow snagged a waiter and provided another round of drinks. No one mentioned how exceedingly unlikely it was that the huge person known among Legal Aids as the Prince of Darkness should happen to be passing the time with a trio of distinctly junior lawyers. It was not an uncomfortable meeting, however, because Murrow took charge

155

charmingly, and the chatter flew about, anecdotes about law-school life, the courts, the various characters associated with same, lawyer jokes. Deena talked fetchingly about her sad-sack clients, and about some of Jessica's as well, and the many travails of what she called the Guilty Girls' Club and Save-the-World Marching Band. Karp, not a charmer himself, was grateful and grudgingly impressed. He frankly admired these young women. He expected that his daughter would turn out to be something like them.

Then, through some social magic, Murrow had pried Deena from her chair and spirited her off, leaving Karp and Jessica Siegel together, as planned. Karp was impressed with the trick, something he himself could not have pulled off in a hundred years.

"Actually, I wanted to talk with you," he began, no beater about bushes he.

"With me?"

"Yeah, about Lola Bustamente."

Her face stiffened. "This is a funny place to do it in. And I thought Mimi Vasquez was handling the state's case."

"I don't mean negotiate. This isn't official in any way. Mimi doesn't know I'm talking to you, and neither does her bureau chief. And it would be embarrassing to me if they found out. Hence the dark corner." He observed her calculate. A very bright woman, he concluded.

"This all was a setup, Mookie and all? So you could talk to me?"

"Somewhat. I'm also a great and longtime admirer of Timothy X. Monahan."

She burst out laughing. She had a deep laugh that flashed little dimples on her cheeks.

"Oh, my! Well, talk away, Mr. Karp. I'm all ears."

"Butch, please." Karp took a breath and began his spiel, hoping that by the end of it he would have explained to both of them why he had arranged this peculiar interview. "Okay, clearly with the events of the last month, infanticide has emerged into the public eye. The public is confused. A woman killing a newborn violates some basic notions of what's right, but unlike say a violent rape-murder, the public doesn't have a good villain on whom to cast guilt, and, well, defuse it. It's disturbing. It unleashes strange and dark social forces. Obviously, my office is affected, too. I mean after all, not only do we represent the People, but we also *represent* the people, if you know what I mean."

"I thought that was the jury's job."

"It's everybody's job. A courtroom is a little government assembled for a limited purpose

—judiciary, executive, and popular representatives."

"Is that why you're coming down on Lola like a ton of bricks? Because you think that's what people want?"

"I don't think I want to defend the People's current position in re Bustamente."

"So why don't you change it? Aren't you the boss?"

"Does your boss stick his nose into your plea bargains? Second-guess your advice to your clients?"

She flushed. "No, but that's not exactly the same thing."

"Why? Because you're on the side of the angels, defending the helpless poor, and we're the forces of the monster state?" He waited, but she didn't respond, which was good. Anyone who thought that wouldn't be worth talking to. In a milder tone he said, "Tell me about your client. What's she like?"

"Lola? Oh, Lola's nobody's fool. A good native intelligence. Youngest of six kids, mom's an LPN, father's estranged but supports the family, he works in a liquor store. She likes clothes and dancing. Not interested in school. She wants to be on MTV. Failing that, she'd like to work in a nail joint. Her brother-in-law, a charmer named Emilio Perez, raped her at her sister's apartment last spring. She didn't tell anyone about it, including herself. She was in a dance hall when she felt her water break. Went into the toilet and had the baby."

"Stupid question: Why did she throw it out the window? Did she say?"

"She doesn't know, really. The best I can get out of her was that she went black for a while and then the baby was gone. She cleaned herself up and went back to dancing. Hi ho, Lola. She thinks it doesn't count because she was raped, and believe me, it took some doing to get the rape out on the record."

"You don't have many cards, do you?"

She smiled and sipped at her drink, a whiskey sour. "We never have any cards."

"So you'll accept the plea."

"Oh, *I'd* accept it in a minute, but the family doesn't want to. The mother, especially, and since she's a minor . . ."

"Why not? Did you explain —"

"Of *course,* I explained," she replied sharply. "What it is, they're outraged. This guy, Emilio Perez, raped their girl and he's walking free and their kid's going to jail. They want the kid up there telling her story. They think when the jury hears it, they'll do the right thing. Basically, they want their day in court."

"Despite the risk of a conviction for murder."

"Which I have explained in great detail, believe me." She finished her drink, licked the foam of it from the glass's rim with a surprising pink flick of her tongue, and popped the maraschino cherry into her mouth.

Karp wanted to believe her. He liked her, and we want to believe people we like. She was poking the foam in her glass with a plastic straw and sucking it off. He asked, "How are you going to approach the defense, if you do go to trial?"

"You want to pry out all our Guilty Girl secrets? Prince of Darkness."

Karp realized, with something of a shock, that she was slightly drunk. "No, really," he said. "The law is against you, the facts are against you, so as the saying goes, you appeal to the emotions of the jury. You think that will work?"

"Oh, of course, and me being a woman, I should be good at emotional arguments. Are you familiar with the British law on infanticide?"

"As a matter of fact, I am. Murrow cranked out an analysis for me the other day, also a general study of the crime of infanticide."

"Little Mookie?"

"Not in my office he's not. Would you

like to take a look at it?"

"Yes. Yes, I would. Thank you." She seemed to have sobered up. A peculiar look was on her face, as if she were struggling to slip out of a mask.

"I'll send it by. But I'm afraid you won't find much help in it, not in New York law."

"The law can be changed. As you've just informed me, juries are tiny little legislatures."

"I was speaking figuratively."

"Were you?" She smiled. Karp caught the little wolf gleam in her eye. He knew it well; he saw it in the mirror all the time.

6

The loft was full of divine fragrances when Karp returned home that evening, and he stood for a moment inhaling them, dripping raindrops on the oak as he hung his raincoat on the brass stand by the door. Beneath the cooking he could detect other scents, of lemon oil and tung oil and floor wax, sweet and acrid, and the sharp pong of Windex. The loft, he observed, was clean, sparkling, glowing; unnaturally clean, for the loft, while never actually filthy, had clearly shown the habitation of six people, two of whom were boys of seven years. Suspiciously clean. It could only have been Marlene herself who had accomplished this cleansing, for Posie, while possessing many child-care virtues, was (before her conversion, at least) a mere jolly slut, and Lucy, although demonically neat within the confines of her room, was unlikely to have volunteered; teenaged geniuses are teenagers still. Besides the aroma, music also filled the air, an operatic soprano, at high volume, coming from the kitchen, undoubtedly from the small, greasy, powerful boom

162

box Marlene kept on a shelf above the sink.

Karp went into the bedroom (also shined, he saw), changed into chinos and a faded sweatshirt and floppy, decayed sneakers, his only other sort of outfit besides the full suit rig. In the kitchen, he found his wife poking at something in her big black iron frying pan. He came around behind her, inhaled the wedded scents of food and wife, sighed theatrically, and kissed her on the cheek. Marlene turned down the gas on the Vulcan and herself around, waving her wooden spoon in time to the final strains of the aria. He could see that her eyes were red. The singing ended; she switched the tape off.

"What was that?" he asked.

"That was Maria Callas singing 'Vissi d'arte,' from *Tosca*. In 1953."

"She kills the guy and jumps off the tower," said Karp, summing up his knowledge of the opera in the manner of a tone-deaf man acknowledging one of his wife's passions.

"That's the one. Funny. It's the only opera about an opera singer. Why are you looking at me like that?"

"Have you been crying or is that onions?"

"Oh, you know, I always get weepy listening to that," said Marlene unconvincingly. "Go round up the kids; this is ready."

"Lucy's in?"

163

"For a change. Posie's out, more or less permanently, I think. She's been moving stuff out of her room for a couple of days. I hope we get an invitation to the wedding. Amazing. I picked her off the street as a drowned-rat, junkie semiwhore, took her into my home, gave her the care of my children, and now she's a Muslim bride and I'm barely good enough for her."

"Good thing you're home, then," said Karp, never a Posie fan at the best of times, and got a sharp look.

"Oh, I can see *you're* enjoying this, all your long-suppressed patriarchal-hegemony receptors are bursting forth. It's disgusting."

"Hey, you knew I wasn't a sensitive New Age man when you married me. I do enjoy getting fed delicious food, I do enjoy a spotless home, I do appreciate not having to worry about hypersonic missiles flying about the heads of my kids, thank you. On the other hand, *the* most important thing to me is are you happy. Which you should know by now. Are you?"

"Oh, Butchie, you know, it's sort of a limbo, now. Neither heaven nor hell, and if you twisted my arm, I'd have to say, for now, it's okay. What I wish, though . . ."

But this wish was not voiced because of the clattering and whooping as the twins burst into the room and swarmed upon their father, talking, giggling, vying for attention, finishing each other's sentences, hurling invectives at each other. Karp settled them, heard the day's news, including the latest second-grade bathroom jokes, and got them into the dining room, where he supervised their setting the table. Lucy entered and helped her mother bring the meal in: pork chops in Marlene's version of *Neapolitana*, over penne, and the salad Lucy had made. Karp sat at the head of the table and could not keep a satisfied grin from his face. His daughter caught the look and grinned back. "Yes," she said, "it's just like *The Wonder Years*. Or, what's that one they're always talking about? Not *Leave It to Beaver . . .*"

"*Ozzie and Harriet*," said Marlene sourly, sitting down, but then it was demonstrated to Karp why it was not, quite, as his daughter said a Catholic grace and his wife and his three children crossed themselves. It had long been explained to the boys why Daddy did not go to church, and in the new Church, of course, there was a good deal less explaining to do, the recent doctrines having played down Christ-killing and the damnation of those outside the bosom of Rome. Still, a slight twinge. Lucy, to her credit, also kept the intensity of her religious life hidden from her family. Quite apart from a natural diffidence — she was the rarer type of genius, who did not want to be made much of — she had a horror of appearing pushy regarding morality and belief. She was, however, to the dismay of her parents, an outspoken opponent of abortion.

So that when Karp happened to mention that he had heard that Marlene's friend Shanahan had been booted off the Goldfarb infanticide case, the normally avoided subject was in play, if indirectly, the boys wanting to know about why people killed babies, and how they did it (the families of surgeons learn to put squeamish feelings aside at the dinner table, but they have nothing on the families of public prosecutors), and this naturally led to a discussion of the recent upsurge in infanticides, and Marlene, unthinking, mentioned that she couldn't quite comprehend it, given the wide availability of abortion services, to which Lucy said, "Well, that's just it. Once you accept killing babies in abortion clinics —"

"Fetuses, dear," said Marlene.

"— *babies* in abortion clinics, why stop there? They probably thought, What's the difference? And it's free besides."

"Quite aside from the illogic of that statement," said Marlene, "because the difference between a baby and a fetus has been established for years by statute following *Roe*, in practical terms, people who want abortions are going to get them. They always have. The public decision is whether they're going to be safe, one, and available to all income groups or only to the rich. It's a no-brainer, Lucy."

"People are always going to do drugs, they're always going to abuse kids, they're always going to rob banks, so let's make all those things legal, too, according to you."

Karp, who had been enjoying a truly delicious dinner and did not want to see portions of it flung through the air, put in what he thought would be a cooling fact, retrieved by his unusually sticky brain from Murrow's document. "You know, abortion was perfectly legal in New York up until about 1850. Abortionists advertised in the newspapers. And it only became illegal because the docs wanted to expand their monopoly on medical treatment, to drive the non-MD abortionists out of business. The docs pushed the legislation, not the Church. The Church didn't have a big stand against abortion until a lot later."

"So?" said his daughter.

"So, morals change over time. And the law is only indirectly moral. At bottom, it's based on what people want. They want, the majority anyway, abortion rights, and they don't want child abuse and bank robbery."

"That doesn't make it right," said Lucy in such a tone that her mother thought, How did *this* come into our home? I expected sex, maybe drugs, maybe bad grades, but not this, and half to herself, and unwisely, she voiced the old Monty Python tag: "*No one* expects the Spanish Inquisition . . ."

At this, the daughter who had been speaking quietly with downcast eyes raised her head and looked at Marlene and said in a much louder voice, "You'll see, those girls are going to get off. They committed *murder* and they're going to get off."

"Good Lord, Lucy!" Karp exclaimed. "What do you think they should get? Twenty-five to life?"

"The same as that man that Mom shot last week would've got if he killed that little girl instead of his wife. What, are you going to say, Oh, she was a girl instead of a grown-up, so knock off a couple of years? I don't see the difference. And whatever you say, there's no difference between what the guy did, and what those girls did, and what they do in abortion clinics."

"Excuse me," said Marlene, "exactly when did you turn into a fundamentalist prig? Did I miss something?"

"And you're a hypocrite," snapped Lucy. "Did *you* ever have an abortion?"

"No, but —"

"Would you ever *have* an abortion?"

"No. I mean, I've never been in that kind of jam."

"You mean no. You only defend it to keep in good with your liberal feminist pals."

This last was so grossly unfair — Marlene was, in fact, so un-in with the liberal feminist establishment of New York and (truth be told) had a view of abortion rather closer to Lucy's than she would ever publicly admit — that for an instant she was struck dumb, mouth actually agape. She brought up a number of devastating rejoinders to the surface of her mind, but since the verbal mutilation of children was not something either Karp ever did, what came out (which was bad enough) was "Oh, shut up!"

Lucy flushed and shot to her feet, knocking over her chair, and said something that no one in the family could translate but which was clearly vile in intent. Into the awful silence after this, Giancarlo Karp let out a high-pitched shriek, holding his hands over his ears. When he had secured everyone's attention in this way, he said, "Why are we talking about dead babies all the time? Why don't we talk about nice stuff?"

More silence, except for the sound of Lucy retrieving her chair and the clatter of eating. Then Zak whispered to his mother, "What do they do with the dead babies in the abortion place?"

"Not now, Zak."

"Do they put them in bottles?"

"Zak!"

Marlene considered her twins, so-called. Giancarlo was wearing a blue flannel shirt hanging out, over a T-shirt with the logo of a local gallery on it, and jeans and blue leather slippers. His hair was a mass of chestnut curls. Zak's treatment of the same equipment was to demand and get, eventually, a 1950s buzz cut, and he wore a camouflage shirt and baggy fatigue pants, resembling, to the extent allowed in this house, the child of an Idaho survivalist. Some weird trick of mitosis had poured double portions of a temperament into one twin, and its opposite into the other, dividing the traditional male domains, art and war, down the middle. I am not responsible for this, she told herself, yet again.

They ate on, the silence just hovering on the edge of toxicity, then Giancarlo clanked his fork down and said, "Let's have *talking!*"

Karp and his wife burst into laughter, which all joined, Lucy last, but she did join, and she said, "Sorry, Mom," and Marlene said, "No problem, kid, my fault really," and then Lucy said, "This is really good. What's in it?" sincerely, because she was really interested in cooking, and the table came back to life.

The phone rang in Marlene's office at the end of the loft while they were washing up, the dog precleaning the dishes with his efficient tongue, and all hands involved, and Marlene, thinking it might be (perhaps even hoping it was) some emergency, went to answer it.

She was away a long while. Karp closed down the kitchen, got the boys through their bath and into pajamas, sent them off to watch TV, and restored the bathroom to reasonable dryness and order. Coming back through the hall, he paused by the door of his daughter's room to knock.

She was at her desk, doing what looked like homework, Walkman earplugs in her ears. She removed these and looked up. He said, "Nice save, there, at dinner."

"It was my fault. I shouldn't let myself get angry like that. It was Giancarlo's save anyway."

"Credit for the assist, then. You are a little hard on her. She's going through a rough time."

"Everybody's going through a rough time,

Dad. It's a vale of tears."

"Have mercy, then."

She nodded. "I try. We seem to be good at pushing each other's buttons. I think it's better than it was, though."

"A lot," he agreed. "You know, I have to say, just speaking legally, you're adopting an untenable position there."

"I wasn't thinking legally. I was thinking about what's right and what's wrong."

"That's just the point. Contrary to popular belief, the law isn't about right and wrong in the way you mean. It's basically about force, and how far the power of the state can be used to make people do things they don't necessarily want to do, like keeping their hands out of pockets that don't belong to them. And you don't want to use that power unless you absolutely have to, for what they call a compelling state interest, and our country has decided that the state interest in preserving the life of an early fetus has to yield to the right of a woman to the privacy of her body. It's about what's properly regulated behavior, not morality."

"I know that, Dad, I'm not *stupid,*" said Lucy, thinking, how much easier it is to talk to him about this kind of stuff than to her mother. "But like you always say, we need good laws because there are bad men, and good men because there are bad laws. So this is a bad law, like slavery, or segregation. People who believe it's bad should resist it."

"Yeah, but if you decide to do that, you should think it through, all the way. Let's say it's illegal. Who do you jail? The abortionist? Sure, throw away the key. How about the mother? She's complicit. And *her* mother and father, too, if they provided the money. And the fetus's father, too, if he knew about it and didn't stop it. In practical terms, do you really want *your* father to bring cases like that? And only against poor women? Because believe me, as long as there's airplanes, those're the only kind we'll ever see. I won't even mention the ones that'll be dying in hallways from illegal abortions."

"I understand all that," Lucy said. "Also people made the argument that there'd be violence if they stopped segregating races and they did anyway and there *was* violence. It was still wrong, and *this* is still wrong."

She has the same set in her jaw that her mother has when she's locked into something nuts, thought Karp. The apple doesn't fall far from the tree. Time to change the subject.

"What're you doing there?" He pointed at her desk.

"This? Latin. It's funny learning a language that no one speaks. I seem to be as bad at it as everyone else." She looked up at the world map pinned above her desk. Little pins marked the homelands of the languages she spoke fluently. There were a lot of them, and it seemed to Karp that new ones were added every couple of weeks.

"You can't have everything."

"No. But speaking of people who do, I invited Caitlin Maxwell to stay over this weekend. The floors are being done in their new place and the Maxwells are going to Vail to ski. They wanted her to stay with her grandfather, but she doesn't much like him, and it's all right with Mrs. Maxwell, I asked."

"Yeah, that's fine with me. Doesn't Caitlin ski?"

Lucy snorted. "On the million-dollar legs? Get out of here!"

"I'll do that," said Karp, smiling. He paused in the doorway. "Oh, one more thing, speaking of wrong. I don't want to hear you cursing out your mother, in any of those languages. Okay?"

"She doesn't understand it," mumbled Lucy, looking away from him.

"Ah, *you* can be legalistic, too, when you want. It doesn't matter if she understands it or not. *You* shouldn't do it. Now *I'm* talking right and wrong — it's in the Bible, too — honor thy mother. You're the one who believes in God — you don't think He under-stands Cantonese?"

An hour later Karp was sitting on the couch watching television, the two boys curled up asleep on either side of him, when Marlene came back. He looked up at her and said, "What's wrong?" He pressed the mute button on the remote.

"Nothing. I think. That was Shanahan from Wilmington. I got the whole sad story."

Marlene moved Giancarlo and sat beside him on the couch. Karp said, "How sad is it?"

"She's pretty broken up, actually. Her first shot at a really big case and she blows it, or rather, the judge screws her. Have you been following it in the papers?"

"You know I only read sports and local crimes. What'd she do?"

"Oh, well, the judge issued a gag order. No, that's not the real beginning. You know how you guys are always mooning about the great white defendant?"

"Us guys?"

"You know what I mean. A juicy case, mid-dle-class people who've done a big no-no, the kind of thing that makes the rep of an ambi-tious prosecutor and takes off some of the guilt for what you do ninety-nine percent of the time, which is putting underrepresented sad-sack minority kids in jail."

"Point taken. So the DA down there is a hotshot?"

"State's attorney, yeah. Name of Jason Abt. And his boss, the attorney general, same thing. Nan Whiting; she got elected on a platform of just-because-I'm-a-girl-don't-mean-I'm-not-tough. Anyway, with all the stuff that's been going on recently, the baby-killing business here in the media capital of the universe, when these two white kids allegedly killed their baby — white, prosperous, non-mentally-retarded college kids to boot — saliva started to flow, and Whiting and Abt started to get calls for TV interviews. Abt went on a local station and did an interview to explain what scum these kids were and why the state was trying them for capital murder. Delaware's a death-sentence state. Then Whiting went on the Geraldo show, *Rivera Live,* and did the same thing — the kids deserved to die for killing the baby. So the judge goes ballistic and issued a gag order, after, of course, the damage was done to the defendants. Okay, the day after this, Maureen walks out of her house and the street is full of newsies. They stick a mike and a camera in her face and ask for her reaction. So, you know, she's not used to this, she's been doing drunk drivers in magistrate's court her whole life, so she says something about how she's disturbed that the state's attorney and the attorney general saw fit to prejudge the case on television, and some more in that vein, five minutes out there on the lawn, and that was it. She told me she thought the gag order just applied to actually consenting to a formal appearance, like the prosecutor's side did. The lawn interview goes on the evening news for a fifteen-second sound bite. Next day, the judge calls her into his chambers, reams her up one side and down the other, and tells her she's off the case."

"That's amazing," said Karp. "Cite her for contempt, fine her, toss her in the can for a couple of nights, but *removal?* I've never heard of anything like that for violating a gag order. On the other hand, the Court says you have a right to counsel, but not a right to any particular lawyer, so he can do that if he wants. *Morris v. Slappy.* Who is this bozo?"

"Speaking of Morrises. His name's Holden Morris Shearing, as in the Morris who signed the Declaration of Independence, not Morris in *schmattes* from Delancey Street. A very high-class fellow, according to Shanahan, very careful of his dignity and prerogatives, and also a little over his head, if you want my opinion. I don't think he's ever had a media case in his courtroom, and he's nervous as a cat."

Karp shifted the sleeping Zak, who had started to drool on his thigh. "Well, he's made a fine start. I'm sorry for your pal, though. And for the girl. What's she going to do? The family."

"Get another attorney, obviously. The family's problem is Shanahan wasn't the first lawyer. They hired a literal Philadelphia lawyer, this fellow Slotkin —"

"Max Slotkin?"

"Yeah, do you know him?"

"Slightly. Used to be a Baxter Street regular, before your time. Mostly criminal courts work, gambling, pross, assaults. He had to be talked to a number of times, as I understand. But I didn't really know him. I think he left the city under something of a cloud."

"It wouldn't surprise me."

"Why, what'd he do?"

"Cashed checks, basically, and sat on his ass, and let Sarah rot in jail. As far as Maureen could determine, he was hanging around playing footsie with the boy's lawyer. Oh, yeah, he's somebody you *do* know — Phil Loreno."

"Phil Loreno." Karp whistled appreciatively. "They've got some serious money, then. Phil don't work cheap, and for him to schlepp down to Baltimore . . ."

"Wilmington. The boy's dad apparently lives in New York, and that's how they made the connection with Phil. Anyway, he talked Slotkin into getting the Goldfarbs to sign a joint defense agreement, but meanwhile the family's hearing noises that Loreno is sniffing around the state's attorney for a deal, and Slotkin's stalling the Goldfarbs, telling them not to worry, the state's just blowing smoke, the indictment for capital murder's just a political ploy, and if Sarah and Peter Jorgensen — that's the boyfriend — just stuck together, the prosecution couldn't lay a glove on them."

"That sounds like good advice," said Karp.

"Yeah, it would be, if Jorgensen's family weren't running so scared. I didn't get the full story — I'm not even sure Maureen knows it — but my sense is that this wacky murder charge has just upped the ante so high that everyone is starting to do crazy stuff — the state, the judge, the boy's family . . . and there's a public hysteria: God, they charged them with murder, they must be monsters. To the gallows with them! You know how it goes."

"I do, I do. And of course, with what's been going on here, it's déjà vu all over again. You know, I still don't get it. Okay, forget a bunch of hicks down in Delaware — Roland is one sharp big-town prosecutor and he's about to go down the same road with this kid Busta-mente. Try her as an adult. Murder two the top count."

Marlene said nothing to this, but stared blankly at the muted, glittering screen and twirled her fingers around Giancarlo's curls. The child mumbled in his sleep and bur-rowed deeper into the piled cushions. They were getting too big to fall asleep on the couch, to be hauled back-breakingly to bed. She was aware of her husband's eye intently upon her and almost longed for their earlier marriage, when he had been far less sensitive.

He said, "And . . . ?"

"And what?"

"The end of the sad story. Who's the girl going to get to represent her?"

"Oh. Well, actually, that was why Shana-han was calling. She wanted to know if she could give them my name."

Karp did not respond to this for some time. He pinched his nostrils and took a long breath. Speaking carefully, he said, "I see. And what did you tell her?"

Marlene spoke just as carefully. They were, as so often before in this marriage, abroad in the country of careful speech. "I told her that she could. And that I would be willing to talk with Sarah and her family."

"Uh-huh. So . . . you're at least, um, *entertaining* the idea of defending Sarah Goldfarb?"

"Yes. Are you going to tell me all the reasons I shouldn't?"

"No. I do that a lot at work. It's boring. For a change, why don't *you* tell *me?*"

"This is a trick, right?"

"No, but ever since you quit packing a gun for a living, I've been waiting for the shoe to drop. If this is going to be it, let's at least be together on what the consequences are. No unpleasant surprises in the middle of the night."

"Oh, that's your game — you're going to pretend to be calm, rational, and supportive. All right — take this, sucker! One, I've never defended in a criminal case. Two, I haven't tried *any* case in nearly ten years. Strike three, it's a different state, so I won't know the law, the precedents, or the people around the courthouse."

"And the batter is out," said Karp. "Tell me, why do you think Shanahan called? I mean you in particular?"

"Probably my international reputation for senseless violence. It's a hopeless case, so the only thing to do is break Sarah loose in a hail of lead. Christ, you're actually looking at me to see if I'm serious! No, really, she said what the kid needed was somebody tough. Tough was more important than the purely legal stuff at this point, because the kid's being railroaded. Oh, I just thought of another reason. The Goldfarbs are essentially broke. They weren't that rich to begin with and Slotkin stripped them pretty good. Shanahan was essentially working for expenses. So it's going to be, I mean if I do, a practically pro bono deal. Anyway, she's got a good PI, although I might do some of the PI work myself, and I'll have a local counsel Maureen's going to arrange, and he'll show me the ropes." Marlene was silent for a moment, studying her husband's face out of the corner of her good eye. He had his blank, deep-thought look on, a good sign.

"So, what do you think? I mean just going down there and looking at the setup."

"What do I think? Jesus, Marlene! It's a capital case. It's a little much to ease yourself into practicing law defending someone for their *life*."

"There's that, but I've been in the life-and-death business for a while. It's not something that's going to reduce me to jelly. On the other hand, I can't get terrifically excited about it right now. I haven't made a commitment. I don't know anything about the case except what Maureen's told me and the crap in the press. Let me go down there and take a look and I'll see if I can handle it, and if I think I can do some good." She laughed. "At least it's out of town. I could be defending Lola Bustamente."

"Marlene, bite your tongue!" said Karp, and they both laughed.

The next morning exhibited more than the usual chaos engendered by five people with strong personalities attempting simultaneously to start their day. Marlene found herself, for the first time in a decade, agonizing about what to wear. A court suit would be too formal, as if she wanted the job. Her bodyguard outfits, which ran to leather and rip-stop nylon, did not give the right impression either, unless the Goldfarbs were really thinking about an escape. The rest of her closet came from retro thrift shops, okay for stepping out on a Sunday in SoHo, but too weird by far for Wilmington. While his wife was so engaged (high-pitched shrieks and muffled cursing coming from the big closet in their bedroom), Karp was getting his sons ready for school. Never had he valued the absent nanny so much; she might be a slob, but she knew their little ways, and they had a surfeit of little ways. Seven-year-olds are kin to the priests of old Egypt in their devotion to routine, and

now their sacred morning rites had been over-
thrown and they were cranky and yet more
determined that everything be as it always
was. Giancarlo could be driven mad by the
outrage of pouring his Cap'n Crunch into his
special bowl *before* adding milk instead of after, and *No, Daddy!* the milk had to come up
to the blue line not the red line. Nor did Karp
slice bananas the right way, apparently; the
ones he presented to Zak were nauseatingly
thick and yucky. Karp steamed; he became
snappish. The boys blubbered. This was a
different Daddy than the genial fellow who
was long gone when they had their school
mornings and was happy to see them in the
evening. Karp kept looking at the clock; the
van would be by in nine minutes to take the
kids up to St. Anthony's school on
MacDougal Street, and if he missed it, disaster! Where are your shoes, Giancarlo? You
don't *know?*

The shoes were in fact in Lucy's hand as
she waltzed into the kitchen in her crisp quasi-
uniform of black jumper and white shirt. "He
always loses his shoes," she explained. "And
don't let them game you on breakfast. Let
'em starve. You're spoiled rotten, aren't
you?" She noogied both their skulls until they
shrieked. Karp left them in their sister's merciless hands and escaped to finish dressing.

Good-bye, *Ozzie and Harriet.*

Meanwhile, Marlene had found a pair of flannel trousers and a navy blazer, which, with a pink oxford shirt and a sleeveless sweater, made an acceptably neutral outfit, suitable for the sticks. She used to wear a similar rig when she visited Lucy's elementary-school teachers. Ankle boots. Clean hankie. Gun.

She was sitting at her desk in her office with the gun safe open and the weapon out when she realized she didn't have to pack heat anymore when she went to work. She let it rest in the palm of her hand. It was seven inches long and weighed only twenty-five ounces and was about as thick as two cigarettes, a SITES Resolver nine millimeter, especially designed by the clever Turinese to be carried all day, every day, without discomfort.

Behind her, a voice said, "Don't do it, Mom. Life is beautiful."

Marlene laughed. "Yeah, right. I just realized I don't need it. I didn't even clean it, after."

Lucy came in and stooped to retrieve something from the low cabinet where her mother kept office supplies. "I need a file folder for my Stendhal essay." She pulled one out of a pack and stood looking at her mother. "That must be weird, after all this time."

"Yeah, baby, it is." Marlene put the pistol down on her desk. "I should clean it, but I don't have time right now, and I know I'll forget. Maybe I should just let it corrode."

"No, just leave it," said Lucy blithely, "I'll do it after school." She kissed the astounded/delighted Marlene on the cheek and left.

Disorder also reigned, Lucy was glad to see, even in Mrs. Maxwell's palace of perfection, although she had to admit that here there was at least an excuse. When she and Caitlin arrived at the Maxwell house after school, the front door was wide open, drop cloths were laid throughout the house, and the furniture on the two lower floors was being stacked into the empty top floor by a crew of grunting men in coveralls. The girls found Mrs. Maxwell in the stripped living room with two men and a single piece of furniture. One of the men Lucy had already met, Oren Lorel, the decorator. This person was thin, late thirties, and wearing a black T-shirt, a charcoal Armani shot-silk suit, and woven-leather loafers. He had bright blue eyes and a pink skin that seemed too stretched over the bones of his face, as if he had been treated for burns. He wore small, slightly tinted, oval wire-rims perched on the bridge of his bony nose. Mrs. Maxwell invited the girls to admire the piece of furniture, which sat on a carpeted dolly.

"It's my reisner secretaire. Isn't it marvelous!"

The girls looked and tried to detect marvels. They saw a desk in dark gold shining wood, with gracefully curving legs covered with bronze acanthus leaves, two drawers down each side, a rolltop decorated with elaborate urn and foliage inlays, a little clock at the top, and four candlesticks supported by reclined cherubs in gilded bronze.

"It's nice, Mom," said Caitlin politely. "But isn't it broken?" She pointed to where some marquetry strips were missing from a drawer panel.

Mrs. Maxwell and Mr. Lorel shared a giggle at this. Mrs. Maxwell said, "Oh, darling, it's over two hundred years old, real Louis Quinze. Mr. Lorel found it for us in London. Of course, he's going to make it as good as new, but he couldn't wait to show it to us." She beamed at the decorator. "Oren, I simply can't wait to see it refinished."

"Yes, well, the sooner we start . . ." He snapped his fingers. "Moussa . . . ?"

The other man, who had been waiting silently a few feet away, swept up a padded cloth, wrapped the desk up like a baby, and rolled it carefully away. Mr. Lorel said something into Mrs. Maxwell's ear that Lucy didn't catch, but which made the woman laugh. "A good place for all your love letters, Jeanne," he added in a suggestive voice, and then he gave a little shriek and rushed forward to supervise his assistant, who was steering the antique through the doorway.

Lucy was rather more interested in the assistant than his employer or the desk. The man was black; not one of the brown shades called black in America, but literally charcoal black. A man of medium size, dressed in a baggy blue coverall, he had a small, elegant, closely cropped head on a long neck, with small, round, delicate ears, and high cheekbones, each marked with three parallel scars. His demeanor was perfectly calm as he jockeyed the awkward piece through the door, unbothered, it seemed, by the decorator's nagging direction.

Mr. Lorel returned, dusting his hands on a yellow silk handkerchief, with a what-can-you-do? expression on his face. "Actually, he's a very good boy. From Mali, speaks French. Spent some time with a man I know in the fourteenth arrondissement." He lowered his voice to say, "And . . . a lot easier to work with than the *locals*." His face assumed a puzzled frown. "Jeanne, what *is* that awful racket?"

A high-pitched whining was coming from

the dining room, punctuated at intervals by loud thumps. They all walked through to investigate. There they found Brian Maxwell racing a large, red, radio-controlled Corvette in circles around the parquet, crashing it from time to time into the freshly primed baseboards.

During what followed, Lucy had an illumination about family life. She thought that the difference between the Karps and the Maxwells was that in the Karp family, each member was sometimes the hero and sometimes the goat. At dinner the other night, she had been the goat and Giancarlo had been the hero. At breakfast and afterward this morning, Giancarlo had been the goat and Lucy had been the hero. Her mother was often the goat, her father less often, but occasionally he, too, would drop the ball in a big way. In the Maxwells, Brian was always the goat, and everyone else was perfect. Lucy wondered if this was the difference between a happy family and an unhappy one. But the Maxwells seemed reasonably happy; they were certainly successful and content with it, except Brian, of course, and even he seemed happy in his goofy way. Lucy often had problems with her mother and her mother's temper, but she could not imagine her mother treating a child, her own or another's, in the way that she had just seen Mrs. M. treat Brian, and over nothing but some marks on pieces of wood, too.

Later, in Caitlin's room, where they were doing their homework, she mentioned the incident to her friend. Caitlin shrugged it off. "He's a jerk, what can I say? But, really, my mom was mad at him to begin with because his school bounced him out the day before yesterday, which makes the second one this year, four in all. The stuff downstairs was like the last straw. My dad's going to take him around to military schools after they ski. He's unbelievably pissed off. I mean, having to miss work and all. Oh, look, can you help me with French dictation?" An unartful change of subject, Lucy thought, but did not press her friend in an area that was none of her business and clearly uncomfortable. She took up Caitlin's French text and read off a paragraph, then read through what Caitlin had written and corrected it.

"It's funny, you don't sound like Ms. Wilcox," said Caitlin, "and you're supposed to be the great language whiz. Or is she wrong?"

"No, she is not wrong," said Lucy in French, precisely and wickedly imitating the accent of Caitlin's French teacher. "She speaks correctly in the manner of a French teacher from Boston who spends her summers in Paris." In English, she continued,

"Actually, I speak French with a Vietnamese accent because I learned French from a Vietnamese man. And I guess I want to remember him."

"This was that gangster, right?"

"Yeah. Uncle Tran."

"What happened to him?"

"He got in a jam saving my life. He lives out of town now."

Caitlin rolled her eyes. "Boy, Lucy, some of these stories . . . I don't know. I mean they sound so *weird,* and you toss them off like nothing. Oh, that was before I was pursued by alien drug smugglers and locked in a trunk with a cobra, la-di-da. Like, what were you doing hanging out with a Vietnamese gangster?"

"He worked for my mom, and he took care of me. He was a very bad man and a very nice guy. He taught me a lot."

"Like what? How to kill people?"

"Among other things," said Lucy coolly.

Then the phone rang and Caitlin picked it up and commenced talking in a low voice, with her hand cupped around her mouth, giggling at intervals. A boy. Lucy thought it was rude to take a call when you had a friend with you, but she already suspected that Caitlin was one of those girls to whom boyfriends were a higher level of creature than girlfriends. This dismayed her, but she was not so dismayed as to seek out the company of girls for whom this was not so, who bored her, for the most part. Lucy, truth to tell, would have liked a little of her own giggling with a boy on the phone, but she thought it unlikely to happen in the foreseeable future. Her great dread was that she would become one of those unattractive girls whom attractive girls keep about them, like the trained dwarfs of a Velázquez infanta, as companions when there is no man nearby. She left the bedroom, thinking dark thoughts, and contemplating (as she had a number of times before) a career with the Barefoot Carmelites.

Early the next morning, there was an intermittent whining noise in the house, coming from the floor below. Surely, Brian was not playing with that car *again*. She slipped quickly down the back stairs to see. She actually liked Brian, finding him amusing in a weird way, like her brother Giancarlo, and wished, if she could, to save him now from himself. They would throw him in *jail* for this, never mind military school.

But it was not Brian at all. In the center of the empty dining room, in a squat, was the very black man in the blue coverall, doing something to the floor. A small table saw was set up on steel sawhorses over a drop cloth, obviously the source of the noises. Lucy paused just outside the doorway and observed him. Waiting in silence, perfectly motionless, was another skill Lucy had picked up from Tran Van Dinh.

The man rose and went to the table saw and cut a length of dark veneer to size and then squatted again and fitted it into place in the parquet he was repairing. He was examining another pair of strips, holding them up to check the darkness of the grain, when he saw her watching him. He nodded to her; she nodded back and said, *"Nse, ih ni wula."* After only the slightest pause, he answered, *"Nba, ih ni wula."* Lucy stepped forward and extended her hand. He took it, and she asked, in the same language, "Did you sleep well?" He said that he had, and then she inquired after the health of his wife, and of his children, and if they were at peace, and then he asked whether she had slept well and about the health of her family and if they were at peace, all the time holding her hand and shaking it gently. The hand was large and warm, hard with calluses, and completely enfolded her own.

Then he asked her a question, which she did not fully understand but whose meaning she guessed at, and grinning at him, she said in French, "Oh, all Americans speak a little Bambara."

His eyes widened, and then he laughed and said, also in French, "That was a joke, yes? It relieves my mind. When you first started to speak, I thought you might be a *djenné* inhabiting the body of a girl, but now I see this is not the case."

"What is a *djenné?*"

"A kind of spirit."

"And don't they make jokes?"

"Sometimes, but not that sort of joke. Then, I thought I was dreaming while awake, but this is not true either, although sometimes in this country one cannot easily tell. How did you learn to greet a person in Bambara?"

"From a man who sells fake watches near Union Square. I am interested in languages, but regrettably I know no African ones, as yet. The Bambara language has a structure of shifting tonal values that interests me." He smiled at her blankly, but she was used to such responses. She pointed to the parquet he was repairing. "Where did you learn to do that work?"

"In Bamako at first, from my father, who made furniture in the style of the *Tubabuka,* I mean the French. Then I worked in Paris and now here."

They talked for a while. His name was Moussa Feydé, he was thirty-four, had a wife and a daughter, lived in Washington Heights.

194

Mr. Lorel was okay to work for; he did not cheat his workers as much as he cheated his clients and had the true eye for quality. America was confusing but one could get rich here. He was saving to bring the rest of his family over. He liked restoring beautiful old things, preferred it to what he had done in Paris, which was forging antiques. Yes, he would be happy to exchange conversation in Bambara for practice in speaking English. Now he must excuse himself; he had to get back to work. Yes, a pleasure. *K'an ben sini.* Good-bye until tomorrow. *K'an be somogow fo.* My best regards to your family. *U n'a men.* They will hear it.

Lucy went back upstairs, buoyed by the near-sensual pleasure she experienced when the prospect of learning a new language appeared. As she walked by the door of Brian Maxwell's room, she heard a stream of odd sounds: squeaking, popping, crying. She knocked, opened the door a crack. Brian was at his computer, playing a game that involved shooting prairie dogs. The prairie dogs exploded in a shower of blood when hit; when wounded, they cried piteously.

The boy looked around and saw her. "I'm playing my game."

She could see he had been crying. "Are you okay?"

He shrugged. "I did a new comic. Want to see?"

"Sure." She went into the room. Almost the entire surface of the shag rug was covered with expensive toys, and parts of toys: games, plastic castles, action figures, construction sets of various types, electronic wonders. She tried to avoid the larger items, but her feet crackled on plastic nonetheless. The comic book was typical boy stuff, superheroes blasting villains in elaborate ways with complex weapons lovingly drawn, but well done, Lucy thought, for an eleven-year-old.

"It's very good, Brian. You could be an artist when you grow up."

"I want to be a ninja assassin."

Unlike everyone else Brian had ever expressed this wish to, Lucy Karp did not ignore the statement or make some patronizing remark. Instead, she seemed to think seriously about it. "It's funny, I was just talking to your sister about an assassin who was a friend of mine. Not a ninja, a Vietnamese."

Brian's eyes widened. "For real?"

"Yes. He told me once that the best assassins were very neat and careful, very quiet and usually very kind to animals. The really good ones suffered when they killed people, and these were better than the ones that didn't suffer, because sooner or later their unconscious guilt would lead them to screw up something and get caught."

"Was he ever caught? Your friend, I mean."

"Yes, but not during an assassination. They arrested him after the war was over. They put his hands in a meat grinder. You ought to think more about this, Brian."

He stared at her for a moment, an astounded look on his face, and then laughed hilariously, doubling over with it.

Poor kid, thought Lucy as she giggled along, not many laughs for old Brian chez Maxwell.

7

They forecast snow, but Marlene took the Volvo anyway. That way she could drive fast down the turnpikes, which she loved and hardly ever got to do, and bring the dog, a bit of eccentricity she felt was not entirely out of place, since tough had been ordered, and if they didn't like it, to hell with them. Love me, love my dog, thought Marlene, and said it, to the dog, who was curled in his usual place on the passenger seat. Occasionally, he would sit up on the seat and press his awful face against the side window, which was by now coated with a frosting of dried drool. This caused several cars passing on the right to swerve violently, but yielded no actual accidents. There was no snow, however, although the sky over the Jersey turnpike country looked like what you emptied out of a vacuum cleaner's bag, with tatters of gray hanging down and blending with the industrial smokes below.

"How about if we keep on going, Sweets? Just you and me, out on the highway, start a new life, live in trailer parks. Butch'd get a new wife, one of those buffed young ladies I see around the courthouse, with two eyes and ten fingers and no blood on their hands. Not crazy. A regular person. The twins would take about three weeks to forget me. And Lucy . . . no, Lucy would probably track me down and drag me back at gunpoint, just for the satisfaction of tormenting me unto death do us part. Sweets, explain this to me: last night it's daggers, it's daggers for weeks, and then this morning it's, 'I'll clean your gun, Mom.' Is this a plan to drive me crazy? Crazier. And also, 'I'll clean your gun'? That was not one of the lines I ever passed through my girlish imagination when I was thinking about how it would be when I had a daughter. 'Oh, let's bake cookies, Mom!' That would be one. 'Oh, Mom, when I grow up, I want to be just like you.' 'Mom, you're the greatest!' Silly me. Yes, Sweets, I know, I'm being shitty, none of this is true, I'm just nervous, I'm going on a *job* interview! Christ Jesus, I haven't been on a fucking job interview in twenty years, and me being Marlene, naturally it's a fucked-up job I don't particularly want, that pays no money, and that's likely to end in complete disaster. Hi ho!" She laughed maniacally and fiddled with the radio, which was out of range of New York by now, and got a black station in Philly playing Etta James, and she rode that all the way into the greater Wilmington area.

Maureen Shanahan had offices in a four-story prewar building on King Street, just within walking distance of the courthouse. It had a Kinko's copying shop on the ground floor and a small, claustrophobically slow elevator done in dark paneling, once elegant, now scratched and shabby.

Her office was in one of those arrangements where four or so low-end attorneys shared a central waiting area, law library, and secretary/receptionist. What would have been vaguely depressing if the office had been in a soulless new construction retained in this older venue the virtues of distinguished decay; the ceilings were high and rimmed with flamboyant plaster decorations, and the windows were the large, old-fashioned kind that could be opened on fine days, and the details were real oak. Marlene gave her name to a dark brown woman in a neat red suit and almost immediately Shanahan popped out from one of the offices that lined the room and embraced her. Shanahan was wearing a charcoal suit skirt and a round-collared blouse with a little gold pin. She looked worn and had gained a few pounds she didn't need.

They went into Shanahan's room, which was three times the size of the office Marlene had occupied at the DA, the last time she had actually worked as a lawyer. It had walnut paneling, and relatively new furniture, and a couple of pleasant still-life canvases on the wall. Shanahan caught Marlene looking at them and said, "My daughter, Shannon."

"They're very good," said Marlene. "Reminds me of Morandi, but a little brighter."

"Thank you. If I didn't have her and David, I'd be going nuts right now. Sarah was an art major, too. Is, I mean." Shanahan shook her head.

"Well, you seem to be holding up pretty good to me," said Marlene brightly. "You look well."

"Don't start that, Champ," replied Shanahan sourly. "I look like shit and feel like shit, but thanks for lying."

"Hey, no problem, I'm a lawyer," said Marlene, and got a smile.

Shanahan said, the smile fast fading, "The goddamn press. You won't believe what's going on. We're under siege. Well, I'm not anymore — yesterday's news, but the family . . . I'm glad you came, Champ; I think you can really help out here. I'd like to take you out to the Goldfarbs."

"Sure. We'll have to take my car, though."

"Your car?"

"I brought my dog. I'll let him sniff out the

situation, and if it's okay with him, we'll go from there."

So in Marlene's car they drove back north on Route 295, then on 47A, and finally south onto 541 through the little nineteenth-century towns eaten by the burbs — Salem, Quinton, Peck's Corner — until they came to Mt. Holly, where the Goldfarbs lived in a substantial split-level under old maples. It had snowed here recently, and the lawns and walks were covered with slushy snow and patches of melting ice. Two vans and a couple of cars with Pennsylvania and Delaware plates were parked on the street.

"See? The jackals are still here," said Shanahan. "They want to get a statement from the Goldfarbs. 'How do you *feel* now that the judge has given your lawyer the boot?' Pull right up into the driveway, Marlene. We'll make a dash for the side door."

Marlene did so and stopped the car. Reporters and two TV crews swarmed out of their vehicles onto the lawn. Marlene left the car and opened the rear hatch and Sweety got out. The dog stretched and yawned. Marlene leaned over him and said a few words into a velvety black ear. The dog growled, then barked, a deep, hollow sound like something from inside an old oil tank, and counter-charged against the charge of the press, baying, slavering, and showing his implements of destruction. Marlene shouted in a high-pitched voice, "Oh, no, Attila! Bad dog! Attila, come!" and ran after him, but not very fast. The press, who usually did the slavering and baying, were not prepared for this. Sweety knocked them over like ducks at a shooting gallery. Expensive equipment flew through the air, expensive reporters covered themselves in slush trying to escape, and one unwise soundman attempted to defend the First Amendment by striking at Sweety with his mike boom.

"Oh, no!" cried Marlene, jumping up and down in a parody of ladylike frustration. "Attila, bad dog! Get off that man! Don't drool on the nice man's face! Oh, *please*, Attila! Please, don't bite the man's face!" Marlene grabbed the dog's collar and hauled him off the soundman. He staggered to his feet, wiped his face, and walked off with the characteristic short stride of one who has soiled his underclothes. The rest of the press were cowering near their cars, filthy and bruised, and threatening lawsuits.

"That added ten years to my life," said Shanahan, dabbing tears of laughter from her eyes. "Attila! Did you train him to do that?"

"I didn't have to. Attila is a Sicilian press-hound. Journalists are his natural prey."

"You're going to get sued."

"*Moi?* A bunch of trespassers on private property fall down in terror when a playful dog runs into the yard while his mistress tries to control him? No one was bitten. Case closed." Marlene said a few Sicilian words to the dog, who trotted off and sat in the center of the lawn.

Shanahan rang the side-door bell. A curtain was pulled aside and the face of a woman appeared, stared, smiled, and opened the door.

This woman, the mother of the client, was wearing a navy tracksuit and Nikes, similar to the sort of outfit Marlene's own mother had adopted for around-the-house wear. As they went through introductions there in the shining kitchen, Marlene actually thought of her own mother, although Mrs. Goldfarb could be no more than five or so years older than Marlene herself. A small woman, slight, sparrowlike, large-eyed, and with a neat, sharp, little nose, she wore her dark hair in a short, shiny mass, the product of a suburban beauty parlor. As she ushered the visitors through the kitchen and up several stairs to the living room, Marlene felt that odd temporal dislocation, as if she were a teenager again, greeted by the mother of one of her friends and shown around the house. The living room had drapes, of some gray-green, shimmery material, and broadloom wall-to-wall in a similar shade. The furniture was solid and unimaginative, medium-colored wood, vaguely Scandinavian, the sort of suite couples starting life in the late sixties bought or received from prosperous parents: sofa and armchair set, covered in navy cotton slipcovers, somewhat worn, the usual glass-and-oak coffee table, the side tables with paper-shaded, ceramic-based lamps, simple and undistinguished; oak bookcases, holding neatly racked best-sellers and family memorabilia, a china cabinet with the good china and some porcelain figures, silver candlesticks, and a heavy brass menorah; on the walls, the kind of landscapes and still lifes one bought at local art fairs, pretty colors, pleasing shapes; a spinet, the keyboard covered against dust (although no dust was observable) with a Chopin étude on the stand; and the only unusual feature, dominating the far end of the long room, a great black modern home-entertainment center, racks of consumer electronics of the latest type, and dominating all, a forty-eight-inch rear-projection TV. Around this altar were ranged a set of comfortable leather and wood chairs. This is a mommy-and-daddy house, Marlene thought. *I don't have a mommy-daddy house, although I'm sure Butch would love one. He'd be comfort-*

able enough here; he could watch games on that big screen and mow the lawn. And Lucy and I could go quietly crazy together. No, I'm not being fair to Butch; he married me, didn't he? After living in my loft for a couple of years so he couldn't really claim to be surprised by the way I live. She shook her head and refocused on the here and now.

Shanahan and Marlene were seated on the sofa, while Mrs. Goldfarb trotted off to fetch coffee, her husband, and the potential client. There were home-baked sugar cookies with the coffee. Marlene had two; delicious. Sarah had baked them, her mother announced, when they were all sitting around the coffee table. Sarah bobbed her head shyly and remarked that the conditions of her bail left her little to do except bake cookies. She was dressed in a tracksuit, too, this one pale pink with thin black piping, but with pink plush slipper-shoes on her feet. Above one of these was the black ankle fetter and electronic box that told the state of Delaware that Sarah was where she was supposed to be.

"It's better than being in jail," remarked Mrs. Goldfarb, and Sarah smiled again. She had a ready and charming smile. A pretty girl of eighteen, small like her mother, and even more delicate. She wore no makeup; her dark, clean hair was pulled back into a short ponytail. She was pale, though, and had worried smudges under her eyes. These met Marlene's look with one so mild and innocent as to be faintly shocking. Born yesterday, indeed. Marlene had not realized that this sort of look was still possible in a girl of eighteen, in the current general depravity. She thought of her own daughter, two years younger and a thousand years older, and of the penetrating, pitiless glance that was often in Lucy's eyes. Marlene would have bet anything that this kid's bed was covered with little stuffed animals.

Mr. Goldfarb had seated himself in an armchair, clearly his usual seat, and his wife perched on its arm, her hand lightly on his shoulder, as they all passed through the social-chat phase. Mr. Goldfarb was small, too, and balding, a few years older than his wife, with an open, boyish, honest face. He was wearing a V-neck, gray sweater over a white turtleneck and jeans below, perhaps an error, for he was running somewhat to fat. He distributed electronics for a living, Marlene learned, and was the largest wholesaler in the state.

The usual pause occurred, and Marlene dived in. "Well, let me say this first. Besides what Maureen here has told me, I know nothing about your case. I expect to fix that after I leave, and then I can give you a better sense of whether it's worthwhile going on. In the meantime, there are some things you should know about me. The first is, I have no experience as a defense attorney. Zero. The second is, I have a somewhat colorful past. I worked for a long time as a security agent, and in that capacity I shot a number of people. I've killed three men and been involved in any number of violent confrontations. We can expect this background to be reported by the press, and this may have an effect on a jury, assuming there ever is one. You'll have to judge that for yourselves. Next, I'm a stranger here. People may have opinions about a New York lawyer, maybe negative opinions, that a local counsel wouldn't generate."

"Peter has a New York lawyer," said Sarah, almost to herself. She dropped her eyes.

Marlene could find nothing to say to this, so she continued, "Added to that, as I said, I've been out of the law business entirely for ten years. You may want someone with more recent experience, more proven in defense." The three Goldfarbs were all looking at her, as if she were telling their several fortunes at once, three pairs of big, friendly brown eyes, touched with apprehension and glimmering with hope. Marlene cleared her throat. "On the other hand, at one time I was a pretty fair prosecutor, and I have almost seven years experience at that, in the best prosecutorial organization in the country, in homicide and in sex crimes. I know felony law, and it's extremely unlikely that the state's attorney in Delaware is going to pull any tricks I haven't heard of or get away with any nasty shenanigans on my watch. Finally, and there's no real modest way to say this, I don't scare. This is both good and bad from your point of view. It's good if you want to make a fight of it. I'll fight in the last ditch and give you everything I've got, for as long as it takes. It's bad if, and only if, you want a low-risk approach to this whole thing. If you think your best bet is to throw yourselves on the mercy of the state and the court and accept what they're willing to give, with maybe some negotiations around the edges, then someone like me is going to upset people and make them less willing to play nice." She spread her hands. "That's all I can say right now, folks."

The Goldfarbs looked at each other. They had clearly expected a more enthusiastic pitch than this, and while not exactly downcast, they seemed a little confused. Mr. Goldfarb spoke first.

"No offense, Ms. Ciampi, but what's your interest? I mean, what do you get out of defending Sarah? I guess Maureen's told you we're just about broke. I can probably raise a little more, from relatives and my life insurance, but this case is not going to pay you New York rates for your time."

"That's an interesting question," said Marlene after a moment. "What's in it for me? I think the simplest answer is that I need to get out of the business I'm in for . . . let's say, personal reasons. I don't care to go back into prosecution, also for personal reasons, so that doesn't leave much unless I want to forget about the law degree, which I find I don't want to do. This is a big case: drama, publicity, the works. It's the kind of case that can put a lawyer on the map, which is one reason why Mr. Abt and Ms. Whiting are trying to hang your daughter, and the same goes for whoever goes to court on your side. I'd be lying if I said that wasn't a consideration at this point in my life. Also, I spent the last ten years doing some extremely unpleasant tasks in order to rescue women from messes they got themselves into. Maybe it's habit-forming."

She said this lightly, but Mr. Goldfarb didn't smile. He said, "So, you're proposing to, like, get some . . . what, experience? . . . on this case, at Sarah's expense, and make a name for yourself? I don't think I like the sound of that, Ms. Ciampi."

"I was being excessively frank. One of my

unlawyerly traits, but you did ask. But the only critical question for you is, Will I sacrifice Sarah's interests to make myself look good, if it came down to something like that. You'll have to judge that for yourselves. The fact is I carried a gun for ten years and put my life and my family's safety at risk to help women in trouble. I've had guns and knives stuck in my face because of that kind of work. And you have to ask, Is someone who'd go through that going to sell out a client for personal advantage? I'm not trying to sell myself here; I haven't even decided if this is going to work. I'm just trying to show myself to you warts and all. It's a trade-off, folks, no question. You get a lawyer inexperienced in defense for minimal outlay, and I get a shot at a big case. You may not see that as the greatest deal, but that's the only one I can put on the table."

Mrs. Goldfarb said, "Well, thank you for being frank, Marlene. I happen to appreciate it. But we have to discuss this as a family before we come to any decision."

Marlene said she understood, and five minutes later Shanahan and she were walking toward the car. The news vans were still there, but the newspeople had locked themselves inside them. The reason for this unusual behavior leaped to his feet and came bounding back

211

to the Volvo at Marlene's whistle, for a glorious caress.

"Did you eat any reporters while we were gone? Let me see your teeth. No hair gel? No false smiles? Good dog! Get in the car! No, the backseat, you idiot!"

Midway back to the bridge the sky began to spit the promised snow.

"They forecast ten inches," said Shanahan. "Do you want to head back to the city?"

Marlene craned her neck to look up at the sky. "I never pay attention to forecasts. No, we'll go back to the office, we'll have lunch, and I'll read up on the case, like we planned. Worse comes to worst, I got chains in the back."

"It's up to you, but you're welcome to stay with me, if it gets really nasty," said Shanahan. "So, tell me, what did you think?"

"Frankly?"

"No, I want you to start being diplomatic."

Marlene laughed. "Okay, frankly, I didn't particularly like the chemistry. I think these are very cautious, normal, frightened people. I think they'd do better with someone more like them."

"Like me, you mean."

"Don't be stupid, Shans. You know what I mean. A suit. Soothing."

"You're the one being dumb. Did you see

the look on that poor girl's face while you were talking to her dad?"

"Disgust?"

"*Worship*, you ninny! Marlene, the dad came at you that way because he's desperate. He thought he knew how to be a dad, take care of the family and all that, and now he's helpless. He picked a lawyer and got screwed. They got me and I dropped the ball . . ."

"Come on, Shans, it wasn't —"

"Doesn't matter, the result is the same. This is a family got hit by a truck, and you come in — you got the transparent airplane, you got the magic bracelets, you got the red-white-and-blue teddy outfit. The kid is sold. The dad is making patriarchal noises, but he's shit out of options and he knows it."

"What about Mom? I sensed she has the veto power in that family."

"Good call. Selma's got some depth, and she's tougher than she looks. They both lean on her. But I could tell she liked you."

Marlene sighed. The snow seemed to be falling faster, large flakes that looked black against the glare of the afternoon sky. Shanahan wanted this to work, so she was seeing the positive. As for herself, Marlene was trying hard to reserve judgment. She had a great deal of experience with victim women, and Sarah G. seemed to her to fit the pattern.

They showed you their sores, appealed to your natural sympathies, to sisterhood if they were more politically sophisticated, and then they'd suck you dry if you let them, because the one thing they were never, never going to give up was their victimhood. Okay, there were exceptions: Sym McCabe was one, gone from victim to Terminator III: congratulations, Marlene! Could Sarah make the transition? The big question.

"Okay, let me go back to your office," said Marlene. "I'll read the case, see what I can make of it. See if the lawyerly chops are still there."

"I wouldn't worry about that, Champ," said Shanahan. "As you'll recall, law is mostly about making lists, long ones, in longhand, which is why those yellow pads are longer than regular paper. You'll see, this is going to fly."

By late afternoon, Marlene was not so sure, having filled twenty-five or so long yellow pages with notes. She and Maureen had eaten lunch in the tiny library where Marlene was working, somewhat to Shanahan's disappointment, because she had wanted to buy them both a grand meal at the Hotel Dupont, but Marlene had wanted to get through the paperwork and get back to the city before the snow made that impossible.

She pushed away from her the final document in the foot-thick pile, the state autopsy report on Baby Boy Jorgensen, made a few more notes, and left the windowless room for the outer office. She went to one of the large windows and pressed her nose and forehead against the cold glass. The snow was sticking all right and still coming down, heavier now than earlier. A mess. I should not take this as an evil omen, she thought, and then, I can't do this, and a good thing I bad-mouthed myself to the Goldfarbs. They'll think it over, and it will occur to them that there are a hundred criminal defense attorneys in the state and a thousand or so nearby in Philly or D.C. In fact, I should just tell Maureen right now that it was a bad idea. I'm not a lawyer anymore.

"Ms. Ciampi?"

It was the secretary. "Phone for you. A Mr. Karp, on line three."

Marlene sat down in front of an empty desk and pushed the blinking button.

"So?" said her husband.

"As you would say, *oy vay!* Anything wrong?"

"No, but I assume that unless you really are Supergirl, I'm going to have to leave right now and be there for the boys when the van drops them off."

"Posie didn't come back?"

"No. I called the number you left and a guy

answered with a thick accent and said that Jalila couldn't talk to me, only to you. She's definitely not coming back to work."

"Oh, boy. That's a problem. I'm sorry."

"No big thing. The damn courthouse is closing down anyway. Just about every judge is dumping the afternoon calendar to make it home before the snow hits. And it's the weekend tomorrow anyway. We'll figure something out. Is it snowing down there?"

"Tons. Don't expect me home before midnight."

"Marlene, don't be ridiculous. Stay over. Shanahan'll give you a bed. Or stay in a motel. Maybe you'll meet a handsome lawyer in the cocktail lounge."

"Yeah, right. Speaking of lawyers . . . I met the D and her family. Nice people, completely wiped by this. And I just finished reading the case material."

"And?"

"I took a lot of notes. You know the kind of stink you get when the cops have concocted a case? The everything-a-little-too-pat feel to the material? The extra corroborating detail."

"I know it well," said Karp. "The state must be nervous."

"I think they're scared shitless, maybe more scared than Sarah and the Jorgensen kid.

216

They've painted themselves into a position where they've got to make Sarah Goldfarb into Lizzie Borden, and she's not. Some of it may be sheer incompetence. The state autopsy is . . . I don't know, wacky. The baby was messed up all right, but the assumption that the kids did it premortem seems unsupported. I mean, the poor thing was in a Dumpster that was in active use for hours. Anyway, stuff like that. But, Butch, it's so overwhelming. I mean, a case like this needs a team of people who've been working together for years on big cases."

"Yeah, it must be scary," said Karp. "A capital case."

"So I should ditch it."

"If that's what you think is best."

"You're being very judicious."

"It is my stock-in-trade."

"You still think I'm stupid to be even thinking about it, don't you."

There was a long pause, after which Karp said, judiciously, "Don't *involve* me in this, Marlene. This is your *baby,* yea or nay. I will support you whichever way you go."

"I don't know. My instinct is to look up this asshole state's attorney and break his legs, that's where I'm coming from nowadays. I'm not enough lawyer for this anymore."

"I don't know, Marlene. You have a law degree from Yale. And you have what it takes to be a good litigator."

"Really? And what might that be?"

"You're smart, honest, and aggressive. Most lawyers I know have two of those. There are plenty of smart, honest wimps. There are plenty of smart, aggressive crooks. There are even some honest, aggressive morons. But you need all three."

"I'm not that honest, as you well know."

"Well, yeah, you're an unindicted felon, but that doesn't bear on the present case. For the purposes the Goldfarbs want you for, you're honest. You won't screw them. You'll tell them the straight skinny. You won't compromise their best interests to make yourself look good. You'll stand up to intimidation. Given where the family is coming from right now, that's not chopped liver."

"I guess," said Marlene. "That's Shanahan's line and it's nice of you to say so, too. This is better than you yelling at me all the time about what I do. I could get used to it, and what then?"

"Heaven on earth. Divine accord."

"What, because I'm a *lawyer?*"

"No, because you're not slipping out of bed at three-thirty A.M. when you think I'm sleeping and putting on a black jumpsuit and a gun and going out to commit class-A violent felonies. Any jobs where you don't do that have my unconditional support."

A long pause followed here, after which Marlene asked, "Is it snowing there, yet?"

"She says, changing the subject. Yes, dear, a few flakes. The storm's coming up from where you are. I want to hear more about this case, though. What's been done so far?"

"Quite a bit actually. The PI is very good. Mike Brewster, a local guy, former FBI. He interviewed the people at the hospital where Sarah was taken, and at her dorm, and at the crime-scene motel. Some interesting variations from what the state claims the same people said to them, which is a good start, I think."

"Yeah, it is," Karp agreed. "But it doesn't give you a handle on your number one problem."

"The boyfriend, yes. I need to talk to Loreno at some point, try to get a feeling about what he's up to."

"Phil is layers and layers; keep your hand on your wallet and give him my best."

Another pause. She said, with mild surprise in her voice, "Gee, I guess I'm going to do this, if they want me. Holy shit."

"*Mazel tov*," said her husband. "So you'll stay over?"

"Yeah, my prospective hostess just came

out of her office and is making gestures indicating a desire to haul ass before we can't get out at all. Kiss the babies for me and I'll see you whenever."

"You're a little late," said Karp. It was nearly eight o'clock; the boys had long been stuffed with take-out pizza and prepped for bed, and for the last half hour Karp had been eyeing the telephone, suspended between waiting for a call and using the instrument to call every one of Lucy's friends.

"I know, I'm sorry," said Lucy as she took off her dripping parka. "I got hung up talking to Moussa, and then something went wrong with the train and we all had to bail out and wait for another one."

"You should have called."

"I did call. I left a message on Mom's service like I always do."

"Oops! My foul. I'm not used to this. Who's Moussa?"

"A guy from Mali. He's teaching me Bambara. He was working on an antique desk at the Maxwells. It cost two hundred and twenty-five thousand dollars."

"That must be quite a desk. Would you like me to get one for you?"

She laughed and began loading wrapped items out of the large shopping bag she had brought in. She stacked half a dozen loaves of Wonder bread on the kitchen counter.

"What's all that, Lucy?"

"Oh, it's for sandwiches. I'm making meat-loaf sandwiches for the homeless on Sunday. Where's Mom?"

"She's stuck down in Wilmington by the snow. But anyway we're all going to have to change our signals. She might not be around as much, one, and Posie being gone, two . . . we'll have to figure out some way of handling things."

"Why, is she going to defend that baby-killer, down there?"

Karp clenched his teeth and hissed. "Please! First of all, it's *alleged* baby-killer. If there's one thing you should have picked up from being in this family, it's that people aren't guilty just because the cops have arrested them and some grand jury has handed down an indictment. Second, it is very much in the interests of this family to give your mother total and unconditional support for whatever she does at this point in her life. She's trying to make a big transition here, in a good direction."

Lucy's eyes narrowed and her lips disappeared into a thin line. Her face looked unnaturally pale in the light from the open refrigerator. "Okay, great! What do you want me to do? Quit school? Stop going to the lab?"

"Don't be stupid, Lucy! I'm just asking for a little flexibility and support until we can get somebody to watch the twins after school. Meat loaf for the homeless is okay, but, like they say, charity begins at home. And it's a lot harder."

Karp disliked lecturing, but he thought this was a fairly gentle one, and so he was surprised and dismayed when his daughter slammed the refrigerator door, broke out in bitter sobs, and ran from the kitchen. Another door slammed in the distance. Karp sat in a chair and eyed the cooking wine by the range, becoming envious of those who could use the grape to alleviate the little agonies of life.

He heard the patter of slippered feet, and his son Giancarlo entered. "We want popcorn."

"Okay by me. You know where it is."

The boy dug out a bag, put it carefully in the microwave, and pressed the button. Popping commenced. "Is Lucy mad at us?"

"No, we just had a little spat, that's all. Don't worry about it."

"When is Mommy coming back?"

"I don't know, maybe a day or so."

"But Posie's *never* coming back, right?"

Karp reached out and swung the kid up on his lap. "Posie's getting married. She'll have her own family, just like we have our family.

Are you worried about it?"

"Yes. I like when everything is regular and nice, and people don't go away. Except if they die. The popcorn's done." Giancarlo slid off Karp's lap, scrambled onto the counter, and retrieved a mixing bowl. While Karp opened the dangerous steaming bag and poured the popcorn, Giancarlo asked, "Are we getting divorced?"

"Of course not. Where did you get that idea?"

"Walter Franklin in my class said, first the Mommy goes on a trip, then she gets a new house, then you have to go to her house. That's divorcing. I could ask Lucy if she wants popcorn."

"Good idea, kid."

"Why is she crying?"

"I don't know. Maybe she just needed to cry. Don't you ever cry for no reason?"

The boy thought about this for a moment and nodded. "Yes. Sometimes I think about sad things, like clouds or angels, or if you fell off your spaceship and fell down and down forever. Sometimes people cry when they're happy. Did you know that?"

"Actually, I did."

"Could I call Mommy, where she is?"

"Not now, GC, tomorrow. And she'll probably call anyway."

The boy scooted off, carrying his bowl delicately before him, like an offering. Karp heard him knock on Lucy's door and go in, and shortly he heard Zak go in, and then sounds of amused chatter. He sighed in relief, went into the bedroom, and spread files comfortably around the bed (an infamous act in Marlene's book, but one Karp had performed since law school) and worked moderately hard for an hour, when it was time to settle the boys into bed. He found Giancarlo curled up already, so he redraped the quilt, kissed the flawless brow, scooped up errant popcorns. Zak's bed was empty. Karp found the other twin in Marlene's office, with his big sister. They were both in sleeping costume, and Lucy was cleaning Marlene's pistol, Zak watching avidly. The room smelled sweetly of Hoppe's cleaner and 3-In-One oil. Karp was not charmed; this family scene was not among those in his dream book.

"Dad, Lucy's going to let me help," cried the boy.

"Do you have to do that now, Lucy?"

"What, cleaning it? Yeah, I said I would, but I forgot. I'm almost done."

He watched her long, white fingers pick up the slide, snap it into place. She worked the action once and handed the weapon butt-first to her brother. "Is it loaded?" she asked.

"No, we took out all the bullets."

"But . . . ?"

"But we have to *pretend* it's loaded all the time."

"Right, and . . . ?"

"Never point it at a living creature unless you want to shoot it," repeated Zak in a well-rehearsed singsong. He held the pistol in a two-handed grip, sighted carefully out the window, and squeezed. Click. Karp balanced his visceral dislike of the scene against the look of rapture on his son's face and made his own face benign. *My son the gun nut.*

The next morning, Caitlin Maxwell arrived, deposited by a Lincoln Town Car, and shortly thereafter came Mary Ma, on sturdy feet. Lucy switched into angelic mode and made a pancake breakfast for everyone. Karp was allowed to do nothing constructive and thought he could get used to being surrounded by attractive young ladies plying table dainties and amusing his children, himself occasionally making a light joke, drawing tinkling laughter. It also interested him to see his girl in the light of her friends: a different girl, more relaxed, more confident, a young woman among her peers. Well content, Karp sipped the excellent coffee and settled back to draw deep upon the forbidden hashish of patriarchy.

But a more abrasive sort had apparently obtained that morning at the Maxwells, as Caitlin told it. "Daddy went ballistic. Everything's upset in his study, right? So he was up reading this incredibly important paper, a prospectus or something he was supposed to give to this guy in Vail, and he left it facedown on the coffee table in the family room after he finished reading it last night, and Brian finds it and thinks it's scrap paper, because he's always leaving his own stupid papers around, and he draws on the blank sides of half the sheets, so of course Daddy has to call someone to run off another copy, and they miss their flight, and there's no first-class seats until tonight, which screws up some meeting he was going to have in Vail. Oh, wait, but the best part was *before* that, when Daddy starts yelling, and Brian figures he'll escape upstairs and hide where they piled all the furniture and stuff, on the fourth floor, and he runs through the dining room, full speed, and that black guy, from the decorator, has got this like flimsy table set up in front of the door, on sawhorses? He's heating this pot of glue, to fix the parquet with, and old Brian, of course, picks that minute to come crashing through. He knocks the table over, the glue, the burner, and everything, and the glue like *ignites,* all over the floor, black smoke is pouring

226

up, and the black guy —"

"Wait a second, Caitlin," said Lucy, "this is Moussa?"

"Yeah, I think that's his name. Anyway, he runs into the corner of the room for one of those furniture pads to put out the fire, and then my mother starts screaming and we all run into the dining room, and Daddy starts trying to stamp out the fire in his thousand-dollar custom-made boots, but the flaming glue is like sticking to the bottoms of the boots and pretty soon they're on fire, too, and he's like dancing around trying to make the flames go out. And the black guy throws the pad on the fire and stamps on it, and then he puts out Daddy. By this time Daddy is all red, like with *veins* bulging? And he starts screaming at the black guy, how stupid he was, et cetera, and how he's going to have him deported back to Africa and he's fired right now and all, and yelling at Mother about this is her fault, if she could only hire a competent decorator, and she's crying . . . it was unbelievable. You know, like it was horrible, but I was trying not to laugh, too. I just got my stuff and said, 'Bye, I'm going to Lucy's,' and booked out. I don't think they even knew I left. I forgot my dance bag, too."

Much amusement around the table, and although Lucy seemed downcast by what had happened to Moussa, Mary came back with a family horror story of her own involving a missing lobster, told in her dry style, which had them all coughing pancake flecks, and (in the case of the boys) making milk gush from nostrils.

After that, a harmonious weekend. Marlene called to say that she was totally snowed in, reassuring the boys that only drifts of Greenlandic scale kept her from their little bosoms, and informed Karp that if the Goldfarbs definitely wanted her and confirmed that, by God, she was going to go for it. Karp wanted the details, but the boys were clamoring so piteously to talk to her that he gave the instrument over.

Later, Caitlin offered the use of her limo for a tour around the shopping parts of town, which she did not have to offer twice. The day was bright and cold, for the great blizzard had turned inland at the Delaware Valley and only a few inches had fallen on the city. The limo dropped Karp, his boys, and their flying saucers off at Central Park, where they skidded down hills and ate *dreck* and had a glorious afternoon.

As for the girls, after some modest shopping, which consisted mainly of trying on ridiculously overpriced clothes and driving a number of tony salesclerks to distraction, they swung by the Maxwell town house to pick up the dance bag and found the place silent, then went to watch Caitlin rehearse at the ballet school. In the evening, Karp took the gang out to dinner at the Golden Pheasant on Pell, where Mary's parents worked, and they were, as usual, treated like royals, and later Lucy cooked five meat loaves and made the sandwiches, helped by her two pals (not that Caitlin was much help) with loud music and excessive giggling, and Sunday passed, amid the usual cartoons and piles of newspapers. Caitlin slept in; Lucy was up for eight-o'clock mass and then fed the starving multitudes, returning with her usual look of exhausted peacefulness. Late in the day, after a series of increasingly frantic phone calls, Karp hooked up with an organization called Nanny-on-Demand, who promised to look after the twins on Monday afternoon for an hourly rate only a little shy of what Patrick Ewing makes during a basketball game in Madison Square Garden. They played Scrabble, hilariously, for hours after that, Lucy demonstrating yet again her inability to spell, and Karp won, with very little cheating, and took to his lonely bed content.

8

Marlene awoke with a start from a familiar and awful dream, the one about the following man with no face, and Lucy hurt, and for one disorienting moment could not remember where she was. Bright sunlight was streaming into a small room painted eggshell blue, through sheer white curtains dancing slowly in the draft from a heating register. She was in a high bed under a merry patchwork quilt. The ceiling was close to her face and sloped at an alarming angle. Her soul reassembled itself then, and she recalled that she was in a dormer room in Maureen Shanahan's house, in Sherwood, Delaware. It was Saturday morning.

She threw off the quilt and groaned with an incipient hangover. She was wearing a flowered flannel nightgown that she could not recall donning, always a bad sign. Marlene descended from the bed, a shiplike thing in walnut from a former age, and got to her feet. An unfamiliar taste was in her mouth, unpleasant and cloying, like curdled molasses. With the taste came the memory. They had taken Maureen's car, an all-wheel-drive Subaru, and even so it was a horrible, slow, tricky ride south on 95 in the teeth of the blizzard, then off on unplowed suburban roads to her house, which had the shape of a Tudor mansion, but at about 1:3 scale, like an extremely ambitious doll's house: beam and stucco, leaded windows, slanted slate roof, ornate chimney pots — all wee. Inside, coziness with a vengeance: cluttered Victoriana, dark furniture, Eastern carpets, horse brasses, shadowy oil paintings with museum lights, a brick fireplace and a broad mantelpiece, upon which was a bronze clock draped with reclining nudes, telling the incorrect time. Marlene couldn't have lived in it a minute, but she could see that it suited her friend. The orphan had created a traditional ancestral manse.

Shanahan, she now recalled, had made a blaze in the fireplace, and both women had sat before it and gratefully soaked up the heat. They were alone in the house; the daughter, Shannon, was at a friend's, the son away at school. They were hungry but did not want to leave the fire.

"We could toast wienies and melted cheese and roast mickies and have sticky marshmallows for dessert," said Shanahan.

"What if our kids found out? We could be expelled from the Mom Association."

Shanahan replied that they would just have to take that chance, and she brought a tray full of the necessary items, hot dogs, rolls, potatoes, marshmallows, and the condiments, and they had a pig feast, cackling like madwomen about the stupidities of men, the insanity of child-rearing, the absurdities of sex, and similar subjects, and then Shanahan decided that nothing would do but that she prepare hot buttered rum in actual tankards, which she just happened to have on hand. After that it got blurry. Shanahan had a weepy, Marlene remembered that, about how much better Marlene's life was than hers, how the men she got to go out with were rats or married, and she got laid about twice a year and how unfair . . . Good God, Marlene thought, and groaned again, hot fucking buttered rum! A shower, now! She stripped off the nightie and grabbed a ratty chenille robe she found behind the door and went through it, tripping headlong over the dog.

Marlene climbed painfully to her feet cursing a blue streak. The dog looked at her unconcernedly and said (with its expressive eyes), As you very well know I am a mastiff and mastiffs have slept across the doorsills of their masters ever since there *were* mastiffs, so as to defend them with their *lives* if need be, and if you get drunk and *forget* about me, well

. . . and licked its balls.

Sometime later, clean of body, but dressed in yesterday's clothes and still foul of mind, Marlene, preceded by her dog, descended the stairs and came into the kitchen, following the scent of coffee and toast. Two teenaged girls were there, both of whom yelped when Sweety padded in and sniffed them to determine whether they were a danger to his mistress.

"He's perfectly harmless, unless you mean evil," said Marlene, and added, to the girl who looked very like her mother had looked at that age, "You must be Shannon Moody. I'm Marlene Ciampi, one of your mother's disreputable friends."

The girl took her hand and introduced her friend, a short, plump, dark girl with braces on her teeth — Denise — and asked, "Is that the same as Champ?"

"You got it."

Shannon blushed and looked away. Marlene could imagine the stories her mother had told. Shannon whispered to her friend and then asked, "Did you really work for *Madonna?*"

"Briefly. Look, is there some coffee?"

Shannon scurried, and shortly Marlene was furnished with a steaming mug and a plate of sticky Pop-Tarts. She consumed both gratefully and retailed a few stories — suitably cleaned up and legalized — about her contacts with the famous and got any number of wows. After that the two girls left to go cross-country skiing along the various trails provided by the village of Sherwood. Marlene drank another cup and went out to the Subaru and got a ten-pound bag of Purina chow she had bought the previous evening and fed the monster.

She settled down to read the Wilmington paper. There was nothing in it about the Goldfarb case except a pair of letters to the editor, in response to a previous editorial about the gag order. One writer thought it was disgusting that the media profited by hideous crimes and that the judge should have put the reporters in jail, too. The other writer similarly deplored media circuses but held that they arose from the same decay of morality that fostered abortion clinics and babies in Dumpsters. Not good, if these were representative of the potential jury pool. Marlene also recalled, painfully, her own daughter's conflation of infanticide and abortion and wondered how prevalent this notion was. She looked around for something to write on, found a shopping-list pad and a pen magnetized to the fridge, and started to make notes. She would need press clippings from the time the original story broke, local news and national commentary. And she would need focus groups, representative of prospective jurors, both in New Castle County, where the trial was scheduled to take place, and in distant areas, in case she wanted to move for a change of venue. She made some more notes on the small pad, labeled the sheet "trial prep," and started another, marked "motions." First, a continuance, because the trial was scheduled to begin three weeks from Monday, which was far too short a time for her to get up to speed, and next . . .

She stopped suddenly and put down the pen. I must be crazy, she thought. I haven't even been retained yet. She assembled the sheets she had used into a neat stack and was about to tear them across, but folded them instead and shoved the wad into her pocket. She paged listlessly through the rest of the paper, the usual dull mix of local events and scandal mixed with wire-service versions of national stories. Marlene was not a news junkie, but she liked a real paper every morning, meaning the *New York Times.*

Maureen Shanahan walked into the kitchen. Marlene continued to read the paper behind whose shield she heard Shanahan pour herself a cup of coffee and work the toaster and the refrigerator door. When she thought her friend was sufficiently fed and medicated, she lowered the paper and looked her over.

"You look like you feel like I did," she said, smiling.

"You're not going to be cheerful, are you? The best thing about the Odious Ron was he hid behind the paper every morning. Did you see my kid?"

"I did, and her friend. I regaled them with lies and sent them off on skis."

Shanahan sipped coffee and groaned. "Hot buttered rum! Whatever possessed me? I had a fifth of Myers's with only a fruitcake's worth of rum missing from it and now it's empty. You're a bad influence, Ciampi."

"Yes, and as I recall at school, you were always thinking up outrages you were too chicken to pull off yourself and getting me to launch them and then blaming me when we got nailed."

"Oh, shut up, Champ!" Shanahan snarled without much heat, as this was perfectly true. She flicked a finger at the newspaper. "Anything in there about our case?"

"Just a couple of letters. Speaking of which, I came down here bubbling with things-to-do thoughts about it and realized that I'm not exactly on the case yet. And I either want to get started instantly or forget it forever. So why don't you call the Goldfarbs and see if they've come to a decision, and if not, you'll drive me back into Wilmington and I'll head back to the city."

"Can it wait until I stop being nauseous?"

"No, call them now!"

Karp spent Monday morning in a series of meetings that had nothing to do with the law, or interesting moral or political issues or current cases, but only with insuring that in the coming year the office of the district attorney would have a roof over its head and walls that were painted, and furniture and office equipment, and that its minions would be paid with checks that did not bounce. Karp's function at meetings of this kind was to act as referee among the operating bureau and division chiefs and the chiefs of the administrative services — budget, personnel, information, and so on. It amazed him that grown men and women could get excited about paint and desks and how many people would work for them rather than another, but it was so. Remarkably, he was good at this refereeing since everyone knew he didn't care and never played favorites. (Karp felt in his heart that it would be good for everyone if they all had to work out of skin tents and be paid in fish.) His reward for this was to be kept on as indispensable chief assistant and never to get to do anything he really liked.

After the last of these dull groups had trickled from his office, he told Flynn that he was going to disappear for a few minutes, and did so, in the direction of the homicide bureau. There he found Mimi Vasquez, in her cube, buried in work.

"Vasquez, let's get a coffee."

This was not a negotiable invitation. Vasquez smiled nicely and threw a lined raincoat over her shoulders and they went out the Leonard Street entrance, through the park, and into Arrow Donut on Mulberry. The virtue of Arrow Donut was the unlikelihood of anyone of note entering it and looking around the corner of the bright L-shaped room and spotting them. Arrow sold a lot of doughnuts to the courthouse, but in bags; it was not a rendezvous. Karp, of course, had every right to speak to any one of the 457 lawyers who worked for the DA, but he did not, if he could help it, want Roland to know that he was talking to this one. Roland would get on Vasquez's case, perhaps even delivering his famous lecture/threat on loyalty as a two-way street. Karp wished to spare Vasquez that if he could. Vasquez understood all this and was grateful. Nor was she loath to spend time in Karp's company. She liked Karp; no, somewhat more than liked, but it was hopeless, and she at bottom was a good girl. Karp had at last grasped this after perhaps two years of its being made clear to everyone in the office down to the janitors, and after it occurred to him, he treated her with a certain jocular gallantry.

"So, what's this about?" she asked after they were settled with coffee — and in the rearmost booth. "You drag me away from my vital work to this intimate cabaret, ply me with a coconut glazed —"

"I'm pregnant," said Karp, straight-faced.

After they cleaned off the spit-up coffee, Karp said, "How's Bustamente?"

"She made bail. We asked for the moon because the top count was murder two, you know, we usually ask for a mil on that, but the judge looked at me like I was crazy. The defense suggested fifty K and we went with a hundred. Tell you the truth, I felt a little crazy myself."

"What's on offer?"

"Still man one, like before."

"Any nibbles from Ms. Siegel?"

"Not a one. Ms. Siegel strikes me as excessively cool in the present circumstances, because I can't see anything much standing between her client and twenty-five to life. She hasn't filed a motion or asked for a continuance, like they almost always do; she seems to be anxious to go to trial. She hasn't given psych notification, either."

"What?" exclaimed Karp. "Now, that's a surprise. What else does she have to go on except extreme emotional disturbance as a . . ." He stopped and frowned. "Wait a second, that doesn't make any sense. She can't be going only for mitigation."

"No, that's what's confusing me, too. Even if the judge charges and the jury finds extreme emotional disturbance, the best she can do is a verdict of guilty on first-degree manslaughter, which we're already willing to offer her. I can't figure it."

Karp thought about that for a while. "Neither can I. That brings me to the other thing I wanted to talk to you about. What's happening with Emilio Perez?"

Vasquez cocked her head and showed a confused look. "Excuse me?"

"Emilio Perez, the brother-in-law, the alleged rapist. What's his status?"

"Jesus, Butch, I have no idea."

"Well, you should. Find out, and if he's not being aggressively prosecuted, make sure that he is. See me if you need any fires lit."

"I'm sorry, am I missing something? What does the rape prosecution have to do with the Bustamente case? I mean, you think she'll try to present the legal status of the alleged rapist as . . . what? Some kind of weird mitigation?

In the first place, I'd never allow it, and . . ."

Karp was shaking his head. "No, no, you don't get it. Look, we agree that Siegel has no case except insanity, and there's no insanity present of any generally recognized form. Nor has she in fact notified that that's what she's going to do. No case, but she wants a trial, and she thinks she can get an actual acquittal or at least make a showing strong enough so that we give her client a better deal than we're offering now. So what does that tell you?"

"It tells me that either she's nuts —"

"Believe me, she's not nuts."

"Or she's going to turn it into a circus, play the emotional card, play the race card." Vasquez was biting her lip, playing with a paper napkin, her brow furrowed.

"And the feminist card, don't forget that," said Karp. "She's going to have Lola up there in a white confirmation dress and patent leather Mary Janes, looking about eleven years old, and she's going to tell the jury that this innocent child was brutally raped, and made pregnant, and here's the state persecuting this child while the man who caused it all is walking around free. Oh, it'll be rare."

"This is why you want us to come down hard on what's-his-face — Emilio?"

"No-o," said Karp patiently, "it's because if the guy raped a kid, he should get his lumps, and he should get them from you. It'll put hair on your chest when Siegel starts implying you're a moral imbecile."

Vasquez nodded impatiently, irritated at herself, and starting to become a little annoyed at Karp. "All right, all right, I get the point. But none of that takes away from the fact that she did the crime. And the insanity plea is nonsense. What did she think she was throwing out the window, a Frisbee?"

"That won't matter. You're not going to have an all-male jury. You're going to have five or six women on there, and they're all going to be thinking, That could be me or my daughter or sister. And I'll tell you something else: somehow or other our Ms. Siegel is going to bring into evidence the law regarding neonaticide as it stands in other countries —"

"No way! That's completely irrelevant."

"Doesn't matter. You know very well that there are ways for the defense to insert just about anything they want, in the form of questions, for example. So you object, so the judge tells the jury to disregard — big deal. Minds are not cassette decks, you don't just push a button and erase the tape. And it won't matter what the judge says in instruction, he can go on for an hour about how the state statute reads and why what they do in the UK is not germane."

Vasquez thought and shredded her napkin and Karp watched with satisfaction as the light dawned on her smooth brown face.

"Wait, you think she's going for a nullifying jury?"

"I do. And you know what? At some level, I agree with her. There *is* a moral distinction between what Bustamente did and a mutt gunning down a clerk and making a widow and a couple of orphans out of his family, or a scumbag getting loaded on a Saturday night and shooting his wife during an argument, and the law does *not* make that moral distinction. It's all murder, one flavor. And you feel it, too, Vasquez. Don't you?"

He stared at her, and she said in a didactic tone, "Well, it doesn't matter what I think, or feel, we're supposed to represent the People and enforce the laws as written." But he kept staring at her, and after a long minute she dropped her eyes and said almost inaudibly, "Oh, yeah, fuck it, yes!" and then, louder, "All right? It sucks. You think I don't see *me* when I look at Lourdes Bustamente? Want to hear *another* sad story? I'm fourteen, I'm down in the laundry room of my building doing the wash, and some sick fuck comes in and grabs me around the neck and starts yanking my pants down. I had a cup of Clorox all poured out, so I tossed it over my shoulder into his face, and I got away. A minute earlier or later I wouldn't have had the bleach handy and I would've got raped. I could've got pregnant. Would I have ended up like this kid? I like to think not, but I don't know. For damn sure I would have been different. Anyway, there but for the grace . . ." She stopped and he could see her jaw stiffening, as anger congealed. She gave him a fierce look. "So what was this, the opposite of a pep talk? I wasn't depressed enough?"

"No, it was only a matter of time before you figured all this out for yourself. Look, you bring passion to your work. That's why you're good at it. You see a mutt like Purcell and you don't have any liberal guilt about him; he did bad, he chose to do bad, and you put him away, because if you don't, among other things, it dishonors all the vast majority of kids who look just like him, or like you for that matter, and come from the same shitty neighborhoods who *didn't* become mutts. But this one, as we see, is different. Here there's no passion. Here you're a pure functionary of the state, doing something that, any way you cut it, is inhuman. And I wanted you to know that I understood that, what you might be going through."

Looking stunned, Vasquez said, "You say that but you're still going to let it go ahead?"

244

"I've told both Roland and Mr. Keegan that I think it's the wrong thing to do. Beyond that I can't go. I'm a functionary of the state, too. Still a little human though, down in the corners." He smiled.

She did not. "And what about the DA and Roland, what are they? Martians?"

"Well, human according to their lights. The Jesuits got hold of Mr. Keegan at an early age, and he's skilled at figuring out how he can be on the side of the angels and one up politically at the same time. He doesn't shout out orders, but everyone knows what he wants. It's one of his great talents, not shouting and getting what he wants. Roland . . . ? Roland has many admirable characteristics, but sensitive humanity is unfortunately not one of them. When Roland was a little boy, the Hungarian revolt broke out, and he was running down a street with his mom and dad when a Russian tank's machine gun opened fire on them. His mother was blown into rags, blown all over him as a matter of fact. He and his father sneaked across the border that night with his mother's blood and brains soaked into his clothes and hair."

"Jesus!"

"Yes. Roland hates murder, and he hates murderers. None of us are particularly fond of it, but Roland is in a class by himself. I mean I

245

was a good homicide chief, but I had doubts sometimes, moral doubts. I had to work on them, so I could function. I was a really good swimmer, you could say, but Roland is a fish. He never has to come up for air, so to speak. No doubts; you kill on his watch, you get the full treatment, which is one reason why we're all trying to hang Lola. By the way, practically no one but me knows what I just told you about Roland, and I will be extremely upset with you if I hear anyone else telling this story or if it gets back to Roland that I told you. I only mention it by way of explanation as to why Roland gets cranky sometimes, and why I cut him a lot of slack in the milk-of-human-kindness department, and also so that you won't start looking for someone to blame when you start feeling like shit because of what you're doing to Lourdes Bustamente. There's no one to blame. The main thing is for you to come through this more or less intact as a person."

Now she smiled. "So you don't want me to throw the case."

"No, of course not!" said Karp with more volume than he had intended. "I expect you to represent the People vigorously and to the best of your very considerable abilities. Let the judge and jury carry some of the shit. That's what they're for." He looked at his watch, finished his cooling coffee. "I have a meeting."

Vasquez seemed to shudder. "Gosh. I'm jelly. Should I say thanks? Or what?"

"Just don't get rotten on me." Karp squeezed her arm and felt undesired electricity shoot up his hand. "You know? Stay human as long as you can." He turned to go.

They left the booth and the shop. On the sidewalk, she looked up at him and asked, "So why aren't you like Roland? What's the secret? Or is it just he couldn't deal with the thing about his mother?"

Karp was becoming uncomfortable with this. He didn't mind being a mentor on occasion, but from the way Vasquez had started to look at him, they were now moving in on the guru zone, where he did not wish to tread. And there was that little physical shock, too, when he touched her. He started to walk back to the office swiftly, requiring that the young woman almost trot to keep up with him. He said, "You know, I've thought about that a lot, and I have to say it might just be fate after all. I lost my mom myself at an early age, too, which I guess is another reason I cut Roland a lot of slack, so maybe it's just the difference between a machine gun and a cancer ward. Fate. God. Like your cup of bleach. I take no credit whatsoever."

★ ★ ★

Caitlin had a cell phone, a sea-green Nokia, and Lucy was with her near the lockers at Sacred Heart while she used it to call home. For the fourth time, nothing.

"Damn it, they're still not there!"

"Maybe they stayed longer in Vail," said Lucy.

"They would have called me at your house. You know my mom, she's a nut for communication. I'm going to call my dad at his office." She did so and spoke with someone for a time, and when she disconnected, her face was grave and pale.

"Now I'm really worried. Even they don't know where he is, and they called the condo in Vail and there's no answer there, either."

"Maybe they went to look at schools for your brother."

"Yeah, but they should have called. Jesus, my dad's never out of contact with his office. The world would come to an end." She stared at the cell phone like a pagan at a fetish that had failed to produce good fortune and said forlornly, "I don't know what to do."

"You don't have to do anything. Go to ballet and then go home. Vida will be there to make you dinner and they'll probably call later. It'll be something like being stuck by a road accident and the phone breaking down."

Caitlin threw the phone angrily into her bag. "I can't stand this! Will you come with me to ballet? I don't want to be by myself."

Lucy felt a brief surge of resentment. She did not say that Caitlin would by no means be "by herself" at ballet, but instead at the center of a crowd of gorgeous young people and the object of every gaze, *as usual,* or that Lucy herself had an appointment to sit in a grubby cubicle and learn words from a card while scientists recorded her brain waves, or whatever it was that they did. Instead, she agreed, and even smiled, because she rather liked that whenever something even faintly frightening arose in the lives of her friends, they turned to her, Lucy, who might not be all that decorative or at the head of the class, but was definitely the one to go to when things started to come unglued.

Besides, Lucy rather enjoyed going to practice with Caitlin. Being odd man out — the only turkey in a flock of swans — was no great burden to her, and she enjoyed playing the moon to Caitlin's sun, less bright, but far more mysterious. There was always a Russian or two to converse with, and astound, and there was, of course, the dancing.

Today, Caitlin was nervous and whiny with it, snappish with the other dancers, and she appeared stiff during the school's ferocious warm-up exercises. Madame had to speak to her, which was highly unusual. In exercise, at least, Caitlin was always perfect. When they took their places for the prologue to *Sleeping Beauty* (Caitlin with a lavender ribbon around her waist and the other principals similarly decorated to indicate their roles) and the music started, the magic kicked in; or, as Lucy preferred to think of it, the finger of God reached down and transformed her friend, an ordinary, slightly stuck-up, wealthy Manhattan teenager, through some suspension of the law of gravity and a thickening of the air, into a creature of consummate grace and beauty.

Madame, however, was not satisfied with mere grace and beauty. Madame had been a famous prima at the Kirov back in the sixties. She had a hawk face that was going leathery and immense black eyes, and her bun was graying, but there was an emotional current around her when she demonstrated movements, a current that even Lucy could see was not matched by the American children. Now Madame clapped her hands sharply twice, the music stopped, and she walked forward and went through the series of moves that Caitlin had just accomplished. The Lilac Fairy is the symbol of goodness and generosity; as Madame danced, goodness and generosity poured off her like heat shimmers off a highway. But when Caitlin danced, though she floated like a bubble, like a bubble she was iridescent, perfect, and empty. Lucy was surprised that she could see this and that her friend clearly could not. After three tries, all more or less the same, Madame waved her hands and let the rehearsal continue.

Afterward, they hurried back to the Maxwell house in a cab, Caitlin with her street clothes pulled on over her sweaty leotards, anxious and tight-faced, punching obsessively at her cell phone, getting nothing. At the Maxwells, they found that the chaos Caitlin had left on Friday, and which they had seen briefly during their visit over the weekend, had been repaired. The floors shone, the paintwork had been renewed, cleansed of smoke and smudges. They went into the kitchen, where they found Vida at work, sautéing something. She did not know where the Maxwells were, had received no communication from them, was planning on dinner for four, as usual, but if Lucy would be staying, it was no trouble.

The presence of Vida and the homely smells arising from her kitchen seemed to calm Caitlin down somewhat. She changed her clothes and took a shower. Lucy wanted to go home, but felt committed to stay with her friend until the Maxwells returned. The girls obtained diet Cokes, drifted into the family room, switched on the TV, and watched cable for a while. Caitlin kept flipping back to CNN to see if some newsworthy disaster might be implicated in the absence of her family.

"Caitlin," said Lucy, "do you think it's possible that you just forgot that they were going to be gone longer?"

"No, but even if I did, Dad's office would know where he is. I mean, he calls them when he's going to be in the bathroom. He's on the phone when he's standing on a movie line."

"Maybe they called and left a message on the answering machine."

Caitlin's face brightened. "Yes! You're brilliant. I'll go check." She dashed off and returned a few minutes later, dejected.

"Nothing, just some stuff from the decorator saying he did the work and apologizing for what happened."

"You just have the one machine?"

"No, my mom has a set in the bedroom, on her private line, and I have one, too, but why would they call those? They'd use the house phone if they wanted to leave me a message."

"Maybe they got confused. Maybe they were at a wild society party with drugs and they wanted to stay for days, debauching

252

themselves with vile practices, and they called the wrong number."

Caitlin giggled and rolled her eyes. "Yeah, right. Okay, I'll check both the upstairs machines, just to make sure."

Lucy twiddled the remote and settled on a rock video. She didn't particularly like Pearl Jam, but sometimes she liked to watch the pretty pictures and allow waves of barely meaningful sound to wash over her. She punched the volume up a couple of notches and was just getting into it when she realized that some of the sounds weren't coming from the speakers. Screaming sounds.

And footsteps. Vida in the doorway, her face fearful, her hands knotted around a towel. Lucy hit the mute. Long, powerful screams, punctuated by sobbing breaths. Lucy was off up the stairs at a run.

She skidded to a stop at the door to the Maxwells' bedroom. Caitlin was just inside the door, with her hands clutching her face in the classic pose of horror. Lucy grabbed her around the shoulders and shouted at her, "Caitlin, Caitlin! Stop it! What's wrong?"

Caitlin's face had turned the blue-white of skimmed milk, her lips were darker blue, her eyes blank. She took a long, deep shuddering breath, as if she was preparing another scream, but no scream emerged. Instead, her eyes rolled up in their sockets and she went limp. Lucy caught her and lowered her to the ground.

Then Lucy became aware of the smell. She stood up and went farther into the room. Both Maxwells were lying in bed, Mrs. Maxwell on her side, Mr. Maxwell on his back. She walked closer to the head of the bed. The smell was awful: butcher shops and backed-up toilets.

Lucy was surprised at how calm and unafraid she felt, as if someone else were in control of her body. When she was close enough, she could see that blood had soaked the sheets around both the Maxwells' heads, like a dark halo. There was not a lot of blood. Lucy had once watched her mother shoot a man through the head with a nine-millimeter round, and that had splashed a gout of red ten feet down the pavement. This was not like that. Mrs. Maxwell's blond hair was slightly matted with a brown crust at the temple, and there were two small bruised holes, smaller than a pencil's thickness, in Mr. Maxwell's forehead. The cool part of her mind registered this fact: both shot with a small-caliber weapon. Lucy went to the bedside phone, dialed 911, and when the operator answered, she pitched her voice low and reported the crime. Then she called her father, telling the secretary that it was an emergency; the secretary told her to hang on, he was in a meeting.

She waited two minutes, struggling to stay in the cool place, breathing shallowly against the nausea.

"Lucy? What's wrong?"

"Dad, I'm at Caitlin's house. Dad, Mr. and Mrs. Maxwell have been murdered."

A brief pause. "You're sure?"

"Yes. It looks like they've been shot in the head. They're in bed."

"Okay, you called 911 already?"

"Yeah, but Caitlin's fainted, and I'm not feeling too good myself."

"Is there an adult in the house?"

"Yeah, Vida the cook, but she barely speaks English."

"All right, Lucy, I'm leaving right now. Get Vida to help you with Caitlin. Wait for the cops." He paused. "Lucy? Is the boy dead, too?"

"Oh, God! I don't know. He's not here. Should I look for him?"

"No. Just take care of Caitlin and wait for the police. I'll be there as soon as I can."

This was, in fact, very soon indeed, since Karp had a driver on call and an unmarked police car with flashing light and siren, and the services of a radio patrol car from the Seventh Precinct to run interference for them up

Madison Avenue to 76th Street. Two RMPs were there already, and an ambulance from Bellevue, and several other dark, double-parked Plymouths that meant detectives and bosses from the Nineteenth Precinct. The Nineteenth Precinct has the lowest violent crime rate and the highest concentration of rich and important people in Manhattan, and its leaders get extremely upset when anything raises the former by eliminating the latter. Yellow crime-scene tape already festooned the decorative ironwork that bordered the front entrance to the Maxwell residence. Karp approached it and nodded to the patrolman on guard outside the door, who eyed the gold shield pinned to Karp's topcoat and lifted the tape.

Inside, Karp looked around for someone he knew. At one time, Karp would have known a majority of the detectives likely to show up at a homicide in Manhattan, but the years had promoted most of them to desk jobs, while others had retired, and Karp rarely hit the streets himself anymore. He spotted two cops talking in low voices in the corner of what must have been the living room. It was empty now of any furnishings save a substantial four-legged object draped in padded cloths. A sandy-haired, tired-looking fellow in a tweed topcoat sporting a gold lieutenant's shield looked up as Karp approached, checked out his ID, and introduced himself as Larry Bell, the shift lieutenant at the Nineteenth. The other man was the detective second grade who had caught the case, a short, bright-looking man with a brush mustache, Frank Soldi. Karp didn't know either of them, but Bell knew who Karp was and was surprised. When important people got killed, the police called the homicide bureau of the DA, which would send a junior member, assigned by rotation, down to cast an eye, show the flag, and make certain that the police could never be blamed for screwing up the legal aspects of the investigation.

"I called it in to your office, but I was looking for the guy on the chart, not you. This is going to be a big one."

"No, Lieutenant, I'm not here officially. I'm looking for my daughter. She should be around here someplace."

Bell stared at Karp for a moment, his cop's eyes picking up the family resemblance. "That's your kid? The one called in the incident?"

"That's her."

"She's in the kitchen," said Soldi. "Hell of a thing, two kids walking in on that."

"Yeah, it's not something you expect either, this neighborhood," said Karp. "Are you finished with my girl?"

"Oh, yeah," said Soldi. "She couldn't tell us much, but the daughter, the friend, is completely out of it. Curled up in a ball. By the way, that's some cool kid you got there, man. How old is she, seventeen, eighteen?"

"Sixteen," said Karp. "Where's the kitchen?"

He found Lucy sitting on a stool, watching a couple of crime-scene techs bagging the contents of the garbage pail.

He hugged and kissed her. "Are you okay?" he asked.

"I'm fine. They won't let me see Caitlin."

"No, apparently she's still in shock. They'll probably take her to the hospital. Did they find the brother?"

"I don't know. I told the cops he was supposed to be here and I haven't heard anything since. Could you find out?"

"I'd like to get you home."

"Please, Dad!"

"Okay, wait here a second."

Karp went back out and found Soldi and asked him.

"Yeah, he was in the back of a big closet in his room," said the detective. "A mess. He'd been there since Friday night, looks like, pulled a bunch of toys and clothes and stuff down on him, pissed and crapped all over himself. He didn't make much sense, but I think he might've seen the perp, maybe even

258

saw the crime. There's your guy."

Karp turned and saw Pincus coming in, coat flapping, red from the cold and looking flustered. Karp grabbed the young man's arm and led him to a quiet corner.

"Pincus, listen up. This is a big one, first of all, major heat, the DA will be personally interested in it, and so will I, because my daughter is a friend of the family and was one of the people who found the bodies. Therefore, after you make your report to Roland, you will come and see me privately and tell me everything the cops found out, and I mean everything, not just what they think they can get by with telling you. I want you to bird-dog this case from now until I tell you to stop. Is that clear?"

"Absolutely. And . . . I mean, you mean it'll be my case up through trial?" Pincus's eyes were bright. This was a step up from scumbag-on-scumbag.

Karp gave him a glare. "That's up to the bureau chief, but you do a good job for me and I can almost guarantee you at least second seat when we pick up whoever did this."

There was a rattling noise and they stepped out of the way of a pair of gurneys pushed by paramedics in white pants and reefer jackets, one holding the still form of Caitlin Maxwell, and the other that of her brother. The brother

stank, and Karp wrinkled his nose involun-
tarily as the boy went by.

He went back to the kitchen then and got
Lucy and took her to the unmarked car, and
they drove home. Lucy sat silently, pale, erect
and stiff in the seat. Karp watched her and
waited. She began to come apart at around
34th Street, just silent tears at first, but by the
time they crossed 14th, she was in his arms,
shaking and wailing like a baby. Her mother's
daughter, he thought as he rocked her and
stroked her head.

9

Lucy was shivering when Karp got her back to Crosby Street, aguey, teeth-chatteringly, and from some interior chill, for the loft was toasty warm. He made her get out of her clothes and into a hot shower, and then dismissed Ms. Schoensky, the Nanny-on-Demand, an ordinary-looking young woman recently arrived from middle Europe, a knitter and a wearer of colorful, hairy sweaters. She did not look like a vicious sadist, but Karp knew that looks were deceiving, and both boys assured him that they had been whipped, starved, cursed, and made to eat disgusting substances. Giancarlo threatened suicide if Ms. Schoensky returned; Zak threatened murder and spelled out, with some care, how he intended to perform the act. Twenty years experience in worming the truth out of felons stood Karp in good stead now. The bottom line was that she had served them the wrong kind of cheese, which they had refused to eat, as a result of which they had been denied *Mighty Morphin Power Rangers* on TV. Karp ordered a pizza, with extra of a correct cheese, and laid down the law in re Nanny-on-Demand. Lucy did not emerge for pizza; when Karp peeked in, he saw a still lump under her Italian-flag quilt. He called Marlene in Wilmington, but the girl who answered the phone said she was out.

Some hours later, the twins tucked away, Karp was watching the Knicks lose to the Bulls in Chicago when Lucy came into the living room and sat down on the couch. She was wearing a white quilted bathrobe decorated with pink flowers, smelled of herbal shampoo, and looked twelve. They watched the game in companionable silence for a quarter or so.

During a break, she asked, "Is he really the best basketball player in history?"

"As Larry Bird says, he's in the top two," Karp responded. "But I don't know much about this kind of basketball. I see walking, I see fouling that never gets called. I see guys getting millions of bucks who can't shoot a foul consistently, who don't ever move if they haven't got the ball. It's a different game. Maybe it's faster and more exciting; they all say that. Are you going to go out for it this year? You said you might."

"I don't think so."

"Why not? I've seen you at the Y. You got

262

the hands, you got the height, you have some moves . . ."

"I don't think I'm competitive enough."

Karp hooted. "Oh, really? How can you not be competitive? God, look at me and your mom! If you're not competitive, Gregor Mendel was blowing smoke."

"No, I'm serious. I like to play, and I'm good, but I don't have that killer edge that makes you work and work at it. Like you. Like him." She pointed to the screen where Jordan was flying through the air. "Okay, he has tremendous talent, but *that* also comes from thousands of hours of training and practice. Like Caitlin. Since I met Caitlin, I understand all that a lot more. I could never work like that in a million years. And besides, even if I wanted to, I can't spare the time. There's the lab, and school. I'm not doing too well, if you want to know the truth. I'm bombing chemistry, and the only reason I'm barely passing math is that Mary practically carries me on her back." Lucy sighed and looked so woebegone that he reached out and drew her into the hollow of his arm.

"I'm a one-trick pony, I guess," said Lucy.

"Even if true, it's a hell of a trick, that one trick."

"Yes. Sometimes I feel like I'm one of those little boys riding on an elephant, like I'm supposed to be in control, but if the elephant really wants to go somewhere, there's nothing I can do to stop it. Like there's practically no me left, just some *thing* I didn't ask for inside me that wants to eat up every language anyone ever spoke, *thousands* of them, and for what? I pray about it all the time. I have to believe God has some purpose, making me this way, and He'll let me know what it is at the right time."

Karp did not respond to this last. He had never quite become used to his daughter's piety, and like many modern people he was vaguely embarrassed by it, as the Victorians used to be by public mention of sex.

After a moment, she said, as if reading his thoughts, "But once you start thinking about God's purposes — I don't mean *you,* because you don't believe in God — but if you do, you have to think about bad things happening to good people, evil and stuff, like what happened to the Maxwells, or women killing innocent babies. If God is really good, how does He let things like that happen?"

Karp waited. He *really* wanted to know the answer to that one. "Yes?"

She pivoted around so she could look at him. Her eyes shone like new pennies in the flickering TV light. "Well, the short answer is that God made the world to include pain and suffering, and not in some other way. Why did He? We don't know. He started with one that didn't have any pain and suffering and that didn't work out. We don't really even know why there's a creation at all. I mean, if God is perfect, why does he need creation and us? Mary Ma says that one of the big unanswered questions in physics is why is there something rather than nothing? Scientists baffled, like they say in the headlines. To be totally honest, I don't think about it much, although if you say you're religious, that's the first thing people hit you with: If God is so good, what about earthquakes and cancer?"

"What do you say?"

"Oh, I usually just shrug and quote Thomas Aquinas, that God in the act of creation limited His power so that He could act only within the nature of things, and then they say, Why didn't He fix the nature of things so there'd be no suffering, and I say, Well, He made heaven, where there's no suffering, and became Jesus to lead us there forever, which is a pretty good deal when you think of it, and besides, He didn't just stand off and play with us like toys, He suffered, too, which counts for something. That usually shuts them down, and then I smile in a beatific fashion." She demonstrated this.

Karp laughed and asked, "So have you

made any converts?"

Rolled eyes. "Oh, please, Dad! The Church doesn't want instant converts anymore. In fact, it's real hard to get in nowadays if you aren't born Catholic. Anyway, it's pretty easy to talk about that stuff in the abstract. It's different when you're suffering pain yourself, or when someone you care about is. Comforting is the hardest thing to do, especially if the person doesn't believe. Like Caitlin. All of a sudden, her parents are gone, and in a horrible way. It doesn't make sense. What am I going to say?" She mimicked briefly the oleaginous voice of the false comforter: "Oh, it was in God's plan, my child, but that plan is far beyond our imagination or knowledge."

"Well, what would you want said, if it happened to you?" Karp asked.

"Oh, I'm different. I have all this support. I have faith, I'm in a community of believers, I have all kinds of rituals and practices that would make something like that bearable. My gosh, I've spent three-quarters of my life waiting for a phone call that my mother's been shot dead, or charged with murder, and it almost drove me bananas, and it would have, if I hadn't had the faith. I mean, death is not the same thing, if you do."

"You think that contributed to you choosing to be religious? What your mother did?"

266

She looked at him oddly, as if he had said something in one of the increasingly fewer languages she did not understand. "Choosing . . . ? Oh, you think I sort of thought about it and decided to stay religious, like choosing a college. No, it's not like that. It's a *gift*, what we call a grace. It's real. Like this." She rapped sharply on the coffee table with her knuckles. "Or like seeing or hearing. It's just there, inside of me. It's not like I read the stories in the Bible and said, 'Hey, makes sense, I think I'll be religious.' It *doesn't* make sense; in fact, it's wacky."

"I'll buy that," said Karp lightly, but she nodded, her face serious.

"I know. It used to make me sad, too. But now I figure, everyone finds their own way to God. Even Mom."

"She always says she's a good Catholic mother."

"I know, in that slightly sarcastic tone. I think she was just waiting for me to lose my faith the way she did. It's funny, because you know, she had it for real, back then."

"What happened, do you think?"

"Oh, you know Mom. She likes getting away with stuff. It was one of the bad things about the old Church, too, I mean before Vatican Two. As long as you punched the clock, did the rituals, kicked in the cash, they didn't bother much with the spirit. Mom must've said eight million Acts of Contrition and not one of them sincere, and besides . . ." Lucy stopped, snorted a laugh, and rolled her eyes. "Oh, see, you got me started on Mom's imperfections. Anything to distract me from mine. It's my secret vice."

The phone rang. Karp said, "Speak of the devil."

"Is that her?"

"I'll bet it is." He went to the phone in the kitchen.

"Let me talk to her after you," she called.

When Karp picked up, Marlene said, "I just got in and Shannon gave me your message. What happened?"

Karp told her.

"Oh, Jesus, those poor kids! How's Lucy taking it?"

"Very well, I think, after a little breakdown at the start. We've just been having a discussion of good and evil and the benefits of faith. That's a pretty deep kid we got here."

"That must be *your* genes. I'm as shallow as a gutter puddle."

"In Carlsbad Caverns. What are your plans?"

"Oh, I'll be back tomorrow, see the brats, take care of some business, shop for some decent clothes, kiss my husband a couple of

268

times, and then it's back here. I'm seeing Judge Shearing on Thursday, which means I have about forty-eight hours to learn the material and enough Delaware law not to make a fool of myself, meet my support staff down there, and draft a continuance. The state is pushing for trial right away."

"Have you talked with Phil Loreno, yet?"

"No, and that's *another* thing I've got to do," Marlene replied with some asperity. "Cripes, I just came from getting hired."

"How did that go down?"

"Funny. We drove out early because I wanted to clear it up or clear out. Only Sarah and Selma were there, the dad was at work. So we go in, there's coffee, cake, and then Selma says, We talked it over and we want you to represent Sarah. Sarah is mum, so I look at her and I ask her if that's what she wants, too. She looks at her mother, you know, just to check, and then she nods and says yes, too. Butch, it's hard to describe this, but the kid's eighteen, and it's like, 'Would you like a piece of candy, little girl?' and the kid looks at Mom to see if it's all right."

"You're thinking she won't stand up?"

"Yeah. I don't think these people have any idea how grueling a trial's going to be. Anyway, Selma went to the bathroom and I grabbed Sarah and I said, 'Let's go for a walk.' She gets to move a half mile from her house without notice before the ankle thing goes off. And she didn't want to, and I practically shoved her into a coat and I shot a look at Shanahan that she should take care of the mom, and we went out. Okay, winter wonderland, clean rural snow, Sweety's having a ball bounding around in the drifts. There's a couple of newsies there, shouting, but Sweety won't let them get close. The poor kid hasn't been out of the house without being hounded for God knows how long. We cut down a hiking trail, where they can't follow in their vans. What's the weather like in the city?"

"The usual. Overcast, windy, around forty."

"Well, this morning it was one of those bright days you get after a big blizzard. Not a cloud in the sky, totally calm, I swear it was like walking through one of those shake-up snow globes after it's been sitting for a while. We're just chatting, I tell her about my family, she tells me about hers, harmless stuff. After a while, we come to a little park with a creek running through it, Bethany Creek, the traditional babbling brook, gleaming icicles, and she brings me to this bench, it's a sun-trap, in a little cove of rocks above the water, it's ten degrees warmer, all the snow has melted off it, and we sit down. This is where she used to come with the boyfriend. And we talk some more and watch the dog splashing around. It was weird, Butch, I flash on doing the same thing with Lucy, when we were in DC, at that park we used to go to, and I get the same, like, affect off her. Lucy was four and this kid is eighteen, and I'm getting the same please-take-care-of-me vibes you get when you're relating to a very young child. And I find myself falling into it, talking a little more slowly, listening a little more carefully — it wasn't an interaction between two adults. And all of a sudden I realize — fuck! This kid is on trial for her life and I'm her lawyer and we're waltzing around in candyland. She just kind of expects that someone is going to take care of her, that as long as she's nice and doesn't offend, nothing bad will happen to her."

"So what did you do?"

"Honestly, I felt like shaking her, tossing her in the creek, anything to knock her out of that fuzzy pink dream. It was exactly like some of the shelter women — oh, he didn't mean it, he really loves me and the kids. And then I thought, Oh, easy does it, Marlene, you got to bring this kid around slowly. So I steered her to talking about the boyfriend. You know, she still sees him."

"Good God!"

"Oh, yeah, all the time, apparently. He calls

271

her a couple of times a day. They chat. He comes over."

"You're going to need to bring your lunch on this one, kid," said Karp. "I'm surprised your pal allowed that, if the boy looks shaky."

"Yeah, well" — here she dropped her voice — "between you and me, I get the feeling that Maureen was reaching a little on this one. I have the sense that her strategy short-term was to hunker down and say novenas in hopes that the state would come to its senses and drop the charges down to something reasonable so she could plead out. She was not set up for trial, psychologically at any rate. She hasn't even met personally with the medical experts."

"She *hasn't?*"

"No. That's another thing that's up there on my agenda; I got a list of twenty things and they're all number one to do." Marlene groaned, then laughed at herself. "Anyway, it was nice to walk in the snow. I started my rapport with my client. They've got a pretty little house. The Goldfarbs. And Shanahan, too. I thought of you, how you're always mooning for suburban life, and because of me you have to live in a loft above a Chinese fruit market."

"Not mooning, as such . . ."

"Mooning. Shanahan's got a hoop and

backboard over her driveway."

"*Now* I'm mooning."

Marlene giggled. "I have an image of you sticking your butt out a car window."

After this, laughter, some domestic details, the nanny debacle described, love plighted in the half-ironic way they used when connecting over the wires, and when Marlene said she had to go and hit the books before retiring, Karp said, "Wait, Luce wants to talk to you. I'll see you when I see you, babe."

Marlene said the same, and then her daughter came on the line.

"Hi, kid, how're you doing?"

"Okay, I guess. Sad. You're going to defend that girl?"

"It looks like it. Do you have any problems with that?"

"Did she do it? They said they smashed the baby's head in. I read a magazine article on it. This woman wrote an editorial in *Newsweek* about privileged teens without souls. It made them sound like monsters."

"I saw that, too," said Marlene. "Goes to show you not to believe everything you read. I haven't figured out the full story yet, but it seems to me right now that the only thing wrong these people did could be classified as felony stupid, not murder. My client was apparently in a coma while the baby was born, if, in fact, the baby was ever born. It could've been a stillbirth."

Lucy made a noncommittal noise in response to this. Marlene asked, "Why are you sad? Because of Caitlin?"

"Yeah, partly. But . . . it's starting to seem like whenever my life is going along halfway decent, some big catastrophe comes along and wrecks it, like there's something about me personally that draws bad things, like a lightning rod."

"That's not a profitable pattern of thought, Lucy."

"Yeah, I know. 'Sufficient unto the day is the evil thereof.' I shouldn't dwell, but I do."

"Do you consider that a lot of the violent, the catastrophic, things that you've been involved with had to do with my so-called career and had nothing to do with you personally at all?"

"Yeah. I used to hate you for it."

" 'Used to'? You mean I'm off the hook?"

"Oh, don't be a jerk, Mom. Everybody hates their mother at some point. You should hear Nona go on about what you were like. Compared to that, I'm *Little Women*, for crying out loud."

"Inadmissible hearsay."

"Yeah, right. But . . ." A long pause here, both of them listening to the seashell hiss of the line. "Caitlin was like that, too, and her mother like practically lived for her, and Caitlin was always putting her down, not nasty stuff, but, you know, my *mother* this and my dumb *mother* that, like kids do. I mean you can't say, well, all your mothers might be jerks, but my mother is, like, perfect or something. It's regular life, and you expect that it'll all work out someday, but then — wham! She's gone and it's never going to work out, and so, I just wanted to say I'm glad you're doing this, being a lawyer, I mean, and not shooting people anymore. Dad's real happy, too. He was singing earlier tonight."

"What! He never sings. He doesn't know how."

"It was pretty awful, but it was singing. 'The Yellow Rose of Texas.' And also, despite everything, I love you. I mean, in case you still get killed."

Karp looked the man over appraisingly and said, "Pincus, you look like you've been up all night."

Pincus brought up a wan smile. "Yeah, well, you know what they say, the first twenty-four hours after the crime, and the cops were hot to go on this one. I figured, I'd ride around with them, it was better than waiting around the precinct or going home and getting dragged out of bed at three in the morning when they pulled in a suspect."

"You have a suspect, hmm?"

"Yeah, I figured we would. It was clearly an inside job — no signs of forced entry, the perp obviously had a key, and it was a robbery, so . . ."

"Really? What was taken?"

"Some jewels and cash. The guy's, Maxwell's, wallet was empty, and he always had five hundred or so on him. A tipper, apparently. The maid said the Mrs. always wore a set of emerald and diamond clips, and they were gone, too. And the pistol."

"What pistol?"

"Maxwell's target gun. Hey, you know, I'm not telling this right. Why don't I give you the straight chronology and if you have any questions, I can answer them at the end."

"Why don't you?" agreed Karp. The man was clearly a little uncomfortable being in Karp's office without Roland present. A good bureaucratic instinct. He would go far.

"Okay. Four people in the house, two of them kids just got there, one of them the boy, who's completely out of it, and one the cook. So they interviewed the cook, Vida Montoya, for sequence of events and, obviously, because she had one of the keys. The woman's terrified, apparently — her husband doesn't have a green card and he's working two jobs, so Soldi calms her down, tells her he's not the *migra,* a different kind of cops entirely, and he won't let on about the husband if she plays it straight up. Which she does. She's clear, by the way: at work during the time of, which the ME puts at sometime on Saturday night, or early Sunday morning. So's her old man, same alibi. Next we got Carlotta Penrose, the cleaning woman. She's a grandma, unlikely to be guilty of execution-style shootings of a couple of rich people, been with the wife's family since the year one. Lives with her daughter and the daughter's three daughters, all tucked in bed the time of. Could there be a connection with a male relative, did the deed? Yes, possibly, but nothing sticks up right now and we have better. Now we come to the decorator, Oren Lorel, who also had a key, or actually two keys. Oren was a hair naughty, which we had some trouble getting out of him. It seems Mrs. M. gave him a key and he made a copy of that key for his workmen, so he didn't have to schlepp to the Maxwells' any time a workman had to get in there; he could just call the worker and have him go do the work. Okay, now's where it gets good. It seems that one of his workers, a guy named Moussa Feydé, an African–non-American type, had a violent argument with Mr.

Maxwell on Saturday morning. This Feydé was careless and started a fire, and Lorel canned him on the spot. Then he had to organize a repair crew and push them to get the place fixed up by the time the Maxwells got back from skiing on Monday or Tuesday. It turns out that they were actually working all Sunday on the ground-floor rooms while the Maxwells were dead upstairs and the little boy was hiding at the top of the house. In the confusion, with the argument and the fire and all, Lorel forgets that Feydé's got the extra key. Okay, hold that thought for a second. While this is going on, Soldi's troops are going through the whole house. Up top, they've got rooms full of the furniture from some of the rooms they're renovating on the lower floors, all jammed in there. They find one of those big display cabinets that gun collectors use: locked and barred glass doors above for long guns, locked drawers below for handguns, ammo, and other gun stuff."

"Maxwell was a gun nut?" asked Karp, surprised.

"Not as such, but from various items in his 'den' furniture, we can assume he doted on the manly pursuits. Fly-fishing, horse-riding, skeet, hunting, target popping. Had shotguns, rifles, and four pistols, a Colt Commander .45, a Freedom Arms .44 mag revolver, a Glock 17L nine-millimeter semi-auto, and a target pistol, a Benelli five-shot .22, which is the only one missing. The thief punched a hole in the glass door, reached in, and got the spare keys to the drawers. Maxwell had left them in the little envelope supplied by the maker. I guess he figured since he had the key to the glass doors and the drawers on his key ring, he didn't have to worry about the spares, or else he just forgot they were lying there. Plenty of people do; they take the keys they need and leave the spares in the desk or whatever, in those little brown envelopes. Kind of thing a decorator or cabinetmaker would think of, though."

"The plot thickens."

"Yeah. Okay, after Lorel publicly fires the African to calm down his clients, he grabs the guy and tells him to go back to the workshop where the guy's been working on —" here Pincus consulted his notes — "a Reisner secretaire, apparently an incredibly valuable piece he was fixing up for the Maxwells, which he was the best guy in town to work on."

"So he wasn't really fired."

"Off the Maxwells' job, yeah, but not for the special cabinetwork. According to Lorel, Feydé was incredibly pissed at Maxwell. They had some harsh words about whose fault it was setting the place on fire. Maxwell seems to have had a short fuse. So Feydé goes back to the workshop, finishes up the piece, works on it the next day, too, and midday Sunday, a deliveryman brings the thing back to the Maxwells', where it still is. Lorel was there and received it himself. Feydé doesn't return the key at this time. So, needless to say, the cops wish to converse with Mr. Feydé right away. I got the Q and A here, if you want to see it, but I can summarize."

"Go ahead."

"Right. First off, Feydé tells his side of the fire story. It was Maxwell chasing his son through the house that did it, knocked over a worktable, and then Maxwell blames Feydé, which he felt was wrong."

"Excuse me — this fellow speaks English?"

"Adequately. He's not going to read the news at six, but he seems to understand pretty good. Okay, his story is after the dustup at the Maxwells, he heads back to the workshop in SoHo, fixes the inlay and the catch on the secretaire, and goes on home. He lives in Washington Heights. He says he went to a café in Brooklyn on Saturday night, he was there from eight to around ten with his African pals, eating and drinking tea, and then comes home and spends the rest of the weekend with his wife and kid. No alibi from around eleven P.M. Saturday to eight in the morning Sunday when he came to the workshop, except the wife, who's not all that sure about when he rambled home on the Saturday. This is a regular Saturday-night thing with them. So, there's opportunity enough. Now, obviously, I'm riding this pretty close, and this guy is looking good. His answers are a little unsure, he smiles where he shouldn't. He's got these shifty eyes. He's got the damn key right in his pocket. So I think I have enough with the fight, the key, and the opportunity to apply for a search warrant — apartment and place of work."

"That's a little thin."

"Yeah, but totality of circumstances is still satisfied, and the warrant is real narrow. All I want to find is, one, those emerald earrings, and two, the gun. Five pounds of dope, bloody handcuffs, hey, it's a free ride. So the cops go in there and they look in his toolbox down at the workshop, and the earrings are there, wrapped in Kleenex at the bottom of the box. So, of course, we confront him with this and he denies it, and we read him his rights and arrest him."

"No gun?"

"No gun, but it's a short walk from his place to the Hudson. ME confirms cause of death, no surprise there, and ballistics says that the four bullets were consistent with the missing pistol — .22 long rifles. I figure the guy was fuming all day about how badly Maxwell had treated him and late that night he decides to do something about it. He gets into the house with his key, he knows where the gun locker is because he's been in the place a dozen times, he gets the gun, goes into the bedroom. He shoots the man, and then the wife when she wakes up. He takes the jewelry and cash on impulse. Anyway, that's it. It's all in the Q and A, and I defy anyone to find a procedural glitch anywhere in the case."

Karp smiled and nodded genially and slipped a look over to Murrow, who had sat through all this silently. "Well, congratulations, Pincus," said Karp. "A good job and a good case. Very impressive. Convey my compliments to the detectives involved. I'm sure Jack will be extremely happy to move this one off his plate."

Pincus made the appropriate noises in response. While he was gathering his papers to leave, Karp asked, "This guy is a resident alien, right?"

"Yeah, a green card."

"Then you've informed his consulate?"

Pincus grinned. "Absolutely. They sent a consular official over, too. They were speaking at length in their native tongue."

"And Feydé still denies it, even after you confronted him with the earrings?"

"Yep. And that means we're definitely going to try this sucker because with something like this any plea but guilty to the top count is out of the question."

After Pincus was gone, Karp said, "Confidence is vital in a prosecuting attorney, Murrow, and there goes a prime example. Besides that, he's lucky. He goes out on a routine chart run and he lands the biggest murder case of the year. Socialites slain in bed by African venting fierce primitive grudge. Pincus will get more TV time than Whoopi Goldberg. And it's a perfect slow grounder to the mound. Perp has a public beef with the vic, shoots the vics, retains incriminating swag, no lineups, no conflicting witnesses, no fiber experts wrangling on the stand. They say that chance favors the prepared mind, but in this case chance has favored a practically blank one. God bless him!"

"Dave's not *that* bad," said Murrow.

"Is that his name? Yes, I guess he *is* a Dave. No, you're right, he's not that bad. None of them are. The dirty secret is you don't need a first-class mind to be a good prosecutor. One like Pincus's will do just fine ninety-five times out of a hundred."

"And the rest?"

"Oh, you'll get a serious defense lawyer who'll blow you out of the water. Somebody once said that the mark of a first-class mind is the ability to hold two contradictory thoughts at the same time. A really bright prosecutor is going to be able to hold his own case and the defense's case in his mind at the same time. He'll be able to entertain doubts without losing his concentration on pressing the case."

"I thought there weren't supposed to be serious doubts."

"There are always doubts, Murrow. 'We see through a glass, darkly,' as my daughter often says. The mediocre prosecutor ignores them. The superior one absorbs them and learns to live with them."

"So as to predict what the defense will do? Or are you talking about a deeper, more existential doubt?"

Karp chuckled. "Murrow, you are supposed to deposit your existential doubt in the receptacle provided for that purpose in the outer office. Failure to do so may result in inadvertent humanization, which might put a crimp in your career. You won't always be lounging away your days on perfumed couches as a special assistant. You might have to represent the People in court someday. How will you attain the crisp confidence we just saw in young Pincus there if you're always maundering on about existential doubt?"

Murrow bobbed his head. "Sorry, sir. It won't happen again, sir," he said cringingly. "And speaking of maundering existential doubt, I guess you saw that the grand jury returned on Bustamente yesterday."

"I did see that. It's going to be an interesting trial. You should attend."

"Really? Why interesting? It seems to be as much of a lock as Dave's African socialite-killer."

"Not for the outcome, for the texture. I think seeing Ms. Jessica Siegel in action on this one is going to be a treat, not to mention our own lovely and talented Mimi V. As for Pincus — you notice how he dismissed the absence of the murder weapon. The guy tossed it in the river, it's gone. No attention to the question of why a guy who's so scrupulous about ditching the murder gun keeps the swag in his tool chest and the incriminatory key in his pocket. Finally, we might wonder why someone who has a choice of three — count 'em, three — powerful, deadly handguns picks out a pissy little .22 target pistol to commit a double murder."

"So you have doubts?"

"Yes, and I just dealt with them and decided that, all told, they weren't worth pursuing. Murder ain't rational. I once had a case in which one partner in a pawnshop killed the other partner after work one day. The place had within easy reach three dozen pistols, a bunch of shotguns, racks of knives, fucking samurai swords hanging from the ceiling. The killer used a metal stool to bash the guy's head in. And the defense made that argument — was it rational to think that a guy with all that weaponry at hand would use a metal stool to kill with? It didn't play. It almost never does. But my point was that your boy Pincus didn't give that kind of thing any thought at all. Fortunately, this defendant probably has a net worth of one hundred nineteen dollars, so Pincus is going to face one of our fine Legal Aids with a hundred and twenty other cases to worry about and no big hard-on on behalf of an African carpenter."

"Unlike, for example, that which, figuratively speaking, of course, Ms. Siegel bears for Lourdes Bustamente."

"Very unlike," Karp agreed.

Caitlin Maxwell's grandfather, James Pell Warren, lived in a ten-room apartment on the twentieth floor of a building on Park Avenue north of 69th Street. Lucy and Mary Ma went there after school, and it was as they had expected, the lobby ornate, the doorman supercilious and careful, the elevator all brass and inlay and smelling of stale expensive perfume. A maid in an actual black dress and white apron answered the door, showed them in, and asked them to wait in the living room, a huge place with coffered ceilings, walnut wainscoting, comfortable and somewhat worn old furniture upholstered in leather and muted silks, with old and faded Oriental carpets on the floor. Three large windows set off by silvery drapes let in the costly light of Park Avenue. Paintings in gilt frames, lit by little brass museum lamps hung on the walls, portraits of well-dressed men, women, and children, a few still lifes and garden scenes in oils, Sargents and Pissarros, and a tiny Monet. They looked at all this and at each other and rolled their eyes. Neither of them was much impressed by wealth.

Caitlin arrived after a few minutes, looking pale and elegant in a loose black roll-neck sweater and black tights. After a brief greeting she led them down a dim hallway and into a large sunny room furnished in heavy maple of the last age, a four-poster bed, chests of drawers, wardrobes, and an elaborate vanity. They all sat on the bed. There was a certain unease. Both Mary and Lucy were reasonably conversant with world-shattering tragedy, but it was still hard to deal with the instant violent orphaning of a friend. Should you pretend nothing happened? Offer condolences? There was not much advice floating around teen culture on this score. After an awkward silence, Caitlin explained that this had been her late grandmother's bedroom.

"Are you going to live here," Lucy asked, "you and Brian?"

"For the time being. I don't ever want to go back there."

"What will happen to all your stuff?" asked Mary.

Caitlin shrugged. "I guess it'll go into storage, or else they'll sell it. Daddy's affairs are a little complicated right now. I mean there's like *money,* and everything, but he always had a lot of balls in the air that only he knew what it all meant. Teams of lawyers are trying to figure out who owns what."

A silence, which Mary broke in her typical clunky fashion. "I'm sorry about your parents, Caitlin. You must be so sad. If my parents were killed like that, I don't know what I would do. Cry for weeks and weeks."

Caitlin looked at Mary oddly, as if not quite understanding the meaning of this very simple sentiment. Caitlin shrugged and picked at a fingernail. "Maybe I'm numb. I can't feel anything yet. Maybe I never will. Does that mean I'm bad?" She addressed this last to Lucy, whose authority on morals was considered among their crowd the equivalent of Mary's in higher math.

"No, bad has nothing to do with it. You feel what you feel, you know? Nobody will think bad of you because you don't carry on, or doubt you loved them."

"Did I? I guess I did, but, this is a big news flash, we were not like a close family, not like a TV family. Daddy practically only talked to me to explain some deal he was doing, like I cared. And Mom was into having everything just right, perfecty-perfect. I was just thinking a little while ago that it was, like, fated that she got killed by a decorator. She actually shopped till she dropped." Her friends stared at her, trying unsuccessfully to keep the horror from their faces. Caitlin made a strange choked sound, somewhere between a sob and a giggle, just before collapsing in hysterics.

The fit lasted some minutes. Lucy and Mary wrapped themselves around their friend while she shook, making soothing noises. After she recovered, Caitlin ran into the adjoining bathroom and stayed there for nearly fifteen minutes. When she emerged, she looked cool and Caitlin-like, with only a little reddening around the eyes to show what had just happened.

"Would you like some *goûter*?" she asked.

The two girls agreed that a snack would be

nice and got up, intending to go fetch it from the kitchen, but Caitlin said, "No, I'll ring," and pressed a button on the wall, and shortly the woman in the maid costume came in and Caitlin told her to bring tea and cakes, and when Lucy remarked, "Gosh, this is just like *Masterpiece Theatre*," Caitlin said, "Yes, it is. My grandfather is sort of old-fashioned."

The tea came, with little cakes of various types, and a delicate china service with tiny rosebuds on it. Lucy could see that Mary Ma was embarrassed to be served by an older woman, but Caitlin seemed to be well at ease and gossiped and told little anecdotes, rather in the manner of her late mother. The recent breakdown was not mentioned.

Lucy asked, "How's Brian?"

"Oh, Brian. Beautiful Brian's fine. Grandfather likes him because he's a boy. He wants Brian to change his name to Pell Warren so that the glorious ancestors don't die out."

"But what about your father's ancestors?" asked Mary, concern on her face.

"Oh, them," said Caitlin dismissively. "Not in the same league. No New York streets named after *them*. Anyway, the little retard is in hog heaven. No military school for Brian. Grandfather's taking him around to show him off today. He'll probably start a fire in the Harvard Club."

"I don't see why you're so nasty to him, Caitlin," said Lucy. "He always seemed like a perfectly okay little kid to me."

"Right, and everything he touches turns to crap. If it hadn't been for him, my parents would still be alive."

"Caitlin, that's really unfair, and you know in your heart it's not true. Horrible things that happen don't have to have an explanation or someone to put the blame on."

"Oh, are you going to *preach*, now?"

"No. But the fact is he's the only family you have left."

"Dancing is the only family I have left."

Caitlin was glaring at her and Lucy had to turn her eyes away, because whatever was inhabiting her friend was not the person she knew, was no one she would ever want to know. Lucy stood up and retrieved her book bag.

"I have to go to the lab now," Lucy said. She looked at Mary, who seemed on the point of tears.

Mary said, "When are you coming back to school, Caitlin?"

"I don't think I am coming back. Sacred Heart was my mother's idea. The ballet school can arrange tutoring to get me a diploma, and then I'll just move straight on to Juilliard or someplace."

Lucy saw Mary poised to speak and knew that she was about to make one of her gormless remarks and that Caitlin, in the mood she was in, would say something cutting, and Lucy could not bear to see that, she knew she would flare and snap back at Caitlin, and then there would be no hope of salvaging anything from this. So she filled the air with chatter — clothes, gossip — and moved them through the hallway again, Caitlin walking ahead, Lucy observing again the curious toes-out waddle of the ballet dancer, and thinking, as she had so many times before, that they're only graceful when they're on duty, like that joke about the short guy in a bar, and the other guy asks him what he does, and the short guy says, "I'm the giant in the circus. Yeah, but it's my day off."

Parting at the door, Caitlin said, "Oh, I almost forgot," and ran back to her room and came back with a pair of envelopes.

"Tickets to *Sleeping Beauty*. Next Saturday." And she smiled at her two best friends.

10

The Delaware local counsel was named Kevin Mulcahey; the car, his, was a Honda Prelude; the traffic was light going south toward Dover; the countryside whipping by was flat, boring, colored dun and white, like a mutt dog. Marlene, always irritable in the passenger seat, became annoyed at the state motto on the highway signs and said, "What is all this with The First State? Isn't that a strange motto? Sort of empty, like nothing interesting happened since 1791. Or like those businesses that try to distinguish themselves by being the first in the yellow pages: AAAAAA Auto Glass."

"Yes, but consider the obvious alternatives," said Mulcahey. "Only Slightly Larger than Rhode Island? Small but Featureless? A Wholly Owned Subsidary of E. I. Du Pont de Nemours, Inc.? None of these sing to me."

Marlene laughed and sidelong reexamined her companion. She still believed that Shanahan had given her a local counsel who looked like Mulcahey did in some antic mood, or out of some weird resentment, because Kevin

Mulcahey was precisely the sort of angelic-looking Irish kid Marlene had made a fool of herself over time and again in high school. He was around ten years younger than she was, she estimated, and had the strawberry-blond hair and the strawberries-and-cream complexion, the sea green eyes, the lipless grin, insouciant, challenging, and the golden eyelashes. His body, she knew, would be smooth, creamy, nearly hairless, chewable, a bite would leave a red mark for . . . She shook her head and snapped back out of what was starting to be an erotic daydream, and damn Shanahan to hell.

"What?"

"Oh, nothing," said Marlene, feeling the blush upon her cheek. "Are we there yet?"

They soon were, Marlene trudging glumly through the melting snow across the picture-postcard courthouse square. Mulcahey led her into the courthouse. Marlene felt as though she were entering a movie set about a small-town scandal. The courthouse was small and colonial and bordered by snow-swathed lawns and big, bare trees, with other state buildings in the same style standing nobly about, like a diorama explaining life in a former age. There should, she thought, be a Lionel train clattering around it.

The only thing metro in the area was press,

news crews from Philadelphia, Wilmington, and smaller stations lined up on the steps pointing gunlike mikes at them or holding out little black boxes in hopes of catching a salable remark. Mulcahey efficiently bulled them through these and into the relative quiet of the courthouse's entrance hall. Marlene checked her reflection in the glass of a bulletin board. Under the leather trench coat, she was wearing her most conservative court outfit, a charcoal suit of severe cut over a white, round-collared shirt, with a little black grosgrain bow at the throat.

"That was nicely done," said Marlene, primping her freshly cut hair into a more perfect fall. "Basketball?"

"Too short. Lacrosse. I missed my stick, though, just now. It's right up here." They climbed a staircase. "As you probably know," said Mulcahey, as they reached the landing, "Judge Shearing is president judge of the Superior Court of Delaware. This court is his usual stomping grounds, but he comes up to Wilmington on a rotation to hear felonies. Just our luck."

"A prosecutor's judge?"

"Not especially, but he's a great one for control. Knows all the state's attorneys of course, and most of the defense bar. You're a ringer, a foreigner, a New York foreigner.

Judge won't like that. Are you deferential?"

"I have the greatest respect for the judiciary and their vital constitutional function."

Mulcahey rolled his gorgeous eyes and ushered her into the courtroom.

It was the sort of courtroom used to illustrate the social studies textbooks. The walls shone white; the jury box, the spectator seats, and the presidium were dark wood, clean and shining, lit by the clean winter light that poured in from four tall, many-paned Georgian windows. There was no peeling paint or the smell of too many people or the noise of aggressive crowds. Not Centre Street, thought Marlene as she and Mulcahey arranged themselves at the defense table, and then a moment later, the reality of what she was doing struck her, and her knees got shaky.

"You okay?" asked Mulcahey.

"Yeah, why, do I look like I'm going to puke?"

"Somewhat. Don't worry so much — it's only the life of a sweet young girl at stake here. Now, if you would direct your attention over to your right, that tall gentleman in the cheap suit who looks like the sole Republican undertaker in Chicago is our adversary, Jason Q. Abt, representing the state of Delaware."

"Almost New Jersey," said Marlene, and broke into loud giggles, which she was able to turn, not very convincingly, into a coughing fit. When she looked up again, through tearing eyes, she saw Abt staring at her as at an unexpected but fascinating insect, a staghorn beetle perhaps, he had found in his garden. Abt was about Marlene's age but looked older, the sort of man who makes a virtue out of appearing unattractive. He had protruding ears, rimmed in red, made more obvious by the way his tan hair was cut short on the sides. A fleshy nose drooped slightly over a deep-grooved upper lip, the small bun of a chin bore a dimple in it, and a prominent Adam's apple bulged over a shirt collar a size or two too large. He wore glasses, and of course they were Clark Kent black horn-rims. He nodded to Marlene and turned back to his cocounsels.

Then the door to the courtroom opened with a dramatic bang, and down the center aisle swept a short, dark, elegant man in a fawn camel-hair overcoat over a double-breasted, navy pinstripe. He carried a thick, shiny briefcase and walked with a bounce, and his face bore a nice even tan. His hair was worn long and combed straight back, and he looked to Marlene like central casting's idea of a mouthpiece for the Mob.

"Phil Loreno," said Mulcahey in her ear unnecessarily.

Loreno went immediately to the prosecution bench, shook hands with Abt and Abt's two assistants, made some remark that summoned amused noises, and then turned and approached the defense table, upon which he dropped his briefcase.

Marlene's hand was pumped enthusiastically, and she got to see a lot of very white teeth, gleaming nicely against the tan.

"Marlene Ciampi!" Loreno cried. "Well, well. I'm delighted to be working with you." He nodded to Mulcahey. "Kevin. How's the boy?" and "Good, good!" before Kevin had answered. "Look, Marlene, we need to have a meeting, real soon, in fact, immediately."

"I'd like to do that, Phil," said Marlene, "but probably not today. I have to make the eleven-fifteen Metroliner back to the city."

Loreno smiled. "The city. See, Kevin, you can always tell a New Yorker, the way they say 'the city.' You know she doesn't mean Wilmington. Okay, this here in court won't take long — you're asking for a continuance? Good, but not too long of a one, I hope, because His Honor wants to close this thing out as soon as he can — anyway, I have a car, you can ride back to Wilmington with me, we'll talk, I'll get you there in plenty of time."

"Phil, today's not good."

"No?" Loreno seemed amazed that anyone

would not want to spend an unbilled hour and a half in his company. "Okay, then we can just drop in next door for a cup of coffee. Just to get all our ducks in a row." Another charming smile. "Also, I want you to meet Peter and his folks, all sweet, decent people. You know, what I can't figure is . . ."

But this remarkable puzzle was never revealed because at that moment the door behind the presidium opened, and Judge Holden Morris Shearing entered and assumed his throne. The bailiff did his act, they rose and sat, and then Marlene rose and addressed the court. She introduced herself as Sarah Goldfarb's new counsel and asked for a two-month continuance, until the second week in April.

The judge stared at her as she explained the reasons for the delay — the complexity of the case, the suddenness of Ms. Shanahan's departure — and she stared back at him. This seemed to make him angry; perhaps he was used to lawyers dropping their eyes when he stared. Holden Shearing was a fleshy, reddish man with a big, blocky head, painted with short, crinkly hair going nicely gray above the ears. His jaw was square and determined, his forehead was broad, its brows dark, bushy, potentially menacing; his eyes were blue, the nose long, flat, and slightly upturned at the tip. The impression of rocklike strength was, however, diminished by the man's mouth, which should have been a stern, bold line, but was instead a small, puffy rosebud, bright pink, with a dear little indentation in the lower lip, like a baby's. Marlene ordinarily thought that character made physiognomy, but perhaps in Judge Shearing's case the opposite was true. She would not like to have been a chubby twelve-year-old in a schoolyard with a mouth like that; it cried out for the fist.

"Miss Chianti, do you really need a whole two months?" asked this mouth peevishly. His voice was deep, with a cultivated upper-middle mid-Atlantic accent. "This case has been dragging on for well over a year."

"Yes, Judge, but I can't provide the competent counsel my client is entitled to if I haven't the time to prepare my case. And, Judge, it's Ciampi, not Chianti. Chianti is a wine produced in Tuscany. The poorer vintages are often sold to Americans in straw-covered bottles."

Twenty minutes later, Marlene, Mulcahey, and Phil Loreno were seated in a booth in a coffee shop a block from the courthouse, and Loreno was chuckling and shaking his head. "Christ on a crutch, when you brought out that line about Chianti, I thought old Shearing was going to spit a tooth. You've got a set of them, I'll say that for you, babe."

"So to speak," said Marlene. "Meanwhile, I got my continuance. What was it you wanted to talk about, Phil?"

"Do you want something? A late breakfast? They have great blueberry muffins here." He called the waitress over and bantered with her, to Marlene's eyes no different from his performance with Abt and several of the courthouse regulars on the way out. Marlene divided the world's assholes into arrogant or palsy, and she observed that Phil was the palsy kind. She guessed that Abt would turn out to be the other sort.

Coffee came, with one of the great muffins for Loreno, a mottled thing the size of a small throw cushion. He took a big bite, dabbed crumbs; she sipped, found the brew insipid, classic American out-of-town diner coffee. She made a mental note to lay in some real stuff in Mulcahey's office in Wilmington.

"Okay, like you so perspicaciously said, Marlene, a difficult and complex case. What's the key to it? We got to stick together. Am I right?"

"Great minds, Phil. I was just thinking the same thing."

"Really?"

"Yes. The Romeo and Juliet angle. All the world loves a lover. And no one knows what

301

went on in that motel except the two of them. Without testimony as to a culpable act from one or the other of the kids, and aside from the medical examiner's report, which is extremely vulnerable, from what I can make out so far, there's no felony case. We have illegal disposal of a body, period, next case."

"Romeo and Juliet, huh? They loved not wisely but too well?"

"That's *Othello* actually, Phil. I think we need to stay away from *Othello.*"

He gave her a big grin around the crumbs. "I love it! We're going to be a great team, Marlene, I swear. But seriously, now: the problem is, that's not going to fly, because we are definitely not going to be able to try this case."

"We're not?"

"No. My guys have run half a dozen focus groups on this, urban, rural, every realistic jury mix. Delaware's a little tiny place, it's all one media market. So forget a change of venue. Every half-ass chicken farmer in Delmarva, every redneck crabber out in the Bay, knows all about this case, and they've made up their minds. From one end of the state to another it's these rich, white college kids snuck a baby into this world and sent it out again by crushing its sweet little head. I've discussed these findings with my client and his parents, and they all agree that a trial is a no-no. The only way of getting out of this mess is to plead out, and the only question that's worth two minutes' thought is getting the best plea going."

"What do you think that would be, Phil?"

"I like criminally negligent homicide. A traffic accident kind of thing. The baby was born, it had some medical problems, they should have called for help and they didn't and the baby died. A typical sentence would be eighteen months, of which they'd serve maybe half in a minimum-security place. They could take college classes. It'd be like going to a Jesuit college back when I was in school. Maybe a little softer, when I think back."

Loreno took another bite of his muffin, mugged its yumminess in a clownish way, smiled, dabbed. He's acting a little silly, trying to disarm me, thought Marlene, he's smiling at me, but his eyes don't go with the picture. They're calculating. He can't imagine that I'm dumb enough not to see through this act, or maybe he's been doing it so long and so successfully that he believes it himself.

"I see what you're saying, Phil," she said after miming a slow person thinking hard, "but . . . gee, what I guess I don't see is why the state would go for a sweetheart deal like that for a couple of people they just indicted for intentional murder."

"Oh, you know, they made their point already," said Loreno, waving a dismissive hand. "They got their exposure, their political brownie points in the bank. You know how these state people are. Schmucks, not to put too fine a point on it. They had anything on the ball, they would've gone private, except they're hoping someone will notice them, nominate them for something. Well, they got their notice, and the last thing they want is to try to defend these horseshit charges in open court."

"Phil, you're saying two different things. You got the focus groups hanging the kids, and you've got Abt and company avoiding a trial . . . it doesn't mesh."

A smile from Loreno, a glance at Mulcahey to reestablish male solidarity. He's going to try to patronize me, thought Marlene, observing this; can he possibly dare? He could. "Marlene, let me just say this, and I mean no offense, but you don't have a whole hell of a lot of experience on this side of the net —"

"Actually, I have none at all."

"Right, yes, and that's why, if we're going to continue in this joint defense agreement, moving toward a joint plea bargain, then I'm going to have to ask you to be guided by my expertise."

"I think that's a great idea, Phil, as long as the interests of our clients coincide."

A big smile this time. "Hey, how could they diverge? Like you said, it's Romeo and Juliet."

"Who both ended up dead, if you'll recall," she said, returning the smile, and looked at her watch. "Phil, got to go. We'll be in touch, okay?"

"Right, I'll call you," said Loreno, looking somewhat discomfited as the two others withdrew. Marlene got the feeling that he was usually the one who determined when the meeting was over.

In Mulcahey's car, heading north on Route 13, Marlene asked him what he thought of the morning's doings.

"You certainly impressed Judge Shearing."

"He hates me."

"You're not his favorite counsel, let's say that."

"Good. Shearing tried to push me around, I snapped back at him, and now we have an understanding. I expect our relationship during this case will proceed along lines of icy punctilio."

"Icy punctilio. I like that. Sounds like a minor Mafia figure."

"Or a ballplayer. Frank 'Icy' Punctilio, played second base for the Reds, 1956 through 1967, lifetime average .223. Do you think I'm right?"

"No, actually, I don't. I think he doesn't like a hotshot girl lawyer from Jewtown barging in and trying tricks in his court. He wants this case, and its two principals, to vanish in a politically advantageous manner."

Marlene sputtered out a laugh. "Um, just speak your mind, Kevin, don't beat around the bush. You're saying it's uphill?"

"The North Face of the Eiger."

"Marvelous. What do you think of our pal and ally Loreno?"

"Oh, him. I never heard such a load of codswallop in my life. He must think we're jerks."

"Well, dear boy, given the track record of counsel in this case, and I have to include my old pal Shanahan, he was making a good bet. Contra Mr. Loreno, the state is out for blood on this one. They'd like both of them, but if they can only get one, Sarah will do just fine. And since she was apparently out cold for the whole event, Peter's the only one who can possibly do a deal. Phil basically wants us to sit and do nothing while he makes just such a deal with Mr. Abt. Have you heard any good rumors about that?"

"I know the Jorgensen family is crazy to get past this. Know anything about them?"

"Divorced. The dad's loaded."

"Right. Interesting people. The boy lives with his mother, but the split was fairly cordial. They've both remarried. The dad, Karl Jorgensen, is an engineer. He invented a kind of automatic valve for the chemical industry and he runs a fair-sized firm that manufactures them. Rich is right, and he dotes on Peter. My sources suggest that if things look like they're going sour, Peter's on a plane for Venezuela with a new identity."

"Do you get the feeling that Sarah's fate is not much of an issue there?"

"Less than zero. They didn't much like her even before this happened. Middle-class Jewish is not what they envisioned for a daughter-in-law."

"I guess you got this all from the PI?"

"Yeah, Brewster. He's great. You'll see when you meet him. So — are we going to sever?"

"Oh, eventually," said Marlene. "But first I want to see where Loreno goes while he thinks we're still sleeping. He needs to tell a story about what went on in that motel room, and I'm dying to know what it's going to be."

"Do you think it will depart from absolute veracity, counselor?"

"I do, sad to say. And when it does appear, I want to have enough material on hand to let me shove it back past his shiny capped teeth."

Mulcahey's office was in the same building as Shanahan's, nestled in the same arrangement of rising lawyers and old courthouse duffers sharing services and working out of cubbyholes. Mike Brewster, the PI, was waiting for them when they arrived, and Marlene liked him immediately. He was a big, lantern-jawed fellow with the blond crew cut of an astronaut getting gray above the ears, and the reasonable drawl of an airline pilot. He was wearing a white shirt, a plain tie, a gray shark-skin suit of unstylish cut, and immense black cap-toe oxfords. Mr. Hoover would have been pleased at the turnout.

They chatted amiably, sharing edited stories about their former lives. Brewster had worked at the New York FBI office in the early seventies, and they knew some of the same people.

Then to business. Marlene said, "Kevin tells me you've been checking out the search warrant affidavit. Any good news?"

Brewster chuckled. "Yeah, I guess. It was sort of amateur hour that night. Detective Yeager, the affiant here, was a little inventive."

"He lied?"

"Hmm. I'd put it more like he heard what he wanted to hear and didn't check. Let me go through the whole story so you'll get the picture from his point of view, okay?" Brewster opened a spiral-bound steno notebook and flipped pages. "At about ten-thirty P.M. on November 12, year before last, the Newkirk, Delaware, police department logged a call from a duty nurse named Myrna Bottoms at Dover General Hospital. She reported that a college student named Sarah Goldfarb had delivered a placenta there approximately an hour previously and bore the signs of having recently delivered a full-term baby, but there was no baby. Shortly after that, the same department gets a call from the police in Chambersburg, Pennsylvania. They have in custody a student at Chambersburg College named Peter Jorgensen. Apparently, Jorgensen had told his roomie that his girlfriend had delivered a baby early that morning in a motel on 301 outside of Newkirk and that he had, quote, gotten rid of it, unquote, by placing it in a plastic bag and throwing it in a Dumpster. The cops by now are pretty interested. They canvass the likely motels, and at the Hospitality Inn on Route 301 they come up with a registration for that Mr. P. Jorgensen, in at four-thirty A.M., November 12, checked out midmorning. The cops go into the room and there they find the sheets bloodied and soaked with fluid. By now it's the middle of the night, three, four A.M. on the following day, the thirteenth. They call in every available cop, including Yeager, and they fan out to look in Dumpsters. This is a strip development here, motels, gas stations, restaurants, and they all have Dumpsters. They see a garbage truck starting to load a Dumpster at the Mother Hubbard Restaurant, about forty yards from the motel, they stop the driver and check out the Dumpster. In it they find a gray plastic trash bag with yellow ties, and in that they find a dead newborn and some bloody towels. Yeager is by this time at the scene, and his boss, Detective Lieutenant Raymond Hill, tells him to write up a search warrant for the dorm room of the supposed mother, Sarah Goldfarb, and after obtaining it, search said room."

Mulcahey said, "Just a second, Mike. Let me get out the actual affidavit." He dredged through a folder and handed a single sheet to Marlene.

Brewster resumed. "Okay, there are three substantive points sworn to in order to establish probable cause for the search. One is that Sarah was taken from her dorm room by paramedics because of excessive bleeding, implying that there might be evidence of forensic value there. The second was that Goldfarb made statements about delivering a baby in the Hospitality Inn and implicated Jorgensen in the disposal of the baby via plastic bag into a Dumpster. Third was a statement attributed to Jorgensen, saying he had picked Sarah up at her dorm room — get that — and that the baby was alive when he placed it in the bag. We have documentary evidence that none of these statements are true." Brewster bent over and pulled a manila folder from a worn leather briefcase and handed it to Marlene. Each document in the folder was neatly labeled in heavy red marker.

"Number one is the paramedic report, which states clearly that Sarah was taken out of her dorm room because she was in convulsions. There's not a single mention of blood. Number two there is the write-up of an interview I did with Lorraine Deutsche, an ER nurse at Dover who helped with the delivery of the placenta and took care of Sarah before she was sent to intensive care. Not only didn't she make any statement about delivering a baby, she was completely out of it, in a coma, for over twelve hours. The cops didn't even interview her until the following morning, *after* they'd searched her room. I also interviewed the attending physician, Dr. Hari Patel. He stated that when she started to come around the next morning, he asked her where the baby was and she said, quote, What

311

baby? I had a miscarriage, unquote. Number three there is the transcript of the Chambersburg police interview with Jorgensen. He never said the baby was alive when he placed it in the bag. They asked him was it crying. I don't know. Was it breathing? I don't know. So, basically, Marlene, on all three substantive points the affidavit is a crock."

"Okay, very good. I'll draft up a motion to suppress tonight. Where are we on the medical end?"

"Sarah, or the baby?"

"Sorry, I meant the postmortem, the forensics."

"They screwed that up, too." Brewster pulled another steno pad from his briefcase and thumbed through its pages. "The autopsy was done by state medical examiner Maryanne Bollinger, who is not a diplomate of the American Board of Pathology. She brought in a finding of death due to blunt trauma and shaking."

"Right," said Mulcahey, "but that finding was based on an examination of the external brain only."

"They didn't section the brain?"

"They did not. Didn't you read her report?" Mulcahey raised an eyebrow.

"I did, I did," said Marlene testily, "but I've also read about a thousand pages of assorted legalese in the past week and I haven't got the details jelled yet. I'm playing catch-up ball now, and you guys are going to have to carry me for a little while longer. But we did eventually get the brain sectioned, yes?"

"Uh-huh. Maureen petitioned for a re-autopsy and we had our forensic guy do it, Dr. Samuel Chapin. He's positive the trauma was postmortem. There was no swelling at the base of the brain, which there would have to have been if the fractures occurred while the baby was alive. Even Bollinger recorded that there was no swelling at the fontanels. Those're the soft areas —"

"I know what fontanels are, Kevin. Okay, I'll reread Chapin's report, and I'll want to see him personally, too. He's in Chicago, yes?"

"Right, and while you're seeing docs, you need to get with Kathleen Palmer, the neonatologist. She's at Hopkins. We have a preliminary report from her, but it's too tentative to do any good. She needs stroking and Maureen just didn't get around to it."

"I'll see her this week. Could you set it up? Meanwhile, tentatively, what does she say?"

"Gross brain abnormalities. She doubts the kid ever drew breath. She thinks it probably expired in utero."

"It would be better if she said definitely

313

stillborn. Remind me why the state thinks the baby was a live birth."

"Oh, they did a float test on the lungs," said Mulcahey carelessly.

"*That's it?* Jesus, Kevin! The float test hasn't been definitive since the nineteenth century."

"Nevertheless. Like Mike here said, it was amateur hour."

"Okay, so now our story's going to be we have a stillbirth tossed in a Dumpster, and the question is where do the postmortem fractures in the baby's skull come from? I assume we have the contents of the Dumpster in evidence?"

She saw it in their faces. "We don't?"

Brewster shook his head. "The contents of the Dumpster were disposed of by the police after the medical exam came out positive for homicide by blunt-force trauma."

"Making it impossible," snarled Marlene furiously, "to demonstrate by means of presenting in evidence the materials under and over the dead baby that could have and probably did crush its skull. Shit! But that's a *People v. Lolly* motion for sure."

Mulcahey smiled. "Very good, Marlene. We'll make a Delaware lawyer of you yet."

She looked to heaven. "Yeah, great, my girlhood dream."

★ ★ ★

Murrow emerged from his cubicle a little past seven-thirty P.M., yawning and scratching at his person, reasonably sure that he would be alone in the DA's suite. The district attorney's office never slept, but those unsleeping were down on the fourth floor processing criminal complaints. The eighth floor was almost always empty at this hour. Murrow went into the copy room, ran off some copies, poured himself a half cup of stale coffee from the pot that was kept there, laced it with sugar and Cremora, and drank some, making a face. The wide box that had held the day's supply of doughnuts was empty, but Murrow used his wetted finger to scoop up crumbs and bits of glazing. Hunger was gnawing and he thought of going out of the building and bringing back a take-out dinner. He decided not to, as he despised the odor of cooked food in an office, and decided to tough it out until he had finished his task, which was an analysis of the disposition of all cases of neonaticide in the state of New York, for the past twenty years. A significant piece of work, and one that had to be done in what his boss blithely called "your spare time." Murrow was one of the vast and unsung legion of young men and women on whom the legal system largely depends. They draft legislation, research cases, pen political speeches, and generate mountains of memos, proposals, and policy papers, always teetering, like their cousins the interns of medicine, at the last extremities of exhaustion. They know little and make numerous mistakes, some of which are caught by their masters, and others of which escape, to become the laws we all must live by.

Thinking vaguely of food, Murrow returned to his office, sat down, and thumbed through the day's notebook pages. The notebook was like the dozens of others racked in his filing cabinet, a college-ruled spiral, common and innocuous. In this and the others, Murrow had recorded verbatim every word of every meeting he had attended in Karp's office. One summer during law school, Murrow had attended, as the only male student, a course in stenography, thinking it would be useful in law school. It was, very, but when he had mentioned it to his fellow students, they had looked at him as if he were crazy, and so he had stopped mentioning it. As far as he knew, it was his little secret, which was fine with him. Murrow liked secrets.

He looked up from this after a while and noticed the gash of light under his boss's office. Thinking that Karp had forgotten to turn the light off, he went in and was surprised to discover the man himself. His desk was covered with thick drifts of yellow felony case folders, one of which he was reading.

"I thought you were leaving early," said Murrow. "Don't you have to pick up your kids?"

"They can squat on the sidewalk in the cold and the rain for a couple of hours. It won't kill them. Besides, people give them money and food. Every little bit helps, Murrow."

"What are you doing? If I may ask."

"If you don't ask, you'll never learn. Since I've been leaving early, I haven't been doing as much case review as I'd like. I like to keep it up enough to rattle cages."

"Anything of interest?"

"Oh, the usual flouting of the Bill of Rights. They're poor mopes and probably guilty anyway, so who cares? What you look for mainly is stupid cop tricks. Somebody slides one by, say they get Charlie to say that Jocko whacked the vic. Charlie supposedly heard it on the street, the so-called reliable informant, and so they arrest Jocko, who has a yard-long sheet, maybe some arrests for murders that didn't pan out, and on the basis of Charlie they get an arrest warrant, making sure they serve it at night so that they can enter his place and scarf up anything in plain view, ha ha. They find the murder weapon, sitting on a dresser where murderers like to keep them. Or maybe they found the murder weapon in a Dumpster and somehow it ends up on Jocko's dresser, right next to the picture of Mom. Case closed. Then the word gets around, and for the next couple of months any cop who thinks he knows whodunit gets Charlie on the line for a chat. Charlie knows about every murder from Inwood to Coenties Slip — a useful citizen, Charlie."

"Framing? I thought that was rare."

"Oh, no, it's rare all right. But cops always know more than they can prove, and it irks them not to be able to grab up the bad guys because of legal quibbles. As quibbler-in-chief, I need to kick butt once every so often, not so much for the cops, because they're incorrigible, but for our guys. Our guys start to snooze on shit like this and the next thing you know we're living in Guatemala. Or New Orleans. Meanwhile . . ." Karp stood up, stretched massively, and rubbed his face. "Meanwhile, I've read this goddamn page three times and it won't make sense." He rolled down his shirtsleeves and reached for his suit coat.

"I guess I'll head off, too," said Murrow, "although properly I should bravely pretend to keep on working until you leave and then sneak away."

"I know that trick. My hidden cameras would detect it. Got any dinner plans?"

"I was invited to dine at Le Pavilion with the Trumps. That or Chinese takeout, I haven't decided. Why do you ask?"

"Come home with me," said Karp. "Maybe the kids have collected enough by now for all of us. How does half a kielbasa sound?"

It was almost unheard of for Karp to bring people home from the office for dinner; in fact, he was famous for keeping a Chinese wall between office and home life. Office gossip had supplied Murrow with some background — the unusual wife and the prodigy daughter — so he was intensely curious as to what he might find when he followed Karp out of the loft elevator. Before he quite knew it, he had been sniffed all over by the largest and ugliest dog he had ever seen and was ensconced on a stool in the steamy kitchen, surrounded by marvelous smells, a garlicky breadstick in one hand, an enormous glass of Barolo in the other, and engaged by the wife and the daughter in a conversation about his life, his hopes, his fears, his beliefs (in between answering or being stumped by a series of infantile conundrums presented by the twins), as if he had been an old family friend.

Around the table (after the girl said grace;

319

and Murrow, a modern pagan with the usual thin and divided family, realized with a shock that he had never sat down to a dinner where grace was offered) they dug into the chicken soup with escarole, the linguine with clams, and a big plate of pickled vegetables so vinegary that they made the sweat pop. They ate, amid light and congenial chat. Murrow got slightly drunk. Over the empty plates Karp raised his glass to Marlene and said, "To the author of the feast. She fights for justice, she travels hundreds of miles, she rushes home through snow and ice to prepare terrific meals. Let's hear it for the divine Ms. C."

They all applauded. Marlene held up her hand. "Thank you all so very much," she breathed. "And now I'd like to thank all the little people without whom this would not have been possible. For the delicious soup, my daughter, the very, very, terrific . . . um . . ."

"Lucy, Mom," said Lucy.

"Right, her, and for setting the table and getting the knives on the right side, and for choosing the dessert, those irrepressible twins, Zik and Zak."

Who both applauded themselves, and Giancarlo said to Murrow, "They think it's cute to call me Zik, because my brother's *real* nickname is Zak, but I prefer Giancarlo. My father's real name is Roger, did you know that?"

"Actually I did," said Murrow.

"Is my father the boss of you?"

"He is."

Zak asked, "Do you have to do everything he says?"

"Certainly."

"Even take off your pants?" Fits of giggles.

Karp rumbled, "Take off your pants, Murrow!"

"Yes, sir." Murrow stood up and started fumbling at his belt. The twins were falling off their chairs.

Somewhat later, when order had been partially restored, Murrow asked Marlene about how she was wreaking justice, and she summarized her involvement in the Goldfarb affair thus far.

"That's amazing," said Murrow. "Whatever possessed them to go for capital murder?"

"A shortsighted lust for fame and political advantage," Marlene answered. "That's the reigning view. Clearly my first job is to make it seem less politically beneficial to do so."

"Without violating the gag order?"

"Murrow, vee haff vays."

Karp rolled his eyes and laughed. "Darling, I am *so* glad this is all happening out of state.

But, you know, I'm not all that sure that this is entirely shortsighted political garbage. Zak, drink out of your own glass! Jack said something when our own infanticide cases broke. People are angry with what's happening regarding children, irrationally angry. They swallowed abortion, but they didn't like it, and of course, a lot of people haven't swallowed it at all. They're scared, they think they don't understand how to raise kids anymore. That's the root of the drug hysteria, for example, why no politician can propose a sensible drug policy, why the prisons are full of dumb kids caught with a dime's worth of coke. Everyone's terrified that they're going to walk into little Jennifer's bedroom one morning and she'll have green hair and a nose ring and tracks."

"We saw a lady with purple hair yesterday, Daddy," said Giancarlo.

"That's nice, baby. Don't share any body fluids with her, okay? It's the same with the child molester witch-hunts in these day-care centers. Fear and insecurity build up, and politicians seize on that and focus it on a scapegoat. The Leo Frank effect."

"Who?" asked Murrow.

"How soon they forget. Maybe you have to be Jewish. Okay, late twenties, the South is being transformed by Northern bankers.

They're buying up everything, rationalizing agriculture, squeezing out marginal farmers. A lot of resentment against Wall Street. The pols are in bed with the Klan, for them Wall Street equals the Jews. Un-American blood-suckers. Frank's a Jew, runs a factory in Georgia. A raped and murdered young girl is found in his factory. The white folks go crazy. All the resentment and fear is focused on one man, Leo Frank."

Karp drank some wine. "What happened to him?" asked Murrow.

"He was tried and convicted, of course, and when the governor commuted his death sentence, a mob dragged Frank out of prison and lynched him. Maybe a similar thing is happening with Marlene's kid there. Interesting that she's Jewish, too."

Marlene uttered a hollow laugh. "Thank you, darling. I think I'll go put my head in the toilet. That's some theory! Blaming it all on women's lib. I love it."

"Hey, I didn't say I endorsed. Besides it's significant that Jack Keegan came up with it, spontaneously. Say what you will, the man has his fingers on the public pulse."

"Which is also why," Murrow put in, "we're getting ready to burn Lola Bustamente at the stake. It makes a crazy kind of sense."

"Yes," said Karp. "Pass that wine, please.

Let's face it, Marlene, women's liberation is practically the biggest social change of the century in this country. It's the square peg pushing into the round hole. Friction. People blow up abortion centers, you think they have a warm spot for babies? Friction makes heat and pressure, and it boils up in strange places and your case down there happens to be one of them."

A silence fell now, and Lucy was suddenly aware that both of her parents were looking at her. She pinched her lips together with her hand and made garbled noises. The Karps laughed and Karp explained to Murrow, "A vexed subject in this house, Murrow. My wife is soft on abortion and hard on the death penalty. My daughter is hard on abortion and squishy-soft on the death penalty."

"Which at least has the virtue of logical consistency," said Lucy.

Marlene stood up. "I believe this is my cue to get dessert," she said sweetly. "Little boys, you can come help."

"And what's your position?" Murrow asked Karp when Marlene and the twins had gone to the kitchen.

"Yeah, Dad, what is it? Come clean."

"Well, the linkage may be clear on some high moral plane, but I'm just a working lawyer. As for abortion, I can't, as I've said more than once, find a compelling state interest. It's between a woman, a doctor, the father, and God. Capital punishment? To a prosecutor, it's like giving nuclear weapons to a government. Maybe it's a powerful deterrent, maybe not, but who's wise enough to use it? Me, of course, but that little *pisher* down in Delaware? No way. And we're fallible, and we have a Court that's determined to speed up and cut down on routes of appeal, which practically guarantees that mistakes will be made, and with the death penalty of course they're uncorrectable mistakes. Like those police frame-ups we were talking about this evening. Hard enough to live with the possibility of sending an innocent man to prison, but death? I don't know."

"Human life is sacred," said Lucy.

"So you believe, but that's not the point. Even in religious societies human life is routinely sacrificed to social ends. Maybe *especially* in religious societies. The Church itself used to burn heretics."

"Right," Lucy snapped, "and whenever a Catholic says human life is sacred, somebody brings up the Spanish Inquisition."

At that, Giancarlo leaped from the doorway, hands clenched into claws, his face contorted in glee. "*No one* expects the Spanish Inquisition," he cried. "Its chief weapon is surprise. And fear. No, its *two* chief weapons are surprise and fear and ruthless efficiency — no, its *three* chief weapons —"

"Thank you, Giancarlo, take your seat, please," Marlene said, placing a laden tray on the table, and aside to Murrow, "He memorizes Monty Python routines. Try not to mention the SI or parrots. Or buying cheese." She set out china bowls of ice cream.

"Pistachio is disgusting," said Zak. "It looks like throw-up."

"Thank you, Isaac," said Marlene, "that's why we have vanilla. How did you all get on to the criminal excesses of the Church?"

"The sacredness of human life and burning heretics," said Karp.

"Oh, but that makes perfect sense," said Marlene. "If you *actually* believe that this life is merely a short prelude to the one to come, and if you *actually* believe that one form of magic will enable you to live it in bliss and another, slightly different form will cast you into eternal fire, then anyone pushing the wrong magic is the worst imaginable kind of criminal, far worse than a mere murderer. QED."

"We don't believe that anymore, Mom," said Lucy. "As you know."

"Speak for yourself, dear. I am a semilapsed pre–Vatican Two Catholic."

Murrow asked, "So what's *your* position on capital punishment, Marlene?"

"Is that a trick question? You see my dog? I love my dog, but if it had rabies, an incurable disease that makes dogs uncontrollable, I would have him put down. Some humans are uncontrollable, for reasons we don't comprehend. I don't mean the stoked-up kid who shoots a liquor-store clerk. I mean creatures in human form who don't have any souls, or whose souls have been eaten out of them by evil. As Ted Bundy said, 'What's the big deal? There are so many people.' Almost always these guys admit to the crime, and there's so much evidence that the situation that Butch was talking about, where an innocent guy is nailed because of framing or miscarriage or crummy defense, just doesn't arise. It's not psychology or bad home life either that makes them do it, it's evil. I believe in the absolute physical reality of evil, which is good doctrine, by the way, Lucy. They can't repent. *Posse non peccare,* as Dante says, they are incapable of not sinning; they're already in hell, but don't know it, and they're simply too dangerous to stay on this earth."

"Maybe, but *we* can't know that, Mom," said Lucy. "You can't substitute human for divine judgment."

Marlene smiled, and it was such a bleak

smile that Murrow, who had been studying her face, was abashed and turned away and felt the hairs rise on his neck.

"Therefore, kill them all," said Marlene. "God will know his own. Who wants hot fudge?"

11

"Why does she say stuff like that if she doesn't mean it? 'Kill them all.' I mean . . . your guy Murrow looked like he was going to faint."

"And you were extremely forbearing all during dinner," said Karp, dodging somewhat. "I saw your eyes flashing once in a while, but you didn't blow once. I was very proud of you. You seem to be growing up."

They were in the kitchen, late, Lucy in her robe, the two of them drinking milk and eating (dunking, actually) oldish chocolate biscotti, a shared vice. The twins were long abed, Marlene was down at the other end of the loft in her little office, reading Delaware cases. An occasional cry of despair issued from that direction, like the howl of a thin wolf from the steppe, besides which the house was quiet except for the sighing of the dishwasher and the other domestic machinery.

Lucy ducked her head at this compliment, faintly embarrassed; children want to grow up, but they don't like when their parents notice it. "But why does she? To be a pain?"

Karp sipped, sighed. "Lucy, if you have questions about your mother's behavior, you need to talk to her about them, not to me."

"Why? You talk about me to her all the time."

"Don't be dense! You're our daughter, we're *raising* you together. Fine, snort if you want to, but there it is."

"She'd just say something terribly witty, if I ever did ask her. You know how she gets."

"Do I? Maybe we should change the subject. Do you know the saying about the hedgehog and the fox?" She did not. "It goes, 'The fox knows many things. The hedgehog knows one big thing.' Get it?"

"Yeah, it's one of those there-are-two-kinds-of-people sayings. What's the point?"

"You and me are hedgehogs. Your mother is a fox. If you try to understand her, you'll go crazy. I gave it up long ago, and that's my advice to you. Just love her."

"I *do* love her. I just never know what she's going to do. It makes me all, like, nervous. I wish she'd be what Zik calls *regular*."

"Welcome to the club," said Karp, and for a while they sat companionably snacking, and then Lucy said, "Dad, me and Mary saw Caitlin the other day."

"Oh? How is she?"

"Okay, I guess. She's not that happy at her

granddad's. I think it's because she's not the total center of attention, I mean her dancing and all. Her grandfather is more interested in her brother, being an old-time male chauvinist, and it pees her off. It's like she fell out of her spaceship into a vacuum. Sometimes she reminds me of Mom."

"Caitlin?"

"Yeah, because you never know how she'll be, and also she needs to be the center of attention. I guess it's because they're both gorgeous. I guess you get used to things being easy."

"But you always said that Caitlin works like a dog on the dancing."

"Oh, yeah. I mean we wouldn't have anything to say to her if she wasn't a serious dancer. I mean she'd just be another slut-clique girl."

"Slut clique?"

"Yeah, you know, clothes and nails, and dating cute guys. Boring."

"And what clique are you in?"

"It's hard to say. I guess most people would put us in the namby-pamby clique, school geeks, but Caitlin's too gorgeous and I'm too . . ."

"Too what?"

Shrug. "I don't know: weird, dangerous. I should be a Goth, actually, but I can't stand that stupid suicide talk. Anyway, about Caitlin, I think she's going to get even more serious about it, too, make it like her whole life, like a nun. It's funny, it's almost like she didn't really care that her parents are dead, it's like a, I don't know, a *nuisance,* like she'll have to go get some new ones. Strange. But Brian's pretty happy, so . . . what's that expression, an ill wind? And . . . this is embarrassing, the first thing I thought about when it turned out to be Moussa was that I needed someone else to learn Bambara from. It's weird being cut off in the middle of learning a language like that; it's nervous making, like having a hole between your teeth. Are they absolutely sure he did it?"

"It looks pretty ironclad."

"Did he confess?"

"No, he denies it."

Lucy frowned. "What will happen to his family? He has a wife and a baby."

Karp shrugged heavily. "Don't know, babe. People do crimes and innocent people get hurt, and not just the victims."

"Could I visit him?"

"In jail? I don't think so."

"Why not?"

"They don't allow minors as visitors. Got to be eighteen, and even then you have to be a relative, or somebody official. If you want, I'll make some calls, make sure the family's not completely down the tubes."

Lucy's face lit in a way that made Karp's heart go warm. He put his hand over hers and squeezed. Both of us prickly on the outside, he thought, with a soft, velvety underbelly.

An hour or so later, the chief hedgehog was in bed, reading the first volume of Page Smith's take on the American Revolution, for Karp's One Big Thing was, of course, the Law, and its dysfunctional mom and dad, History and Politics. He looked up to greet his wife, who came in dressed in her peacock kimono, clutching a thick handful of yellow legal. This she brandished noisily in his face as she plopped down beside him.

"You know, I can write a motion," said she. "I wrote hundreds of motions, in law school and at the DA, and I thought nothing of it. Now . . . I don't know, they say you never forget how to ride a bike, but what if you get on one and you remember that riding a bike was a huge pain in the ass. How can *you* stand it? Giving two shits about what some judge said in 1937? Or what a half dozen drunk and or bribed legislators intended in 1961? This is like resurrecting a dead Marlene."

"It can't be that bad."

"Easy for you to say; you *love* this shit. Do

you think there's even the slightest chance that we could trash all this in favor of a system where we just tossed them in the water and if they sank, they're not guilty?"

"I like it. We could replace Centre Street with a lovely ornamental pool. It wouldn't be as fair and just as the way we do it now, though."

"But close."

"Extremely close. Let me take a look at that." He held his hand out; she quailed dramatically and clutched the papers to her breast. "I'm embarrassed. This is my very first real-life defense motion."

He shrugged. "Suit yourself, babe. It's probably just fine, but if not, what's a little cruel raucous laughter in open court?"

"Oh, all right! Since you insist, here! Read it, and I'll go bring in the supporting documents."

She left and Karp read slowly through the pages. Marlene had retained the fluid, rounded cursive taught by nuns in 1950s parochial schools; it was easy to read and she had made it easier by skipping every other line. Karp had read thousands of defense motions, but, like his wife, had never written one for the defense in a criminal case. It gave him a peculiar feeling, like a slugger suddenly finding himself on the pitcher's mound. Every criminal trial began with a blizzard of motions like this one, to suppress evidence, to toss out confessions, to quash indictments. Their purpose was to hack away at the prosecution's case, if the motions were granted, and if rejected, to form part of the basis for appeal — the defendant was convicted on tainted evidence, the trial judge was in error to allow it, so please reverse the judge, junk the verdict, and see if the state wanted to go for a retrial.

The substance of the present example was perfectly clear. New York and Delaware law were in agreement that a warrant obtained under false pretenses was no warrant at all, and that therefore any evidence produced by such a warrant was inadmissible in court. Here Marlene was saying that the cop who got the warrant had knowingly lied on his affidavit, that he thus had no legal right to search Sarah Goldfarb's dormitory room on the night after the alleged crime. Marlene came in and lay down beside Karp. He held out a hand and she slipped a wad of stapled photocopies into it.

He began with the police affidavit that Marlene was challenging, the sworn statement the cop had used to obtain the search warrant. As he read, Karp tried to put himself in the place of Detective Ralph Yeager of the Newkirk, Delaware, police department. He gets hauled out of bed a little past three in the morning and told to report to a Hospitality Inn parking lot off Route 301, the alleged murder scene. Karp had never been in Newkirk, but he thought it was probably another of the suburbanized villages that dot the length of I-95 from New England to Florida — a sad downtown made of two-story, brick buildings from the optimistic early century, a truncated network of streets lined with oversize wood-frame houses shaded by big trees, a factory or two, ugly sheds of concrete block and sheet metal, a couple of old mills converted into malls or outlets, and in the environs, where the farmers used to be, dull bedroom suburbs. A cop in a place like that would deal with auto crashes and thefts, some drug running, some burglary, a few pathetic wanna-be gangsters, and domestic brawls. Maybe once every couple of years, one of those domestics would go sour, and there would be a corpse. So he must have been excited, to be out there on a frosty night in November, on a homicide, and not just a dumb domestic, but something like a mystery. Yeager reports to Lieutenant Hill, who fills him in on the story, and Yeager concocts an affidavit at four in the morning that shouldn't have convinced a third-grader but obviously did convince a magistrate. Karp handed the papers back to his wife, who had been lying there pretending to read a *New Yorker.* "Good job," he said. "It's a motion."

She sighed theatrically. "Thank you. It's funny, you know when you're going to give a public appearance and you start hallucinating that you look like a clown, your makeup is all smeared, or your slip is hanging down in back?"

"My makeup is always perfect."

"You know what I mean. It's like that, irrational. While I was writing it, I kept thinking, This is dumb, I'm making some awful first-year-law-student mistake."

"It's fine, Marlene. Don't worry so much. You did good; it's a tight, cogent argument." He snorted derisively. "The classic stupid-cop trick — they always add the extra little concocted detail, in this case the bleeding suspect. It's pretty clear this guy's not an experienced homicide dick, because an experienced homicide dick could've faked the affidavit in a way that you couldn't instantly explode by easily obtained paperwork. The ironic thing is that if these idiots had conducted a decent Q and A in the first place, they could have got Jorgensen to testify to enough detail about Sarah and her room to justify a legit search. What did they get, by the way?"

"Not a lot. A trash bag that looked like the

337

one that the baby was found in. A loose-leaf book with some adolescent confessional scribblings subject to malign interpretation. A nail scissors with suspicious stains. A box of heavy-duty sanitary napkins and the cop's observation that there was no baby-care stuff in the room, the implication being that she was prepping for childbirth, but had no intention of bringing home a child. I'd rather not have to deal with that shit, and besides, it's the principle of the thing. You don't catch these guys in their lies, they're going to start lying right in your face. What are you grinning about?"

"Nothing. That was an admiring look."

"You're just glad I'm not operating in New York."

"That, too. Do you realize that it's been years since we were able to just chat about what we were doing and toss ideas around, like regular people, without worrying about you revealing something I wasn't allowed to know about. I might be smiling a lot if you keep this up."

"I hate smugness in a man," said Marlene, occasioning a guilty pang, and she thought, What's wrong with me, the poor guy puts up with my crap for years, and here he expresses a little pleasure in what I'm doing and I snap at him. She was surprised, therefore, when, instead of snapping back at her, Karp put an arm around her and drew her close to him. Could it be he understands me? she asked herself. If true, would this make me happy or sad?

All during the following day, Lucy Karp tried to think of herself as having One Big Thing. It did not work. The language talent was not something she had struggled to learn or had freely chosen. Clearly, she would build her life around it, in the way that a swallow builds its little life around flight, but it did not stand in relation to her essential being as did her father's devotion to the law or Mary's to math or Caitlin's to dance. It was too *biological*. Something of a spiky fox, then, perhaps more like Mom than Dad was willing to see, or capable of seeing.

After school, she avoided Mary Ma and the other friends with whom she usually rode back downtown on the subway. Today she would take the bus, by herself. Today, she did not care to descend the iron steps and feel the pressure of the subways, of the noise and the steamy, electrified air, nor did she want to chat, to occupy the familiar persona of a schoolgirl. Lately she found herself thinking about Tran more often, especially since the Maxwell murders.

Lucy had spent thousands of hours with him, was one of the few people in the States who knew his real story. Tran never rode the subways if he could help it. He avoided descent beneath the surface, was nervous even in a room without windows. He had been buried alive in a tunnel during the war. Upon rescue, after five days in the grave, he had learned that his wife and child had been annihilated by an American bomb. Somewhat later, after his side had won the war, he had been imprisoned and tortured, then escaped across the Pacific in a sailboat and assumed the name of a dead man, a servant of the defeated South, on the strength of whose papers he had entered the Beautiful Country. He had taught Lucy Vietnamese, and French, and fractions, and also, for reasons of his own, many less common skills that he had found useful during his eventful life, so that she was perhaps the only Sacred Heart sophomore who knew how to, say, fieldstrip a Stechkin machine pistol or use a team of irregular infantry to ambush a convoy. Sometimes it felt to Lucy as if the soul of the old guerrilla had taken up residence in her heart and head. She heard gunfire in the sounds of the city; she paused and reversed direction on the street; she ducked into doorways and watched; and then felt ashamed and crazy. He was in there, along with all the languages, and the Faith, and the regular American girlness, all rattling around and making her slew in her course like a badly stowed freighter. Had her mother planned it so? It was sometimes hard to know how much of what Marlene made to happen was by design and how much was a by-product of her strange and violent existence, the sparks shot from a rocket striking fire in the woods. She was doing dangerous work, her family was apt to be threatened, had, in fact, been attacked, and she had engaged Tran to watch her back, and her little girl.

And here was that little girl, nearly grown now, riding on the Fifth Avenue bus, despairing yet again that her life would run smoothly along any ordinary course. She could feel it build up inside her, a premonition of strange and dangerous events to come. She had discussed such feelings with Tran; Tran said that she should always trust them as guides to correct action, as they had saved his life many times in the forests and cities of his war. Or they could drive you crazy, too; he knew of men turned into quivering wrecks by a surfeit of premonition. Suddenly a loud giggle burst from her throat. People stared. She blushed and turned her face toward the window, pressed her hot cheek to the frigid glass, looked out at the bare trees of the park, black as guns against the tissue-paper sky. The incongruity of her thoughts with her present errand was what had made her laugh. Thinking of Tran, of violence, of peril, and here she was on her way to the basement of Old St. Patrick's Cathedral to bake muffins for the poor.

Every morning Karp received a printout of pending cases and a printout of available court dates, and every morning Karp uttered a curse against the anonymous politicians who ultimately controlled the criminal justice system, for there were hardly ever enough court slots for the trials that were legally required to take place. In the nearly twenty years that Karp had been at Centre Street, that system had seen huge increases in crime, in policemen, in the severity of the laws, in prison cells, and in prosecutors, but the availability of trials had stayed nearly the same. This was because trials needed judges, and since the appointment of a judge was, next to a hydroelectric dam, the largest prize in the gift of any Albany hack, and since the state legislature had been divided between the two great parties for as long as anyone could remember, and since neither of the two great parties wished to let the other have such a gift, new judgeships were hardly ever authorized. Add to this doleful state of affairs that pesky

Constitution, which requires a speedy trial, speedy having been precisely defined by the state criminal procedure law as requiring a trial within 180 days of indictment if the defendant is incarcerated. The DA's office was thus placed in a nice pickle: try the guy or let him go scot free. On Karp's list were dates showing which cases were close to having the clock run out, and these, of course, received priority, although it was nearly unheard of for a defendant actually to get a free ride in this way. The saving trick was that, as all defense lawyers knew, delay favored the defense. The defense wanted witnesses to die or leave town or forget, they wanted evidence misplaced and accomplices to recant confessions. So the DA would answer "ready for trial," the defense would ask for a continuance, and with luck no courtroom would actually be needed for some time.

Karp was abetting this fraud in the usual fashion when his pencil halted, and he drew a circle around one line of his printout.

"Murrow!" he called out. The man appeared. Karp handed him the printout. "What do you make of that, Murrow? What I marked."

"Hmm. *People v. Bustamente* is ready for trial next week. What about it?"

"There are no continuances. Jessica is letting it go forward on our schedule. What do you think she's up to?"

"Maybe nothing. Maybe she believes justice delayed is justice denied."

"Are you trying to be funny, Murrow?"

"No, sir. But why should she wait? We agreed she has no case. Why does she need time to prepare? Don't we expect her to make an impassioned speech about the abuses of the patriarchy, jerk some tears if she can, and retire from the field with her guilt assuaged and her feminazi credentials enhanced?"

"Murrow, believe me, they always delay. They're so jammed up over at Legal Aid, it's a conditioned reflex to ask for more time, *especially* if they've got no case. Siegel is up to something. Find some time on my calendar this afternoon and get Vasquez in here, say, for half an hour."

Murrow's silver pencil flashed above his tiny notebook. "Do you want Mr. Hrcany there, too?"

"I don't think we have to bother Roland on this; he's a busy man, as he never gets tired of telling me. And Murrow? Keep your ears open. In fact, this might be a pleasant day for a stroll by Leonard Street, see what your old pals in Legal Aid are up to, catch up on the gossip. In your character as the charming Mookie."

"Gosh, boss, I have a pile of work to do — I thought I'd stick close to the office today."

"Murrow . . . ," Karp rumbled.

The notebook flashed out again. "Got it. Siegel re Bustamente. Gossip."

There were three in the weekly muffin crew besides Lucy, two regulars and one ringer. The two regulars were Sister Agatha, plump, jolly, bespectacled, and officious, and Mrs. DeFalco, plump, dour, beady-eyed, and subservient, the classic Catholic good-works dyad of yesteryear. Both were in their late fifties. Sister A., as she was called, wore a shapeless navy-blue pants suit and a headdress and regretted her vanished habit. Mrs. DeFalco wore black, also shapeless, which she protected by a long, white apron. Lucy got along well enough with the two of them, submitting patiently to the sort of niggling supervision she would not have tolerated for an instant from her mother, regarding this as a necessary spiritual discipline. She understood that she was often a pain in the ass to her elders, but unlike most of her peers she did not regard this as a positive accomplishment. Beyond this duty, the two of them held no interest, which Lucy recognized as a fault, but there it was: had she prayed like Augustine, her version would have been, "Lord, make me bored, but not yet."

The ringer was different. She was a nun, like Sister A., from one of those nursing orders that frequent the unhealthier parts of the globe. Elfin of stature, elfin of face (an unattractive too-literal elfin, triangular, thin-lipped, curiously flattened, with large, protruding, dark eyes), sallow-skinned from the remains of a deep tan and the stigmata of some tropical disease, Sister Birgitta dressed always in the kind of blue cotton coveralls favored by European auto mechanics (and Moussa Feydé, Lucy recalled with a pang). She was quiet, intensely concentrated on the task at hand, and she had the look of someone who had experienced inconceivable horror. Lucy's acquaintanceship was surprisingly rich with such people, and she knew the look. Besides that, two other things about Sister Birgitta attracted Lucy: the nun had been five years in the south Sudan, and she visited prisoners. Lucy had already found that Birgitta disliked talking about the Sudan, nor did she seem inclined to teach Lucy a word of Dinka, Kalenjin, Teso, or any other of the Nilo-Saharan group, which was a pity, because Lucy's score in this interesting linguistic subfamily was a shameful zero. Which left the prisoners as a topic, and here the nun was somewhat more forthcoming. She made a weekly trip to Attica to see hard cases and did similar work on a more irregular basis at Riker's Island, where New York City jailed. Lucy and Sister Birgitta scrubbed cake pans side by side for a companionable hour after the baking was done, and the muffins were cooling, and after that they set out the long trestle tables and folding chairs in the hall of the cathedral crypt, while the other two women fired up the coffee urns and stacked the muffins in golden pyramids on plastic plates, and thick china mugs in towers. Then they opened the street doors and the homeless streamed in.

Lucy had become used to their smell months ago, and now she scarcely minded it, and in any case it was heavily cut by the scent of cinnamon and baking yellow cake and perking coffee. She circulated around the long tables, making polite conversation and little jokes with the mad, the drug-ruined, the incompetently criminous, the terminally luckless. At the end of one table she spotted Sister Birgitta kneeling in close conversation with a black man wearing a greasy headband around a mass of gray tresses that resembled dust bunnies. She was about to approach when someone tugged on her sleeve and asked her if there were any chocolate muffins left. The chocolates were prized far above the cinnamons and the chopped nuts, and some of the men scooped up pocketfuls, which was not allowed. Lucy had heard they traded well on the street, against drink and tobacco. Sister A., however, always baked the same number of each, perhaps inspired by the Federal Reserve's reluctance to interfere with free markets. When Lucy came back from the kitchen with a fresh tray of chocolates, Birgitta was standing against a wall, sipping coffee and staring at the rows of ragged men. Lucy went over to her and remarked, "They're hungry today. Or maybe it's the cold."

Birgitta said, "They don't come for the muffins or the steam heat. They come to sit on a chair, at a table, and put a paper napkin on their laps and eat from plates and make conversation with well brought up ladies like us. They have two hours of being human twice a week."

"Who was that guy you were talking to? In the headband."

"Willis? My spiritual adviser. A bright guy in between the bursts of static. He used to be a bus driver. He says holiness isn't light, it doesn't go *up* towards God, like in the paintings. Willis says God doesn't *need* no more holiness, he got the whole *factory* of it up in heaven. Holiness is heavy, heavier than forty-weight oil, which is why you find most of it in the basement of the church, and in the lower parts of the jailhouse. God's always trying to get holiness way down into hell, and those devils they keep on shoveling it back. Says Willis."

"Is that why you visit prisons?"

The nun gave her a sidelong look. "Oh, yes," she answered dryly, "I'm a seeker after holiness in the dark places. That or a masochist. I tried it for a while in hell itself, but hell wouldn't have me. How about yourself? Like the bad boys, do you?"

"Some of them," agreed Lucy. "I don't think I have, like, a vocation for the work, but I'd like to get into Riker's as a visitor, though."

"In a program, or to see someone in particular?"

"Someone. His name's Moussa Feydé."

"What's he in for?"

"He murdered the parents of a friend of mine."

Birgitta had never smiled that Lucy could recall, but now her peculiar flat eyes flashed something that might be called amusement, and her mouth tugged upward slightly at the corners. "You have to fill out a form and give them a letter showing you're of good moral character, and then they run your records and issue you a card, like this." She reached into one of the many pockets of her coverall and pulled out a large laminated photo card. "But you're too young. What're you, sixteen?"

"And a half."

The nun shook her head. "No, can't be done. You'll have to content yourself with street people for a few years longer. Come to that, you'd probably find a murderer or two in this bunch if you looked hard enough."

The tone here was meant to be hurtful, and Lucy was hurt, but said nothing. People who had suffered lashed out at any convenient target, and Lucy had enough sense to understand that it was better for Birgitta to lash out at her than at the derelicts, or at Sister A. or Mrs. DeFalco. In a funny way it was almost a compliment. But she did not feel it necessary to actually occupy the social category Birgitta had obviously placed her in — do-gooder, middle-class cookie baker — and so after the feeding was over and all had been cleaned up, Lucy went to the vestry, where there was a pay phone, and, using the roll of quarters she always carried for that purpose, dialed a number in Bridgeport, Connecticut, which represented her chief contact with the world of pain, violence, and un-muffin-baking.

"*Chao?*" said a man's voice.

"*Chao,*" said Lucy. "May I please speak with Ong Tran?"

"*Dai la ai?*"

In Vietnamese, Lucy said, "Tell him it's Lucy."

She heard the phone put down and voices in the background. Shortly a familiar voice came on the line, speaking French. "My dear! How good to hear from you. I trust everything is well?"

"Very well, Uncle Tran," she said in the same tongue. "And are you well?"

"Exceedingly so. I prosper and my health is not too bad."

"I am happy to hear it. Uncle Tran, the reason I called . . . no, I mean, if you want to, I need a slight favor."

"I see. Would this be the sort of favor to be spoken of on the phone or only face-to-face?"

"I would prefer face-to-face. Also, I miss you. And I still have your copy of *The Tale of Kieu.*"

"So you do. And what a great many reasons to want to see your old Tran, besides the favor. Very well, I will meet you tomorrow."

"Marvelous! Thank you! Where and when shall we meet?"

"Oh, go about your usual business. We will meet, never fear."

"But you don't know where I'll be."

A whispery laugh. "So you imagine. Until tomorrow, my dear."

Karp could tell that Mimi Vasquez was nervous when she sat down in his office. He was on his couch and she across the coffee table from him, sitting stiffly on the edge of her chair, unsmiling, and Murrow was off to her left in another straight chair, unobtrusive, notebook at the ready. It was the classic setup for a reaming out, especially the reaming out of someone of the opposite sex: the reamer, the reamee, and a witness.

"This is about what, Bustamente again?" she asked.

"You think you did something wrong?" Karp smiled and got a forced smile in return.

"No, but could I be frank?" Karp nodded. "I'm starting to get uncomfortable with these sidebars with you on Bustamente," she said. "I mean I appreciate your interest and all, and your help, but I really think Roland should be here for these meetings."

She was blushing, and Karp felt a pang of guilt. Lawyers who could still blush were as rare as whooping cranes and cried out for preservation. He said, "Okay, I see your position. Here's mine, so you'll know. Mr. Keegan sometimes lays on me personal responsibility for a particular case or cases, which he did with these infanticides. Now, why would he do that when Roland reports to him just like I do, and the other bureau chiefs, too? The reason is, he respects my judgment on tricky cases. Not that he doesn't respect Roland's, but sometimes he wants a different judgment, and in order to give that to him, I have to get information about cases from the horse's mouth, which is you in this case. Clearly, if I had Roland in here, I would get his take on the case, and only his, because as a loyal staff member you'd be obliged to back him up. What you're probably worrying about is whether you're going to get whip-sawed between the two of us, and you're going to have to rely on my word that's not going to happen. Does that make you feel any better?"

"Honestly? No, it doesn't. I mean, I believe you, but I don't understand why we have to play these games."

"We play these games because that's how Jack Keegan runs the office. It's a political office, and public opinion bears on cases like this. We used to have a DA here, Mr. Garrahy, way before your time, who didn't much care about politics at all. That was a different era. The media gave us a break, we were the good guys, people trusted government to more or less do the right thing. That's all gone now, obviously. We're under intense, perpetual scrutiny from people who don't trust us one bit. Then after Mr. Garrahy, we had Bloom. Bloom was nothing *but* politics, and dirty politics at that. Jack Keegan is, let me tell you, a hell of a lot more like Mr. Garrahy than he is like Bloom, for which we should all be grateful. He would never even hint at me to throw a case for political reasons or nail someone for political reasons, but he feels he has to trim his sails to the prevailing winds, or he won't survive in office. And one of the ways he does this is by playing his staff off against one another so he doesn't get blindsided on a politically important case, like I just explained. Is he wrong? I'm not in his shoes, so I'm not going to be arrogant and say so. Hell, Vasquez, the entire job would be a damn sight simpler if it was 1970 again. Plus, I'd be twenty-six and incredibly handsome."

This got a smile at least. "I'd be a zygote," she said.

"And an extremely competent and decent zygote, if I may say so. Also, if you don't mind me mentioning it, the number of female Hispanic ADAs we had in homicide back then was exactly zero. So things change, sometimes for the better, sometimes for the worse. We accept it or bail out. Are we clear now?"

Vasquez nodded, a quick jerk of the head. "Clear." She seemed to relax into her usual cool professionalism. "Okay, on Bustamente.

You know she's been indicted for second-degree murder. The plea is not guilty. She's had a routine psych evaluation for competency and passed."

"And how about for mental disease or defect?"

"Not yet, and obviously we won't ask for it unless the defense offers state of mind at the time of the crime as an exculpatory factor. Which they still haven't shown any sign of doing so far."

"Yes, we discussed this earlier. I'm starting to find it a little disturbing."

"Well . . . yeah, assuming she wants to get this kid off. Maybe she's still shopping around for an amenable shrink." Vasquez hesitated. "There's another factor. The alleged rapist, this Perez character, the brother-in-law, says it wasn't rape. He says she practically fished it out of his fly."

"He would."

"Yeah, and he also says he thought she was eighteen."

"Like hell!"

"Well, the thing is, she actually was carrying a phony ID, which was how she got into the club where she gave birth. He says she showed it to him, so he thought she was legal."

"Gosh, what a prince! He really expects

people to believe he didn't know the age of his own sister-in-law?"

"*I* don't," replied Vasquez, "not that I could swear to. I got four of them and two exes. I could say, Vera's around twenty-nine and Estrella's around thirty-four and so on, but not under oath. Hey, sixteen, eighteen, it's a toss-up. Lola and her sister weren't that close after their parents split, and this is like the first time he met her since the wedding. They'd — Perez and his wife — they'd been living in San Juan. So the third-degree rape charge on the underage point is weak. The first-degree rape charge, the forcible rape, you got her word against his. She kept it secret, there's no forensics. It's his baby, of course, but aside from that, it's the kind of case we'd ordinarily never prosecute. Roland wants to offer him a deal, testify against the girl, plead to misdemeanor sexual conduct with probation and a suspended sentence. The picture we want to paint is a slut and a conniving bitch, she screwed her sister's husband for fun, got caught, kept it secret, and killed her baby to get back to the salsa."

Karp pursed his lips, flexed his long fingers, and regarded her over their inverted V. "And what do *you* think, Vasquez? She a conniving bitch-slut?"

A bitter, short laugh. "Aren't we all? I don't

know, boss, I just follow orders. I think I can nail her on the murder two, absent some really compelling psych evidence. And that's what I intend to do."

After Vasquez left, Karp turned to Murrow. "Thoughts?"

"Lourdes Bustamente seems less of a poster girl for liberalized treatment of infanticide than she once did."

"Maybe. What did you learn at Legal Aid?"

"I chatted with Deena Mitchell."

"She of the lacy underthings in the bathroom."

"She. Her office is smaller than mine and she has to share it."

"Working for Leviathan has its advantages. Anything of interest turn up?"

"I think so. I put it to her as delicately as I could our concern about what Ms. Siegel was doing with the lovely Lola. She, too, was concerned. In fact, there's quite a little buzz going on over there, which I guess is par for the course when they have interlocking cases. Obviously, they're pleased about the Perez deal, but they can't figure why Siegel hasn't front-loaded the psych defense yet. I did get a little news about Ms. S. though. She's formed a committee to run for the State Assembly this year. She's from a liberal district in Brooklyn, and Deena thinks she stands a fair chance, if she can get some name recognition. Which a plea in Bustamente would not do, but a big, messy, sexy trial would."

"Oh, ho, the clouds part. Do you think it's possible that Ms. Siegel intends to use her closing statement in Bustamente as the first speech of a political campaign?"

"It's a good bet. Do you have a problem with that?"

"No, not unless she's setting up to tank this case to make a point," said Karp. "I would have a problem with *that.*"

12

Lucy and Mary Ma were walking east on 91st Street after school, heading toward the Lexington Avenue subway, when a black Ford Explorer with deeply tinted windows slid into a bus stop just in front of them. The front passenger-side door opened and an Asian man stepped out. He wore a green air force parka with a fur hood and sunglasses, though the sky was dull. He nodded to the girls and opened the rear door of the big vehicle and gestured for them to enter.

Mary quailed and uttered a mewing cry. Lucy clutched her arm and hissed, "Don't be scared, it's only Tran. We'll get a ride home." She smiled at the door-holder and stepped into the car, nearly dragging Mary after her. He was there in the corner of the backseat, a thin, middle-aged Asian man with an old-fashioned haircut and worn, dull-colored clothes, a shabby brown suit and a white shirt, buttoned to the collar, no tie. She was glad he hadn't gone over to slick dressing; he still looked like a guy who worked in a restaurant, if you didn't study his eyes. He had a big dent in the side of his head, and most of his finger-nails were warped into baroque lumps. She flung herself into his arms and again smelled the familiar sharp odor: fish sauce and cooking fat and lilac hair oil.

They exchanged news. He was doing well, he had three noodle shops in Bridgeport and some bars and other business interests he did not specify. He had a little house in the suburbs, and mutual funds. An American immigrant success story. They spoke in Vietnamese, until Tran remembered Mary shrinking in the corner and switched to Cantonese, and they all spoke in that language during the drive downtown, Tran drawing Mary out like a polite host, trading apparently amusing mathematical brain-twisters on a level that Lucy could not follow in any language, and she recalled that he had been a teacher in some earlier incarnation. They dropped Mary off near her parents' restaurant on Mott Street, then drove to Crosby Street and parked in front of Lucy's building.

Tran looked around and smiled. "My old stomping grounds."

"Do you miss it at all, Uncle?" Now they were speaking French again.

"The great city? Not in the least, except for you and your mother. How is she?"

"All right, I guess. She went back to being a

lawyer. She's given up the gun."

"Has she? Well, she was always of two minds about violence."

"Uh-huh." Lucy did not wish to discuss her mother. "Uncle, do you ever . . . this will sound strange . . . do you ever have a kind of waking dream about guns going off? Not just pistols, but big guns, cannon even, firing and recoiling, that sharp, clean sound and the gout of flame and the recoil. *Clang-ka-chang!* And the smell. And also explosions, not like in the films, with all that orange-fireball business, but real ones, a flash, and all the dust, and then the sound and the shock wave strike you in the face? Do you ever get visions like that?"

He considered this gravely for a moment. "No, I do not. But I will tell you what this is, though, if you wish."

"Yes, please."

"These are the ghosts of violent acts, performed by people around you, in your actual past, and by your ancestors. They wish to seduce you into the delights of murder and destruction."

"But you don't have them."

"No, because I engage in murder and destruction. I am already seduced, already an old whore, you might say."

"I thought you were a noodle king. You

said *pho* was the next pizza."

"Yes, but you understand I also own bars, which are also . . . do you know the term *bia om?*"

"Cozy beer?"

"Yes, our euphemism for places frequented by complaisant women. Also, in the back rooms there may be gambling going on. Also some of the money from this business is invested in the Vietnamese community, loans to people who could not go to a bank for money. Naturally, others are in these businesses who feel the competition and wish me to stop, so I must take measures to prevent this."

"Wow! You're a gangster!"

"In a very small way, I assure you, my dear. Now, what is this favor you desire?"

She told him and told him why she needed it.

"Yes," he said after a moment's thought. "This can be done. Suppose, let us say next Saturday, I call you at home about four. You still go to church, I assume? . . . Good, then on this particular Sunday perhaps you can arrange your face and costume so as to look as ancient as possible, and I will tell you a place to go after church. They will need a photograph. And tell me, whyever did you cut off all your hair?"

★ ★ ★

Marlene shipped her draft motion off to Wilmington and it was duly filed by Mulcahey, and a week later she put on the old harness and drove down to Dover to argue it before Judge Shearing. She left the city at dawn and arrived at the Goldfarbs just as the parents were leaving for work. They both wanted to go to the motion hearing, but they were nearly broke and had used up all their sick leave and holiday time, and Marlene had convinced them that no conceivable harm would befall their girl at a hearing with Marlene holding her pale white hand. Besides, didn't they want to save whatever free time they might accumulate for the actual trial?

In fact, there was no legal requirement for Sarah to be present at a motion hearing, but Marlene had wanted very much to get her client away from the hovering parents and determine, if she could, what made the girl tick. Sarah was wearing a roll-neck, tan sweater and a full skirt of heavy, black wool with a broad leather belt, stockings, and short, fur-lined boots, all under a tweed coat with large buttons. It was the sort of outfit that suburban moms bought for college-bound daughters in John Wanamaker's. Her hair was shiny and pulled back into a ponytail held by a silver clasp, her face nearly bare of makeup.

Marlene had chosen a calf-length, gray wool skirt, and a gray blazer over a black turtleneck, and knee-high cordovan leather boots: tough, she thought, but not menacing.

The day was bright, wintry, in the low forties, the sky's blue rags peeping from behind mottled clouds. Marlene drove slowly and carefully; they had plenty of time and she wanted to use it. Sarah asked if she could play the radio, and when Marlene agreed, the girl selected an oldies station. "A Whiter Shade of Pale" was playing.

"Not a hip-hop person, are you?"

"No, I can't stand it. Or punk. Or metal." Sarah giggled.

"Good, nor can I," said Marlene. "And forgive me for saying this, but when I think artist, someone very different from you comes to mind. I mean, black clothes, haunted look, spiked hair, tattoos, piercings . . ."

"Oh, I could never be like that!" Sarah exclaimed. "God, my parents would kill me! My friend Louise has a tattoo of a rose, though, on her ankle." She sounded wistful, making this claim to association with the demimonde. And then, more primly: "I don't think you have to do all that boho stuff to do art. Not washing and all. Besides, what I mostly like to do is teach children. That's what I want to be, an art teacher. I don't expect to, like, have pictures in museums." She laughed shyly to underscore the absurdity of this expectation.

"And Peter — I take it he wasn't part of the artsy crowd either."

"Oh, no! Peter's, like, extremely clean-cut and preppy, but he's creative, too. He's going to be an engineer like his dad."

Not if he goes up for murder, he's not, Marlene thought, and asked, "How did you two meet? What was the attraction?"

"Oh, he's gorgeous," she said spontaneously, and then laughed. "No, but, really, he's so sweet. I remember the first time I saw him, it was on the soccer field, a bunch of us were watching the team work out. This was at the beginning of sophomore year. He wasn't from Mt. Holly, he'd just moved here from New York, and he was on the team. And I saw him, he was running down one side of the field with the ball, just running, he looked so beautiful, it was like a movie or something, his blond hair. Did you ever meet him?"

"No, but I'm looking forward to it," said Marlene. "So, what, you went up to him right then?"

"Oh, God, no! I was just a sophomore. A boy I knew, Benny Green, was on the team, and he came over after the practice and Peter came over, too. I couldn't look at him. But I could see out of the corner of my eye he was

365

looking at me. And we started to hang out, you know, in a gang like kids do, we were just around, going to the movies and driving. He had an electric-blue Mustang. His father's loaded. Anyway, I was sort of finding my niche — you know how it is, in high school. Everybody in cliques? And I was sort of hung up between the arty clique and the preppy clique, not really fitting into either one. The preppy clique was like, what labels do you wear, what kind of car and stuff, and I thought that was so boring, but the kids I could talk to about painting, I don't know . . . I didn't want to be that weird. Peter made me feel, I don't know, anchored. Safe. Then in the summer that year we saw each other a lot, and like it got too sort of overwhelming . . ."

Sarah hesitated and Marlene offered, "You mean sexually?"

"That, but mostly I think we were worried about how strongly we felt about each other. I mean, we were sixteen. Peter said we should see other people in junior year, and I thought that was the right thing to do. My parents were crazy about him, though, even though he wasn't Jewish."

"So you both dated other people in junior year?"

"Yeah, but it was like, you know, marking time. We were both real busy. Peter was on the soccer team and the tennis team and I was volunteering at the Y, teaching art classes to little kids, and cheerleaders . . . it was a lot. Then he asked me to the junior prom and that was it. He gave me his soccer team jacket. We saw each other practically every day that summer, and we went steady all senior year." She sighed. "That was the best year of my life, that senior year. It was like everything was pastel, and soft, you know?"

"I can dimly recall," said Marlene. "When did the sex start?"

"In senior year, around Christmas. December 23, actually. His mom and stepfather went away skiing the week before the holiday, and Peter was supposed to go, too, but he twisted his knee. So the house was empty, and we started. He had protection and all, and we loved each other so much it seemed okay. And we kept doing it all senior year. Then when we started college, we talked and we agreed that it would be okay if we saw other people. Like it was too *intense* again, you know? But he would drive down on weekends and he'd stay with me in the dorm. My room-mate Sheila went home on weekends mostly, so we had the room to ourselves."

"Did you see other people?"

"Oh, I went on dates a couple of times, but it was just like, you know, to pass the time, bunches of us, going to movies, nothing serious. And Peter did, too. We used to talk about it. We can talk about anything, that's what's so great about him, he's like a friend, not just a *boy*friend, if you know what I mean."

"Did he?"

"Date? Yeah, but it was just the same as me, casual."

"So no sexual relationships, for either of you?"

She seemed aghast. "Oh, God, no!"

"Okay, so now tell me about this baby. When did you start it?"

Marlene felt the girl stiffen next to her and turn to look out the side window. "Don't you know all about that? I've told the whole thing about a thousand times already, to the cops, to Mr. Slotkin, to Maureen . . ."

"Yes, but you've never told it to *me*. Also, I'm afraid you're going to have to tell it many, many more times. It's a critical part of your case."

The girl sighed. "All right. I figure it must have started on the weekend of January 31. Peter came down that weekend, I know. I had just had my period and we figured we were safe. After that I didn't have a period again until July 2, or that's what we thought. Peter and I had sex on July 13, and I didn't have any period at all after that, which is why I thought that's when I got pregnant."

"But on July 2, as we now know, what you saw must have been second-trimester spotting. Didn't you think that's what it might have been?"

"No. My periods have always been pretty irregular."

"Yes, but nothing from January to July? Didn't you think that was odd, being that late?"

"I don't know, I didn't think about it," said Sarah quickly, "and then on July 21, I had my precollege medical with Dr. Seaborn. And I told him that my last period was July second, and he examined me and didn't say anything about me being pregnant."

"At which time we now know you were six months gone. You weren't showing at all?"

"No, not at all. I thought I was a little overweight, and I went on a cottage cheese diet. My weight fluctuates a lot anyway. I went to YMCA camp that August and I wore a bathing suit every day. Nobody said a thing. And I never felt anything anyway."

"Did you mention to the doctor that you were sexually active?"

A brief pause, another look out the window. "He asked, but I said I wasn't. I mean, my mom was sitting right there. What was I going to say?"

Marlene could think of any number of things to say, and could also think about going, age eighteen, to a medical exam without your mother, but she only nodded and said, "Right. And then what?"

"Okay, August I was at camp, and towards the end of the month I started to feel funny — logy, tired all the time, dizzy, and my ankles were all swollen. I put on about fifteen pounds. I started to get worried. Peter was in Europe with his folks, and when he came back, I talked to him about it. He wanted me to take a pregnancy test, go to a clinic and get tested, so at least we'd know what was going on, and we made one appointment with a clinic in Christiana, but I chickened out at the last minute. He drove me there and I wouldn't go in. I was crying right there in the parking lot. I figured if I went there, they'd take all my information and it would get back to my mother. I didn't want my mother to know."

"Sarah, you're over eighteen. Medically, you're an adult. Didn't you realize you had the right to complete confidentiality?"

This comment had no effect. "I didn't want her to know. I always went to the doctor's with my mom, so I just couldn't. Then school started. I was totally messed up. I didn't know what to do. The main thing I was worried about was one, my parents finding out, and two, that Peter would stop loving me because I was so fat and swollen. September, October, I was dizzy with headaches all the time. I was exhausted. But nobody noticed. Everybody thought everything was fine with me. And the times I saw my folks, I just couldn't bring myself to do it, to tell them. I decided to wait until Thanksgiving, when the whole family was together. I said to myself, Thanksgiving I'll tell them. Okay, now we're at November 12. Late, maybe eleven at night, I start having strange pains in my belly. They wouldn't go away. I called Peter at his school and told him I was having these pains. Maybe a quarter to one, this was. Then I must have fallen asleep."

"You got right through to him? You didn't speak to his roommate or leave messages on his machine?"

"No. Why?"

"Oh, nothing. It might be important. Okay, go on — you fell asleep . . ."

"Yes, and when I woke up, I went to the window and there was Peter's Mustang pulling up. I felt so grateful! I went right down to the parking lot and we hugged and I said I thought I might be having a miscarriage. I fig-

371

ured I got pregnant in July, so now it's early November, it's a twenty-week miscarriage. And I felt glad, it was like a miracle. Peter asked me if I wanted to go to the hospital, but I said no, just away from the dorm, so he got a blanket and we climbed into his car and he drove out to 301 and we stopped at the Hospitality Inn."

"Why didn't you want to go to a hospital?"

"Same reason, I didn't want my parents to know. Anyway, there we were in the motel. I lay down on the bed, and my stomach was really hurting by then, and I was shaking, I couldn't control it. I could barely talk and the light hurt my eyes. Peter wet a washcloth and put it over my eyes."

"You had that washcloth on all the time?"

"All the time until we left. Peter helped me pull my jeans off and my underpants. I felt a squish from down there, wet, I thought I had peed. I was embarrassed because Peter was there. Then — this part is hard to remember — it was like I was awake, and then I was asleep and then I was awake again, you know like sometimes when you're in bed in the morning and you drift in and out of sleep, but it was like more violent, awake, asleep, awake."

"You were convulsing, according to the medical reports."

"I know that now, but then it was just weird. And I was so tired, like nearly paralyzed."

"What was Peter doing while this was going on?"

"I don't really know, to be totally honest. I remember him standing there, and hearing the door opening and closing, I think twice. I asked him what happened and he just said, 'Don't worry, baby, everything's going to be all right.' Then I rested for a while and we left. We went back to my dorm room and fell asleep together. When I woke up, it was light, morning, about eight. I was bleeding, but I was like still pretty out of it. Peter said, 'I should get you some Kotex,' and he did, and I put one on. Then he left to go back to Chambersburg. I went to a twelve-thirty class, it's like an art 101 class, just showing slides. I think I dozed off in it. And I went to another class at four-thirty, my studio course, which was also a blur. I remember I just splashed some paint on newsprint. I couldn't concentrate. Then I was back in my dorm — don't ask me how I got there — and my roomie, Sheila, said I had a call, and I was going to the phone, and then, like in the next second, I was lying on the floor, and my tongue felt like a catcher's mitt in my mouth, and Sheila was kneeling there and yelling for someone to call 911. I just lay there. I could see Sheila's face up there like at the end of a tunnel, and some of the other kids. They looked scared to death. I was still going in and out, in and out. Then there were two paramedics, one of them was a black man. They took my blood pressure and I tried to tell them I was okay, I just wanted to rest for a while. They said I was real sick and I had to go to the hospital, that I was having convulsions. I didn't want to go, but they took me anyway; Sheila signed me out. I don't recall the ambulance ride at all. The next thing I remember I'm in a hospital bed and a nurse is saying to me, 'Sarah, Sarah, where's the baby?' and I go, 'What baby? I didn't have a baby, I had a miscarriage.' "

They were off the highway now, threading through the streets of Dover. At a stoplight, Marlene took a moment to study her passenger. The media typically focused on rebellious teens and all the trouble they caused, so Marlene had never considered that it was possible for a teenager not to be rebellious enough. There was no understanding it: her own daughter was practicing to be a virgin martyr of some kind, and this kid, a bright, creative, caring kid, was headed for the Dumpster, albeit a more figurative one than the resting place of her late child. She belonged in the nineteenth century, or some traditional society where guys with big mustaches and curvy knives made sure that people like Peter Jorgensen didn't get near their daughters. In a place like suburban America in the nineties she should have had a target painted on her back. Marlene couldn't wait to meet the boyfriend.

Mulcahey met them in the courthouse lobby. He assured Marlene that all their witnesses were present and prepared. They went into Shearing's courtroom. Marlene nodded to Abt and Loreno, who, she was not all that surprised to observe, was deep in conversation with the state's attorney. The judge entered right on schedule, and after the usual preliminaries Shearing asked Marlene to state the issues raised by the motion, which she did: of the seven paragraphs contained in the affidavit present to obtain the search warrant, three spoke to probable cause, and all three were based on false statements. Shearing received this blank-faced and asked Abt whether the state wished for an opening comment. Abt uncoiled his long frame and said that the state would, and gave it, at length, which was that there might have been some lack of clarity in the affidavit, but Detective Yeager had prepared it in good faith, based on information that had been given to him by his superior officer and other law enforcement officers, whom he had no reason to doubt. He then called Ralph Yeager to the stand. The detective proved to be a jowly, swag-bellied fellow of forty or so, with a dull, pink, carefully barbered look. Marlene made him as a typical hick narco cop, which is what he had recently been, a man who could be depended upon to stop any northbound black or Hispanic motorist on the interstate and search his car, and to break up a suburban pot party if he heard the wrong kind of music floating out on the street — not a man steeped in the understanding of probable cause. Abt drew from him the sources of his knowledge and got him to explain how the various inconsistencies between what he had sworn to and the actual truth had come about. An honest mistake by a hardworking cop was the message. Abt turned the witness over to Marlene with a polite smile.

She went over the same material, in the same order, only now the story was a cop so eager to get into a place he had no legal right to be that he simply made up a story to convince a magistrate. He hadn't read reports he could easily have read, he hadn't talked to people he could easily have contacted, if he had really wanted to get the truth.

"But you didn't want the truth, did you, Detective?"

Yeager lowered his head, cowlike. "I wrote down what I believed the facts were, ma'am."

"Having made no effort whatsoever to check those facts?"

"I checked the best I could under the circumstances."

Marlene then went over the police statements that Yeager said he had consulted on the night of and demonstrated that these documents did not, in fact, support his sworn statement as to what Jorgensen had said, or what Sarah had said. Yeager had simply extrapolated a plausible and useful story from hearsay and an incompetent police interview.

When Abt got Yeager back on redirect, his line was to establish that police officers routinely relied on the reports of other police officers in swearing out warrants, without having to verify their accuracy, and that the errors that Yeager had made were honest mistakes that were reasonable under the circumstances; in other words, he did not make knowing and intentional false statements with reckless disregard for the truth.

Yeager stepped down then, and Marlene called her other witness, the ambulance paramedic who had taken Sarah out of her dorm room and conveyed her to the hospital. Abt asked for a sidebar conference, and the two counsels approached the bench.

"Your Honor, we're concerned about an offer of proof here," Abt said. "The state is prepared to stipulate that defendant was not, in fact hemorrhaging and was removed from her room because of convulsions, and we are also prepared to stipulate that this fact was apparent in the ambulance-run report and that Officer Yeager had access to it. What we're concerned about is getting into a long discussion of the defendant's physical and mental state at the time she was picked up, which is not really relevant to the issues here with regard to suppression."

"Miss Ciampi?"

"Your Honor, our witness will establish independently the reasons for Sarah's removal from her room and, more important, establish the routine nature of the transfer of the ambulance-run report to the Newkirk police department. This routine nature speaks to the recklessness of Detective Yeager's ignoring a documentary fact that was virtually before his eyes when he fabricated the supposed excessive bleeding. We're not going to agree to stipulation."

The judge frowned, sighed, said, "Call your witness."

An hour later, Mulcahey and Marlene were sitting in a booth in a restaurant near the courthouse, the same one Loreno had taken them to. Sarah had gone to the bathroom, and Mulcahey used the opportunity to ask Marlene what had gone on in the sidebar conversation before the ambulance man was called. Marlene told him.

"Interesting. You thought Shearing wanted you to accept the stipulation?"

"No question. Nearly audible teeth-gnashing. And, of course, Abt was right. It was our first shot at getting Sarah's mental and physical condition onto the public record."

Sarah came back to the table. People looked up from their lunches. Some of them recognized her. There were silences and a buzz in her wake. She sat down. The waitress brought food. Sarah picked at her chicken salad, morose as she always was in public now. Mulcahey was good with her, though, thought Marlene, better than I am. He's charming. He makes her laugh, an Irish gift I lack.

Sarah asked, "How do you think we did today?"

"Hard to tell," answered Marlene. "I think we made our legal point, which was that the stuff in the warrant wasn't true and that the cop didn't spend any time or effort on finding out what *was* true. But the law in Delaware doesn't require that the facts in the warrant application be true, only that the cops haven't recklessly and deliberately lied. That's in the eye of the beholder, and I get the feeling that Judge Shearing is going to behold it the way the cops and Mr. Abt do."

"Why? That doesn't make sense," said Sarah. "A cop could just tell another cop, like, oh, 'So-and-so has four dead bodies in their house,' and then they can bust the door down? The cop could just say, 'Hey, I heard it around.' "

Marlene looked at Mulcahey and grinned. "See, our client is much too straight, which is why she needs us. No, kid, to any judge who actually cared about the Fourth Amendment, we made our case. If it comes to an appeal, that'll be one of our points. Meanwhile, we have a more serious problem."

"What?" Both Sarah and Mulcahey said it at the same time, with the usual giggles afterward.

Marlene said, "Well, we know we have a case of prosecutorial overkill here; they thought they had a monster mom, as they so charmingly put it in the New York media, but in reality they only have Sarah Goldfarb, an obviously decent kid who made a couple of ill-considered moves. So they're committed, they'd look like fools if they backed down now, and they won't back down unless I can make them look *incredibly* stupid, so that the political costs of going ahead with this absurd charge on the botched evidence they've accumulated are higher than the costs of coming out and saying, 'Hey, we were wrong.' To crank up those costs we have to establish an image of stupidity and incompetence before the public eye, for a considerable time before we go to trial."

Sarah was nodding. "Yes, I see that. But how are you going to do that if you can't talk to the papers and TV?"

"The way I just did. Legal documents are public records. Obviously, I'm not going to crank out a specious motion to publicize our case, but luckily for us, their incompetence has made them vulnerable to legitimate motions that tell our story."

Barking outside, and they looked up to see Sweety, who had been put on post outside the restaurant, holding off a band of newsies. Marlene slapped some money on the table and they made their way out the back, where Marlene had foresightedly stashed the Volvo. She put Sarah in the front seat and drew Mulcahey aside.

"Any news about you-know-what?"

"Nothing definite. The Jorgensen boy apparently went into New York the day before yesterday, with his dad, to meet with Loreno."

"Mike had people watching?"

"Like you told him." Mulcahey had an uneasy look that did not sit comfortably on his choirboy face. "Marlene, is all this really necessary? Sneaking around? Spying on Loreno?"

"You don't think he's spying on us? On you? Bet on it, kid! Who else was at the meeting? Did Brewster say?"

"Yeah, Lieutenant Hill, Newkirk PD."

Marlene whistled. "And what do you suppose he was doing there?"

"Taking a statement probably." His face clouded. "You don't think . . . ?"

"I do think. Peter is about to put it to Sarah. And Loreno will make sure it hits the media, too. Okay, we can't do anything counter until we see where they're coming from. Meanwhile, I'll see you in court tomorrow for argument." Mulcahey nodded and headed off for his own car.

Marlene opened the rear hatch on the Volvo and drove around to the street. She blasted a whistle through two fingers and the black dog stopped entertaining the press and leaped into the slowly cruising Volvo. Marlene accelerated sharply, warned her passenger, and jammed on the brakes at the next stop sign. The rear door slammed down into place and they sped away.

"You've done this before," said Sarah.

"Oh, yes. Many times. The dog loves it."

Sarah dropped into sleep soon after they left Dover. Marlene glanced at her; she looked twelve in sleep, and Marlene felt simultaneously like a white knight and a gothic corrupter of tender maidenhood, because Sarah was going to be blasted out of innocence before this was over, or not survive.

Sarah awoke as they slowed off the state road and turned into Mt. Holly. An electric-blue Mustang with a tan ragtop was parked in the Goldfarbs' driveway. The press vans, she was happy to see, were temporarily absent, probably because the hot story was down at the courthouse this morning. As soon as the Volvo stopped, Sarah leaped out and ran up the drive. The boy got out of the Mustang and embraced her. Marlene got out of her car and studied him from a distance. He was tall, with tight blond curls, and had the sharply cut and somehow forgettable American beauty of third-rank movie stars: Tab Hunter, John Hodiak, Rory Calhoun.

Marlene waited until the embrace had cooled somewhat and then went over to the couple. Sarah introduced her and the boy shook her hand politely and said he had heard a lot about her. Close up, his face was still handsome, but Marlene did not like what she saw in his eyes. The felony flicker they had called it back at the DA, the look of someone not skilled in conspiracy trying to cover something up.

"Come on, let's go inside," said Sarah.

Marlene said, "I need to head on back to Wilmington, so I'll say good-bye for now. See you in the morning, Sarah. And nice meeting you, Peter."

The boy gave a halfhearted wave. To Sarah, he said, "Let's go for a walk."

Marlene watched them stroll off down the road, locked together at the hip like Siamese twins. She got back in the Volvo, started the engine, and waited, undecided, becoming nervous. The boy had come over when he knew the parents wouldn't be home. Sex? Crazy but possible, but then why go for a walk? The temperature was in the forties and the sky was now overcast and threatening chilly rain. She switched off the engine, retrieved her cell phone and a pair of Minolta mini-binoculars from the glove compartment, let the dog out, and walked down the street in the direction the young couple had just taken.

She knew where they were going, their special place by Bethany Creek. She took the path, walking slowly, silently, with the great dog like a shadow beside her. She stopped when she heard the sound of their voices, above the burble of the water, just before the path began its descent to the river walk and the bench where the young couple were sitting. She couldn't see them, but she could see the opposite bank of the creek, which was higher and covered with dun winter vegetation, bare vines and bushes, the trunks of trees, the earth beneath strewn with last season's dead leaves, the lichenous gray of large boulders. Some of the trees were white birches, Marlene knew, which was nearly as far as her botanical knowledge went. There was movement there, a flash of something lighter. Marlene held one tube of the binoculars up to her real eye and studied the place. Another movement. It was a man. She could see his head, and the side of his face. He was crouching behind a large boulder and staying fairly still. He wore a soft hat printed with dead-leaf camouflage, and black earmuffs underneath it. No, not earmuffs, headphones.

She backed away, and when she was well up the path, she began to trot. Out onto the street she ran, away from the Goldfarbs' house, until she found another of the rustic brown signs that showed a hiking trail leading to the creek park. She ran down the trail, over uneven ground, tugged at by branches, glad of the boots and the loose skirt and her leather trench coat. When the trail met the creek walk, she ran upstream, away from where the kids were sitting. There was a little wooden bridge and she crossed on it and then bushwhacked up the low hill, hoping that the sound of the water covered her noise. At the top of the hill was a street identical to the one the Goldfarbs lived on, except these houses faced the park instead of backing onto it. She trotted back along it until she came to a car, the only one parked on the street, a Chevy Blazer, black, with tinted windows. She dialed Mike Brewster's cell phone. He answered immediately.

"Mike? We got a slight problem. Can you run a plate for me, like immediately?"

She knew he could. Any law enforcement officer retired to private security work kept contacts in the cops who would do this important service. She read off the number, broke the connection, and waited. Five minutes later, the cell phone beeped.

"Registered to Gerald Zandt," said Brewster. "He following you?"

"Why, do you know him?"

"Oh, yeah. Gerry used to work for the Philly PD. He's been Phil Loreno's PI for years. Where are you?"

"By the Goldfarbs' place. I think this bozo is doing some audio spying on Peter and Sarah, and I think Peter's in on it. This guy carry?"

"Count on it."

"Terrific! Anything else breaking?"

"Not much. My guy called in from Chambersburg. Apparently the prince had been boffing a girl up there pretty regular since the start of the school year. Willa Shields her name is. According to sources up there, it was pretty intense." Brewster paused. "Poor kid. I guess she'll have to know."

"Yeah. I'm not looking forward. Meanwhile, I need to go see Mr. Zandt."

"Uh-uh. Wait on that, Marlene, I'm leaving now, don't do anything until I get there. Marlene . . . ?"

She broke the connection, put the phone in her pocket, and then she and her dog entered the woods, going downhill through the bushes. Marlene was far from a Hawkeye, but even she could see the scrapes in the earth and the broken branches that marked the path Zandt had taken carrying his bulky equipment. She found him in a little clearing, set up behind a flat boulder. At the edge of the boulder that pointed toward the creek was a shotgun microphone, a black tube sixteen inches long, sitting on a low tripod. A cable went from this device to an amplifier and then to a tape recorder, an expensive-looking reel-to-reel model, into which the man's headphones were plugged. Zandt sat on a folding canvas stool. Besides the hat, he was wearing a hunter's coverall, in the same dead-leaf pattern. The folding stool was camouflaged, too. A good plan, Marlene thought; they didn't want to risk the boy wearing a wire, not if he was subject to loving hugs from the girl he was betraying.

Marlene walked closer. Zandt in his headphones was oblivious to her presence. She told the dog quietly that the man was an enemy and that he should go sniff the man and stay on guard. Sweety darted forward and jammed his nose against the man's buttocks where they hung over the edge of the canvas stool. Zandt shot to his feet and whirled around, ripping cables out of the recorder, knocking the microphone off the rock, yanking the headphones askew, while his hat flew off. Sweety showed him the grin of death and growled. Zandt took a step back, stumbled over his stool, and went down on his butt.

Marlene stepped into his view. "Hi," she chirped, "what are you doing?"

"Jesus! Get that goddamn dog away from me!" He said this not in a shout, but in a strained near-whisper, still hoping to conceal his activities from his targets across the creek. He was a beefy guy, with a pig-eyed, foolish-clever face and a wide, red boozer's nose. He looked like someone who would fit right in on the Philly cops, maybe in vice.

"He won't hurt you. He's a good dog, aren't you, Brutus?" Sweety took this as a cue to do his famous imitation of the creature from *Alien*, but with more saliva. "So what are you doing with all this equipment?"

"Bird-watching," said Zandt, a phony smile appearing on his broad face. "I'm a bird-watcher. I'm recording birdsongs."

"No kidding? But it's the middle of winter. All the birds have flown south. 'Sad, deserted shore, your fickle friends are leaving, how do they know, it's time for them to go?' "

Zandt stared at her, then at the dog, then at her, his eyes bulging with fear and the effort to keep the smile on his mouth. She saw his fingers pop open a button at the front of his jumpsuit, then another. Marlene said, "You think you can get your gun out before my dog rips your face right off your skull, but let me assure you that you are mistaken." She snapped out a few words in Sicilian. The dog jumped toward Zandt and placed his gaping mouth three inches from the man's ear. A thick rope of drool fell down the collar of the camouflage suit. Marlene said, "Please, please, don't even move a muscle. When he gets like this, I'm not even sure *I* can control him."

She strolled over, leaned down, reached inside the jumpsuit, and withdrew a short-barreled .38. She removed the bullets, scattered them, and tossed the empty weapon far into the bushes. Then she stopped the recorder and took both reels off it.

"Hey, you can't do that!" Zandt said weakly.

"Oh, yes, I can. I have always loved the silent songs of the invisible birds. See you in the springtime, Mr. Zandt."

13

Marlene went back to the Goldfarbs' house, sat in the Volvo, and turned on the engine, the heater, and the electric seat-warmers. She was cold, and not just from the chilly air. She waited forty minutes or so, snapping distractedly through a muddy, dog-tromped *New Yorker* from the previous summer, one of the permanent library stored in the footwell of the rear seat. The icy fury she felt at the boy and his parents and Loreno and his idiot minion slowly shaped itself into a plan. It would be hard on the girl, though, bitter as the death of love.

They came back, walking side by side, no longer embracing. Sarah looked downcast and serious; Peter looked as if he wished to be somewhere else. The girl did a double take when she saw Marlene's car still in her driveway and came over to the left-side window.

"Hi! Is anything wrong?" Sarah's voice seemed strained.

"Yeah, there is, a sort of emergency. I have to talk to you right away, and it has to be alone. Is Peter leaving?"

"We were going to hang around a little until my folks get home."

"Would it be too much if I asked you to cancel that? This is critically important."

Sarah looked glum, but complied. Marlene saw Peter's glare directed at her over Sarah's shoulder as the girl hugged him good-bye. The last hug, in all probability, Marlene thought grimly. Time to grow up.

Sarah let Marlene into the empty house. "Would you like some tea?"

"Sure, Sarah, tea would be great," said Marlene absently, tossing her coat on a chair. "I need to just set something up on your tape deck."

The stereo wall held a JVC reel-to-reel machine. Marlene fitted the stolen reels on it, rewound to the leader, and pushed play. Nothing. Fiddling with a complex of cryptically labeled switches took some time. A teakettle whistled in the kitchen. She played part of a Streisand CD, then an FM easy-listening station, then produced a series of hisses, then the sound of an afternoon TV soap opera. She cursed softly and tried another combination of switches and got lucky; the room filled with atmospheric sound: the wind, the noise of the creek. Rewinding again, she rolled the tape from the beginning. The wind, the creek again, then the voices. Marlene adjusted the volume and fiddled with the graphic equalizer to suppress the background, then sat back in one of the comfortable leather chairs. It was Sarah's voice, at first some lover chat, I miss you so much, I wish this was over, pitched high and sweet, some kissing sounds, murmurs, then Peter's voice, Yeah, me, too, baby, and so on, insincere to Marlene's ears, but maybe that was mere cynicism, based on what she knew about the situation.

Peter said, *Look, babe, um, we need to get our stories straight now, so they can't like whipsaw us against each other, you know?*

What stories? asked Sarah.

You know, what happened in the motel, with the baby.

God, Peter, I told that story a million times. I don't know what happened in the motel. It was all a blur. You did everything.

Sarah's voice, in real life, strained, from behind Marlene: "What is this? What's that tape?"

Marlene stood and faced her. "It's a recording of the conversation you and Peter had down by the creek."

"You *spied* on us!" An outraged shriek.

Well, well, thought Marlene, the girl is capable of anger. "Not me. A private detective employed by Peter's lawyer got it from across the creek using a special microphone. I took it away from him."

Dropped mouth. "I don't believe it."

You could remember if you tried harder, baby, Peter's taped voice urged.

Sarah was standing with a tray full of tea things. Her knees seemed to give way. Marlene grabbed the tray, stashed it on the coffee table that stood before the set of armchairs, and sat Sarah in one of them.

Come on, please, for me, Peter urged. *You don't want me to get convicted, do you?*

Of course not . . . but I don't get it — I just told them the truth.

No, that's not how I remember it, Sarah. I mean I was trying to protect you when I said what happened, but it wasn't true. And now you've got to help me.

Help you?

Yeah. Look, you were lying there on the bed in the motel. The baby came out. You sat up. You saw the baby. We both looked at it. And you said, "Get rid of it! Get rid of it!" And I said, "No, we have to call an ambulance. It could still be alive." And you said, "No, get rid of it. You have to make it go away. This can't be happening to me." That's the way it happened, baby.

Sarah threw her hands up to her face as the penny dropped. She was as white as the china tea mugs. "No!" she cried at almost the same time as her recorded voice cried, *No!*

No! Peter, that's not what happened. I was

394

*having convulsions . . . I blacked out. I don't re-
member saying anything like that.*

So you're saying I'm lying? The voice had become angry, petulant.

No!

*Then what? I thought you trusted me. I thought
you loved me.*

*I do. I do, but . . . this is crazy. It's driving me
crazy . . . honest to God, Peter, I don't know
what to do.*

The voice turned softer, insinuating. *Hey,
take it easy, babe. I didn't mean to get you upset,
but, you know, they say that when people have
traumas, they, like, forget things they did and
said. Maybe that's what's going on. You said
some things, and then you forgot them. Maybe
that's it, huh?*

A long, hissing silence on the tape. Then
Sarah said, in a voice almost too low to make
out, *Yeah, I guess. Maybe that's it.*

*Yeah, you said, "Get rid of it," and all that,
and then you sort of suppressed it. Maybe you
were embarrassed, huh?*

*I guess. Could we stop talking about it now,
could you just hold me?*

Sure, honey, whatever you . . .

A clattering sound, and the tape went silent. Marlene said, "That's when I must have
arrived. It interfered with his recording, I
think." She stopped the tape machine and re-

wound the tape. When she faced Sarah again, the girl had wrapped her thin arms around herself and was rocking slowly, the classic attitude of despair.

"He was just scared," she said, mainly to herself, "he was scared and they made him do it. They brainwashed him, like those cults."

Marlene knelt at the girl's feet and took her hand. Ice; and the face pale, lips the color of earthworms and quivering. Marlene said, falling again, irresistibly, into the gentle way of talking to a child, "That may be true, Sarah, but here's the thing: he *did* do it, and it's part of a plan. It wasn't just random. He was trying to get you to confirm, on tape, something we think he's already told the police. He fed you a story that set you up as the director of the criminal plan. We know he had an interview with them the other day in his lawyer's office. We think, no, we're almost certain, that Peter's about to make a deal with the state, which has got to include testifying against you. He didn't think up those questions by himself, down by the creek. He was following a script, trying to get you to admit culpability, that you knew you had delivered a baby, and that you ordered him to kill it."

Sarah drew away, pulling her hands to her chest. "No! He wouldn't do that. He'd never do that. He loves me."

"Yeah, he says." Marlene took a deep breath, fixed the girl with her one eye, and said carefully, "Sarah, I'm sorry, but I've had people looking into Peter's doings, private detectives, I mean. It's a part of my responsibility to you as a client. And they've just informed me that he's been carrying on a serious affair with a girl named Willa Shields, up at his college for at least seven months."

Sarah's face transformed itself into a tragic mask, the mouth stretched down, the eyes empty. An instant later, she howled and struck out at Marlene with her fist. It wasn't much of a blow and Marlene barely felt it glance off her chest. This sort of thing happened to Marlene all the time. When the realization at last penetrated the woman's love-drugged mind that the guy *didn't* care, that he *really* wanted to hurt her, that he actually *liked* it, rage and self-contempt was the normal reaction, and the rage was often directed at the nearest human, who was likely to be helpful, caring Marlene Ciampi. She'd been shot at in similar circumstances.

After this, the expected waterworks and screaming. The tea tray got kicked over, making a mess. Marlene got paper towels and a wad of tissues from the kitchen, stuffed the tissues in the girl's hand, and started to clean up the mess, reflecting sourly that private eyes in the movies, not to mention lawyers, were never shown cleaning up any messes, but somehow she always wound up doing it.

The front door opened and in came Mom. Marlene sighed. It was Mom who was *supposed* to clean up the mess, but here Selma Goldfarb dropped the briefcase she was carrying and cried, "What's happening! What happened!" then raced to her daughter's side. Clutching the moaning girl protectively, she glared at Marlene. "What did you do to her?" she shouted.

Marlene stood and deposited a dripping, crockery-filled wad of towels into a nearby wastebasket. She explained briefly and indicated the tape machine. "Play that tape when you get a chance."

The mother took this in blankly and clutched more tightly at her daughter. Sarah had descended into mere hysterical sobbing. The two of them swayed together in the traditional way. Marlene thought her work was over here, it was the "Hi-yo, Silver" moment. And she had her own family to look after. She cleared her throat and said, "I'll let myself out. I'll be in touch. Don't speak to anyone about this, and absolutely not to Peter or his lawyer. Do you understand?" Selma nodded and Marlene grabbed up her coat and left.

Back in the car, Marlene rubbed her face

and considered her next move. In all, she was glad this crisis had come. Hell hath no fury, right, and the kid was going to need a little hellfire in her to get through the coming months. Marlene took out the cell phone, raised her troops, and conveyed orders based on the changed situation and her expectations of what the opposing forces — and these now, of course, included the codefendant and his lawyer — were likely to do in the next few days. Then she turned the nose of the Volvo north toward home. The dog nuzzled her thigh and she absently caressed his ears. "Sweety, you know why I'm so good at this job? It's because I just *love* people."

After a week in which she was increasingly nervous and distracted, Saturday came, and Lucy Karp went up to Old St. Patrick's to confess. As Lucy, unlike her mom, and like the priest concerned, was definitely a post-Vatican Catholic, this took place not in the traditional little booth, but in an office in the rectory, a dark, paneled room lined with muddy oil portraits of nineteenth-century prelates. Beneath these, miscellaneous furniture stood forlornly against the walls, interspersed with wooden and steel filing cabinets and document boxes. The center of the room was occupied by a thick, black oak table, which was surrounded by straight chairs covered with worn, faded red velvet. This must have been an important room when the church had been the actual cathedral of New York, but now it was used for occasional vestry meetings and storage, and for occasions such as this. The priest sat at the center of one side of the table and Lucy across from him. He was named Michael Dugan, and the Karps, *mère et fille,* both thought he was a spectacular find in these, the slim-pickings days of the Church. He was an Irish-American of the dark-skinned, blue-eyed, black-haired type, with a long-skulled, bony intellectual face set atop a tackle's body. He was a former Jesuit, booted out of the very highest circles of that order for some unspecified crime, which would in itself have fascinated both Lucy and her mother, but besides that, he was just exactly the sort of thinking priest both of them required. It was all very well to say *ex opere operato,* not the worker but the work, and it didn't matter to whom you confessed, it was a sacrament, but the plain fact is that opening your heart is hard enough without having to cope with a jerk. For Father Dugan's part, he considered that the pair of them presented him with an almost medieval feast of spiritual conundrums. He was not happy as a parish priest, although of course a good soldier, not a complainer, and regarded this particular duty as a cup of water in a dry place and took it as a sign that he was not entirely abandoned.

After the usual schoolgirl faults had been dispensed with — anger, sloth, petty cruelties — Lucy turned to the meat: "I have to do something that's illegal, although I think that morally and spiritually, it's the right thing to do."

"Really. That's setting yourself pretty high, isn't it? Our Lord commanded us to render unto Caesar."

"Yes, I know that. But morality and the law are never an exact match. Those priests in other countries, in Communist countries, and in Salvador. The law offended their consciences, and they resisted."

"I grant your general point, but sin consists in particular acts. What exactly are you planning to do?"

"I'm going to visit a prisoner in jail, using false papers. They won't let me in otherwise because I'm too young."

"I see. So you're actually breaking one of God's commandments — not to bear false witness — in order to accomplish what you believe is a great good. That must be quite a good. Is this person in jail a close friend of yours?"

"No, not at all. He's . . . gosh, it sounds weird to say this . . . he's the man who murdered the Maxwells, my friend Caitlin's parents. We found the bodies."

"I see," said the priest blandly. It was not nearly the most outrageous thing he had heard from the female Karps over the years. "And why do you want to see him so much that you're willing to break the laws of God and man?"

"I don't know; I just feel it's the right thing to do. He's all alone, and he did a terrible thing. He must be suffering. He's a Malian and he can barely speak English and he's in a strange country, and I don't even know whether his wife knows how to get in touch with him."

"Lucy, there are official agencies for that kind of thing."

"I know. And I know it's not just that, although I would be glad to help in that way, if I could. It's . . . like, I didn't know this man very well. His name is Moussa Feydé, and I was attracted to him because he was going to teach me Bambara, and we spent a little time together at the Maxwells, and, well, I liked him. He was nice, polite, he wanted to learn and do well. And he seemed religious. A Muslim, but devout. And, for him to do this horrible thing, to kill sleeping people and steal, it just knocked me out, you know? Like, how could I have been so wrong, why didn't I see it in him? And I want to see him again. I want to ask him why he did it. If he knows. Does this sound crazy? I was talking to Sister Birgitta the other day, at coffee and muffins, about good and evil being mixed up down in the depths, and it came into my mind that I had to see him. Had to."

Father Dugan took a moment before replying. Lucy had intimated from time to time that directions came into her mind as from Elsewhere, although thankfully she was too sensible a girl to claim these as divine messages. So far. As a priest, he was, of course, obliged to believe that heaven occasionally spoke directly to people, choosing with some frequency devout young girls like Lucy Karp as recipients of such communication. As a modern man, on the other hand, he was hard-pressed not to assume that people who heard voices telling them to do illegal things were crazy, especially when such people had brains that were clearly out of the ordinary, such as Lucy's. Fortunately for Lucy, he was an extremely intelligent man, and thus, like Lucy's father's ideal prosecutor, capable of holding two conflicting ideas in his mind at once.

"Have you considered," he asked, "whether it might be your injured pride urging you in this way? You thought the man was decent and he was not, and so you have to expose yourself to him again, hoping to find some evidence of depravity to make you well with yourself again?"

Lucy nodded vigorously. "Yes! Yes, I did consider that. Is it just pride? And I don't think it is. It's like you always say, Father, you have to consider the character of the presumed wrongful act. Is it easy, something that gives pleasure? No, it scares me, going to a jail, talking to a murderer. An alleged murderer. Will it make me look good and get praise? No, the opposite. Will it injure anyone? No, except maybe me, and it might do some good." Here she dropped her eyes and colored slightly. "So, you know, it's probably not, um, demonic urgings. St. Teresa said that the way you distinguish messages from God from messages from the devil is that the ones from the devil make you feel proud and the ones from God make you feel humble."

Father Dugan allowed himself an inward sigh. This was far, far from "my boyfriend wants to do it," a more usual issue among six-teen-year-old girls; and it engaged priestly muscles long out of practice. St. Teresa, indeed! "You know, in the old days I would have either ordered you to clear this nonsense out of your head, and forbidden you to break the law, on pain of mortal sin, or else I would have gone running to the bishop with the news that the parish had produced a saint. You're not thinking about trying out stigmata, I trust?"

"I thought it wasn't something you tried, it was something you got," said Lucy severely. "Anyway, I don't think I'm the type. I didn't ask for all this, you know."

"I know. I didn't mean to seem facetious, either. For the record, I have to tell you not to do what you're contemplating. What you actually do, of course, is upon your conscience. Is there anything further?"

There was not, and the priest performed the necessary absolutions. Walking the girl out of the rectory, he said, "We haven't seen your mother around lately. I hope she's well."

"She's fine. She's working out of town a lot. She's a lawyer now."

"Really. All that . . . shooting and the rest, she's given it up?"

"So she says."

Father Dugan held his palms out wide and gazed upward. "Yet another instance of the power of prayer." He grasped the girl's shoulder. "And I'll pray for you, too, kid."

Having sanctified her spirit, Lucy now tripped down Mulberry Street on a mission to puff up her vanity. Lucy's vanity was ordinarily unpuffy in the extreme, a small, lean animal the size of a vole, living in a deep burrow. But now that adornment carried a higher purpose (necessary to make herself look older for her jail expedition), she found herself quite looking forward to buying a new outfit. As a side benefit, she would get to go to Caitlin's *Sleeping Beauty* in a garment that made her look like something other than the complete dweeb she was. The ballet-school performance was likely to be the most glamorous event she would attend anytime within the next decade, and, she told herself, she did not want to embarrass her friend. Lucy was superior to most of her age cohorts in self-examination, but still distant from saintly perfection.

The place she now visited (nearly the only place, in fact, where she ever shopped, where she had been buying her own clothes since the age of thirteen) was the St. Anthony of Padua Resale Shop on Mulberry. Because of the neighborhood from which it drew its contributions, St. A.'s was overstocked with black, dowdy garments, cheap suits, bowling shirts, and one of the metropolitan area's largest collections of used parochial-school uniforms. This was fine with Lucy. Her school no longer demanded uniforms as such, but, to her mother's despair, she chose to dress herself in strange combinations of crested jumpers, little cotton, collared shirts, and plaid skirts, accessorized with the sort of scarves, bangles, and embroidered gear favored by recent third-world immigrants — the Catholic schoolgirl from Mars.

The proprietor, Maggie Burke, was a retired union organizer with a cigarette-scrunched face and a wild shock of dyed-orange hair. She looked up from where she sat behind the counter as Lucy entered and, smiling broadly, greeted the best customer for her most sluggish stock.

"I got a Holy Rosary outfit for you, from 1955," she said. "Maroon. It's got a Communion medal on it."

"Not today, Maggie. I need like a real outfit."

Maggie put down her *Nation* and raised an eyebrow. "What, like a prom dress?"

"No, more of a suit. I want to look older, a professional look, dark, you know, conservative but classy. I have to wear it to a concert and a party, too."

Maggie stood up and looked Lucy over. "If you don't mind me saying so, it's about time. What, a seven? Turn around. Jesus, what a waist! I had a waist like that for about twenty minutes back in the third Roosevelt administration. Let me think." She thought. "Something just came in that might work." She went into the rear storeroom, rummaged noisily, returned with a black garment on a hanger, and spread it before her on the glass counter.

"God knows we don't see many of these. This is from an estate load: Bishop Murragh's sister died last week. She was loaded and she never threw anything away. Look at the label."

"Chanel," Lucy read. "Like the perfume?"

"Exactly. What you got here is the concentrated essence of the exploitation of the working classes." Maggie turned the suit jacket partly inside out. "See this? Tiny, tiny stitching. Girls your age ruined themselves making this, went blind and crippled. Feel it. That's all cashmere, and the lining's heavy silk. Thing'd stop a bullet. I figure late forties, early fifties, the so-called little black suit. Go try it on."

Lucy did and looked at herself in the dusty full-length mirror, with Maggie fussing behind her, tugging. The jacket was double-breasted, with many small cloth buttons, and satin ribbon trimming the lapels.

"I don't know," said Lucy, looking. It was like wearing a costume for a play, or armor. The suit had a faint smell, of camphor and a flowery perfume. An old-lady odor, somewhat creepy.

"Don't be crazy, it fits you like a glove, and you're taller than she was so the length is right. I got shoes for you, too, from Bendel, same era."

"I hate heels."

"These are low. Black calf, worn maybe three times, probably cost a month's salary for a brickie. The rich!"

Lucy walked out with the suit and the shoes and a strand of paste pearls that Maggie said were actually imitations of real ones that the wives of plutocrats wore in public in order to keep the insurance down, all in an old Saks shopping bag. Lucy dropped the suit off at a dry cleaner's and then went back on Prince and up Broadway to the Village, where she stopped in at a hair joint and had them do what they could with her hack job. They gave her a trim and a moussed look, the short hair slicked back like a taxi dancer's in a twenties movie. After that she went into Tower Records on 4th Street and flipped through CDs, getting up her nerve for the requisite next step. This was located half a block away and called Faces.

Behind the counter was a young, round, seraphic Latina woman, dressed in a powder blue smock, and surrounded by glass shelves loaded with every cosmetic product manufactured in the civilized world.

"Do you know about makeup?" asked Lucy.

The woman grinned and mugged, looking around her in that New York gesture that denotes amazement the question was ever asked.

"Okay, I don't know *anything* about it," Lucy admitted, "but I have to look older. Could you show me how and sell me the stuff I need?"

"Absolutely. Sit down there in front of the mirror. You want to get into clubs, right?"

"No, into jail," snapped Lucy with some satisfaction.

The plan was to hang out in the Village for the rest of the afternoon, shopping for the other things she needed, grab a bite out at around six, pick up the suit on the way back, slip into her room, get the call from Tran, dress in the new outfit, redo the makeup, and scoot out without anyone noticing. The call from Tran came through, but the plan was doomed in its final goal, there being two skilled criminal investigators on the premises, who knew very well that something was up. Karp nabbed her as she was slipping out the door.

"Whoa!" he cried. "What is *this!*"

"Dad . . ."

"Hey, Marlene, come here!"

The Mom trotted down from her office. The boys came out of their room.

Marlene walked up to her daughter, smiled, and extended her hand. "How do you do, I'm Marlene Ciampi. And you are . . . ?"

Zak explained, "It's really Lucy, Mom."

Giancarlo said, "Lucy looks like a TV lady."

"Mom . . . ," said Lucy, flushing under her makeup. She had on an almost black shade of lipstick, false nails to match, bronze eye-shadow, mascara, false lashes, a powder base, and blusher under her cheekbones.

Marlene said, "Turn around." Lucy turned, mumbling under her breath. Marlene palpated the suit. "This is gorgeous — where did you get it?"

"Maggie's, at St. A.'s. It's a Chanel."

Marlene raised her eyes to the ceiling and crossed herself. "Thank you, Jesus." To her husband she said, "My daughter's wearing a Chanel suit, I can officially die now."

"I have to go now, Mom," said Lucy, easing toward the door.

"You don't have a coat."

"I don't need a coat, Mom."

"Of course you do, it's thirty degrees outside. You can wear my leather." Marlene ran off and came back with the lined trench coat and a smoky Hermès scarf.

When these were emplaced, Lucy asked, "*Now* can I go?"

"Are we actually going to let her go out like that?" asked Karp.

"Of course not," said Marlene. "Lucy, go back to your room and get undressed."

"*Mom!*"

"Take a gun," said Mom as Lucy sailed through the door.

"When will you be home?" yelled Karp. No answer. He felt a familiar fear, but in a new, disturbing flavor. His daughter had been shot at by professional murderers, but this was different.

It was past two-thirty in the morning when Lucy rolled in.

"Well?" said Marlene. She was leaning against the kitchen doorway, in her flamingo gown, smoking a cigarette.

"Tell me you weren't waiting up for me," said Lucy warily.

"Actually, I got up a little while ago. I've got this case on the brain. Things are starting to break open, and . . . I don't know. It's hard to cope. So, how was it?"

"It was great. Thanks for the coat, by the way," Lucy added, hanging it up. "It *was* cold."

"Don't mention it. Did Caitlin do okay?"

"Oh, a lot more than okay. I mean she's not the star, that's Sleeping Beauty, Aurora, they call her, but she's onstage more than any other dancer, and she has this incredible solo in the prologue. Anyway, when she danced, a kind of sigh came from the audience. I was crying, it was so beautiful. My mascara was all over my face. Does that always happen?"

"It's one of the burdens of womanhood, my child."

"Anyway, I kind of felt sorry for the girl who danced Aurora, I mean Caitlin just blew her away. She was mobbed afterward, and it was neat, like in the movies, there were all these people around her with flowers and stuff, congratulating her, and when she saw me, she kind of pushed through all of them and hugged me, and Mary, too. I thought that was kind of terrific of her. I mean *I* would do that if I was getting famous, but Caitlin's, I don't know, you could say she's easily distracted. And I heard people arguing, she was another Darci Kistler, no, another Allegra Kent, no, another Suzanne Farrell. Ballet people are apparently always doing that, who's like who, or better than. And it really was kind of fantastic, the way she danced, you could feel it, like dancing was all she had left, she was spilling her guts up there. She was always gorgeous and talented, but tonight she had something extra, and everybody knew it. Madame Vernova was crying, and Mr. Rodenski came backstage, which apparently he never does at a school performance, and gave her strokes. Then we all got into limos and went to the Plaza, where the school threw a party and everyone was being totally la-di-da, and some dance bigwig gave a speech and mentioned Mrs. Maxwell and what a great person she was, and how they all wished she could have seen her daughter's triumph. Everybody was looking at her, and they had a spotlight there, right on her. I thought Caitlin was going to lose it, but she was like ice, just nodded and smiled. Incredible applause, but, really, it was a little scary, how calm she was. Then we went to a party at a loft on Broome, which turned out to be Caitlin's boyfriend's place. I was freaked because he was like thirty or something, but nice in a kind of disgusting way, very artsy-fartsy, and there were some other old guys there, kind of lusting after the dancers, which I thought was pretty gross, but apparently that's part of the life, and not just, or even mainly, the *girl* dancers, if you know what I mean. They played tango music and everyone danced, and it was great, to see them just dancing for love, for themselves, not to impress anyone, it was sort of heavenly, like being in on a secret, like on *National Geographic*, where they show you, I don't know, the unknown life of cheetahs."

"And did you dance?"

Eye-rolling. "Oh, right! Be serious. I stood in a corner and watched. I was a little drunk, too, all that champagne. I never liked champagne before, but now I do. Maybe it was the brand. Is Taittinger good?"

"Many think so. And then what? Opium dens?"

"Please. No, just dancing. Tango, and then some weird pygmy music, and samba. Girls were flying through the air, it was incredible. The only strange thing was that I went to the john and it was locked and I heard crying, and it was Caitlin, and she let me in and like totally fell apart. She said I was her only friend, and all the people who were making nice to her really hated her or were after a piece of her, now that she was going to be famous, and she hated her grandfather, and wanted to move in with Mitchell, that's the boyfriend, but she had to wait until she was eighteen. So I hugged her and I said I'd always be her friend, and so on, and we fixed her up and went out again. I took the phony eyelashes off then, too. The funny thing was, when I went to leave, she was hanging out with Mitchell and a couple of his friends and it was like I didn't exist. Or maybe that's love, it gives you tunnel vision."

"It does," said Marlene, "but remember, the poor kid has had an incredible blow, losing both parents, and just now a huge emotional night, on top of the fact that artists tend to be a little peculiar at the best of times. If you hang out much with them, you should be prepared for some rough rides." Marlene yawned. "I'm going to crash. See you in the morning, kid." She kissed her daughter tenderly. She thought, with Yeats, Oh, my flourishing hidden tree. "You looked great tonight. One tip, if I may: ease up a little on the makeup. You go around looking like you're twenty-two, guys are going to start treating you like that, which you may not like. I don't think Caitlin is a role model here."

Lucy smiled weakly, suppressing a pang of guilt. She *had* danced at the party and *had* been treated as twenty-two by a couple of decrepit thirty-something lechers, and she was not sure how she felt about it. In general, it was thrilling in a sort of sick-making way, like a particularly sadistic amusement-park ride, but she was happy to be able to do it at all, the clothes and makeup part of it, and accepted it as another in her bag of useful skills.

"You going to the ten-o'clock tomorrow?" Lucy asked.

"Yes. You?"

"No, I'm going to the eight. I have some things to do early and then I'll probably crash all day."

After the early mass, Lucy, in her killer outfit, after a stop in a coffeehouse rest room to put on the paint, proceeded to the address she had been given on Saturday afternoon. It was on Lafayette off White, a typical Chinatown hole-in-the-wall place, with handmade signs in a variety of Asian languages announcing the availability of pagers, money orders to the Far East, phone cards, gold chains, cutlery, and passport photographs. Lucy went down the four steps and into an area about the size of a suburban kitchen, with glass display cases showing the shop's unlikely assortment of wares, with the prices clearly marked, and a glass counter, behind which stood a young Asian man with the usual bad haircut and burning Marlboro.

Lucy said who she was, in Vietnamese, and got a smile without much warmth, and an invitation to please step into the back. He locked the street door and led her through a green cloth curtain to a dim, narrow hallway smelling of anise and cooking rice, and a little alcove holding a straight chair, a blue background cloth, and a big Polaroid camera on a stand. Lucy sat in the chair and the man took two flash pictures. He told Lucy to wait outside. She waited, thumbing through a Vietnamese magazine, for fifteen minutes, after which the man returned and handed Lucy a plastic card with a clip attached. The card had Lucy's picture on it. Thanks to the alchemy of the ID camera, she looked to be in her late twenties with a lot of hard miles. The card was issued by the New York City Department of Corrections to Juliet F. Murphy, of the Social Sciences Department of Marymount College, and was a three-month facility pass of the same form issued to legal types and others with a need for a free run of Riker's Island. Lucy put it away, wondering vaguely if there really was a Juliet Murphy who was missing a pass, or if Tran had just caused the identity to emerge out of thin air onto a counterfeit pass form.

"How much do I owe you?" she asked the man.

A broader smile. "Oh, nothing. It's all taken care of. Please give my respects to your friend." He unlocked the street door and showed her out.

Lucy walked to Canal and Broadway and descended into the subway. She was happy to get out of the chill, for she was wearing only her old, unlined raincoat, disdaining to don the pea coat she usually wore to school, as being ridiculous on top of her suit. She took the number 6 train uptown to 51st, switched to the eastbound F, and traveled to Queens Plaza, among a sketchy crowd of sleepy Sunday riders. She crossed the street and shivered in the wind at the bus stop, along with a straggling line of waiting women and children, nearly all of them black or Hispanic. It was a day for visiting prisons, that wind slashing down through the broad thoroughfares of Queens, the sky ten feet high and pressing, an Akhmatova day. After half an hour, a Q101 bus arrived with "Riker's Island" showing in its destination window. The bus filled, and as the sticky diesel warmth sank in, the atmosphere picked up, becoming congenial in a sisterhood-of-the-damned way, anticipatory and noisy, like a factory picnic. Lucy struck up a conversation in Spanish with a young woman not more than two or three years older than she, with a toddler in her arms. She was visiting her boyfriend, a junkie burglar, but nice to her and the child, she hastened to add, no hitting, not like some of them. And you? Visiting your boyfriend? No, just a friend. What's he in for? Murder. Lucy had the odd experience of being deferred to by someone older, an artifact, she supposed, of her dress and makeup, and maybe the nature of her visitee's crime. Lucy gathered from various remarks that the woman assumed Lucy was a Mexican, and a courier of the sort through which big-time *narcoleros* kept tabs on their empires. She found this oddly flattering.

At the visitors' center, a modern building at the end of the Riker's Island bridge, Lucy went to the gate designated for pass-holders and was waved through without a second glance. She learned at the desk there that Feydé was being held in the John A. Thomas Center and boarded a Corrections bus for that destination. There are ten jails on Riker's Island, and as Lucy could observe out the grimy windows, most of them were low concrete structures that looked, except for their corsets of razor wire, like the most undistinguished type of motel. The Thomas Center, formerly the Men's House of Detention, is a one-man-cells maximum-security clink, where Riker's keeps its hard cases, and was unmistakably a prison. It was tall and made of orange brick and decorated around its entranceway in that peculiar faux-Babylonian style beloved of thirties public architects. It looked, and may have been meant to look by that less sentimental age, like the gates to hell.

Her pass was checked again and passed muster, and she found herself in the traditional room with the long tables and the glass shields and the heavy telephones that communicated across the few inches between the prisoner and the visitor. Moussa Feydé looked frail and very black in his orange jumpsuit, but he had a look of anticipation on his face when the guard led him in, a look that quickly changed to confusion. He sat on his chair and picked up his phone. Lucy saw that his lip was split and swollen, as was the skin around his eyes.

It occurred to Lucy, with something of a shock, that he might have no idea who she was, so she said into her phone, speaking French, "M. Feydé, I'm Lucy Karp. We met at the Maxwells' house. You thought I was a demon and you were teaching me Bambara." She saw the knowledge come into his face, but he did not smile.

"Yes. I remember. But you look very different. Like a young woman and not a schoolgirl."

"This was to enable me to come here and see you. A disguise."

"That was a lot of trouble to take," Feydé said after a staring moment. "You must wish to learn Bambara very much."

Lucy felt herself blushing and her throat

went dry. She had, as he said, spent considerable effort arriving at this place and now found herself unsure about her purpose. Temporizing, she said, "I thought you might need something. Or I could help your family."

"This is a charitable visit? Then, thank you, but we require nothing. My family is being taken care of by the Muslim community, and I have no needs that you can satisfy. We only have fifteen minutes. It will be hard for you to learn my language in pieces of time fifteen minutes long."

This was going all wrong. "How did you get hurt?" she blurted.

He touched his bruised mouth. "This? A fight. I was assaulted. I have never been in trouble with the law before this, or in jail, and I did not know how to behave. Now I am in a cell by myself and never leave it, so there is no more trouble."

A silence now. Lucy listened to the crackle of the phone and hated herself for a pretentious jerk. Did she think this man would be *happy* to be visited by a strange girl who couldn't but remind him of his crime? He interrupted these vile thoughts with, "So, now you have seen me, that the beast is safe in a cage, you can go and sleep safely."

"That's not why I came," she snapped.

"Why, then?"

"I wanted to know why you killed them. I knew you, and I liked you, and felt bad about myself that I didn't see you were evil. And I prayed about it, for what to do, and I . . . got told to come."

"Told by God?"

She was sweating now, in embarrassment and shame. "Yes."

"God speaks to you often?"

"Not often, but sometimes I have a sense of a voice, yes."

"I, too. It is very comforting. As to why I killed them, it is very simple. The man insulted me and I killed him, and his wife awoke and I got frightened and killed her, too. We Africans are violent and have very little control of our impulses, as all the world knows. There, you can go home now and tell God you have obeyed His command."

"I thought you said you didn't do it. You pleaded not guilty."

He made an elegant, dismissive gesture. "A matter of form, on the advice of my lawyer. I am sorry you are shocked. Listen, in my country, we believe in fate. We don't struggle against it, wiggling like frogs, as you do. This is my fate. I had an interesting life, more interesting than the ones most of my countrymen have, and had work that gave me pleasure. God was generous with me. Or so I thought.

Then I wished to travel to far countries. When my father advised me not to leave Bamako, I didn't listen to him, but he was right, and see, now my life is over. I wish the trial would be soon, because here there is nothing for my hands to do, and when my hands are idle, my mind grows worms. It is very distressing. They tell me that in the prisons, there is work, building furniture and so on. Is this true, do you know?"

"I believe it is, in some places."

"I hope so. If not, I will go mad, and not be Moussa anymore, and it won't bother me. I am very fond of furniture. I am amazed by the care and labor that goes into a fine piece. Some will say, For what, so a rich fool can be proud? But the love that goes into the thing itself is what matters. This is of God. That piece, the reisner I was working on, was a lovely thing. Did you see it?"

"Yes, before you worked on it."

"Oh, well, it is more beautiful now." And he drifted into a technical discussion of what he had done, and Lucy gladly let him talk until the guard came to take him away. She asked him at the end whether she might visit him again and he nodded, and for the first time, she saw the startling white line of his smile.

14

"I'm not going to do anything," said the district attorney. "It's not in my job description."

"Not even if she's throwing a case for political reasons?" asked Karp. "Isn't that a kind of corruption?"

It was just past eight, a Monday morning, at the beginning of March, and Karp was meeting his boss for their usual start-of-the-week meeting. In a few minutes, the bureau chiefs would file in for their own weekly. The purpose of this premeeting meeting was to eliminate the possibility that the DA would be surprised by anything these people were likely to tell him, and to chivy them about whatever Karp had learned that the DA was not officially supposed to know about the works of his high satraps.

Karp got a bleak stare. "You don't know that," said the DA, which was true. "You added two and two and came up five, because you've turned into a goddamn bleeding heart on this Bustamente case." He was sighting at Karp down his big Bering Churchill, a bad sign. "Look, Butch," the DA continued in silkier tones, "the only real fact here is what's-her-face's got no case at all."

"Jessica Siegel."

"Whatever. She's got no case. Her client killed her baby, tossed it out a goddamn window of a dance club, and went back to dancing. The facts are not in dispute, the law is not in dispute. It's an easy layup, and you're trying to move the basket?"

"She's trying to move the basket, not me."

"This is your idea that she's going for a nullifying jury?" The cigar sketched a dismissal. "Never happen. On a drug charge? Yeah, maybe. You get a Bronx jury in there, thinks the homeboy shouldn't go away for ten years for selling a little dope, everyone else on the street's doing it, I'll give you that, and maybe the odd Bernie Goetz case, a man supposedly defending himself by pulling a gun and blasting a couple of teenagers, people are scared of kids on the subway, they want to send a message. But not this, not a baby out the window, no way. Especially not with Ben Urey on the bench."

The DA leaned back in his thronelike judge's chair and gazed out his window. March was doing its lion entry, spitting sleet against the glass. "Listen, Butch, nobody's ever called me vindictive. I don't give hang-

'em-high speeches, you know that. I've opposed the death penalty just like the cardinal has, and I'll continue to. But there's a reasonable offer to this girl on the table, and it's tossed back in our faces. What am I supposed to do? You know we always deal, especially on prison time. She pleads to man one, hell, you know we'll go with three and a half to ten, a minimum-security joint, and she'll serve the minimum, like most of them do. She can go to college, if she wants."

"Jack, for crying out loud, you're making my point for me," replied Karp with some asperity. "*I* know that, *you* know that, Jessica *Siegel* knows that — why the hell don't we have a deal that'll put this horseshit behind us? Why is she putting this kid up this week to face a goddamn second-degree-murder charge? The case cries out for a diminished-responsibility defense, and she hasn't asked for a psych review. Why not?"

"I don't know, and as I thought I just made clear, it's not my business to know, or yours either. That's why, if you ever noticed, they got *two* tables up there in front of the courtroom. You got a professional problem with Siegel, go yell at Milt Freeland, not me."

This was sly. Keegan knew very well that Karp would not speak to the head of Legal Aid if Mr. Freeland's pants were on fire. "Or talk to Siegel," the DA continued. "Maybe she could use a little more legal research, courtesy of the People." He looked at Karp closely to note the reaction. Karp showed little; he seemed to take it for granted that the DA would eventually find out about the infanticide paper.

"It wasn't legal research, Jack," said Karp tiredly. "It was a historical survey shared with a colleague in the interests of developing a fair solution for a vexing case. You know, I try to tell my guys that it isn't a game. We got different roles, but we're all working for the same outfit. You don't think it's a game, do you, Jack?"

"No, I do not," snapped the DA, the silk turned to something like emery cloth, "but the media does. Who won, who lost. That's what sells the papers, boyo, and gets the folks to tune in, and I've got to give lip service to the idea, or come next January, you'll be looking at another fellow across this desk. And Butch? I know you like to fool around and play it close so that things work out the way you like, the hell with what the law says and what I want, but you need to be real careful here. We can't look bad on this one. If we end up looking bad, the wolves will be out prowling, and it's not my fine white Irish heinie they're going to be eating off of. Are we understanding one another?"

"I think I get the message, Jack."

"Good," said Keegan, and mashed the intercom button, calling, "Send 'em in, Mary!" at the little box.

During the ensuing meeting, Karp was uncomfortably conscious of the sports terminology in the language of the men (just one woman was present, in charge of the rape-and-sex-crimes bureau) who ran the DA's office. Concentrating on an issue was a *full-court press;* moving aggressively against an opponent was a *red dog* or a *blitz;* plans were always *game* plans. Karp realized that this was part of the ordinary metaphorical equipment of most American men — he often talked this way himself — but today he found it intensely annoying. Also annoying: Roland's digs as he described the *slam dunk* he projected for the Bustamente trial. Karp had his lone-wolf tendencies, nothing like his wife's, naturally, but all in all he was a team player. He liked passing to the free man, and it discouraged him when others failed to see what was obvious to him. Bustamente might be won, all right, but not by a slam dunk. It would be more like a nasty elbow fight under the boards, with fouls aplenty, and a disabling injury or two.

Jury selection in the case was proceeding at the moment, at an even more glacial pace than usual. Karp wandered upstairs to Part 50 after the chiefs' meeting and watched the paint dry for a while. Judge Urey, a small, sharp-featured man with an aureole of silver frizz around his pate, was looking none too pleased with the process, but Urey was famous for irascibility at all stages of the trial, and famous, too, for taking things into his own hands if he didn't like how they were going — Benjamin Urey, Judge and Jury, as the courthouse saying had it.

Siegel was up now, asking juror 74, a white man with the look of a retired union guy, to expatiate on how he felt about the sanctity of human life. The guy thought human life was pretty sacred. Had Mr. Umph been in the service? He had. Would he have taken human life if ordered? Not only would he, he had, the man replied. Siegel smiled benignly and asked whether he thought Hispanic people tended to be more sexually free than other Americans. He said he didn't know about that. Did he know the defendant or anything about her case? The juror turned to look at the defendant. Karp did the same. Lourdes, as Karp had predicted, looked prepubescent in a little pink, flowered dress, her black hair in side barrettes, lacking only a wreath and veil for the First Communion snapshot. The juror said all he knew was that she tossed her baby out a window. Siegel thanked him nicely and asked for a dismissal for cause, the cause being prejudice. Urey grumpily granted this and told juror 74 to return to the jury pool.

Karp stayed for a couple of more voir dire to get a feeling for the style of the two attorneys. Their game, he thought (*game* again!), was perfectly simple. Vasquez needed law-abiding citizens, easily cowed by a judge's direction. Siegel needed people with a grievance against society. Vasquez wanted men or wives; Siegel wanted single mothers, college students, longhairs, the lower depths. Each side had but twenty peremptory challenges, so the art here lay in booting people of the wrong type by asking questions whose likely answers would get them dismissed for cause, thus saving your peremptories, as Siegel had done with juror 74. While Karp was there, Vasquez blew off a thin, dark woman who didn't know if it was right to judge people, and Siegel got a well-groomed matron to suggest that she was frightened when traveling through Latino neighborhoods. This had been going on for three days, and but two jurors had been confirmed.

Karp caught Siegel's eye and she nodded and smiled at him, a smile too pert for his liking. She thought she was going to win this thing in selection, and she well might. Karp himself believed that, barring cases in which major social issues were in play, any jury could be won over with a well-presented case. Was this one a major social issue, a Bernie Goetz case? Jessica Siegel certainly thought so. Karp pulled out his wallet and made a note on an ATM receipt to call Vasquez at the end of the day to find out how it had gone.

Walking down the steps, he thought about the tedium of the law, and what Marlene had asked: How can you stand it? How indeed? It took a certain personality, he knew, a patient, focused one, heavy on fortitude, with a long view. The kind of person who could shoot baskets by himself for five to seven hours of a weekend afternoon, *bump ka-thump, bump ka-thump.* A hedgehog, like him, like Vasquez. Not like Marlene.

Another dawn drive for Marlene, slow, the roads nasty with icy rain. She should take the train, she thought, she could work and sleep on the train, but they'd make a fuss about the dog. The dog was important now, not only girl's best friend, of course, but a link to the previous Marlene. That thing with Zandt, putting the dog on him, she had felt the old shameful thrill, not professional, not the same as scoring a point across a courtroom. She had to stop that, let it fade. She had the will-power, but . . . tapering off, she needed the big dog. Tapering off motherhood, too, the sight of Lucy in that suit, and made-up, had been gravely shocking, if only in retrospect; in the event Marlene had been able to joke through it. A whiff of mother guilt here: Had she unconsciously kept the kid a kid, sending secret ugly-duckling vibes across the parental ether? No, surely not, but here, at any rate, it was, the sexual debut of the daughter, the mother moving more or less gracefully into dowager status, which she definitely was not ready for. Relation between lust for violence and sexual lust? Who, *me?* Yes, a twisted creature, but trying, and there were still the twins to raise, matronhood was not the same as death, not really. And we have to cut down on the sauce, that's another thing, have to guard against that cross-addiction, although all things considered, being a semi-lush was not as bad as shooting others, and maybe her own dear family gets in the way of a bullet.

Marlene got tired of eating the spray from the semi in front of her and tromped on the gas. The Volvo still had some legs on it, and she tore past the streaming silver flank of the monster and back into lane. Another, indistinguishable, semi. Symbolic. And there was the other girl, the client, she wasn't looking forward to that either, or the mom. Maybe there was something screwed up in that dyad, too. The kid fucking like a mink with that bastard, but can't go to the doc by herself, not without Mom. Virginal Lucy in contrast would arrange for brain surgery by herself if she thought she needed it and casually drop the fact, clunk, on the dinner table. Marlene missed her boys, so uncomplicated by comparison, such simple creatures, some hugs (but not too many), a little encouragement, and they were fine, and taking this job, driving this goddamned road three days a week, working all weekend on this case, which, at heart, was like all the other things she'd done with her life so far, cleaning up a family problem.

Mulcahey looked disgustingly fresh when she arrived at his office, and bursting with news. He brandished a sheaf of papers. "Wait'll you see this."

"What is it?"

"The reinterview Jorgensen did in Loreno's office. They submitted it yesterday."

She sat on Mulcahey's tatty sofa and took the papers from him.

"Coffee, please?" she gasped. Mulcahey hesitated just a second, then went off to get it from the secretary. Youth must serve, thought Marlene, and my God is he ever a cream bun, I could lick the sugar right off . . .

no, Marlene, focus. As Marlene had already surmised, Loreno had worked it so that Jorgensen looked like the patsy of the demon girlfriend. Jorgensen claimed, contra his statement just after the event, that Sarah had been awake and aware, had seen the baby, and had pressured him to dispose of it. It had been Sarah's plan, too, to have the baby in secret. He had wanted to call a doctor, an ambulance; she had refused. Loreno had telegraphed this move, but Marlene had not picked it up. Jorgensen was now positioned as one who loved not wisely, but too well, the hapless dupe, paralyzed by love, turned into a tool. There was a clipped op-ed and a news story attached to the back of the photocopied statement.

Mulcahey came back with the coffee. It was serious coffee, smuggled in from the metropolis by Marlene, and she took a deep slug of it, black as her mood. She waved the clippings. "How in hell did the press get this so fast?"

"Oh, the papers and TV have a direct wire to the prothonotary clerks in the courthouse," said Mulcahey. "Any filings might as well get sent straight to the newsrooms."

"Terrific," said Marlene, and read on. The op-ed was a discourse on evil women and passive men, written by a woman. Ma Barker and Bonnie Parker were mentioned. The writer questioned what the feminist perspective on such women should be and warned that even though it was good that women were more assertive, it was still not good to be bad. Perfect.

"So? What's your take?" Marlene asked. "What's the state's response going to be to this?"

"Well, it's going to make their job easier with respect to our client," said Mulcahey. "They'll be happy to give him up to get her on a heavier charge. She masterminded the plot, she showed intent."

"So they'll hold at capital murder, you think?"

"For now, but if we asked them nice, I guess they'll let her off with a maximum term on man one, to avoid the trial risk."

"Fuck that," said Marlene vehemently. "He goes in for twenty months and she gets ten years. Over my dead, twitching body." She drank some more coffee and wished for a cigarette. Unfortunately, she no longer officially smoked, and there was no one nearby to bum one off. Brewster would have some.

"Everything set up with the nation's premier polygrapher?"

"Nine o'clock," answered Mulcahey. "And he really is good, even though he tends to boast. Mike swears by him."

"I'm glad to hear it. It's sadly the case that

some conceited assholes are actually good at what they do. Were I skilled at that art, I wouldn't print 'Jerome Dettweiler, The Nation's Premier Polygrapher' on my stationery, but I guess it takes all kinds. I suppose we're all the nation's premier something or other, too."

"The nation's premier owner of man-eating dogs. I still can't get over that business with Zandt."

Marlene let this pass, as she was having the same trouble. "I assume we'll all meet them there?"

"Right. Brewster's driving Sarah and her mother. The press is rabid behind this latest, by the way. He's planning to use evasive-driving tactics. Meanwhile, I assume we are no longer going to stay in bed with Loreno and his client?"

"Not unless we want to get fucked worse than we've already been. There's no question in my mind anymore that he's wangling for a plea and offering up Sarah as a human sacrifice. It's a perfect *Bruton* case for severance, plus we got conflicting defenses. If the state wants to use Peter's story against Sarah, they're going to have to bring him in as a witness and let us cross-examine him. We need to get started on the severance motion right away."

"Okay. What about the polygraph? How do you want to handle that?"

"Hm. Some interesting possibilities here. It's a *Scheffer* motion. The Armed Forces Court of Appeals has just ruled that under certain circumstances polygraphs are admissible. And I think we need to append not only this recent statement of Jorgensen's, but the original statements he made just after the offending event. Our position is that our client's veracity has been impugned, here is the demonstration of that, and here is the polygraph material that supports Sarah's recollection of the events in question. That it also shows Peter Jorgensen is a damned liar is an inevitable inference, but . . ." Marlene smiled and shrugged elaborately.

"If you file that with the prothonotary, it'll be on the air within five minutes," said Mulcahey. "Loreno will go ballistic and so will the judge."

"That may be, but it's a perfectly legit motion that we have a perfect right, nay, a *duty* to file. If Judge Shearing's court leaks like a sieve, that's his lookout. I'm not going to get down to their level, Kevin. I'm not going to leak, and like I've said all along, I'm not going to file frivolous motions, but if the motions I do file contain material that helps Sarah, that redresses in some way the grotesque pollution

438

of the jury pool that these pigs have allowed over the past year, then I'm not going to blush and say, 'Heavens to Betsy! How awful.' " She put the coffee mug down, got up, and looked out the window. Two lawyers in three-piece suits, holding newspapers over their heads against the rain, were running toward the courthouse. A van braked and honked and let them by. Probably didn't know they were lawyers, Marlene thought. She turned to Mulcahey. "What else is cooking?"

"Motion to dismiss on the Dumpster-contents issue. We're still thinking *Arizona v. Youngblood* on that?"

"Yeah, and the law in Delaware is helpful for us; we'll move to dismiss the indictment because of the unavailability of potentially ex-culpatory evidence. We admit the baby's skull was fractured, but we say that it was fractured postmortem by heavy objects placed on top of the baby, said heavy objects having conveniently disappeared. We link that to obvious and stupid inconsistencies in the statements of the police who searched the Dumpster and witnesses. The cops claim they didn't tromp around in the Dumpster, but we know they did, and we have testimony of restaurant workers as to what was in it that evening, pipes and metal junk and so on. And whoever heard of anybody searching a goddamn

Dumpster without walking in it? I want the jury to picture big cop boots grinding junk down on the baby's skull."

"And we have the medical evidence for that, too."

"Which reminds me, thank you: Did you set up all those appointments?"

"My secretary did. And your flight tickets, too. It's going to be a busy week."

"Yeah, but it's key. I need to look all these guys in the face and find out how they respond to impertinent questions." Marlene checked her watch. "We have some time, let's see the schedule."

Mulcahey went out; again a little moment of stiffness. Marlene appreciated his resentment. They were colleagues, she was in no way his superior, but she found herself giving him orders, and he found himself obeying them, functioning as an efficient second. It had to be that way: they were competing against the state, a vast hierarchical organization under a unified command, and there had to be a single commander for the good guys, too, or the defense team would dissolve into squabbles, as it had once already, before Marlene came. Mulcahey saw that, Marlene thought, and suppressed his not inconsiderable ego in the good cause, bless his Irish heart. He returned with a folder.

"Chapin's in Chicago," he said, "but we need him because pediatric forensic pathology is pretty rarefied and he's the best guy for that according to everyone around here. Dr. Vostok's a neonatologist, at Hopkins, who'll weigh in on the abnormalities in the baby's brain, the viability question, and Morgan Brody, who's head of ob/gyn at Delaware General, and the local big expert on eclampsia and problems of pregnancy. Then we have Cyrus Wohler, who was our guy on the baby's autopsy. He used to be the ME in Pittsburgh. He's got a national reputation, and he'll support Chapin's findings, and also we'd like him to crap all over Maryanne Bollinger, our own Delaware ME, for raging incompetence."

"Will he really do that? Docs may disagree, but they don't usually want to piss on their colleagues."

"Oh, he'll do it all right. He was outraged, and he's a tough, street-smart hombre with Yale and Harvard credentials up the wazoo. You'll like him. It also helps that he's like a national monument in forensics and Maryanne doesn't even have full board certification in the field."

"I'll be sure to bring that up, as long as we can stay away from my own qualifications." Marlene handed the folder back. "Well, good. Dueling experts, including the nation's premier polygrapher, just my kind of trial. Do you think it's Mr. Abt's kind of trial?"

"I'm not sure any kind of trial is Mr. Abt's kind of trial. I think he likes it when they cop to a lesser. I think he is very much disturbed to think that he's going to have to face a competent defense across a courtroom, which is why we think he's going to offer a deal to Peter. When we blow their crummy forensics up, all they've got is two kids having a baby, and they need one kid to rat."

"That's very perspicacious of you, Kevin," said Marlene, and then, grinning, she added, "And I love to hear myself called competent. It makes me all shivery inside."

"I love to make you feel shivery," said Mulcahey, surprising both of them, making Marlene's eyes roll. Ah, flirting. It had been a long time.

"Ahem," she said. "And, of course, we now know this rat is a liar, which we are going to nail down with this polygraph."

Their eyes met, a long silence. "Assuming she passes the polygraph test," said Mulcahey.

"Bite your tongue, Mulcahey."

Dettweiler, the lie detector, had his offices in Philadelphia, in a modern building off Chestnut Street, respectable but not grand.

Dettweiler was a small, almost doll-like man with wispy gray-blond hair and clear-framed glasses, and the look of a failing dentist. Marlene and Mulcahey arrived early. Dr. D. (Ph.D. in psych from Lehigh, as the diploma on his wall stated) sat them in his expansive office and bored them for ten minutes with bad coffee and a lecture on the stupidity of not allowing polygraph tests as evidence in court while at the same time welcoming the notoriously unreliable evidence of eyewitnesses. Marlene's gaze drifted to a framed photograph of a large blond woman and two children on a credenza. They looked bored, too.

Then Brewster arrived, radiating his usual competent calm, with Sarah and Selma Goldfarb in tow. Selma looked stiff and nervous. The girl looked deathly — paler than usual, her hair unwashed, her eyes dull and smudged. Her glance was downward, pointedly not meeting Marlene's gaze. The polygrapher led them through a door, down a functional hallway, and sat them in assorted straight chairs in a featureless room. The room had a window through which they could see another small room, this containing an armchair and a straight chair and a table. On the table sat the polygraph apparatus. Dettweiler took Sarah through a door into this room, arranged her in the armchair, and hooked her up to his machine with tape and wires. The rest of the party observed this through the glass. There was no chatter; the scene was creepy, and Marlene flashed on movie sequences of people witnessing executions. Dettweiler sat in front of his machine and asked Sarah questions. The observers could hear what was going on through a small speaker in the wall. The questions were innocuous at first, then relevant to the events of the alleged crime. Marlene had written these out herself.

After a little less than an hour, Dettweiler came through the door with Sarah. He was holding a wreath of polygraph paper. He caught Marlene's eye and made a gesture. She knew it was the expert's policy to offer results first to the principal who was paying the tab. She followed him back to his office, where he indicated a chair for her and sat behind his big oak desk. This was his moment of glory, and apparently he liked to stretch it out. Spreading the polygraph tracings on the desk, he went through each question, pointing out the important data with a red Bic.

"I think there's no question of conscious lying, especially about the intent part," said Dettweiler. "She really thought she was having a five-month miscarriage. I'm prepared to assert professionally that she had no intent of delivering a viable infant and disposing of it. She did not say anything demanding disposal of the infant to the boyfriend either. Questions fourteen through sixteen, that's very clear. Down here, however, the data are more problematical. See the pulse-rate trace?"

"What's the question there?"

"Number eighteen. 'Were you aware that you had delivered a full-term baby?' Answer, 'No.' "

"A lie?"

"Not precisely, in my opinion. Lack of knowledge is more likely. If I ask you something you think you should know, but can't instantly put your finger on, you might say yes. The *Jeopardy!* effect."

"The what?"

"*Jeopardy!* The quiz show on TV. People watch it and blurt out the answers. When they don't know, when they have that tip-of-the-tongue feeling, they generate traces like this."

"But, not a lie."

Dettweiler pursed his lips and smiled a superior smile.

"Not as such. But she said no, and she doesn't know if it's really no. In my opinion."

Marlene went back to the observation room and delivered a slightly edited version and added, "This is good, people. Mainly, it shows lack of intent, which is basic to the state's case, and it directly contradicts Jorgensen's recent statement. The part where she doesn't know, where she's guessing, that's explained by the fact she was out of it during and after the delivery. She doesn't know because she doesn't know."

Both Mulcahey and Brewster looked satisfied; the lawyer pumped his fist and hissed a "Yes!" Sarah rested in dullness. Selma Goldfarb's face was creased with worry. As they walked down the corridor, she touched Marlene's elbow and drew her aside.

"Could we talk?"

"Sure, talk," said Marlene. "We're all on the same side here."

"No, alone. Just for a minute."

Marlene signaled Brewster to take charge of Sarah and then steered Selma back into the observation room.

"What's wrong?" Marlene asked.

"Everything! Sarah . . . I don't know . . . she's falling apart. She can't handle this anymore. We have to get her out of it."

"Out of this? I thought that was the point. She's been indicted for capital murder and I'm trying as hard as I can to defend her."

"No. I mean, I appreciate what you've done, I mean we all do, but there has to be some way to put this behind us. Why can't we

446

get the same deal as they gave him?"

"Meaning Jorgensen? You want me to approach the state and deal for a plea?"

"Yes. I think that would be better at this point. Get it behind her, let her get on with her life."

Marlene took a few deep breaths before she answered. "Well, Selma, okay, but you have to understand a couple of things. One, the state's prepared to paint her as a monster to make their case. That means that, politically, they have no reason to be nice to her at this point, as long as Jorgensen's testimony stands. They need a fall guy. Otherwise, they'll look like fools: they made this big capital murder case and they let both alleged perpetrators plead to negligent homicide."

"But you don't know that. You haven't asked them." Her voice had desperation in it. There were beads of sweat on her upper lip and her eyes looked set to gush.

"No, that's right, I haven't. And in my professional opinion, if we went to them now, they'd take it as a sign of weakness, that we're throwing in the towel behind this cocked-up testimony. They might stick with the capital murder. At the very best, they might go to first-degree manslaughter, maximum term. That's a minimum of ten years in prison."

"But she'd be alive!"

"Yes. And she'd be on public record as admitting that she intended to kill her baby and did kill her baby through the instrument of that poor, deluded, innocent boy. That's the story they'd make her tell in open court, and swear to." Selma was swaying now and seemed about to collapse. Marlene sat her in a chair and reached out a wad of her ever-ready tissue supply. Selma dabbed at her eyes, but did not dissolve. Marlene pulled a chair over and sat, her knees nearly touching Selma's.

"Selma, look — I'm your lawyer, I'm supposed to do what you want, within prescribed limits."

"A deal is what we want," Selma snapped. "I'm telling you, she can't take it. She's falling apart. She doesn't eat. She doesn't sleep. Three in the morning she's sitting in front of a blank TV screen holding her pink baby blanket against her face. I'm losing my daughter. She's going to end up in a mental hospital. The three of us . . . my husband's got a heart condition, it's killing him . . ."

"And Sarah wants this, too? She wants to confess to something she knows isn't true?"

"Sarah's a child. She doesn't know what she wants. I'm her *mother*. I'm trying to save my family. You have a family, don't you? A daughter? You know what this is like."

"Well, yes, I think I do, but right now I have

to function as a lawyer, not a mother. Sarah's lawyer. Sarah's, not yours, or your husband's. I realize that you're paying me, and that Sarah's a legal minor in some respects. But she's over eighteen. Not five."

Selma did not appear to register this. "So, you'll go to them, you'll make the best deal you can."

"Yes, Selma, but only after I hear it from my client. And I need to talk to her alone."

This got through. "Alone? Why? What are you trying to do?"

Marlene stood up. "I'm trying to defend your daughter."

"You're trying to break up my family!" Selma shot from her chair, her fists clenched, her eyes bulging with fury. Marlene grabbed her by both arms and gave her a shake.

"Stop this! Listen to me! You can't help her, Selma. You helped her her whole life, but now you can't. You knew that at some level and what you did was you hired me. I *can* help her, but only if you let me do my job. I need your support, but I have to work with *her*, get directions from *her*, not you. Why? Because it's her life. *Her* life, Selma."

"She can't take it!" Selma wailed.

"Maybe not, but that's what I need to find out. Now, here's what's going to happen right now. I'm going to take Sarah in my car and drive her home. I'll talk to her and lay out the possibilities and ramifications of the courses open to us now. If, after that, she wants to plead out, I will do everything in my power to get her the best possible deal. If you don't allow me to do that, I'm off the case as of this minute. Mr. Mulcahey can wave a white flag as well as I can."

Selma Goldfarb looked at her. What was that in her eyes? Fear, of course, but something else — resentment, envy? Shanahan had said that the mother was tough, and she was that, but Marlene now saw that it was a toughness that depended on her daughter's willing obedience, her softness, her docility. Selma was not going to tolerate anyone getting between her and that image of Sarah. It was her taproot. As Marlene walked away, she thought, This woman is not my ally anymore. It's just me and Sarah now.

Half an hour later, Marlene and a stony Sarah were in the Volvo driving south through New Jersey along the line of the Delaware on 295. The sky was fractionally brighter, but the roads were still slick, and the traffic was glacial. Sarah had replied to Marlene's conversational openings with shrugs and monosyllables, the last bunker of the mutinous teenager. Time to roll out the heavy weapons.

"You like opera, Sarah?"

This clearly didn't deserve an answer.

Marlene said, "I do. People say the plots of operas are ridiculous, but I don't agree. Life is ridiculous, and opera takes the weird things that happen to people and makes them into art. You're sorry your lover betrayed you? Well, here's what *really* sorry sounds like. Take Tosca, for example. A nice kid, artistic, a singer, not a painter like you, but her boyfriend's a painter. The boyfriend gets in trouble with the cops. The boyfriend has a revolutionary pal, he helps him escape, but Tosca thinks he's got a girl stashed away. She's jealous. The cops know this, and the evil police chief uses Tosca's jealousy to capture the boyfriend. They torture him, trying to get him to tell them where the rebel has gone, but he hangs tough. Not like some people we know. Now Tosca finds out the cops have the boyfriend, so she runs down to the clink to help him, cringing from shame, of course, because it was her fault. To make a long story short, the evil police chief says he'll let the boyfriend go if Tosca will screw him. So here she is, the police chief is twirling his mustache and leering, the boyfriend is getting the shit kicked out of him in the next room, she can hear his screams. So what do you think she does?"

The girl was interested but trying not to

show it. "I don't know. What?"

"Oh, since this is opera, she sings. In fact, she sings this." Marlene reached down between the seats, grabbed a grubby cassette, and inserted it into the excellent sound system Mr. Volvo puts in all his vehicles. Callas's voice filled the interior, rich and poignant: "Vissi d'arte, vissi d'amore, non feci mai male ad anima viva!"

When the great aria concluded, Marlene switched the stereo off. "What did you think of that?"

"I don't know. I don't understand Italian."

"Yes, but the music, what she was feeling. What was she feeling when she sang, the character Tosca, I mean."

"Sad. Lost."

"Yes. Okay. Think now, is she going to let him rape her?"

Sarah thought for a while as the car moved slowly past an accident. "No, I don't think so. She's like, too strong." Silence between them; the sound of the wipers. "What do the words mean?"

"The words mean, 'I lived for art, I lived for love, I never hurt a living soul. In secret, I helped the distressed poor. Always, I've offered up my sincere prayers in the chapels of the saints and laid flowers on their altars. Why, why, Lord, why in this hour of sadness have you repaid me in this way? I gave jewels to deck the mantle of the Madonna, I gave my songs to the stars, to the heavens, in tribute to their beauty. In the hour of my sorrow, why, why, Lord, have you repaid me like this?' Sounds better in Italian, but the sentiment is pretty clear. I lived for art, I lived for love, I never hurt a living soul, so why do I get it in the neck? Sound familiar?"

"She's feeling sorry for herself."

"Yep. It's natural. But it doesn't do her any good, aside from producing a gorgeous song."

"She still had love, though. She still loved her boyfriend and he still loved her."

"Yes, well, it's opera. And Tosca, if I may say so, had better luck with men than you. In any case, you have to decide what you're going to do. I just had a good-sized fight with your mom about that. She wants me to throw the case, throw you on the mercy of the state. She doesn't think you can take it anymore. I said it wasn't her decision to make, that I'd have to talk to you. So I'm talking to you. The evil police chief wants to rape you, kid. You going to lie down for him, or what?"

A longer silence. The dog grunted, the wipers swished. Marlene turned off the freeway onto Route 49 south.

Sarah said, "I don't know. My mind's been

numb for days, ever since . . . you know, with the tape. I'm writhing inside. It's funny, I still want to call him, talk to him, because he's the person I would call if something like this happened to me, who I'd want to be with, and that makes me feel even stupider. Stupid! Stupid! My whole life, stupid, stupid! Everything I believed in is a pile of garbage. I wrote him letters, on stationery with little huggy bears on it, at Chambersburg, and all the time he was . . . The cops came and took them, the *cops* are reading my letters to him. Maybe he even showed them to that girl and they laughed."

"I doubt that, for what it's worth. I think he was just a kid, like you, who got in over his head, a shallow kid, not who you thought he was. It happens."

"Really? Not to my folks it didn't. They dated in high school and all through college and got married a month after they graduated."

"And you wanted to live that life? Like your mom's life, again?"

"No!" she said instantly, and then after some silent thought, "I guess. Is that so wrong?"

"No, it's not wrong at all. As a mom myself, I have to think it's admirable. We want our kids to be like us, only better. It's natural. But you've moved over a line into a different world." Marlene flicked her fingernail against the stereo. "Like this. A more, let's say, operatic world. Murder, lies, betrayal, spies, evil police captains. No offense, but I think I'm a better guide to that world than your mom. That's where I dwell, may God forgive me. So you can't be the same person anymore, not and survive, and that's what's messing you up. Am I right?"

Sarah was nodding. "Yeah. And Mom doesn't understand it. Or Dad. When this thing happened, when I got out of jail, he gave me a welcome-home present. It was a stuffed animal, a tiger. It's a family tradition, I guess, and I didn't think anything of it, then, but now . . . I guess I see what you mean. I lived for art, I lived for love. Right, but that's, like, *over*, now, in a way, isn't it?"

"In the form you knew them, yes. But there are other forms. Some say higher ones."

"That's what the song meant, that's why it was so sad. Things being over. That's the saddest thing in the world, isn't it?"

"It's way up there," Marlene agreed.

They were in Mt. Holly now, driving slowly through the narrow streets, under the bare, dripping trees.

Sarah asked, "What happened to Tosca after? In the opera?"

"The evil police chief condemns her boy-friend to death, but Tosca doesn't know that. She says she'll have sex with the cop if he writes her and the boyfriend out a passport, so they can escape together. She thinks it's going to be a fake execution. The cop writes it out, and when he goes to grab her, she sticks a dagger in his chest. 'Here is Tosca's kiss!' is what she says. Then after the boyfriend gets shot, and the cops are coming for her, she jumps to her death from the tower of the prison."

"Wow. That's not a very good omen, is it?"

"No, but look at the upside. You didn't kill anyone, and Tosca didn't have me."

For the first time that day, Marlene saw the girl's face crease with the suggestion of a smile. They were on the Goldfarbs' street now. Marlene asked, "So, what's it going to be, kid? You want to lie down for this, like your folks want, or go a few more rounds?"

The girl chewed her lip and said, "If I take a plea, that means I'm going to have to swear I meant to kill my baby, that I planned it to come out like that, like they're saying?"

"I think so."

Marlene watched as something came into the girl's soft, unformed face, something she had not seen there before: a tightening of the jaw, a stiffening of the angelic mouth, a tiny

456

flare in the nostrils. "Then, no. I won't say that. I'll never say that. I don't care what they do to me."

Marlene stopped the car, got out, opened Sarah's door, and when the girl stood up, embraced her warmly. The embrace was returned, and they stood that way for what seemed like a long time, on the walk in front of the Goldfarbs' house.

"Listen," said Marlene, "it's going to be okay. You'll see, after this week, the tide's going to turn our way. But what you have to do is buck up your folks. Don't let them think you're going crazy. Eat, sleep, bake cookies; even better, start painting. Can you manage that?"

"I'll try. Can I call you?"

"Whenever you want," said Marlene fervently. "And I'll be there for you, whatever happens. We're going to stick together, and God willing we're going to drive a dagger into the evil heart of the state of Delaware."

After a stunned moment, they both started cackling like witches.

15

"How have you been?" asked the priest, which, offered to Lucy Karp, was not entirely a conventional opening. You never knew. They were in the basement of Old St. Pat's, a muffin-and-coffee day, Father Dugan having dropped by to kibitz with the insulted and injured.

"Pretty well, thanks," Lucy answered. Dugan was helping her fill a coffee urn the size of a gas tank on a Chrysler. "Except I still hear those gun sounds in my head."

"Oh, yes? Like how?"

"Oh, just a minute ago. I was just sort of noodling in the kitchen with kind of vague thoughts, and I had this vivid picture of a gun cocking and going off, a machine gun, a big one. Just an instant and then it was gone. It happens a lot and it always makes me a little queasy. I mean, why guns? I never see anyone getting shot, just the guns shooting. What do you think it means?"

"Lucy, I really couldn't say," said the priest after consideration. "The undisciplined mind is active, it throws up waking dreams all the time. When I was in seminary, I used to be afflicted with smells — baking bread, onions, things burning."

"You think maybe demonic intrusions?"

"I wouldn't go *that* far. Maybe radio static would be a better guess. I won't mention the possible Freudian interpretations, guns as symbolic."

"Oh, right, sex." Sneering.

He ignored this. "Do they bother you?"

"A little. My friend Tran says they're the ghosts of violent acts in my past and by my ancestors, trying to seduce me into violence. That would be sort of demonic stuff, wouldn't it?"

The priest gave her a hard look. "I know you like him, but surely a Communist murderer is hardly a suitable spiritual guide."

"Oh, Tran wasn't much of a Communist, really, more of a patriot. A murderer, yes, but the spirit isn't dead in him. He lost everything, but he's not bitter and mean. He tries to do good, and he loves me and my mom. The workings of grace. So that's something. And Moussa, the same."

"You're continuing these visits to the jail, are you?"

"Yes. We talk about religion, mostly. He had some very peculiar ideas about Christianity. You know, it's really hard to, like, explain the Trinity in words, why it's not really wor-shiping three gods."

"It's been noted," said the priest dryly. "And again, I'm telling you, you should stop doing this."

"Uh-huh, I know. But I have to. And I'm glad to learn about Islam, which I had some peculiar ideas about, too. All that hard-on-women stuff really isn't in the Quran, it's cultural, like pre-Islamic. He was amazed that I could speak Arabic. And I'm learning Bambara, too . . . but that's not the main reason I'm going," she added hastily. "Any-way, I cheated and went up to Columbia and spent a couple of days with tapes and books so I could get up to speed in the language. I think it does him a lot of good to speak to someone in his native tongue."

"If you can learn a language from tapes, why do you have to find someone to teach you?" asked Father Dugan, his Jesuits' fasci-nation with languages breaking through.

"Oh, because it's not the same thing at all. It's, oh, like the difference between canned orange juice and fresh-squeezed. You can't get the range of idiom and intonation from a tape or a book. I mean, what does learning a language really mean? Well, at one level, its grammatical structure, the principal conjuga-tions, and about twelve hundred words to memorize, but —"

"Why twelve hundred?"

"That's about what you need to make yourself understood. If you have an English vocabulary that big, you might not know the word for, say, asparagus, but you can say, 'What's that long, thin, green vegetable?' And you have the main roots and the affix rules, so from *stupid* you can get *stupidly* and *stupidity* and so on, and then the cultural overlays, the . . ." She stopped herself; she could go on for days in this vein, but she had a horror of boring people, although the priest was far from bored. "Anyway, what you can't get from tapes and books is the sense of the living language. Anyhow, my point was, it's almost impossible to get to know a person unless you're speaking to him in his cradle tongue."

"And have you? I mean, got to know this man?"

She nodded. "I'm getting there. He's in terrible pain."

"From guilt?"

"Yes, because of leaving Mali. His father told him not to and he did anyway. He thinks all of this is a punishment for that. The Bambara are unbelievably into their families. Like the Chinese, but maybe even more extreme. When you meet a guy on the street, you can't just say hi and move on, you've got

461

to keep shaking his hand and ask how's the wife, how's the kids, the mom and dad, the brothers, the sisters. It was bad enough in Paris where there were lots of Bambara, but here he's pretty isolated. He thought he could make his pile in a short time and go back to Mali like a big shot, but he didn't figure on how expensive everything was here. And his father is sick and he can't go back to be with him, so . . ."

"I meant about the murders."

"No, we've never talked about them." She stopped and reflected for a moment. Something important was rising into consciousness, but had not yet broken the surface. "No, and it's funny because he seems to me to be like a really deeply moral man. He's *full* of remorse, but not for that. Maybe he blanked it all out, like in the movies, suppressed memories. And it's so strange, because the reason I started to go see him, like I told you, was because I liked him and I didn't think he was a bad man, but it just now hit me that my best friend, my best adult friend in the whole world, is a murderer, too, about a thousand times worse than Moussa. But I love him and I'd trust him with my life, and he'd trust me with his, and he has and I have. On the other hand, someone like Mr. Maxwell . . . I know we're not supposed to disrespect the dead, but I wouldn't trust him as far as I could throw him. I mean he was just a complete phony and rip-off lawyer. So if murder is the worst crime of all, how can a murderer, like, seem to be so *decent?* To me, I mean, or maybe I'm just warped."

"*Warped* is not a word I would use for you, not in this respect anyway. And, you know, sin is particular and individual. It's not like crime, where society has to assume everyone equal before the law and judge which acts are worst for the social order and punish them accordingly. You can damn yourself very thoroughly for acts that aren't even illegal. And of course some acts are made excusable by situation. Soldiers kill in war, and soldiers can be honorable, in fact we insist that they be, and that's probably the reason. We license them to kill for us, so they have to be good men."

"And women, Father. And the other reason, I guess, was that I had some kind of arrogant idea that I could, like, *save* him, turn him toward God, but, of course, it turns out that he's practically the most religious person I know. It's sort of ironic. Maybe he's saving *me*. And now I can't *stop* seeing him, or he'd be hurt."

Father Dugan thought briefly that this was the point at which to remind Lucy about that road paved with good intentions, but, being a man of generous soul, a former lawbreaker himself, and no hypocrite, he instead changed the subject. "How're your friend and her brother getting on?"

"Oh, Caitlin's all right," said Lucy, who seemed relieved at the change herself. "She decided to finish up the year in Sacred Heart after all, which I thought was a good idea. Less wrenching, considering all the changes she's been through. The grandfather put Brian in Emmett, up in Riverdale — it's like a school for what they call special students, ha ha, meaning kids who've been kicked out of every school in the world. They have like about two teachers for every kid. So I guess they've made an adjustment, on the surface."

"But not beneath it."

She shrugged. "I don't know. You know, it's like everybody has to worship something. There's a gene or some kind of human thing. Mr. Maxwell worshiped money. Caitlin worships dancing. My other friend Mary worships math. Caitlin's grandfather worships his family . . ."

"You've met him, have you?"

"Oh, yeah. James Pell Warren, and he's the kind of guy when you think of him, you have to think all three names, like Frank Lloyd Wright. Not that I have much to do with him, but I run into him in that apartment — the mausoleum is what Caitlin calls it — and I always think that he's waiting for me to curtsy or something. I say, 'Hello, Mr. Warren,' and there's a pause — beat, beat — like he's wondering whether I'm high enough in status to get a hello back. And then he looks right through you and says, 'Good afternoon,' or whatever, in this slow, creepy voice. Like the butler in a horror movie. The Pells and the Warrens back to the year one, that's the thing he cares about. He's always yapping to the kids about your great-great-whatever Erasmus. Caitlin can't stand it, but Brian can't get enough. The ancestral soldiers."

"Maybe he will be converted to the church of Pell Warren."

"Maybe, but really, Brian worships Caitlin. The way he looks at her sometimes is . . . like he wants to eat her up. She won't pay any attention to him, of course, especially now that she's a star. He did a comic book and showed it to me, about this superhero who rescues this girl from interplanetary villains, and the girl is, of course, a ballet dancer, except she has wings. I try to spend time with him when I'm there, give him a little contact, but Caitlin is incredibly jealous. Weird, isn't it? The whole world is her slave now, and she can't stand it if I sit five minutes with the poor kid."

"Perfectly comprehensible, however. The

worship of things other than God is fraught with peril."

"Yes," Lucy said, her brow wrinkling, enjoying the word *fraught*. "I feel that. There's something brittle there, in the mausoleum, little looks I catch that don't seem connected with what's going on. For example, the other day . . ."

But Father Dugan did not hear what happened the other day because just at that moment Sister A. cruised up, her skirts billowing like the sails of a caravel, and dragged the priest away to see the deplorable condition of the kitchen sink.

Dogless, Marlene sat fuming in a cab caught in Baltimore traffic. They seemed to be making a tour of slab-sided industrial architecture and abandoned construction sites. The Sikh driver was uncommunicative about alternate routes or how long it would take to get to Johns Hopkins, and Marlene wished for her daughter's ability to curse fluently in half the languages of mankind.

Marlene was seeing experts. The previous day she had flown to Chicago to interview Dr. Samuel Chapin, the pediatric pathologist. A nice fellow, unlike what she had expected in a man who made his living cutting up dead children. The cab jerked and stopped between a truck and a city bus. The air in the cab turned to burnt diesel. This was almost worse than a plane, the claustrophobic tube where time stopped. Marlene disliked flying, not because she was afraid of fiery falling death, but because she was not at the controls of the vehicle; and she felt the same about cabs. As a distraction she rummaged in her briefcase for her notebook, cringing slightly as her hand brushed the smooth plastic of the slide box. In that box were dozens of hair-thin slices of the skull of Baby Boy Jorgensen, brought for the examination of Dr. Chapin. Marlene had, of course, waded through blood any number of times, but these things made her squeamish. It was like carrying around a little morgue in her shiny morocco case.

She flipped open the notebook, a steno model of which she always carried half a dozen fresh, writing on one side of the vertical red line and, as now, writing comments and clarifications on the other. Chapin was tall, with thick silver hair and thick black-framed glasses, and a calm, slow, judicious voice; in short, a TV doc, a superb witness. She pulled out his original report, now dog-eared, stained, scribbled on, decked with colored Post-its, and began writing out the framework for a line of testimony, using the report and the information she had gathered from Chapin's mouth.

This was all the biography that Baby Boy Jorgensen would have, or ever would have had, since it was clear that the child had been doomed in utero. The lungs were shrunken and incapable of sustaining life. Chapin said that they had never expanded for a first breath, which was, of course, critically important for the case. The brain exhibited gross schizencephaly, a severe malformation involving the shriveling of one of the cerebral hemispheres. Huge cysts had resulted from the catastrophic loss of brain matter and the efforts of the brain to repair itself. The brain surface, where thought largely dwells, was abnormal, shriveled, and the motor cortex was essentially nonfunctional. This baby would hardly ever have moved in the womb, clearly an explanation of why Sarah had never felt the quickening of a normal child. The cherry on top was that at the time of his birth, Sarah's eclampsia had cut off his oxygen for up to twelve hours, causing severe asphyxial damage to whatever brains the poor creature had left.

Marlene dutifully transcribed her questions: How would such a baby have appeared on delivery? Answer: Dead to a naive observer. Thready heartbeat if any. Agonal. Q:

What's *agonal?* A: Dying. Bring out: Could anything, any medical activity, at time of birth have saved? A: No. Brain and lung development were insufficient to support life. Q: Normal life, or any life? A: Any life.

And the baby had indeed died during or immediately after birth. Chapin was positive that the skull fractures had been made postmortem. Q: How do you know that? A: No blood in fracture lines. Very clear on slides. Means brain did not bleed after fracture, hence no life. No brain swelling, ditto. No blood mass in dura, hence no bleeding, ditto. No brain trauma, ditto. The junk thrown on the little corpse in the Dumpster had crushed its skull, the junk that the cops had let be destroyed.

She experienced a transient wave of rage. These findings were not rocket science. They could have been found by any competent pathologist, but for some reason the state did not employ a competent pathologist, and so here they all were, little Sarah under the ax, and Marlene in a strange city, on the cab ride from hell.

Which ended, eventually, amid the dirty brick and bare trees of Johns Hopkins. Dr. Myra Vostok was a short, rotund woman in her early sixties, of immense authority and tutelary manner. Another good witness. She would remind the jurors of their third-grade teachers, the stern but fair ones. Marlene now learned more than she ever thought she would need to know about the myriad things that could go wrong with a pregnancy between the gasp of consummated sex and the howl of birth. It was a wonder that anyone ever got born at all. Chapin's theories were confirmed, strengthening the case for a still-birth or the next thing to it.

Then a quick lunch in a local fern bar, back into a cab, to the Amtrak station and a train for Philadelphia. Cab to the office of Cyrus Wohler, forensic consultant, a tiny suite in a nondescript building overlooking the oily Schuykill. In Wohler's office, a scholar's den lined with shelves jammed with thick books, bulging files, jars full of brains and other organs floating in murky liquid, Marlene got the story, a dryly witty devastation, of the actual autopsy of the subject baby. Good, she could use this; Wohler was a small, neat man just past seventy, who sported a bow tie and a brush mustache, and was one of the rare medical experts who would criticize a colleague in open court. Marlene didn't ordinarily have much respect for professional witnesses, but Wohler apparently turned down cases where he did not believe he was testifying to the absolute professionally extracted truth. Also rare, and the rep was borne out by the tattiness of the offices, which said, "Not for sale to the high bid."

Her next stop was in offices of far more grandeur, the Broad Street den of Lorrimer, Berg, and Loreno, in a modern office building occupying most of the tenth floor, a place of glass walls, dark paneling, leather chairs, the latest magazines on mahogany coffee tables, glistening receptionists asking would she like coffee or a soft drink. After half a *People* magazine, a slick young man wearing yellow suspenders and a golden tie came out and ushered her back through hushed, carpeted warrens to a corner office. Loreno stood from behind his vast, shiny, near-empty cherrywood desk, smiled, came around, shook hands, they sat (the slick young man to one side, with a notepad ready), Loreno chattered — the crazy weather, a little politics, a little sports. Marlene let him go on: his meeting, after all. He had called her the day after she had filed the motion to allow Sarah's polygraphic evidence, and she had agreed to come, more out of curiosity about how far Loreno was prepared to go in his exploration of the uttermost reaches of chutzpah than from any expectation of benefit to her client.

After what she thought might be a precisely calculated interval of small talk, Loreno plumped up his smile and said, "So, Marlene, you'll recall when we first started working on this thing together, I advised you to let me take the lead in shaping our case, and I thought you were going to go along with that, or anyway I haven't heard any different, and so I was sort of dismayed with you about this polygraph stunt. I mean, everybody's extremely pissed off about it, the judge, the state, and I have to say I didn't expect this of you, this . . . I have to call it an *attack,* on my client."

He was really terrific, Marlene thought. There's absolutely no difference between his face and that of a man who's telling the truth. He must have some way of making himself believe this garbage, but how does he keep all the stories straight? Another minor talent. There must have been something odd in her expression, because he intensified his gaze — how good that must be with a jury! — and continued, "But, hey, I figure, you're inexperienced, you're entitled to make a couple of mistakes . . . ," and here he stopped, because Marlene had burst out laughing, literally burst out, a stifled, honking snort.

"I'm sorry," she sputtered, hand over mouth.

Loreno's smile was still fixed, as by formalin, but his eyes had turned cold, and perhaps a little worried. "Ah, would you like to share the joke with us, Marlene?"

Marlene brought herself under control and replied, "Oh, nothing, really. So, Phil, you think it was a mistake to file that motion. Exactly why is that?"

Loreno tried the patronizing smile again, but it didn't quite work. Her laughter had been discomposing, and his studied face looked like a toupee knocked slightly askew. "Marlene, please! You attack my client's statements to the police, completely out of context, as part of your motion — what effect do you think that's going to have on his credibility? It's devastating. I've already moved to seal it."

"Seal it? That's funny, Phil. You didn't move to seal any of your client's statements that were devastating to *my* client. Why was that? I thought we were running a joint defense here. But you didn't feel it was worthwhile to tell me that you were holding a cozy séance with your client and the cops right there in your New York office, during which he spewed out what was obviously a carefully prepared story designed to shift the blame onto Sarah."

"Now, hold it, Marlene! I don't like the implications of —"

"Neither do I, Phil. Nor do I like the curious dovetailing of that testimony with the state's theory of the case. You'll recall how at the hearing on suppressing the search warrant I pointed out how Peter hardly said anything about the baby to the Chambersburg cops, although the Newkirk cops claimed, falsely we know, that he said the baby was alive. Now comes Peter in act two, and all of a sudden, not only does he know the baby's alive, but Sarah does, too, and she orders her passive boyfriend to, quote, get rid of it, unquote. How terribly, how implausibly, convenient."

The smile was gone now. In its place, Loreno had assumed the threat face: eyebrows knotted, jaw clenched, eyes slightly bulged and staring. "You need to be careful here, Marlene — you're coming mighty close to accusing me of suborning perjury. In front of a witness." He glanced at the slick young man, who was scribbling away. "That would be actionable slander."

"It would, and that's why I used the word *convenient*. How lucky and fortunate for your client that he recovered these memories just in time. And how fortunate and convenient that your *dick*, Mr. Zandt, was stationed with his recording equipment ready to record your client trying to get my client to affirm his new version of the facts."

"I have no idea what you're referring to."

"No, because as you keep on saying, we're

in this together. So why don't you tell me what kind of deal we're working on with the state?"

Loreno threw up his hands in exasperation. "What *is* this with you, an obsession? Read my lips — there is *no* deal with the state. I would tell you if there was a deal. I have to under the terms of our joint defense agreement."

"Wow, that makes me feel better, Phil," said Marlene in the same tone a twenty-dollar whore uses when she tells the john what a terrific lay he is. "So, while we're cooperating, what have you learned from all the people you've been interviewing?"

Loreno's eyes narrowed. A trick question. "What do you mean 'interviewing'?"

"Well, for our case. I've been talking to the medical experts. Mike Brewster's been interviewing witnesses of various types, people in the hospital, up in Chambersburg, around the crime scene. You know, what you high-class defense attorneys always do to build up your cases. The problem is, we're the *only* people these witnesses have spoken with. You're not interviewing anyone that I can see, even though you're the one with the rich client and all the resources. I wonder why that is. Is it possible you're not assembling a case because you know you're never going to go to court here?"

Loreno sighed dramatically. "I'm doing my job. What I'm not doing, as I said, is rocking the boat with motions like this polygraph nonsense. I assume you don't intend to withdraw it."

"I do not. In fact, I'm planning a blizzard of motions."

"Which you'll share with me, hopefully *before* you file, next time?"

"Sure, Phil, as soon as you start sharing with me your negotiations with the state of Delaware."

"I told you, damn it, there *are* no negotiations."

"Right," said Marlene sweetly, "you did." She stood up. "You know what I can't figure out? Why you think you can treat me like a kid two days out of law school. Do I have spinach on my teeth? Am I wearing a clown suit? My bra strap is hanging down? What is it? You were in the DA's office, and I was in the DA's office longer than *you* were, so you have to know that practically the first thing you learn in the felony prosecutions business is how to tell when a defendant's lawyer is sniffing for a deal. And yet you think that somehow I either never learned that or I've forgotten."

"Marlene, come on," said Loreno, placatingly now, "you know I've always had the greatest —"

"But I haven't forgotten," she said, and made for the door. "See you around the courthouse, counselor."

"I think she outplayed me," said Mimi Vasquez glumly. "I shouldn't have used my last peremptory on Mazzik."

They were in Karp's office, going over the final jury list for *People v. Bustamente*, fourteen people, twelve regular and two alternates. Karp flipped to the sheet on Mazzik, Mrs. Erma C., in the folder that contained the scant information on jurors who had been challenged and excused.

"This is the one where Siegel brought out she was an ACLU member and a bleeding heart."

"Yeah, I figured I couldn't leave her in, and then the next two were Hispanic women, one of whom had a baby out of wedlock and another whose daughter had one. That's three Hispanic women on there."

"Mimi, you're starting to obsess about this, and it's not doing you any good. There may be cases that are won in the voir dire, but I've never had one, and I don't believe this is one either. You have a very simple story to tell. There's no obvious ethnic issue here."

"There's a sexual politics issue."

Karp shook his head. "I know Jessica Siegel

thinks there's one, but you don't have to. As far as your three Hispanic women, I think there's something degrading and patronizing about the belief that folks are going to give their ethnic cohorts a free ride on a felony charge. I haven't seen it. In fact, you may get the opposite effect — respectable citizens being glad to see the kind of scumbag that makes life hell up on the block finally getting his lumps. So there's nothing wrong with your jury that I can see."

"If you say so, boss," Vasquez replied, and gathered up her papers.

Karp put his arm around her as they both stood, something he rarely did, and said, "Vasquez, lighten up! It's only a case. Forget about it! Go home, have a relaxing weekend, and come back here on Monday ready to start trial." With these and other similar platitudes of encouragement, he led her out of his office.

"I don't get it," said Karp, half to himself and half to Murrow, who had been sitting silently in his accustomed corner during the meeting, pen flickering, to all visitors as unnoticed as a waste can. "This is an experienced, first-class trial lawyer. I raised her from a pup myself, so I know what she can do. But she's acting like a nervous kid."

"The nature of the case?" offered Murrow.

"Identification with the defendant, you

mean? Yeah, it happens. The there-but-for-fortune thing, and she admits it. So maybe we legal strategists should have put some big white stud in there, right? Then the jury gets the picture of the oppressor beating up on this little minority girl. On the other hand, picking prosecutors because of their skin tone makes me want to puke. What's happened here is that Ms. Siegel isn't playing by the normal rules and she's succeeded in spooking Vasquez, which is part of her scheme. The Muhammad Ali strategy. But all Vasquez has to do is play it perfectly straight, deliver her case, which is actually rock-solid, and stop worrying about runaway jurors. The Joe Louis strategy — you can run but you can't hide."

"So you think Bustamente's going down for the big one?"

"Inevitable. Leviathan will eat her up like a smelt, the poor little twit." Karp sighed and thought for some moments. "I'd give something to have ten minutes alone with the girl's mother. Murrow, do me a favor: get me the mom's phone and address."

"You can't really do that, can you?"

"Technically? It'd be an ex parte meeting, frowned upon, a no-no. But I may think of something." A rapping on the door. "Yes? Come in!"

The door opened ten inches and a large pink head popped through.

"Sorry, I was looking for Roland," said Pincus. The rest of him slid in. "But maybe I could ask you."

"Ask me what?"

"Probably it's nothing, but Dick Kemmelman was out at Riker's and he happened to get into a conversation with some guards and they happened to mention that our boy Feydé has a regular visitor."

"So? He's entitled."

"Yeah, but it's not family. It's some kind of social worker, or psychologist, from Marymount College. Juliet F. Murphy. Ever hear of her?"

"No, but still, so what?"

"Well, I thought, maybe they're thinking of a diminished-responsibility defense, which we had no notice of at all, so I called his lawyer, Horace Wicks, over at Legal Aid, and I said, you know, Horace, what gives? And he didn't know anything about it either, and they've got no intention of going that way on the D. Funny, huh?"

"Somewhat. And what did you want to ask, Pincus?"

"Well, she's been there half a dozen times or so, so maybe they have a rapport. Maybe she's doing like a study of immigrants who commit crimes, how their minds work, or like that. What I'm thinking is, maybe he let something slip. We still don't have the murder weapon. And if she's just like doing a scientific study, then there's no privileged communication. She's not a priest or a shrink or a lawyer. And it's not a custodial interrogation. She's not an agent of the state. So I'm figuring we can use whatever, if anything, she's learned."

"Yes, assuming she's not operating as a psychotherapist. If she's just a researcher, you could subpoena her notes. Have you called her?"

"No, I wanted to talk to someone first."

"Well, call her. Find out what she's doing and what her status is regarding the defendant."

"Just like that?"

"Yeah," said Karp, and he could see from the expression on Pincus's face that the man was disappointed. He wanted some clever legalistic ploy to be revealed. Karp was at the moment sick of cleverness, and so he said, with rather more asperity than he meant, "Hell, Pincus, just ask her what she's doing! The guy's in our custody. You got every right to know what she's doing with him. That's why they call it custody. Be polite, inform her of our interest in the forensic value of her work, invite her out for tea. If she tells you she's a shrink and fuck you, then you'll let me know and we'll forget it. Anyway, as you're always pointing out, we've got the poor bastard cooked as it is."

Sometimes in the month of March the city gets a day heavy with the promise of spring, a promise subject to renegotiation naturally, because the next day could bring twelve inches of snow, or a rain of frogs, but while it lasts the inhabitants dash around like bees at rose time, drunk on unaccustomed sweetness. Not on a weekend, of course, no; it had poured all weekend. But it took much of the sting out of Monday, which dawned with the sky an absolute blue, utterly cloudless, the air washed and fragrant with that wet-concrete smell of clean city. At noon the temperature touched seventy and the streets were filled with slightly dazed workers in shirtsleeves and spring dresses. Citywide, it was estimated that nearly 350 people smiled at strangers, and on two occasions in Midtown, natives gave helpful and friendly directions to tourists.

After school that day, Lucy Karp had accompanied Caitlin Maxwell to a rehearsal hall at the Juilliard School at Lincoln Center to watch her audition for the title role in the Metropolitan Ballet's new production of

Giselle. As Caitlin had impressed upon her, *Giselle* was big, the most famous classical ballet next to *Swan Lake,* and a famous maker of reputations. Lucy thought that her friend would be nervous, but Caitlin had exhibited an almost somnambulistic calm during the preceding week. At the last moment, however, Mr. James Pell Warren announced that he would be attending, too, had, in fact, been invited by the director of the ballet company. Mr. Warren had never demonstrated much interest in ballet before now, but after Caitlin's splash he had convinced himself, with the help of the sort of people he hung with, that a famous ballerina was nowadays an ornament to any family. He therefore proposed to take charge of Caitlin's career, starting with a major financial contribution to the company, and attendance at ballet events. This was not so different from what his late daughter had done, but, unlike her, he insisted, once they were all in his limo and could not reasonably object, on going up to Riverdale and collecting Brian. Brian was part of the family and would also attend. Caitlin threw a fit, which her grandfather ignored.

They made the pickup and drove south, Caitlin in grim silence, her lovely face anger-blotched red; the grandfather, a tall, tanned, fit man, with the usual silver hair and blue

eyes, like someone in an ad for a pricey retirement community, sat bland with entitlement,
insensitive as a truck tire, with his manicured
delicate-fingered hands folded on his lap;
Brian chattered as he always did, about his
comic book fantasies, and what level he had
attained in various video games. Much of this
was directed at Lucy, who, for her part, was
writhing in embarrassment and confusion,
not wanting, out of loyalty to her friend, to
encourage the kid, but having at the same
time no stomach for brutal rejection. She kept
civility going during the hellish passage as
best she could.

At the rehearsal hall they found, instead of
the few parents and company personnel typically present at rehearsals, well over forty people. Some were balletomanes who had
wangled building passes, but most of them
were dance-establishment beggars trying to
get close to James Pell Warren. Mr. Warren
ordinarily exhibited the suspicious stinginess
of the very rich, but he enjoyed being made
much of, as now. Lucy sat a few rows back
from the stage in the small theater and took
off her beret. She was wearing a white shirt
with a navy sleeveless sweater over it and a
green plaid skirt and a forest green blazer with
a St. Bridget's parochial school seal on the
pocket. It was not exactly a parody costume;

Lucy enjoyed looking like a 1950s parochial schoolgirl when she went to school. The resale shop had also sold her a navy blue nurse's cape, which she prized. With the cape on, and the beret, and her thin face and cropped hair, she looked like a partisan of some lost romantic cause fleeing toward the mountains, a look she prized.

The dancers came out onstage in leotards, slippers, and leg warmers and began their stretches. This was boring. Lucy dragged her homework out of the khaki military satchel she used as a book bag and concentrated on that until the music started. Then, entrancement. Caitlin seemed to have thrown off the disturbing events in the limo and radiated Giselle-ness — innocence, vanity, compassion, nervousness, fantasy — and in the famous madness and suicide scene at the end of act one, she was devastating. Somehow, while maintaining grace and precision and keeping tempo, she was able to convey the discordant, distracted movements of a girl maddened by grief. Lucy was chilled by it; she had seen those gestures before, in real life, unfiltered by art. Caitlin wasn't acting all that much. Rehearsal audiences rarely clap, but this one did.

A covey of cultural leaders were preparing to cosset Mr. Warren even more, making plans to scoot off to some tony joint for a bite.

485

Like many another rich bore subjected to this treatment, Mr. Warren was dizzied. A lifetime of managing trusts and attendance at tedious family suppers had given him little resistance to such glittering parasites. He had detained Caitlin for some time to schmooze with these types, but as soon as she could, she grabbed Lucy and led her back to the dressing room, which by that time was empty.

"I'm not going out with those people and I'm not going back in that fucking limo," announced Caitlin. "We have to escape."

"James Pell Warren will be steamed," said Lucy.

"Oh, fuck him! I'm the star, not him. How can we get away?"

"Out the fire exit. Turn left instead of right when you leave the dressing room, down a flight of stairs and through a door, and you're on 65th."

"How do you know that?" asked Caitlin in surprise.

"I never like to go into a place without knowing how to get out," said Lucy portentously. "Besides, there's a big sign over the door that says fire exit."

"Great! Let me change." Like anyone in show biz, even at the exalted levels, Caitlin had no physical modesty at all and immediately stripped naked. Lucy was used to this

486

and didn't mind seeing Caitlin nude. It was rather like an anatomy lesson — every muscle was visibly working under the translucent skin — interesting in itself, and besides, Caitlin was the only girl Lucy knew with less breast than she herself had. The dancer had been dressing recently in imitation of her downtown crowd, and so she now put on a turtleneck, a miniskirt, tights, short boots, a felt slouch hat, sunglasses, and a long silk duster that reached to her calves, all of it black.

Out of the dressing room, suppressing girlish giggles, and to the fire door, which they found, to their dismay, was alarmed.

"Oh, the hell with it," Caitlin cried, and pushed through, and they escaped running and screeching with the siren whooping behind them. They ran straight down 65th Street and did not stop until they had reached Central Park West. The balmy day increased their spirits, already high from the escapade, and they skipped gaily along the great park's edge, cracking jokes and in general making a spectacle of themselves. Caitlin was, of course, used to this — it was her métier — but Lucy was not, and she found it intoxicating.

"We can get a cab at 72nd," said Caitlin. "Have you got any money? I came out without my wallet." Lucy laughed and rolled her eyes. It was truly remarkable how so many of the very rich girls she knew somehow always managed to be without cash. She said, "I have, but I don't want to blow any on cab fare. Let's walk back to your place."

"Walk?"

"Yeah, through the park. It's a gorgeous day."

"*Walk* home?"

"Yeah, Caitlin, look, it's easy, it's like ballet except you use your whole foot and there's no music. One-two, one-two. That's it! By George, I think she's got it!"

Giggling again, they entered the park. It was by this time nearly five-thirty, and although the shadows were lengthening as the sun sank toward its home in the Jersey suburbs, the air was still pleasant, slightly cool and soft. The oaks had dropped the last of their leaves, and their twigs were covered with fat buds. The maples and plane trees were showing the first hesitant glimmer of pale green. They walked north on the path paralleling the West Drive, crossed over the top of the lake, and entered the Ramble. They bore east, threading the maze of twining paths through the heavily wooded area.

Caitlin said, "Crap, I have something in my shoe," stopped short, and sat on a bench.

Snap!

For an instant, Lucy thought she had imagined it, that it was another and more insistent violent ghost, but only for an instant. Few Sacred Heart girls have been under hostile fire, but Lucy Karp was one of them and she recognized the sound that a high-velocity missile makes when it breaks the sound barrier a few inches from the ear of its target. She yelled, "Get down!" and flung herself at Caitlin, knocking her off the bench.

"Ow! Get off me!" Caitlin yelled. "What're you, crazy!"

Snap! Pop!

This time Lucy recognized the report of the weapon, coming infinitesimally behind the passage of the supersonic bullet.

"Shut up! Someone's shooting at us."

"Are you nuts? This isn't funny, Lucy, I banged my —"

Snap! Pop!

This time a shard of wood sprang up from a bench plank six inches above their heads. Caitlin's eyes popped and she gasped.

"Roll under the bench! Crawl behind that tree!" hissed Lucy, and jabbed Caitlin hard in the ribs to get her moving. The tree was a sycamore three feet across at the base, and there were prickly ilex hedges on either side of it. They crouched behind the tree.

"Who . . . who . . . who's shooting at us?" asked Caitlin.

"I don't know. I didn't spot anyone following us and I'm usually good at that. It must have been the nice day. I got sloppy."

"Someone wants to kill you?"

"Oh, yeah, all the time. Or my mother. Give me your hat." Caitlin seemed paralyzed. Lucy snatched it from her head and held it up on a long twig beyond the cover of the tree. Two quick shots cracked by and the hat flew into the bushes.

"Guy's good," said Lucy. "He's got a rifle, sounds like a .22. He's firing down the sun from the west so we're all lit up and we can't see him."

"I can't believe this! What're we going to do?"

"Nothing right now. He can't get us from where he is, and if he tries to move, we'll hear him. Oh, Jesus, stop crying! Listen, someone's coming."

Feet sounded along the path, crunching leaves, scattering pebbles. More than one person. A gang? Caitlin was chanting, "Oh God, oh God, oh God," in a low, strained voice, which Lucy would not have found so annoying had her friend actually been calling on the deity, but she knew it was only a reflex: it was what people in movies did when they were frightened. The steps came closer, and the sound of conversation. Not English, and a number of different voices. Lucy strained to make out the language. Staccato, atonal, lots of vowels. Closer still. Then comprehension. Someone was having a polite argument, in Japanese.

"I think we have come too far this way," said one voice, a male. "We should have turned back there."

Another voice said, "No, there is the sun, which is west, and we have to go east. Look at the map!"

Lucy grabbed Caitlin's arm and drew her up into a crouch. Together they walked around the tree and the bench and came out onto the path. There were ten of them, five couples of Japanese tourists, all in late middle age, neatly dressed, with the expected festoons of high-end optics on the men and the bags from pricey shops in the hands of the women. Bent almost double, keeping east of the group, Lucy approached them and said, in perfect Japanese, with her voice pitched a tone higher than normal, "Good day, honored visitors. Is it possible that I may be of assistance?"

They all goggled and murmured. The map holder said, "You speak Japanese?"

"All Americans speak a little Japanese," said Lucy blithely. "If you would allow me, I could easily lead you to your destination, pointing out sites of interest along the way."

"We are going to the café by the Conservatory Pond," said the man, dumbfounded.

"An excellent choice, sir. If you would turn to your left up here . . ."

Good, thought Lucy, they were moving east and away from the shooter, who clearly was not up to a massacre. After a minute or so, the man asked, "Why are you walking like that, bent over?"

"Our teachers advise it, sir," answered Lucy brightly. "One hour per day. It helps to strengthen the spine and improve the posture."

The man grunted. He himself was a school administrator in Yokohama, and he made a mental note to inquire into this method.

When they passed under the East Drive and into the more open area leading to the Conservatory, Lucy made a show of consulting her watch and straightened up. Caitlin, still a little stunned, copied her. "The hour is over," Lucy announced, giggling with her hand over her mouth, and then, in a more formal tone, "This path will lead you past the Alice in Wonderland statue, a famous place for photographs. Go left around the lake and there is the café." She bowed. "Thank you for allowing us to be of assistance."

Lucy pulled Caitlin away and took off running, toward Fifth Avenue and 76th Street. At a phone booth, she dialed 911 and called in the shooting. Then she dialed a number known to barely half a dozen people in the city, the very private, emergency-only number of the chief assistant district attorney of New York County.

"Dad? . . . Good. It's me. Look, I'm okay, I'm not hurt, but a couple of minutes ago someone took some shots at Caitlin and me in Central Park. . . . No, I *said* we're okay. . . . Yes, of course, I called 911 first. But they're not going to bust themselves over a couple of kids saying they got shot at, so I thought you could, like, shake things up. . . . Fifth and 76th. . . . Okay, I'll wait right here. . . . Dad, no, he's definitely not chasing us; if he wanted to kill both of us, he would have just waited behind a tree and made sure, so no way is he going to follow us out into the street. I can hear the sirens now. I'll see you."

She hung up the phone and went over to the bench on which Caitlin was sitting, trembling as with the flu. By the time the first cops arrived, the two of them were wailing like babies.

16

Detective Lieutenant Larry Bell had expected to be home in Grasmere in Staten Island by now, but he was not and would probably not be until late this night. He was instead in the office of the chief assistant district attorney, confronting that person, his daughter, and a police captain named Clay Fulton, the head of the DA squad, the district attorney's personal band of investigators. What had started as a routine shots-fired call-in to 911 had become very big very quickly, when it turned out that the shots fired were aimed at the chief assistant DA's daughter, and a fairly famous young ballet dancer, both of whom had been involved as witnesses in a huge double murder on Bell's turf. Bell's people had put that one away in record time, the guy was in jail, and the last thing Bell wanted to think about was that somehow that brilliant success was about to come unstuck.

He was also uncomfortable being in the DA's office at all this early in an investigation. The NYPD is a gigantic quasi-military organization, and it likes to feed the legal authorities facts about cases only when all the loose ends have been tied up or, in some cases, suppressed. But in fact, the police are the legal subordinates of the district attorney. From writing a traffic ticket to arresting a killer, every cop operates under the authority vested in that person by the sovereign people. Thus, technically, the DA is in charge of every investigation. Most assistant DAs are content to let this slide, largely accepting as givens the cases the cops prepare, and checking only for legal sufficiency. Karp, famously, did not see it that way, as every senior detective on the isle of Manhattan well knew, so Bell had to swallow his discomfort and get through his report as best he could.

"We threw out a canvass along both sides of the park, from 65th to 85th," said Bell, "and we ran a sweep across the park from the Great Lawn down to the Sheep Meadow. We must've had a hundred and fifty, two hundred guys on it, horses, bikes, the works. No one saw anyone with a rifle."

"And you're sure it was a rifle?"

"Pretty sure," said Bell carefully. He reached into his suit coat pocket and drew out a bunch of plastic evidence envelopes. "Shooter fired five times. One of the slugs was squashed pretty good, but the others ended up in dirt and we should be able to match them, if we ever find the piece. All .22 long rifles. We found the shell casings about thirty yards away under some bushes. Some fibers there, too. The guy waited for them to come around on the path. Thirty yards is a hell of a long pistol shot, and the shooter plugged the girl's hat twice, so . . ."

"Okay, say it was a rifle," said Karp. "So tell me, how could someone walk through a city street around rush hour with a rifle, and no one saw him?"

"I'm thinking it could have been one of those light folding rifles," said Bell. "The Feather company makes one that breaks down to seventeen inches, weighs a little over three pounds, without scope. Stick it in a sports bag, a shopping bag."

"That's pretty fancy," said Karp after a brief pause. "Sounds like something a pro would use. Any ideas, Clay?"

Karp had, of course, called Fulton the instant he got off the phone from Lucy's initial call, and it was Fulton who had shaken out the police resources. Fulton was Karp's oldest friend on the police, the first Ivy League–educated black police captain in the history of the NYPD, a man whose career was equally divided between brilliant achievement and being an enormous pain in the butt around police headquarters. This was why he was a captain instead of a deputy chief at age fifty-one. Fulton did not mind this very much, as he liked the work and disliked politics. He said, "Well, the obvious question that's got to be on everyone's mind is the possibility of a connection between the Maxwell murders and what looks like a professional attempt on their daughter. That would suggest a gang, or at least some kind of conspiracy, a vendetta against the family."

"It could be a coincidence, too," Bell objected. "Some nut in the bushes and the girls just happened to be there. Come to that, we got no idea which girl was the target. It could have been Lucy here they were after."

Everyone looked at Lucy, sitting pale and silent in the corner of her father's couch. Much to their surprise, she cleared her throat and said, "I don't think so. They were definitely gunning for Caitlin."

"Why do you say that, Lucy?" asked Karp gently.

"Because the first shot went right through where Caitlin was the second before she suddenly sat on the bench. Then I knocked her off the bench and the second shot went right through the plank where she was sitting. I was on top of her then and the shooter had a clear shot at my back, but he didn't take it. Then we crawled under the bench and behind the

497

tree. When I held up Caitlin's hat on a stick, he put two rounds through it. He wanted her, not me."

"Okay, granted," said Bell, "but there's still no evidence of a connection, between this and the parents' murders."

"No, but I hate it that both shooters used a .22, once at point-blank range and then at long range," said Karp, "and so I'd like you to run a match between the Maxwell murder bullets and the ones you've got there."

"The Maxwells were done with a pistol — this was a rifle," said Bell.

"Yeah, but the murder weapon is still missing, and as I recall, it was some kind of target pistol. Couldn't a pistol like that have made those shots?"

"Possibly," Bell admitted. "But . . ."

"So we have to eliminate the possibility that it's the same weapon. If it *is* the same weapon . . ." Karp waggled his hand. "Oh, boy . . ."

Bell shrugged. "So Feydé killed the Maxwells and gave the gun to a friend and the friend is taking revenge on the whole Maxwell family, including the daughter. Hey, the guy's an African, who knows what kind of sh— stuff, weird stuff, they're into."

"Right, Larry, but our case is not built on African weird stuff," said Karp impatiently. "It's built on a very simple story. Man gets angry, man breaks in, man steals gun, man kills people, man escapes with jewelry. If someone is using the same weapon to commit further crimes against the Maxwell family, then it's a whole different case, and a much weaker one. Then we have the real possibility that Mr. X did the Maxwell killings for reasons unknown and planted the jewels in Feydé's toolbox. But it's stupid to speculate or talk about the case anymore until we've definitely eliminated the possibility that it's the same gun. So . . ."

This was a clear invitation for Bell to leave and go down to the police lab on 20th Street to run the ballistics check. He did. When the door closed, Fulton shook his head and chuckled. "That poor son of a gun! Here he had a big high-profile case wrapped up with next to no effort, and he thinks it's about to come unglued. One thing I hate to see is a cop looking for an African revenge society to make a case."

"There's probably fourteen of them listed in the yellow pages," said Karp, laughing, too. But he sobered instantly and turned to face his special assistant, still in his corner. "Murrow, get with Pincus and give him a heads-up on this development. Break it to him easy that we may have to reopen the Maxwell case. And go by public affairs and have them get ready for a press assault. No, we don't know if this sniping attack is connected with the Maxwell murders. We're treating it as a random shooting. The news peg is how coincidental, how tragic, these god-awful times. And absolutely no comment on the weapon similarity. If the cops leak, which they will, we're waiting on lab tests, and so forth; when we have more information, they'll be informed. You know the drill."

Murrow scribbled in his tiny book and left.

Karp went over and sat next to Lucy. "How're you holding up, kiddo?"

"Okay. I'm really tired, though. Can I go home now?"

"Like hell. I'm going to tie you to my leg until you leave for college."

This raised a faint smile. "Is Mom coming home today?"

"No, she's in Wilmington. She's got motions all this week. And you shouldn't be alone."

"I'm all right."

"Uh-uh. It's a Karp family policy — when we get shot at, somebody has to keep us company after."

"Could I go to the bathroom myself?"

"Be my guest. But come right back here."

After the girl had gone out, Fulton said, "That's some kid you got there, Butch. I'd be real proud, kid throws herself in the line of fire to save her pal."

"I am proud," said Karp. "I'm proud and scared to death. I practically puked my guts when she called. Marlene is bad enough, but when Lucy does it . . ." He raised his eyes heavenward.

"It wasn't her fault, though."

"No, but she's got the gene. You know, I didn't expect this. I figured, public-service criminal law, it's an interesting life — I won't get rich, but on the other hand I won't get fat and boring, maybe do some good, get married, settle down. Settle down — doesn't that phrase imply to you calm, stability, basketball hoops in the backyard, little faces around the fireside? I didn't figure on eighteen years of Bonnie and Clyde. Okay, Marlene says she's retiring from being a thug, great, so now I got to start worrying about Lucy? What is this, a tag team? You watch it, the boys are next. Zak's going to join the SEALs and Zik is going to take up parachute skiing on glaciers. My heart won't take it, Clay."

"You love it," said Fulton, laughing. "It keeps you young."

Lucy came back in and resumed her place on the couch. Fulton was making leaving noises when a familiar rap sounded on the door.

"Yes, Pincus! Come in!"

In came that man, holding some papers. He looked distraught. Glancing about the room, he spotted Lucy and froze, jaw gaping.

"My daughter, Pincus," said Karp. "Lucy, this is Dave Pincus. He's prosecuting the Maxwell case." Lucy extended her hand like a duchess and Pincus took it limply.

Karp asked, "Did Murrow fill you in on this shooting business?"

"Yeah, yeah, he did." Pincus seemed unable to take his eyes from Lucy. "He said we were waiting on the ballistics. Meanwhile, there's two things. You remember Juliet Murphy, the social worker who was visiting Feydé? Well, I called Marymount and talked to the head of the sociology department. Murphy's in California on a study grant. She hasn't been there for three months. The woman said Murphy did have her purse snatched sometime last year and lost all her ID. So I called the guard office at the Riker's jail where they got Feydé and had them make a print from the tape. All the visitor rooms are under video surveillance, and Feydé's, um, visitor came there on Sunday. They just faxed it in." He extended to Karp the paper he was carrying.

The photograph was grayed out and grainy, but there was no mistaking who it was. Karp looked at it and without a word handed it to his daughter.

"Well?" he said.

She stared up at him, defiant, but when she met his eyes, she understood that she was in real trouble. Her father had not looked that way at her before. It was a famous look around the courthouse and had broken far more experienced criminals than Lucy Karp. She dropped her eyes and mumbled, "I'm sorry."

"God in heaven, whatever *possessed* you to do something like this? Hand it over!" he snapped.

She gave him the jail pass. He looked at it carefully. "You didn't do this yourself. Where did you get it?" Silence. "Lucy, answer me!"

She said, "I wish to remain silent at this time and I would like to speak to my lawyer."

Fulton made a sound that could have been a startled laugh converted out of prudence into a heavy throat-clearing sound. Pincus was still standing there goggling at it all.

Karp said, "Pincus, could you wait outside for a minute? I'll need to talk to you later."

Pincus vanished. Karp tromped around his desk and sat in his chair. He swiveled it so that he faced the window and sat there in silence for a full minute. When he spun around again to face Lucy, he was calmer, in control, but far from warm when he spoke. "Let me explain to you what you've done. The law reads, 'with intent to defraud, deceive, or injure another, possesses or utters an instrument he knows to be forged.' That's criminal possession of a forged instrument, PL 170.20, a Class A misdemeanor. Then, since this Murphy is an actual person, there's criminal impersonation, second degree, 190.25, quote, with intent to defraud, he impersonates and acts as another person, unquote, also a Class A misdemeanor."

"Kids use phony ID all the time," said Lucy sulkily.

"Excuse me, are you waiving your right to silence? Do you wish to make a statement at this time?"

"No."

"Then shut up! Two Class A misdemeanors, each of which carry up to six-month sentences for youthful offenders, plus a fine of up to five thousand dollars. Beyond these, there may be other charges, based on what passed between you and the defendant prisoner. Your involvement with this man also casts a shadow on the events of this afternoon, and your version of those events, if it turns out the shooting in the park is connected to the Maxwell case. This is quite apart from any damage that may be done to the People's case against —"

"But we didn't talk about the murders," Lucy protested, "not really, we just —"

"I said *shut up!* Listen to me! You are on the edge of a meat grinder. You could get ground up, and not only can't I help you, but I am specifically abjured and disqualified from helping you by virtue of my position here. *How do you think that makes me feel?*"

Lucy sat stunned. She was far from naive about the way the world worked, but the notion that her father might be tormented in this way, by something she had done, had never entered her mind.

Karp said, "Go make your call. Use one of the phones outside."

She left the room immediately, found a phone in the DA's waiting room, and dialed a number.

"Mom? It's me."

"Hi, honey — look, I'm in the middle of something. Can I call you back later?"

"Me and Caitlin got shot at in the park, and I think I'm under arrest or something. I'm in Dad's office."

A digital nothingness for some seconds. "I see. Let's have it, from the beginning."

Lucy told the story, both stories, and their intersection, leaving out only the part about how she had obtained the false pass. "And Dad's incredibly steamed," she concluded. "He thinks it's going to mess up his case against Moussa. But, anyway, I don't think he did it."

"Yes, well, I wouldn't stress that point to your dad, if I were you. Why don't you let me speak to him now."

"Are you coming back?"

"Eventually, but all hell broke loose today, and I have to stay with my client. I'll call Uncle Harry and get him to meet you at the courthouse. He'll bring one of Osborne's lawyers and you should be fine for the time being."

"But I want *you!*" wailed Lucy.

"I know, baby, but you can't have me. Surgeons don't operate on their kids and lawyers don't defend their kids. When you love someone, it clouds your mind, and you have to have a perfectly clear mind in this business. And I do love you, you know that."

"Right, but you're never here," said Lucy with petulance suddenly breaking through. She regretted it immediately, acting like a baby, whining for her mommy. But it was true. She was absolutely cool under actual gunfire, but now she found herself reduced to disgusting jelly. That her father had turned into Darth Vader didn't help either.

Marlene ignored this last remark and said, "Lucy, it's going to be all right. Now put your father on."

Lucy mashed the hold button on the set and slammed down the phone. She marched into Karp's office and said, "My lawyer wants to talk to you."

Karp said, "You wait outside." When Lucy stalked out again, he pressed the flashing button and picked up the receiver.

"Here's a fine howdy-do," said his wife.

"I assume you're coming home."

"Not right away. Things are a little unglued right now. We went down to Dover today to argue the polygraph motion, and when we got back to Mt. Holly, some shithead had spray-painted Nazi stuff all over their house. 'Jew bitch die,' 'kike baby-killer,' the whole works."

"Ah, shit, Marlene!"

"Yeah, there's been a nasty little undercurrent of anti-Semitism attached to this case from the get-go, and now it's filtered down to the rednecks. Selma is hysterical, she wants to plead out like yesterday and move house, the mister is medicated for palpitations, and Sarah, if you can believe it, is carrying the show. But I can't leave just yet."

"Oh, that's marvelous, Marlene! It's a good thing you dropped the boys off at your mom's. That's all I need right now is a call from Nanny-on-Demand. Could you remind me once more why we don't have a normal life?"

"Because we're not normal people. I hear you came down pretty hard on her."

"I did. I lost it for a bit. First the shooting business and then she pulls a bonehead stunt like that. If it was just a matter of trying to sneak into a club and getting busted for false ID, hell, a stern lecture and a court appearance, but this, as you can imagine, is different. I realize it's not her fault, but she could not have picked a worse time and place and prisoner."

"Why place? Oh, God, your thing with the jail!"

"For starters. I understand they still regale young corrections officers with tales of how Butch Karp betrayed the criminal justice system, lo, these twenty years ago, by pressing a case against three guards who beat a prisoner into a coma. I put them away for a long time and Corrections has never forgiven me. The director is probably on the horn with Jack, as we speak, demanding punishment to the full extent of the law. Even if I resigned this minute, the office would still have to come down on her like a ton of bricks. Equal justice under law is what it says on the front of the building, and every so often we have to nail someone to make the point. They came down on your Delaware kid for the same reason. And Jack is not apt to be sympathetic, because the fact that she's my daughter colors the illegal visits and clouds the prosecution of the highest-profile murder case of the year. Why is the kid of the chief assistant DA visiting a defendant she hardly knows? Could Karp be using this ploy to wangle incriminating evidence out of said defendant, violating the spirit if not the letter of numerous Supreme Court rulings on custodial interrogation? And then someone tries to shoot her? Why?"

"I thought they were after Caitlin."

"On Lucy's say-so, which is also now clouded."

"Oh, come on, Butch!"

"Well, Jesus, Marlene, *I* know she's not bent, but look at it from the standpoint of someone trying to make trouble. The press hates both of us, I got a bunch of people don't particularly like me right here in the court-house, and our kid has walked right into the crosshairs. If she has to serve any time in their fucking jail, God knows what they'll do to her."

"Surely there's no chance of that?"

"Well, a good kid, clean record, a misde-meanor charge — ordinarily it'd be a fine and

509

probation, maybe a suspended sentence. But this ain't anything near ordinary. I just don't know, and there's not a thing I can do officially." Neither spoke for a while. "You've arranged representation?"

"Yeah, Harry'll be coming with the Osborne A-team. Is she furious with me?"

"Probably."

"Are you?"

"Ah, shit, Marlene, don't start that! Look, I have to go, Flynn is standing in my doorway gesturing. I'll call you." Karp hung up.

Flynn said, "He wants to see you. Now."

Karp quickly maneuvered to the anteroom outside his office, where Lucy was waiting. "Tell him I'm on my way, and tell Pincus not to move. Oh, and Flynn? If Lieutenant Bell calls from the police lab, I need to talk to him immediately, wherever I am. Go! Captain Fulton, you need to take this young person into custody, read her her rights, and escort her into the system. I'll meet you back here after, assuming I still have my job." And he left.

Fulton said, "Well, kid, you going to come quietly, or do I have to slap the cuffs on you?"

"I was hoping you'd hit me a couple on the head with a phone book," said Lucy. "I feel so *stupid*. Uncle Clay, is my dad really going to lose his job?"

Fulton shrugged. "Anything's possible. I

think what gripes him right now is that he really can't do anything to help you. You might have to take some lumps."

"You mean jail?"

"It's always a possibility. But look at it this way: even though you're not going to get any special treatment on the good side, your dad's not going to let them shaft you on the bad side, just to make a point. He can do that much. It's going to go down by the book."

The district attorney was pacing back and forth in front of his windows, clutching a long, green, unlit Bering in his teeth, the worst possible body language. His face was mottled red. This meant he was really angry and not merely pretending for effect.

Karp approached and asked mildly, "You wanted to see me?"

"Can't you keep that damn family of yours under control?" the DA cried. "Jesus H. Christ! First Marlene, now it's Lucy. And she would pick the goddamn Maxwell case to screw with."

"Would you like my resignation?"

The DA glared blue sparks. "It may come to that, boyo. I just got off the phone with my esteemed colleague over at Corrections. You'd think the girl smuggled a pound of heroin and a box of hacksaws into his precious facility. They're out for blood, mister, and they're going to get it one way or another. And, of course, they leaked it immediately, so the jackals are out. I got half a dozen calls in — is the DA using kids to worm their way into the confidence of defendants in custody? What the hell am I supposed to tell them, huh?"

"You could try the truth."

"The *truth!* What the hell does the truth have to do with it? This is a public relations disaster. Speaking of which, please oh please tell me that neither you nor Marlene had anything to do with this."

"That's insulting," said Karp, tightening his own jaw. The two men stared hard at each other, until Karp said, "Before you kick me out, I want to offer my apologies on behalf of Lucy. I think she went into this in all innocence, to try to bring some good out of a bad situation. She felt sorry for the man."

"The man murdered her friend's parents in cold blood, for God's sake, and she felt *sorry* for him?"

"What can I say, Jack. She's a Christian. A good Catholic girl, in fact. Unfortunately, she's a good Catholic girl who knows how to get hold of high-quality forged documents."

The DA fumed for some time longer, although at a lower level, making various comments to the effect that when he was a lad, good Catholic girls hung out at the Order of Mary and didn't utter any false paper at the goddamn jail, and then he sat down in his big chair, removed the cigar, studied its chewed end, tossed it in the basket, ordered Karp to a chair, and demanded, "Okay, what do you suggest we do to climb out of this?"

"Okay, one, it's a serious offense and we're taking it seriously. Lucy will be subject to the full rigors of the law, without favor. On the other hand, I'm not going to allow her to be hung to satisfy the Corrections Department, who you know have had a hard-on for me for some time. Nor am I prepared to ask them to play nice, in return for us overlooking some of the shit they pull from time to time. We run it straight up, just like she was any kid caught on a bad ID. Let the judge decide. Two, as far as Feydé is concerned, we promise and launch a full investigation to see if his constitutional rights have been violated." This did not go down well. The DA snorted deep drafts of air and shook his mane from side to side like a horse trying to dislodge a fly. The district attorney is the chief investigating officer of any county. For him to investigate his own office, especially at the highest levels, is the most excruciating process imaginable. Yet if he did nothing, other investigative units, at the federal and state attorneys general, would be delighted to jump in with both feet, dancing on his head.

"We'll go with a blue ribbon," said the DA. "A couple of judges, the ex-governor, a select group, including some of my more respectable enemies, so it doesn't look like a whitewash. They'll fart around for a couple of weeks and that'll keep the press off us, and by the time we come up clean, no one will give a rat's ass." He looked sharply at Karp. "And we are clean, aren't we? You're absolutely sure there was no culpable motive here, no helping Daddy at his big job, no revenge on behalf of the friend, no Nancy Drew horseshit . . . ?"

"Jack, the only critical question is was Lucy Karp acting as a covert agent of the state? There's not the tiniest scrap of evidence that she was. She was not sent by us, nor did she convey tainted information to us. I will deny it, Roland will deny it, Pincus will deny it, and the charge is absurd on the face of it. The kid is a do-gooder, she bakes cookies for the poor, for crying out loud, and I guarantee you, if anyone tries to make her a scapegoat, there'll be relays of nuns with signs and candles outside this courthouse, led by me."

The DA's big face cracked the faintest grimace of amusement. "It'd be worth it just to

514

see that, fella. Okay, we'll play it that way, but you're out of it, totally recused from any involvement in Maxwell henceforth. I want a statement to the press on that subject —"

There was an interrupting knock on the door and O'Malley stuck her head in. "It's your secretary, Butch. A Lieutenant Bell."

"I got to take this, Jack. It may be relevant to Maxwell."

The DA waved him on and Karp picked up one of the DA's phones and punched the lit button, then listened silently for a moment. "Are you positive? . . . Okay, Lieutenant, thanks. I'll get back to you in a bit." He hung up.

"What was that?"

"From the ballistics lab. You heard about Lucy and Caitlin Maxwell getting sniped in the park today? Well, the gun the shooter used was the gun that killed the Maxwells, a target pistol."

"Shit!"

"Meaning that either Feydé passed the gun to an unknown accomplice, who's pursuing a vendetta against that family, and of whose existence we have not one hint, or we have the wrong guy in jail, who was the victim of a clever frame. So, until we have the new shooter, our case against Feydé is not what it was."

"The earrings . . ."

"Could have been planted. It's reasonable doubt, Jack. And it raises the suspicion of a real conspiracy. We put this thing down so fast we didn't really look into who might've wanted the Maxwells dead. Business rivals, lovers, hell, even the kids or their friends — don't look that way, Jack, it happens, and in some of the best families. No, we grabbed the convenient stranger because the victim blew up at him and because he had pieces of stolen jewelry in his toolbox. Borderline thin, when you think about it."

The DA sighed disgustedly and waved Karp away. "Stop! I don't need any more bad news today. Christ, it'll mean reopening the investigation, full bore. The cops won't like it."

Karp waited, watching the political calculations play across his boss's face.

"Oh, hell!" the DA snapped at last. "Let 'em lump it. Just go and fix this mess so it stays fixed!"

"I can't fix it if I'm out of Maxwell, Jack," said Karp, but got no response from the DA, who was reaching for his phone. Karp left the office and walked slowly to his own. A typical Jack Keegan solution, one that left Karp positioned to take the fall, if a fall was required.

Pincus was still in the outer office, and

516

Karp motioned him in as he sped by. He sat the man down and without preamble told him the latest, and that his beautiful case against Moussa Feydé would have to be re-opened. Pincus cursed fluently and turned from pink to fuchsia in the face, but having been elaborately socialized as to reasonable doubt made no coherent objection to the change. No sooner was this conversation over than Roland Hrcany appeared in Karp's doorway.

"Hello, Roland," said Karp, "I've been wondering when you were going to show up."

"I was across town at a meeting. What the fuck is going on? I'm hearing crazy shit about Lucy screwing up our case in Maxwell."

"Our case is screwed, but not because of Lucy," and Karp went through the whole thing again, including his meeting with the DA. "You have to front it, Roland. I can't," Karp concluded, and was interested in the remarkable expressions that then crossed Hrcany's craggy face. Ordinarily, Roland was delighted to see Karp discomforted, and in his mind the two of them were in strenuous competition for the DA's favor, and for glory. But like many horrible men, he had points of honor, and it would never have occurred to him to take advantage of a family problem to get one up on his rival. He nodded and said,

517

"No problem. What's set up?"

"Murrow!" called Karp. "What's with that press conference?"

"Seven o'clock, the public affairs media room," said Murrow. "I have talking points."

"They'll have to be changed," said Karp. "Now it's the attempted murder of Caitlin Maxwell with the same gun that killed her parents. We're reopening the investigation into their deaths as a result. That should take some of the gloss off the Lucy story, but there will still be questions."

"Yeah, from your good friends in the press," said Roland.

"Them, to which the answer is you're taking it seriously, so seriously that the DA is setting up a commission that he expects will clear his office of any and all improprieties, et cetera, et cetera. I'll stand up, the tormented father, and Lucy will stand up, too, looking suitably remorseful. We tell the simple truth, we don't stonewall, we don't talk about matters under adjudication. Speaking of the devil . . ."

Lucy came into the office with Fulton. Karp's heart went out to her, she looked so beaten down. She had not been crying. That would come later, in gallons. Her mother's daughter, yet again. He looked inquiringly at Fulton.

"Booked and arraigned. The lawyer's named Anthony Scopetta, he seemed pretty sharp. He explained the peculiar situation to the judge, one parent out of town, the other being you. I explained I was a friend of the family and so the judge released her to me, pending hearing."

"Okay, good. Thanks, Clay," Karp said. "Roland, it's your show. Feel free to enlist young Murrow here on the new talking points. And I owe you one."

"And I'll collect, too," said Hrcany, who clapped his hands once and said, "Okay, people, let's get this abortion over with. Pincus, call Feydé's counsel and give him a courteous heads-up on this, and try to feel out whether he's going to go anywhere with it. Murrow, you come with me."

They were all filing out the door when Karp stopped Pincus. "Pincus, what was the second thing?"

"What?"

"When you came in with the jail fax, you said there were two things. What was the other one?"

"Oh, that. Nothing, really. Just something from Feydé's Q and A. Something about the antique desk he was working on. He claimed he went back to the workshop and worked on the desk. This was after he went to the café, the time that we figure the murder went down, and he said . . . wait a second, I got it right here." He brought a stack of papers out of a folder and riffled through them. "He said, quote, I fixed the inlay, and worked on the catch. It was a complicated catch and it took me a long time to do, but it was so interesting I could not stop, and so on. Well, the thing is, there's no catch on that desk, no locks either. It just opens right up. So, I figured, a lie, intent to mislead, it could be useful, and we didn't press him on it then, we had so much more —"

"Not a catch," said Lucy, "a *cache*."

Everyone looked at her. "Excuse me?" said her father.

"The secretaire Mrs. Maxwell bought. It has a *cache*, a secret compartment. Moussa showed it to me and Brian once. The decorator knew about it, too. I heard him laughing with Mrs. Maxwell about it. He said she could keep her love letters in it."

Everyone now looked at Pincus. Karp asked, with deceptive gentleness, "Pincus, did you know about this item?"

"No, I didn't. Hey, that's why it's secret, right?" Pincus laughed, but nobody else did.

Karp and Roland looked at one another and rolled their eyes. Roland put a heavy hand on his minion's shoulder. "Pincus, get a warrant. Get a cop. Get the key to that house. Look in the secret compartment and, if you would, tell us what, if anything, you find there. Do you think you can do that?"

"Sure, but, I mean, how do I get into it?"

Lucy said, "There's a statue holding up a candle thing on the right side. You turn it left until it clicks, then right, then back the way it was, and it makes a side panel pop open."

Pincus repeated this to everyone's satisfaction and left. Roland said, "Twenty dollars the gun's there."

"No bet," said Karp. "We need to talk to this decorator — what's his name?"

"Oren Lorel. What, he aced them because they didn't like the drapes?"

"There are stranger things. The point is, we know nothing about the Maxwells or their affairs. Lorel had an alibi. Let's check it. Let's check his pals. Let's find out what his relationship with the missus was. A sex thing, a money thing, a drug thing?"

"Not a sex thing," said Roland, holding up a hand limp-wristed. "Not with the missus, anyway."

"You're not supposed to do that anymore, Roland," said Karp, "but anyway, my point is, there's something. Why am I telling you this? You know how to do this. And I'm not supposed to participate in Maxwell anymore."

"Lucky me," said Roland, and left. Fulton also left shortly thereafter for home and family, leaving Karp with what passed for his family this evening.

"Want me to order in? Pizza?" he asked.

"Sure, whatever." Listlessly.

"Not hungry? Boy, I'm starving." He dialed a number. "What do you want on it?"

"Are you still angry at me?"

Karp replaced the phone. "No, I was, but I'm not now. I was afraid for you, like when you see a little kid run out in the street. The parent grabs him and whaps him a couple on the butt and then hugs him like crazy. It was like that. A flashback. Instinct. But also . . . hmm, how can I put this? To little kids, parents are almost inanimate, like vending machines. Press the button, get food, comfort, love, protection, sort of for free, and there are buttons that you learn you're not supposed to press. Then one day you wake up and there's an adult living in your house instead of your kid. And you kind of hope that adult will care about you, you know, as a person, that they'll treat you like a mensch and not like a busted vending machine, the kind you kick until the candy pops out. So I felt hurt. I thought you would see the effect pulling your stunt would have on me, but you didn't."

"Mom does it all the time," the girl burst out angrily. "Did."

"Yes, she did, and it was something that was between us, something not good in our marriage. And we can thank God she never got caught. But you're not her, are you?"

"I'm like her."

"Yes, you're a little like her and a little like me. Not an easy combo, kid. I feel for you."

She was struggling hard not to cry now. The rippling spasms of suppressed tears moved over her thin face. A stifled sob slipped out, and he said, "You can cry if you want. Nobody here but us."

Her jaw tightened, and she glared at him; her Marlene look. "I'd rather die," she said, "than go on TV blubbering. And I want anchovies, mushrooms, and green peppers."

17

Night in Mt. Holly, and Marlene found herself missing the sounds of the city, in her
mind symbolic of missing her family and, on
a deeper, darker level, her abandoned former
life. Rusticated junkies must feel this way,
she thought, wandering the country lanes,
seeing dime bags among the wildflowers.
The house was silent, except for the idiot
noises of the appliances; outside, silence, too,
no wind, too early in the year for the suburban insects. The dog lurked under a juniper
outside, invisible, on guard, keeping them
safe, at least from skinhead yokels.

Marlene was at the dining room table,
adrift in legal papers, the long sheets anno-
tated with colored scrawlings and stuck with
Post-its in different colors, a clever scheme, if
only she could recall what it all meant. At
such times, when copious reading was required, Marlene keenly felt the loss of her eye.
She groaned, rubbed her good one, and took
a sip of cooled coffee. Through a doorway,
she could just make out the head and shoulders of her client, sitting in front of the elec-

tronics wall, the head enclosed by thick padded earphones, the shoulders wrapped in a bright wool afghan throw. They were alone in the house; Selma and Mr. Goldfarb were at a local hospital, the former watching through a haze of Xanax the cardiac monitoring of the latter. It was hard to blame them for their reaction. One saw it on television all the time, but the unfiltered reality, lasting longer than the usual thirty seconds, was another matter. Even Marlene, long inured to violence, felt the force of the violation.

Remarkably, the sprayed obscenities were already gone; the garage door and the house wall were again clean. Marlene thought the kid had done well. While her mother wailed and called the dad, Sarah had gone into the garage, grabbed a scrub brush and a can of mineral spirits, and started on the wall, grimly, heedless of what the splatters were doing to the neat navy wool suit she had worn to court. Shortly after Sarah started cleaning, a pickup truck had pulled up, a middle-aged couple had dismounted, and without a word to anyone, the man had plugged in the belt sander he had brought along and begun sanding the defacement off the garage door. His wife followed behind him, wiping dust, and spraying primer, which they had also brought. Another car pulled up, and also without much fuss, a guy in painter's overalls emerged and laid down a neat coat of exterior white. The press arrived in droves and Marlene was busy keeping them in order. The cameras got it all.

Marlene rose, stretched, and walked through to where Sarah was. She sat next to the girl, who took off her headphones, used the remote control to stop her cassette, and offered an exhausted smile.

"How are you liking that tape?" Marlene asked.

"It's great. Opera, I never liked it before. I thought it was phony. All that screeching." Sarah laughed apologetically and wrapped the afghan more tightly about her shoulders, although the room was warm. "Are you going to leave?"

"No, I'm going to stay on the couch here. You shouldn't be alone, and . . ." Marlene hesitated.

"Those guys could come back, right? The Nazis."

"It's a possibility. Are you frightened?"

"Not really. I feel safe with you. This is what you used to do, isn't it? Guarding women?"

"Yeah. I guess you can take the girl out of security, but you can't take security out of the girl. Anyone tries to come after you physically, they will not be happy, I guarantee it. Who were those people who came by? The couple with the sander and the painter?"

"The couple was the McNallys. They live a street down from us. We just know them to wave to. I have no idea who the painter was. He came up to me and said, 'I'm sorry about all this. We're not like that. Good luck.' And he left."

"That's pretty amazing. Our country. Go figure."

"Yes. But you know, when I saw the . . . what they did, I felt this big surge of guilt. Oh, God, what I've done to my parents. It all came back in a rush."

"But you showed a lot of class there today, what you did."

"I was so angry. I felt violated, my home . . . but, Marlene, I don't know now. I can't let my folks go through any more of this. What if my father . . . ?"

"Dies? Sarah, it's their burden. The way it works, parents sacrifice themselves for their children, not the other way around."

"That's so cruel!"

"Yes. Look, things are coming to a head now. This incident today — I know it sounds horrible to say it, but from the point of view of the case, it does us good. Because it makes it harder for the state and the people who buy their line to demonize you. All of a sudden, you're a victim of hatred. Those folks who came by and helped out, that's an indication. Then the motions I've been filing are having an effect. The state now sees that you can't just be squashed. They made you their designated fall guy, but you're not falling. Every time I file a motion, it rocks them a little, and I'm feeding information into the legal system, information they could have obtained but didn't bother. It makes them look bad."

"You mean the lie detector stuff?"

"That, but also the others. I'm painting a pattern of prosecutorial abuse. We moved to void the search warrant of your room and its fruits. Then we moved to dismiss on the unavailability of vital evidence, the Dumpster contents. Look, the victim's skull was crushed. They immediately said the skull was crushed because you guys crushed it, hence murder, but we demonstrated that the skull was crushed postmortem. By what? By the junk dumped on top of it in the Dumpster. Where is that junk? The cops disposed of it. Disposing of potentially exculpatory evidence is grounds for dismissal, under *Lolly v. State*, in Delaware, and *Arizona v. Youngblood*, a Supreme Court ruling. And because of the incompetence and corruption in Dover, the stuff leaks out to the press. People have a very different picture of you than they did a couple of months ago. The state can't handle that, because if you're not a monster, the indictment is an absurd overcharge, a disgusting miscarriage of justice, and they look like fools."

"But we've lost on the first motions."

"Yes, we have, so far. I misjudged Shearing. I knew he was frightened, but I thought that would make him be scrupulously fair. It didn't turn out that way. He's playing safe by going with the state, instead of standing up for what's right. It's a common failing. No judge ever got kicked out of office by seeming too hard on defendants, but a lot of them have been dumped for letting people off on what the idiot press calls 'technicalities.' That's why there are appeals courts. But every time he rejects a motion on specious grounds, it makes a successful appeal more likely."

"Does that mean you expect to lose? I mean, if we go to trial."

"No, I think we can win, and things are moving our way. The state's under pressure, and they're dumb, and so they're going to make a dumb mistake. The newspapers have been full of speculation that they're going to offer Peter a deal."

The girl stiffened slightly at the sound of

this name. "Yeah, I saw that. What does it mean?"

"It means they're going to let him plead guilty to a lesser offense, in return for his testimony against you. We knew this was coming, didn't we?"

A sad nod. "I guess. That's bad for us, isn't it?"

"Not necessarily. It means we sever the cases, separate the two trials. I've already moved to sever. And as for his plea, it becomes a *Bruton* issue. Sorry — *Bruton* is a Supreme Court ruling. Bruton and Evans knocked over a post office. They caught the two of them and Evans confessed. The postal officer he confessed to testified at the joint trial as to that confession. The judge instructed the jury that even though the confession was good evidence against Evans, the jury wasn't supposed to use it to make inferences as to Bruton's guilt. Bruton was convicted, surprise, surprise, and he appealed up to the Supremes, who ruled that even with the instruction, his right under the Sixth Amendment to confront witnesses against him had been violated. I know, boring, but in terms of our case, it means either that if they use Peter's confession against you, I get to grill him on the witness stand."

"That's good?"

"Honey, he's lying. They're not going to let *him* near a polygraph. And if I can't show a jury he's lying, I belong in a different business."

Sarah did not seem cheered by this. Marlene felt a pang of irritation. She was not cut out to be a cheerleader it seemed. She patted the girl's shoulder. "Sarah, I know it looks dark. It *is* dark. But please believe me, it's getting lighter. That's why I think you should hang on." In the dining room, Marlene's cell phone began to warble, for which she was grateful.

"I don't know . . . ," said Sarah, biting her lip.

Marlene stood up and patted the girl's shoulder again. "Just sleep on it, okay? Things'll look less dire in the morning."

Marlene answered the phone. "What took you so long?"

"Sorry," said Karp. "It's been a little crazy."

"How is she?"

"She seems fine. She's curled up on the couch in my office fast asleep."

"You're still in the office!"

"Yeah, we had a break on the Maxwell case, and I wanted to hang around to see how it turned out. We had a press conference. You might be able to catch clips at eleven."

"How did you do?"

"I didn't *do* anything. Roland handled the whole thing, with an assist from Murrow. I stood up and looked grim. Lucy walked through it like a queen. You know how they bay and shove mikes in your face — 'Hey, Lucy, did your father put you up to it?' 'Did you have sex with the killer?' Nice stuff. It just bounced off her."

"I doubt that," said Marlene. "Christ! I should be there. What was her disposition at the arraignment?"

Karp told her and added, "She went through the process in that wacky parochial-school uniform she wears. Fulton said one of the working girls asked her, 'Sugar, what're *you* doing down here?' and she said, 'I broke into the jail.' Apparently they couldn't stop laughing. Anyway, the ex parte aspects of the jail business may be moot."

"This is because of this break in Maxwell?"

Karp explained about Mrs. Maxwell's desk and its secret. "So they went over there, and there was the gun and a box of rounds, in the desk all the time, while the cops are tromping through every sewer on the Upper East Side. The ballistics check out. It's the murder weapon and the gun used to shoot at Caitlin."

"So Feydé's off the hook?"

"Next thing to it," said Karp.

"Unless it's a conspiracy and he's in it."

"Wait, it gets better. So, of course, we were interested in the decorator, who as far as we know is the only one who knew about the compartment besides the defendant, and the kids. And the cops went by and had a talk. He had alibis for the times of both shootings. The question was, because he looked so good, could he have an accomplice, could the alibi be broken? Our great detective minds are cogitating over this while the pistol is being worked over in the police labs. You ever see a gun like this? It's a foot long, heavy, with a big carved handle and a box magazine that drops down from the center, like on an assault rifle. And it was dirty, prints all over it, not Feydé's, not Lorel's either, small prints, they thought it might be a woman, it looked like they were made with mud, like the shooter put his hand in a wet spot while he was lying on the ground. Brown mud, you get the picture?"

"Yeah." The picture was indeed coming up, but Marlene's mind shied away from it.

"But our police laboratories, using the finest scientific analysis, showed that it wasn't mud at all. It was chocolate."

"Oh, Butch, no!"

"Yes. Chocolate with tiny fragments of peanut butter embedded therein. The experts are guessing Reese's Pieces, but, of course, the police labs don't have lots of experience with felons leaving chocolate smears on murder weapons. They're more blood-and-semen sorts of guys."

"The prints match? There's no doubt?"

"Well, funny you should ask. Little Brian didn't actually have his prints taken during the original investigation. The kid seemed practically comatose with shock, accent on *seemed* now, and when they dusted the murder scene, it was easy to eliminate the little, tiny fingerprints they found there. It was his house, and they weren't looking especially hard for any preteen killers. But the same prints are on the release mechanism on the desk, and the secret compartment, and on the box of .22 rounds in the compartment, and there will be partials on the shell casings found at the murder scene, and probably on Feydé's toolbox, and even on the earrings the kid planted there. Once you know what you're looking for, stuff turns up. No, it looks like Brian Maxwell walked into his parents' bedroom and shot them both in the head. He was careful to choose the weapon that made the least noise, and the one that had a hair trigger. Then he stashed the thing in the desk and curled up in a ball in his closet."

Marlene said, "God is a pig," in Sicilian.

"Later, for some unknown reason, he cleverly goes back to his old house, gets the gun, takes it in his backpack to his fancy private school, slips away from the theater while granddad is busy, tries to kill his sister, and cleverly manages to return the gun to its hiding place, meanwhile uncleverly leaving chocolate-smeared fingerprints all over the weapon. Just like a kid. And there you have it."

"There you do. You sound exhausted, love."

"I *am* exhausted," agreed Karp. "It knocks the stuffing out of you, this kind of thing. Not just me, either — everybody's wandering around like *Invasion of the Body Snatchers*, the cops, Roland . . . Pincus looked nauseous, green skin, the works. Every murder upsets the order of the world, and a child murder the worst of all, but a child *murderer!* There aren't any words. And the legal implications . . . Christ, I can't even think about that now."

"What will you do?"

"Oh, the guys are uptown rousting the monster out of his lair as we speak. Probably the first prisoner in history to do the perp walk in Batman jammies. I can't think about this anymore. What's with you?"

She gave him the short version. He said, "Sounds good. You seem to have Leviathan on the ropes."

"Not the ropes, no. But I landed a couple of good ones. If we went to trial tomorrow, at least it wouldn't be a simple massacre."

"The state's going to deal with the boy."

"Believe it."

"And you'll sever and go with *Bruton*?"

"Yes, and if they want to use his testimony against her, he'll have to get up on the stand."

"They won't want that," said Karp consideringly. "I can't imagine they'll persist in this intentional-murder horseshit, if all they have is the testimony of the confessed coconspirator. They'll have to revise the charges."

"I think so, too. I'm waiting. And they'll try something sneaky, too. They're sneaky people."

"So it seems. I got a call here, babe. I'll talk to you later."

The call was from Roland Hrcany. "They're bringing him in."

"How did it go?" asked Karp.

"Granddad was not pleased. He's a tough old bastard. Rich, old money, heavily connected, and a lawyer himself, trusts and corporate, but he knows the rules. It was more like a job interview than an arrest, and we didn't get hired. He implied that the arrest was a cheap stunt to take the pressure off you and Lucy. I'll tell you, man, this is going to be a fucking bear."

"Anything turn up on the search warrant?"

"Sure, comic books and video games. Evidence of depravity. The kid didn't keep a diary where he confesses all."

"No statement, I presume."

"Oh, dream on! Warren told him to shut up and he did. Kid had a little smirk on his face, too, like he was enjoying this. You ever see him? Looks like a fucking angel — unbelievable! Oh, and here's the beauty part. Warren retained Lionel T. Waley to represent his kid."

"A good choice," said Karp after a shocked moment.

"I thought you'd think so," said Hrcany, laughing cruelly.

After Karp put down the phone, he sat without moving for a while, listening to the building and his daughter's soft breathing. There was a sound from the adjoining cubicle, the former closet where his special assistant dwelt.

"Murrow, are you still there?"

Murrow emerged, looking surprisingly fresh. Karp felt as if mold were growing all over his own face and down his throat. "Go home, Murrow."

"You're sure?"

"Yes, it's all over. Or just starting, which-ever. I just heard that Lionel T. Waley is going to represent our young defendant. Is that a look of incomprehension I see? I thought you knew everything, Murrow."

"A defense counsel, I presume."

"*The* defense counsel. The White Shark. Also, as you may have heard, the only person ever to beat me in a murder case. Roland can't wait to get into the ring with him on this Maxwell business. If he wins, it will be the final and inarguable proof that he's a better man than I am."

"Will he?"

"Oh, he might, in a straight did-he-do-it case. The forensics are pretty strong, a mur-der weapon with only the defendant's prints on it, and they'll find some evidence the kid arranged the frame on Feydé. But Waley won't do that, he'll admit the crime and plead insanity, and I'm not sure anybody on earth can beat Waley arguing an insanity plea."

"He's that good?"

Karp leaned back in his big chair and stuck his feet up on the desk. "Oh, he's good, all right, but insanity pleas are a very peculiar le-gal institution. Basically, they exist so that rich people don't have to do heavy time for murders. Juries believe, in their inner hearts, that poor people are depraved and guilty and rich people who kill must be crazy. I mean they got everything, why would they risk it all, unless they were nuts. So you go in with that, for starters. Okay, next — you know the insanity rule?"

"Yes, I know the rule."

"Okay, following *Patterson*, the burden is on the defense to demonstrate that the defendant had the requisite mental disease or defect by a preponderance of the evidence. What is that? In practice, it means we line up the shrinks and the shrinks duke it out, and the prize goes to the most convincing team of docs. In this case, of course, we have the added factor of the defendant's age. In common law, under seven is infancy, presumed without criminal capacity, over fourteen, or thirteen in this state, we assume criminal capacity, and with certain crimes we can try them as adults. Between seven and thirteen there's a rebuttable presumption of incapacity, with the burden on the prosecution to prove a consciousness of the wrongfulness of the act. Then we have the whole juvenile court system, where the criminal capacity is deemed irrelevant, because juvie courts are set up solely in the interests of the child, to rehabilitate. In cases of particularly horrendous crimes, which I'd say this one is, the state can petition to try the kid as an adult."

"Which we'll do?"

Karp thought for a moment and then sighed. "I guess. But the truth is, the law is supposed to have a hole for every peg, but it just doesn't for this one. An eleven-year-old is *not* an adult. Everyone knows that. And he murdered his parents in their sleep. We *want* him to be responsible, we *want* someone to pay for that crime, to clear the books, so we can all go back to sleep and forget about the inner demons. But the truth is, and I mean the *truth*, not the kind of thing that juries deal with, the truth is we don't know what to do with this fucking kid. We don't even have a name for it."

The next day, in Dover, Mike Brewster supplied Marlene and her client with a couple of big boys to move them through the crush of newsies, and another guy to watch the Goldfarbs' house. Sarah was glum and distracted on the ride down and used Marlene's cell phone twice to call the hospital to check on her father. On the second call, whatever her mother said to her made her weep, and she was still crying as they entered the courthouse. The newsies ate it up.

This morning, Marlene was arguing her motion to dismiss the indictment because of the state's failure to preserve potentially exculpatory evidence, to wit, the contents of the Dumpster into which Baby Boy Jorgensen had been tossed. Judge Shearing was up there on his high bench, looking impatient and irritable, like a man kept from an important meeting by the dithering of subordinates. He wanted to get to trial, or in any case bring this increasingly noisome mess to resolution. Of course, he could have done that by dumping the case. Marlene had certainly given him reasonable grounds and was giving him more. He knew the thing was a botch, indefensible on appeal, but he seemed to be reserving his ire not for the state but for this pesky woman from New York City.

Marlene was not to be rushed, however. The state called the Dumpster operator and the officers who had seized the Dumpster and hauled it to Newkirk PD headquarters. The state wished to demonstrate that the disposal of the Dumpster's contents was a simple oversight and did not exhibit bad faith. Abt was relying on the legal theory propounded in *Youngblood v. Arizona*: that when cops trashed exculpatory evidence it was up to the defendant to prove that the cops knew the exculpatory value of the evidence; that the stuff they were destroying was the only reasonable source of such evidence; and that the cops acted in bad faith. Abt was trying to show that the disposal was due to error, hence no bad faith, hence no violation of due process. On cross, Marlene established that the cops who had ordered the junk disposed of knew that the victim in this case had, according to the state's medical examiner, died of blunt-force trauma to the head, supposedly before being deposited in the Dumpster. Then to the crux:

"Officer Claiborne, when you examined the Dumpster in the early morning of November 13, what exactly did you see?"

"Trash," said Officer Claiborne. The officer was a big, good-looking kid with blue eyes that were perhaps a trifle too close together.

"What sort of trash?"

"Restaurant trash, from the Mother Hubbard; it was their Dumpster. Dented food cans, crushed cartons, plastic bags with paper trash, and some big pieces of metal, a fan housing and a fan and a burnt-out motor. They just got a new exhaust fan in there."

"Thank you. So, heavy stuff, metal stuff, and — Officer Claiborne, just how did you and your colleague search the Dumpster? By climbing in, right?"

"Right," said Claiborne, and then his face fell. "I mean, no. We did not enter the Dumpster."

"Interesting. Just how do you search through a Dumpster without climbing into it, and trampling around in the trash? Did you have special high-tech equipment for exploring Dumpsters while standing on the ground?"

"No. We, ah, reached in."

"You reached in. And the victim was lying right on the surface in the gray garbage bag? You just lifted it off, right?"

"Ah, no. It was under, under some junk."

"Under that heavy metal junk. And since we learned earlier that the lip of that Dumpster was sixty inches from the ground, are we to imagine you, Officer Claiborne, on your tippie-toes, reaching way into the Dumpster, and lifting a fifty-pound fan housing off that dead baby?"

"Objection," said Abt. "He answered the question."

"Sustained," said Shearing. "Move on, Ms. Ciampi."

Marlene moved on. This was enough. She had witnesses who had seen the cops trampling around in the Dumpster. If Claiborne or his pals tried to lie at trial, she would impeach them with that testimony, plus that wonderful, inadvertent, spontaneous "right." Of course they had climbed into the Dumpster to search it. That's how you searched a Dumpster, everyone knows that. But when the word got out to the cops that the state was basing its case on blunt trauma, and the cops recalled squashing heavy metal down on what proved to be a baby's skull, someone must have said, "Uh-oh," and the junk vanished. Another stupid cop trick. Marlene called one more witness, to establish that the cops knew about the blunt-trauma autopsy findings before they disposed of the garbage.

Marlene was about to launch her argument from law, which was that the state of Delaware, following the ruling in *Lolly* by its Supreme Court, had adopted a much softer view of the bad-faith issue. Clearly, absent a confession by police, it was impossible to prove the cops had acted consciously and illicitly to suppress exculpatory evidence. Therefore, the burden was merely to demonstrate that the lost evidence would have exculpated, that the cops should have known this, and that by their negligence they had removed an essential and irreplaceable piece of evidence. Before she could start, though, Loreno signaled the judge for a sidebar conference.

Marlene marched forward with him and Abt. Loreno said, "Your Honor, I am asking for protective relief from the court in regards to the motion on admission of polygraph evidence filed on behalf of defendant Goldfarb. I have no objection to the motion per se, nor would I wish to imply that there is a tactical reason for filing this motion at this time, but there is material included in there, to wit, the testimony given by my client, which, if it reached the public, would be catastrophic to Mr. Jorgensen. The jury pool would be contaminated beyond repair, and the gag order you wisely issued would become a nullity. The appropriate action would be for the court to order the prothonotary to seal the motion immediately." Abt, who was nodding through this last, said, "The state concurs with Mr. Loreno, Your Honor. The courthouse is full of press. If this got out, it would do a lot of damage."

Judge Shearing said, "I see. You want me to seal it pending hearing. All right, with no objection —"

"But I do object, Your Honor," said Marlene.

The judge looked down with a tired expression. "Ms. Ciampi?"

"Yes, Your Honor, first of all we strenuously object in principle to sealing motions. The motion in question is evidentiary, is offered in good faith, and is legally part of the public record. We are not going to try this case in a dark basement. Mr. Loreno's concerns about the jury pool are laudable, but I believe that, because of the actions of various parties, we are far beyond that now. I am sure the court will press upon any jurors the requirement to base their deliberations only upon evidence presented in court."

"Thank you, Ms. Ciampi," said the judge frostily. "I will seal the motion temporarily, until it is actually argued. Yes? You have further?"

"Yes, Your Honor," said Marlene, "while we're on the subject of fair and open dealing in this case, I believe we're entitled to know the status of any plea dealings between Mr. Jorgensen and the state. Mr. Loreno is concerned about damage to his client from something in the polygraph motion; fine, I am concerned about the possibility, and the papers are full of talk about this, the possibility that the state is going to treat Mr. Jorgensen differently from Ms. Goldfarb. Therefore, Your Honor, I would ask at this time for an order compelling the state to make full disclosure to us of the status of its negotiations with Mr. Jorgensen, and also whether it intends to treat the two defendants here differently from each other."

Take that! thought Marlene, as Abt snapped back an objection. Of course, the judge, after three seconds of thoughtful deliberation, turned down the request, but Marlene caught the look that flashed between Abt and Loreno, and she knew what it meant. There was no point in their delaying any longer, now that Marlene was clearly and publicly wise to them. The deal would go through, and soon.

The next day Karp stayed away from the office. Lucy was in no shape to go to school, and he did not care to leave her alone. Although she had hung together beautifully during her own ordeal, she had gone to pieces upon learning the news about Brian Maxwell. The boy was being held in Manhattan Juvenile Detention Center, within walking distance of Crosby Street, and Karp wished to avoid even the remote chance that Lucy, in her present frightening mood, might choose to bust in there, too. Lucy thought she should have seen it coming, that there was something she could have done. She would not be comforted. She would not emerge from her room, from which issued sobs and groans. Around eleven, Karp called his in-laws and then trotted down to Grand Street for the papers. The *Times* had a nicely nasty op-ed about incompetence in the criminal justice system. Karp was mentioned unfavorably, his racism adverted to, the association with the rush to judgment on Moussa Feydé noted, the probability that the arrest was a cover-up of the murder by the child of a prominent white man assessed. Lucy was mentioned, too, insinuatingly, and Karp made a note of the writer's name. Karp was a great believer in the First Amendment, but still, if the chance ever arose to savage this fellow, he would. The *News* contented itself with a full-page picture of little Brian, probably a school photo of some sort, looking angelic, with an inset picture of the Maxwells' bloodstained bed, and the fat headline KILLER? Juveniles in the justice system were supposed to have their identity protected, except where the story was really juicy.

Around noon, Marlene's father drove up and delivered the twins, spoiled to the last increment of rottenness, telling of unspeakable indulgences granted, the superiority of Nonna's food (SpaghettiOs! Pop-Tarts!) and the liberality of Nonno, who passed out shiny quarters on the hour, taught them how to blow their noses through their fingers, and allowed them to ride in the front seat of his ancient pickup truck without seat belts (seat belts are for *babies!*).

Still, Karp was glad for the distraction. He played strenuously with his boys, demonstrating that he could be very nearly as indulgent as any grandparent, and hoped that the merry ruckus would lure the girl from her room. But she stayed. He peeked in and saw an inert lump under the quilt. The phone rang every half hour or so, reporters, and he let the machine answer. The office left him alone, for Murrow and Flynn would between them intercept and blockade any call except one from the DA. But the only thing that the DA would want to talk about today was Maxwell, and Karp could not talk about Maxwell, by the DA's order. So he was safe.

At five Marlene called. "Home early?"

"No, I took the day off."

"Alert the networks. How's the kid?"

"Not good, Marlene. I'm starting to get worried. She's been in her room for eighteen hours, nothing to eat . . . this goddamn Brian thing is clawing at her, and I don't know what to do."

"I'll call Mike Dugan, ask him to stop by."

"*Father* Dugan?" asked Karp suspiciously.

"Yes, but you don't have to call them 'father' anymore, just like they don't call you 'esquire.' And he doesn't eat Jews, either. Oh, maybe once in a while, with close friends . . ."

"So, what, you think this is the same as vomiting green stuff with her head on backwards."

"No, Butch, listen: like it or not, your little girl is a devout Catholic and she's got a spiritual crisis, and for that you call an expert. Think of him as a plumber, but free of charge. Are the boys around?"

They were in fact literally around, clutching

at the hem of Karp's shirt and whining in their eagerness to talk to Mommy. They got on simultaneously, with the phone held between their faces, recounted the wonders of Nonna's, asked if they could stay there for a month, were denied, and then found, in the manner of children that age, that they had nothing at all to say, except when are you coming home.

Karp, back on the line, asked, "When are you?"

"Not for a while. Things are about to break here, the state's ready to deal with the scumbag, we have skinheads in the woodwork, the family's coming unglued. I dropped Sarah off at the hospital and I'm here alone guarding the house and using the dining room as my office. Mulcahey's due over in a while and we'll draft our severance motion. Still love me?"

"Sort of. If I could just remember what you looked like . . ."

"One eye, nice ass."

"One eye, nice ass . . . yeah, it's coming back to me now. Yes. Yes, I still do."

18

The priest arrived while Karp was getting the boys into bed, not an easy process this night because "Nonna lets us stay up as late as we want." Dugan arrived at the door damp with rain, looking like a roadie for a fading rock band, in a ratty blue mackinaw, a flannel shirt, jeans, and worn running shoes. Karp, whose image of priests was still based largely upon the Bing Crosby films of the mid-forties, and who was thus somewhat startled by that outfit, let him in, sat him at the kitchen table, poured him a cup of coffee, and went back to settling his boys. Karp was trying not to be grumpy or irritated, but he was nervous around priests, especially this one, whom he could not help but think of as an intruder. The idea repelled him that the two women closest to his heart were sharing their souls, telling things they would not tell *him*, to a stranger, this particular man. Karp returned to the kitchen.

"This is a lovely place," said the priest. "I've never been in one of these fancy lofts."

"Marlene likes it," said Karp.

"But not you?"

"If I had a choice, I'd like the kids to have grass and trees and running space and a hoop over the garage. But with Marlene you don't get a choice, so . . ."

"Yes. A determined woman," said Father Dugan, neatly cutting off that undesirable line of discourse. "Tell me about Lucy. Marlene gave the background, the connection with this dreadful Maxwell thing, but how does she seem to you?"

"I've barely seen her. She goes into a hole when she gets like this. You know: God's on his break, so she's in charge. She thinks she messed up. Not the jail misdemeanor, she's fine with that. I mean she thought she could have stopped the murders if she'd been on the ball."

"Yes. Yes, Lucy takes her spiritual responsibilities very seriously. And, of course, in the current age, when people think there's no such thing as spiritual responsibility, she has nothing to compare herself to, and so she may get herself painted into a corner."

"I'm not sure I follow," said Karp.

"Oh, I mean that two hundred, three hundred years ago, a girl with her talents and predilections would have been in an order, with hourly guidance and a rule to follow. Think of

552

Mickey Mantle being born in, say, Romania in 1830. The talent's there, but there's no cultural space for it. May I see her now?"

Karp told him where to go. He heard a knock and Lucy's door opening, voices, and the door closing again. Then, silence. He cleaned up in the kitchen. He threw himself down on the living room couch. He tried to watch television, grew bored, turned it off. He tried to read a magazine, but he found himself reading the same paragraph several times and flung the thing down. Time crept. He resisted the hideous temptation to linger outside her door and eavesdrop. He heard the sound of water running.

Father Dugan emerged and Karp sprang from the couch like an expectant father.

"So?"

"She'll be fine," said the priest. Karp sat again and motioned him to a seat, and he settled into Marlene's bentwood rocker. "She'll be out in a bit. You know, we're not supposed to have favorites, but, of course, we all do, being fallible humans, and I have to say that your daughter is one of mine."

"Mine, too," said Karp. "You know, I didn't quite get what you said before, about the convent." There was a distinct coldness in the way Karp said this.

The priest met his gaze and grinned

disarmingly. "Order, not convent. And I just meant it as an illustration. Lucy has no religious vocation, if that's what's worrying you. I think her gifts are distinctly to be used in this world. She just needs some help controlling them."

"The languages you mean?"

"No, I wasn't thinking of the languages. I meant her spiritual gifts."

"You mean like she's kind and generous? Things like that?"

"Well, those are the visible signs," said the priest judiciously.

"And there are invisible ones?"

An uncomfortable look now appeared on Father Dugan's face. "Hm, this is always awkward. I think you need to speak directly to Lucy about all that."

"Speak to me about what?" said Lucy, marching in, looking not at all like the demi-corpse she had been for the past day. She had combed her hair and washed her face and put on a long quilted bathrobe. She sat down next to her father and kissed his cheek. "I'm sorry, Daddy. I've been horrible."

"That's all right, kid. I'm glad you're feeling better. Father Dugan here and I were just talking about your invisible spiritual gifts."

"Oh, the consolations." Lucy said *consolations* like, *Oh, the tickets to the dance.*

"The . . . ?"

"Consolations. An immediate perception of the divine presence. Sometimes with like a message attached. It's kind of hard to explain."

"You mean you hear voices?" asked Karp, goggling. "Like Joan of Arc?"

A look passed between Lucy and Father Dugan. Karp caught it and didn't like it at all. He said, more harshly than he meant, "This is what told you to break the law? These 'voices'?"

"It's not like that, Dad," said the girl patiently. "Like I said, it's hard to explain. It was wrong, but it was also right for me to do it. I admit I didn't realize that you'd be hurt by it, and I said I was sorry about that. I am. But the way it worked out . . . if I hadn't done it, Moussa would still be in jail, you wouldn't have caught the real murderer. And he would have killed more people, like he tried to."

"So you're saying that God Almighty reached down and decided his good deed for the week was saving some poor guy from a stretch in the pen?" said Karp, giving full vent to his incredulity. "I mean, forget the cancer wards, and the rapes, and wars, for crying out loud, and we'll focus on Moussa Feydé?"

An embarrassed silence here, which Father Dugan broke. "Yes, it doesn't make much sense. I won't insult you with the God's ways are not our ways, yadda-ta-yadda, but in fact, either you believe that there is an ineffable mystery at the heart of life, or you don't. I do. Lucy does, you may not. Setting that aside, for the moment, it seems ungrateful, perhaps even to an unbeliever, that when a good thing does happen in this unusual way, we should reject it because evil things continue."

Karp was glad to let the ineffable slide, as he always did, and said, "Yeah, but my point is, you just can't go and flout the law because you think you're right, or divinely inspired. No offense, but the divinely inspired have a very bad track record when it comes to running societies. That's why we got rid of them and established representative assemblies, established rights, and wrote laws."

"But the laws are divinely inspired in the first place, aren't they?" said Dugan mildly.

"Are they? You mean the 'endowed by their creator' business? That was just Jefferson trumping the divine right of kings. He had to say something like that. But you don't find anything about God being a coauthor in the Constitution. It's 'we the people' all the way. The laws arise out of social contract; that, and tradition."

"Yes, but absent a policeman for every citizen, most people obey the law not because of a realistic fear of punishment, but because of conscience, which *is* divinely inspired, or so we believe. And surely you'll agree that in some cases the law conflicts with conscience. The Soviets had a terrific constitution, chock-full of rights. The Nazis were strong on legality, too."

"That's not relevant," Karp snapped. "Those were dictatorships, hence lawless by definition."

Lucy stood up and said brightly, "I'm going to get something to eat, I'm starving. Anyone want something?"

Both men shook their heads and she left with an amused look on her face. Dugan said, "But what if they were democracies, with the Nuremberg laws, or similar abominations, what about democratically established bigotry, democratically established torture, or unjust wars? We've had all those right here at home, and in our lifetimes. On what basis do you oppose them? Or do you go along?"

"You work to change the law," replied Karp, knowing it was a weak response. Though argument was his business, he had never gone head-to-head with a Jesuit before, certainly not with a cast-iron, gold-plated one like this, and in truth, he had spent about as much time thinking about the ultimate source of law as the average grease monkey spends thinking about the laws of thermodynamics.

Besides that, he knew that he didn't really believe in his position, and worse, that the priest knew it.

"And in the meantime? Life is short. The grave beckons. Do you spend your days hoping for the better and doing what you know to be evil?" Dugan put on a theatrical grimace and laughed, a pleasant tenor sound.

Karp smiled in spite of himself. "All right, you got me. Philosophical premises — I take it that was a speciality of yours?"

"In a way. In general, I'm afraid I'm more suited to the library than to the parish. I'm not a natural helper of the troubled. I lack patience in the face of stupidity. In a Jesuit parish, I could talk to the other priests, but where I am, it's a pretty dry field."

"So go somewhere else."

Dugan laughed. "Not so easy. As Marlene may have told you, I'm under something of a cloud. The Church wants me in a slot that is both undistinguished, rich in the lessons of humility, and also under the all-seeing eye of a conservative bishop. So no academics, and no heathen jungles either."

"How did you screw up? If I may ask."

The priest's face stiffened momentarily into a mask of remembered grief, just a flicker, before he exerted control and, smiling, said, "Actually, you may not. Let's say I committed a crime. In another country."

They were silent for a moment, in which they could hear Lucy in the kitchen, the thud of the refrigerator door, the rush of water, the clank of a spoon, the dropping of a plate, immediately followed by a cry, *"Putain!"* and some miscellaneous Asian expletives.

The two men laughed. "A side blessing," said Karp. "She never curses in English."

"Yes, but as you pointed out to her once, God knows Cantonese. What did you want to ask me about?"

Karp cleared his throat, embarrassed. "Why do you think I want to ask you something?"

"Well, I may be a bust as a pastor, but I have enough experience to know when someone wants to open an uncomfortable topic. So? What is it?"

"Just a technical question. Is hypocrisy a sin?"

"Hm. Interesting. Well, on the one hand, it's a social construct, 'the tribute vice pays to virtue,' as La Rochefoucauld puts it, a lie, surely, but not mortal. On the other hand, it often covers a more serious sin and enables the sinner to avoid the social consequences of sin, and therefore makes repentance less likely. Hypocrisy also has the quality of insidiously creeping into the mind of the sinner, fooling him as he fools others, until in the end he may no longer believe he's a sinner at all. Thus, you might say that while not a sin itself, hypocrisy is one of the devil's most potent tools. Our Lord was particularly hard on hypocrites, probably for that reason. So what are you being hypocritical about, Butch?"

Karp barked a laugh. "I didn't expect the Spanish Inquisition."

"*No one* expects the Spanish Inquisition," replied Dugan, laughing, too. "Well?"

"Okay, there is a case I'm involved in. Something I consider very wrong is happening, but it's perfectly legal. No, scratch that *perfectly*. I believe a lawyer is using a client for her own political purposes, which is technically a violation of legal ethics, but I can't prove that, and my boss has specifically warned me off doing anything directly in the case. I can't go to the girl myself. That *would* be illegal. Are you familiar with the Lourdes Bustamente case?"

"Only what I read in the papers. Are you suggesting that she didn't kill her baby?"

"Oh, she killed her baby all right. The problem for me is I don't think a sixteen-year-old kid who kills a neonate is in the same moral class as a Mafia contract killer, but that's the way my office is treating her. Her lawyer wants to make a feminist martyr out of her. She's risking everything on the jury's reluctance to put this kid away for twenty-five years. She thinks she can create what we call a nullifying jury."

"And this won't work?"

"That's not the right question." Karp was glad to be back on his turf, where he had few equals. "Nullifying juries are not a good thing. The jurors on them are first of all in violation of their oath to apply the law as instructed by the judge, and second, it throws the whole legal system into disrepute. It's exactly the same thing as when you have juries voting on their race prejudice instead of on the facts as presented. It damages the system, and the system, the law — and listen, if anyone knows how screwed up, how imperfect a system it is, it's me — the law is all we've got. The law may be corrupt and lazy, but it's a paragon of virtue compared to what it guards against. And lawyers using their clients for political purposes, however noble, is also not a good thing, nor, for that matter, is what my own office is doing, crushing this silly kid to satisfy some revenge lust because an unusual number of gaudy infanticides have shown up lately. I despise that whole impulse; the media run everything, yeah, but they shouldn't run the law, too."

"So you're objecting to defend your view of the system, not so much because you have feelings for this girl, that's she's being unjustly treated?"

"Frankly? I have no feelings for Ms. Bustamente either way. I don't know her. She could be a feminist saint or a bubbleheaded slut, or both. My own daughter, who I *do* know and love dearly, is going to feel the full rigor of the law for what she did, and I, because of my position, can do precious little to mitigate that. Justice isn't the point. Bustamente did it, her crime conforms technically to the statutory definition of depraved-indifference murder, murder in the second degree, and so what's happening to her is not unjust per se. But . . . but it's *wrong*. This kid needs counseling. She needs to come to terms with what she did, accept it, experience the remorse, and go on with her life. Maybe she needs to go away for a year. We should be saying to her, 'Hey, you got into trouble, you did bad, and we're punishing you for it.' But not by taking her *whole life,* for Christ's sake. Not that. So call me a hypocrite."

"Not at all. You're in a moral dilemma arising from the pursuit of two incompatible goods. That's quite different from professing virtue while practicing vice; in fact, it's a moral homologue of what your daughter did. The apple doesn't fall too far from the tree." Karp laughed at this and rolled his eyes. The priest said, "I take it you want me to intercede in some way."

No flies on Father Dugan, thought Karp, and said, "I can't say that. I've unburdened myself to you honestly. What you do is entirely and absolutely up to you. I abjure, reject, and utterly detest any implication that you are my agent or an agent of the state of New York in whatever dealing you may at any time have with the legal guardian of a person under felony charges."

Father Dugan laughed. "Okay, your hindquarters are covered. I assume the woman is a churchgoer?"

"Yes, she's apparently devout and I'd guess she'd take what you say seriously, should you choose to do so."

"I see. Perhaps I could explain the situation to her. Perhaps I could get her to understand what's happening to her daughter, make sure she understands about diminished responsibility as a defense. What about their lawyer?"

"A woman named Jessica Siegel, and I think she's part of the problem. I think, but I don't know, that she's actively misleading them. If that emerges as a fact, then I *can* do something. The Bar Association looks askance at stuff like that. But, needless to say, you're under no obligation to tell me anything you may learn."

"All right. I'll see what I can do. Obviously, there's a possibility that the family does know what's going on, and they approve, in which case —"

"Then it's on them," said Karp abruptly. "But somehow I doubt it."

They discussed some details after that, and the priest made his farewells to Lucy. When he had gone, Karp went into the kitchen, where Lucy was rinsing her dishes.

"Well, what did you think of Father Dugan?" she asked.

"Nice guy, smart. You know, I'm ashamed to admit it, but I never said more than a couple of words to a priest before this. I was surprised. He seemed a lot like me."

"They're a lot like everybody, Dad. It depends who they're talking to. The Jesuit motto is 'all things to all men.' It's what they *do*."

Marlene and Kevin Mulcahey were working together at the Goldfarbs' dining room table when she stopped in midsentence and cocked her head, listening.

"What?" he asked.

"Car. Outside the house. Went by, came back, went by again, slowed down in front of the house, and took off, a lot faster than it came by the first time. And the dog is making noises. Let me go check."

"I'll come with you," he said, rising from his chair.

"No, you stick by the phone, okay? I know what I'm doing."

Before he could object again, she left, throwing on her long leather coat as she went out through the side door. She heard Sweety whining then and saw the mastiff prancing nervously near the curb.

"What is it, Sweets? What've you got there?" She pulled out the tiny Maglite she always carried. The beam revealed a large lump of hamburger meat lying on the dead grass of the lawn. She stroked the dog's head and said, "Oh, someone dropped off a present for you, Sweets, and I bet it's got all kinds of drugs in it. Good thing you're in recovery, or you'd be in dreamland by now."

Marlene went to her car, opened the back hatch, and from the well under the rear deck she pulled a small plastic trash bag. She was about to shut the hatch when she paused and reached down into the well again and came up with the breaker bar from her socket wrench set, a steel shaft somewhat over a foot long, with a bulbous head containing the ratchet and key. This she slipped into her coat pocket. She also removed a black ripstop nylon bag. Inside the bag was a black cotton twill mechanic's coverall, and a pair of black Converse high-tops. Marlene used to wear such outfits on nighttime interviews with men she wished to dissuade from abusing their estranged spouses. She always kept a spare in the car because quite often the one she wore to work would become soiled with blood or other body fluids.

After picking up the hamburger with the plastic bag and posting the dog again into the shadows under the hydrangea, she went back into the house. Mulcahey was in the kitchen, looking tense.

"What's that?" he asked, pointing to the trash bag hanging from her hand.

"Hamburger, obviously drugged or poisoned. They didn't know that Sweety only takes food from my hand." She placed the trash bag in the refrigerator.

"You trained him not to?"

"Not just me, actually. It's part of *schutzhund* training. Sweety is a second-level *schutzhund*. That's like a Ph.D. in guard-dog land. And I think we're going to see him do some *schutz*-ing tonight."

"We should call the police."

"We should not. If we call the cops, the cops will come with their flashers on, and our pals will see them and split, and then they might come back when there's no one here, or just Sarah and her mom. Whereas if we sit tight, they will return and attempt to do evil, and then we will catch them at it."

"We . . . ?"

She grinned. "I meant me and the dog, Mulcahey. Your job is to be decorative and charming and sit by the phone in case things go to hell." She held up the nylon stuff-sack. "If you'll excuse me, I'm going to slip into something more comfortable."

She went to the bathroom and returned dressed in the coveralls and sneakers. The breaker bar was in the long, narrow hip pocket provided to contain just that tool. Mulcahey gave her a strange look, but said nothing. They went back to the living room and continued their work. Marlene found it nearly impossible to concentrate. Spiders were crawling over her belly and down her spine. She kept getting up and pacing, sighing, rising and nipping out to the back patio to smoke.

When she returned from the last of these visits, Mulcahey tossed down his pencil and said, "Now you're making *me* nervous. Look, we're not getting anything useful done. Why don't we call it a night, and you'll come to the office tomorrow and we'll bang this out."

Marlene plopped down in the chair across from him, and as she did so, the breaker bar collided with the leg of the table, making a loud, solid thump.

"Marlene, I hope that's not a gun in your pocket."

"No, I'm just glad to see you." Oh, God, a blank face. He's too young. "The old Mae West tag line, Mulcahey, 'Is that a gun in your pocket, or are you just glad to see me?' " She pulled out the tool and showed him.

"Why are you carrying around a socket wrench?"

"Doesn't everyone? What if you suddenly wanted to tighten up some nuts?"

She said it lightly, but his face remained concerned, the smile on it weak. She was getting manic with the waiting. Which, however, ended a few minutes later, with the sound of a car approaching, moving slowly. She stood and said, "Stick by the phone, Mulcahey. If I don't come back right away or if you hear me dying, call 911. Don't come outside, okay?"

She left in the middle of his sputtering reply. Lawyers, always talking, talking. Out the kitchen door, around the back of the house, slipping under the hydrangea, next to the dog, who was quivering tensely and making nearly inaudible high-pitched sounds. The night was cold and damp, and dark with an overcast sky; a faint chill breeze blew, and the only light came from the sky glow of the big cities just north and south. A dark chopped Mercury sedan with its headlamps off sat on the street in front of the house, engine idling. As she watched, the passenger door opened, and in the dome light's instant glare she could see two men in it, both shaven-headed, wearing dark clothes. The passenger left the car and opened the trunk. He bent over the opening. Marlene heard the clink of glass, and a moment later she smelled the reek of gasoline. The dog whined a little louder.

The man closed the trunk softly and stepped around the car. He had a forty-ounce beer bottle in his hand, with a rag stuffed in the opening.

Marlene hissed, and gave Sweety a command.

The mastiff took off like a cruise missile, Marlene right behind him. The man with the bottle heard a scrabbling sound and looked up. It took him a few milliseconds to register what he was seeing, and a somewhat longer time to draw breath for a shout, and then two hundred–odd pounds of bone and muscle traveling at twenty miles an hour struck him square in the chest. The bottle went flying. The man's head cracked against the rear fender with a dull clang.

Marlene was around the back of the car by then. The driver heard the bottle smash and the dull clang, opened his door, and started to get out. He looked up, gaped, and Marlene hit him between the eyes with the fat end of the breaker bar. It was a good solid, two-handed hit. Blood spurted, looking black in the dim light, and the man went down on his back. Marlene hit him again. And again, and he lay still, blowing hideous blood bubbles through his smashed face. She felt the familiar nauseating pleasure. She made herself stop.

She reached into one of her outfit's many pockets and brought out some cable ties, with which she trussed the man. Then she walked around to where her dog was working. Sweety had undressed the man from the neck down and was worrying at the crotch of his jeans. The smell of gas was strong, but underneath it, Marlene's nose could also tell that the man had soiled his shorts.

"You're not going to give me any trouble, are you?" she asked.

The man shook his head violently from side to side, and said "No" and "Uh-uh" more times than necessary.

Marlene called the dog off and bound the man's wrists and ankles with the cable ties. She walked back to the house on shaky legs, and just before the front steps she threw up onto the earth beneath a juniper hedge.

Mulcahey had watched the whole event

from the living room windows. It stunned him, so different was it from the violence depicted in the movies, over much more quickly and infinitely more horrifying. Marlene came into the house.

"Are you okay?" he asked, his voice creaky.

She made a cup gesture with her hand and said, "Drink." She made a dialing gesture. "Cops. Ambulance."

Marlene went into the bathroom. Mulcahey called the cops, then rummaged in the living room until he found a liquor cabinet. He filled an Old-Fashioned glass half full of Teacher's and after a moment did the same again. The two of them drank in near silence, serious medicinal drinking, until the cops came. Mt. Holly was a three-car police force, and two of these arrived, one containing the local chief; shortly thereafter came an ambulance from the local community hospital. There was little for the cops to do, except collect evidence and write things down. The two men in the Mercury were well-known as local nasties, the situation was as clear as could be, and the police were not about to draw fine points about appropriate force in defense of hearth and home. But it all took a while, and then the press arrived in some force and lit up the night and got some terrific news-leading pictures of the blood and the smashed

Molotov cocktail and thug-face, and in the midst of this circus, Sarah and her mother came home.

This further tap upon the cracked vase of Selma sufficed to send her into fragments. Marlene sat and ignored the screams and talked to the police chief and sipped her whiskey. Sarah hustled her mother upstairs with the help of a female paramedic well supplied with the appropriate needles, and soon quiet was restored.

The cops and medic departed, then the press left, sans an interview with any of the principals involved, except the police chief. Sarah did not descend again.

Mulcahey mentioned this: "You'd think someone would thank you." They were sitting in the living room, with the bottle there in front of them.

"You would think that," said Marlene, "but you're not in the bodyguard business. Bodyguards never get thanked, only blamed when the shit hits the client. It is a thankless profession, which is one reason I left it." She poured herself another Scotch. She rarely drank hard liquor, and through the growing haze, she realized that she was downing glasses of it as if it were her usual red wine.

"What were the other reasons?" asked Mulcahey. He had not drunk as much as

Marlene, but things were going soft around the edges. The room was warm, and she had popped the first three snaps on the coverall, and he had gotten a pretty good look when she bent over to grab the bottle.

"I get nauseous," she said in a tone that did not encourage probing.

"I should go, but I'm too drunk to drive. I'll call a cab." He made no move to get off the couch.

"I should take in the dog."

They both lay there, utterly paralyzed, legs stretched out like store dummies. He said, "I guess we're not going to finish that motion tonight." Their eyes met, rolled. They started giggling, and poking each other, which quickly turned into a kind of hysteria, as the tension of the evening discharged. And then, somehow, she was on his lap, her mouth steaming against his, the snaps on her coverall popping like firecrackers. The mouth was as delicious as she had imagined. It was teenage sex, the teenage sex of a decade or so previous, and it passed like a cloudburst. Before he could really get into it, Marlene thrust him violently away from her. She stood up, staggering, fumbling with the snaps, stamping her foot, saying "Shit" and "Fuck" alternately between clenched teeth.

"What? What?" said Mulcahey.

"I can't *believe* I just did that," she said, having buttoned herself up to the neck again. She crashed herself into an armchair across the room from the couch.

"Nothing wrong with it that I could tell," said Mulcahey lightly, and was rewarded by a fierce glare.

"No, it was very nice, Mulcahey. You're a good kisser and so am I, and it's the slippery slope. The thing of it is, I'm an addict, Mulcahey."

"What? You mean alcohol?"

"No, not alcohol! If it were alcohol, I'd be in a church basement breathing smoke and being bored into mental health. No, I'm addicted to what just happened tonight, with those Nazis, and the problem is, there's nothing going on for people who are addicted to socially useful compulsions, like protecting people from violence. Do you know there are firemen who start fires so they can be heroes?"

"That's not —"

"No, of course, different, but the same. You don't see Mother Teresa in a shrink's office: 'Doc, help me before I help again.' You don't see Bill Gates on the couch: 'Please, please, I can't stop making money, I'm sick.' I'm sick. First I kick ass, then I puke my guts, then I get drunk, then I get incredibly horny and want to fuck my brains out. It's a pattern.

And a slippery slope. If I'm not careful, I'm going to wind up as a bouncer in a bar outside Tonopah, dragging stringy cowboys into the bushes. I thought I could get away with it if I just pretended to be a lawyer, but it doesn't seem to be working out that way."

"Come on, Marlene, you didn't plan for there to be violence."

"No, but it's always there, and it always finds me. Or unconsciously, I find it." She rubbed her face. It felt like a cheap rubber toy. "So, how's that fine young liver, Mulcahey. Burned off the booze yet?"

"I'm fine. It all boiled out of me from the heat." He gave her a melting look that must have knocked them over like duckpins in the singles bars, Marlene thought, and she laughed.

"Oh, don't flirt *now*, Mulcahey! I'm old enough to be your mother, and I'm not in my right mind. Besides, if I once lost control, you'd be in a wheelchair for a week and I need you in court. Leave all the case crap here, and scram!"

"You're sure . . . ?"

"I'm *not* sure. That's why you need to get your coat and leave."

Marlene plunged into sodden slumber, which lasted, as it often did, for no more than five hours. She awoke at six-ten, feeling crapulous and guilty, and not remotely willing to face Selma Goldfarb in her cheery breakfast nook. She left the guest bedroom, tripped over the dog, stifled a curse, took a twenty-second shower, dressed in her wrinkled suit and blouse, packed up the legal material, scribbled a note saying she would call later, and was out of the house by ten of seven. She drove into Wilmington, picked up a couple of bran muffins, let herself into Mulcahey's office, and made a quart of Dean & DeLuca's Danisi Gold Can coffee. This she drank black with the muffins, while drafting the severance motion from the notes she and Mulcahey had made the night before.

At eight-thirty, Mulcahey arrived, and if he was surprised to find her there, he said nothing, nor did either of them advert to the events of their last meeting. Around ten, Mike Brewster came by and dropped off some reports. Among these was a report on the competition. Marlene leafed through it; it was not thick. Murder is a rare crime and few public prosecutors outside the very largest jurisdictions have much experience in its prosecution. Jason Abt had exactly one murder trial to his credit, that ending in a hung jury. Marlene had seventeen. But Mr. Abt had managed a substantial number of plea bargains.

"Check out the Maury case," said Brewster over her shoulder. "Marked with a red tab."

Marlene did so. Clarisse Maury's case had been disposed of the previous year, a month before Jason Abt had charged Sarah Goldfarb with capital murder. Ms. Maury, aged twenty, had become pregnant, hid the fact from relatives, delivered the baby in the bathroom of her parents' home, and drowned it in the toilet. She had then attempted to dismember the dead infant, a process interrupted by her mother's arrival. She had been allowed to plead to criminally negligent homicide, received a five-year sentence (suspended), and served five months. She was out on the street now. Clarisse Maury was African-American.

"Makes sense, the little shit," said Marlene, "no good ink in another poor, dead black baby, and what the hell, they're animals anyway. This is good, Mike. I'll have to figure out some way of making sure this surfaces."

"I'm sure you will," said Brewster. "You guys had quite a night out there. It would've been smart to call me, Marlene."

"Mike, if I yelled for every pair of two-bit Nazi firebombers, you'd never get anything done. It worked out fine."

"This time," said Brewster, not amused.

"And there won't be a next time," snapped Marlene definitively.

Brewster grumbled some more, then left, as the phone buzzed. Mulcahey picked it up, listened briefly, covered the mouthpiece, and said, "They did it!" and then listened some more.

After he hung up, Marlene asked, "What did they go for?"

"Criminally negligent homicide."

"I guess. That seems to be a favorite with Mr. Abt. I presume the press has it already?"

"Of course. What's our plan?"

"Obviously, we go ahead with the severance," said Marlene. "Then I think we should call Mr. Abt, who seems to be in a generous mood today, and see whether sauce for the gander is sauce for the goose."

"Seriously? You want to consider a plea?"

"I think it's our duty, and you know damn well Selma's going to be all over me when she finds out that old Peter's caught a break."

Mulcahey made the call. Mr. Abt would indeed see them in his office at the courthouse in Wilmington. At the appointed time they both walked across. Abt had a bigger office than a similarly situated ADA would have had in New York City, with nicer appointments. Marlene thought this might have been to compensate him for having so few cases.

They entered, they sat, they dispensed with the small talk.

"I assume," said Abt, "that you're here to talk about a deal."

"That and to tell you we intend to move for a severance," said Marlene. "Frankly, I was a little surprised. Dropping the charge on Jorgensen from capital murder to negligence, that's quite a comedown, especially since he was the active participant. If Jorgensen gets negligence, it's hard to see what you have left to charge Sarah with."

Abt's narrow face bent in a knowing smile. "That's not how we see it, Ms. Ciampi. We see your client as the instigator and controller of the entire conspiracy, and Jorgensen will so testify."

"Conspiring to be negligent? How would that work, Mr. Abt?"

"Your client had a duty to provide care for her unborn child. Absent that duty, the child was at risk. She had a duty to insure that the child at risk would be born in a medical environment conducive to its survival. Not only did she not do that, she arranged with Mr. Jorgensen to give birth in a secret place and used the force of her personality to prevent Mr. Jorgensen from summoning help, which Mr. Jorgensen was inclined to do. Further, she ordered Mr. Jorgensen to dispose of the infant, thus furthering its demise. I'd say that adds up to depraved-indifference murder."

"Uh-huh. Let me get this straight — while she was unconscious, convulsing, and physically helpless, she conspired in negligence and committed depraved-indifference murder? That seems like a bit of a stretch to me, sir, even in the state of Delaware."

"We have only her word that she was unconscious," said Abt, ignoring the gibe. "Mr. Jorgensen has a different story. In any case, that is for the jury to decide. We think we have a strong case for depraved indifference. I will tell you, however, that to spare the state the expense of a trial, we would entertain a plea of manslaughter, under the diminished-capacity rule."

"Have her examined by the state, you mean?"

"Yes. *If* the state finds that she was impaired mentally at the time of the crime, we let her plead to manslaughter first, and a term of three and a half to ten."

"And the boy?"

"Twenty-six weeks."

"That's outrageous!" cried Marlene. "Half a year for the active partner and three to ten for the passive?"

"The instigator," said Abt blandly. "In any case, that's what's on offer. I suggest you put it to your client." He pursed his lips, paused, and added, "Her mother is very interested in the idea of impaired capacity."

"Her mother! Oh, tell me you're not engaging in ex parte conversations with my client!"

"I never spoke to your client. Her mother called me this morning. She's a citizen and I'm a public servant. She has a right to talk to me."

"Oh, please! I intend to bring this extraordinary breach of procedure to the judge's attention."

"You can do as you like, Ms. Ciampi. Now, if there's nothing further . . ."

Out on the street, Mulcahey observed, "That went well."

"That fuck-head! I can't wait to get him in court. I'll bore him a new asshole."

"Assuming you get to court. Selma will want that deal."

"I know, I know! It's a disaster. Look, you handle the motion, I've got to get back to Mt. Holly right away, before Selma can work over the kid too much. Impaired capacity, my ass! Oh, yeah, find out whatever you can about the state's shrink, the guy who would examine Sarah if we let him, his track record and all. I'm starting to smell a rat. Yet another rat."

"Meaning what?"

"Meaning if a state shrink with bad intent gets hold of Sarah, it could give them a devastating witness. If we don't deal, if we do go to trial, we could have a psychiatrist up there testifying that Sarah Goldfarb is a soulless monster who knew very well what she was doing when she did it."

"That's far-fetched, Marlene. And if you don't allow a state psychiatric exam, you could be barred from presenting favorable psychiatric evidence at trial."

"I don't *need* psychiatric evidence; I mean, it would be good to have, sure, but I can't take that chance. I know it's a scam. Christ, how could Selma have been so stupid!"

19

"You're a youthful offender," said Karp. "Do you know what that is?"

"Like a juvenile delinquent," said his daughter. They were in his office, about to descend to courtroom AP3 (All-Purpose Part) criminal court for her hearing. Lucy was sitting on the couch in the characteristic stillness she assumed when nervous, back straight, hands neatly folded. She was wearing a gray shirtwaist dress that Karp had not seen before, of some coarse, heavy material, with small buttons down the front, and under it, black wool stockings and clunky, black leather, low button-boots, highly polished. Around her neck, on a silver chain, she wore her great-grandmother's silver crucifix. Her face, bearing now not a trace of makeup, had the pale translucency of a new candle.

"Not exactly," said Karp. "A juvenile delinquent is thirteen to fifteen. Except for some listed crimes, serious stuff like rape and murder, they get remanded to family court. The idea is they're kids who went wrong and need protection and counseling. A youthful offender is sixteen to eighteen and is treated as an adult, but he catches a break unless the crime is listed serious or he's got a prior YO or felony conviction, which you don't."

"What's the break?"

"Sentencing's lighter, plus your record gets expunged at eighteen upon good behavior. We don't want to put softened criminals like you in with the hardened kind."

"What about Brian Maxwell? What's he?"

Karp sighed. "Oh, well, Brian is sort of in a class by himself. Legally? Under seven is absolute infancy, no criminal responsibility at all, and over thirteen is, like I was saying, a JD and can be tried as an adult for certain crimes. In Maxwell we have the heavy crimes, for sure, but we're short on the age. It's not exactly a common occurrence, a double murder by an eleven-year-old. My guess is we'll try him as an adult, but Roland's meeting with the Maxwells' lawyer today, so maybe we can avoid that farce. In any case, as far as —"

The door popped open and in walked Marlene, who, as was her habit, had neither knocked nor waited to be announced. They both stared at her for a second. She was crisp in a black Karan suit and looked deceptively like a perfectly ordinary person.

"Wow, this is a surprise!" exclaimed Karp. "I didn't expect you'd be able to get away."

"What're you talking?" said Marlene. "Four great moments in a mom's life — First Communion, college graduation, the wedding, and first adjudication on a criminal offense. I wouldn't've missed this for the world." She sat down next to Lucy. "Well, my thug, how are you? By the way, interesting outfit. You look like St. Joan at Rouen. Intentional, I hope?"

Lucy felt a blush arrive. "*You're* the thug, Mom. Aren't they going to fall apart down there without you?" Said lightly, but there was a challenge in the tone, and no little resentment.

Marlene chose to ignore this. "Oh, the Goldfarbs! The Goldfarbs are, let us say, a high-maintenance client. Let them cry on Mulcahey for a while. In fact, I have the feeling that I am not long for this case, if Selma has her way."

"Are you serious?" asked Karp in amazement.

"Dead." Marlene put her eye on Lucy. "You know, there may have been a few unconventional things about the way I raised you —"

"Oh, no-o-o, why would you say that?"

"Right, go ahead and laugh, but let me tell you something: if, God forbid, any serious poo ever hits the fan in your life, you're going

585

to be able to handle it with grace and spirit. Sarah's a sweet kid, a decent kid, and I like her, and she loves her mother, but every minute I spend with her, I thank God you're the way you are, even if you hate me."

"I don't hate you, Mom." Sighing dramatically.

"No, right now you don't. Give it a few minutes."

"Mom, you keep making remarks like that . . ."

Karp cleared his throat and pointedly looked at his watch. "We should get over there."

Courtroom AP3 was a limb of the Criminal Courts of the State of New York, handling misdemeanor offenses, one-stop shopping for petty crime, and for not-so-petty crime that had been pleaded down from felonies. It was run by Her Honor Judge Barbara T. Phelan with the speed and dignity of a Kmart, Saturday afternoon on the low side of town. The lawyer, Scopetta, a neat, dark man with an egg-shaped head, round, steel-rimmed glasses, and an alert and sensible mien, picked them up in the crowded side aisle.

"What's the situation?" asked Karp.

"Could be better," said Scopetta. "The judge got a blistering letter from Corrections, to the effect that if she wanted to get into jail so bad, they'd love to have her up in Spofford for about twenty-four weeks to a year. That's unusual, and as you know, anything that makes a case stick out in misdemeanor court is always bad for the defendant. It helped that Lucy gave up the source, by the way."

Lucy and Marlene shared a quick look.

"I gather the cops didn't make an arrest there," said Karp.

"No, but we can't be held responsible for that. Apparently the forger took off. In any case, I've arranged for Father Dugan to stand up for her — he's already written a letter — and this professor she works for, Slotkin, wrote one, and we've got letters from Congressman Jennings, of the House Intelligence Subcommittee, Major General Stouffer, Dr. Ruth Leman —"

"Wha . . . wait a second," Karp sputtered. "Jennings, Stouffer . . . who *are* these people?"

Scopetta looked mildly surprised. "Oh. Stouffer runs the Defense Advanced Research Projects Agency, Leman is a deputy director of the National Science Foundation. They fund the project Lucy's involved in. According to them, the quest for how language works and the fate of the free world depends on Lucy Karp's brain. She's a unique national treasure. You didn't know this?"

"Not the details, no, but I hardly ever know

the details until things have been tidily arranged behind my back," said Karp somewhat sourly. "Well, anyway, that crew ought to trump a cranked-up jailhouse guard."

"We can but hope," said Scopetta, "but you know judges."

Karp did. Phelan, a large, red-haired woman, had a rep as a ball-breaker, and it was the custom to try to assign plea bargains that were thought a trifle soft to her courtroom, where she habitually gave them the maximum jail time she could, one year, a "bullet" as the jargon had it, for which reason she was known as Bullet Barb. Karp wondered which of his many enemies had jiggered Lucy into the courtroom with Judge Phelan presiding.

They waited. Father Dugan arrived, dressed to impress in full clericals, and Karp saw Lucy light up a little when he clasped her around the shoulder. A little pang, there, too. Bullet Barb dispensed with small-time drug handlers, prostitutes, petty gamblers, sneak thieves, fare beaters, drunk drivers. Then she dispensed with Lucy Karp.

After the usual legal folderol and the testimonials, she said, her beady blue eyes glowering down over half glasses, "Ms. Karp, you seem to have a lot of important friends, and a great talent. I am setting those things aside, however, because they neither justify nor excuse what you have done. Further, as a child of privilege and opportunity, the crime to which you have pleaded guilty is even more reprehensible than it would be in one without your opportunities and talents. I'm going to sentence you to six months' imprisonment and fine you fifteen hundred dollars." She paused here; Karp gasped, Marlene muttered a foul oath, Lucy stood statuesque, her face white. The judge continued, "Sentence to be suspended, and a year's probation. That means if I see you back here anytime soon, young lady, you're going to jail. Do I make myself clear?"

Lucy murmured that she had, and down came the gavel. Outside, in the noisy corridor, after all agreed that it could have been worse, and Lucy promised to pay the fine herself (her parents in no way demurring), the lawyer was thanked and dismissed, Lucy and her mother left to return home, and Karp buttonholed the priest.

"Any action on what we talked about?"

"Mike," said the priest. "You can call me Mike, like I was a regular person. Actually, a lot. She attends at Nativity on Second Avenue, which happens to be a Jesuit parish, so I had an in."

"I thought you were in bad with them."

"I am, but I was pretty high up before that.

Think of Richard Nixon walking into a Republican precinct in Omaha — horrified fascination and a willingness to show charity. Are the horrible stories true? In any case, I got their attention and talked to her pastor, and I got to talk to Mrs. Bustamente last night. A nice lady, Carmen her name is. The bottom line is you were right in your supposition. She has no idea that she could have asked for a psychiatric examination, or that the state would entertain a plea based on impaired capacity. In fact, their lawyer, this Miss Siegel, has stressed to them that the state is out for blood, and that their only hope is convincing the jury that the law is too harsh."

"So, she would consent to a plea?"

"Would she? She practically kissed my hand when I suggested that it was possible. So what's the next step?"

"Let me contemplate it for a while, but what you've done is very helpful already. Do you think you can arrange to be at my office around five this afternoon?"

"Sure, I'm right down the street anyway."

"Okay, Mike, see you then. And thanks for this."

Karp returned to his office and mooched around with catch-up work, minor tasks he could do sleeping. Somewhat before noon, Roland Hrcany came by. He looked sulky and irritated. Karp let him sit for a while on the leather couch, steaming gently, and then asked, "How did it go with Waley?"

"Oh, with Waley it went fine. Waley is a pro and a gentleman. With the old granddad it didn't go fine at all. The fucker would not shut up."

"What did he have to say?"

Hrcany shot to his feet and began pacing stiffly back and forth in front of the couch, clenching his fist rhythmically, flexing his enormous biceps, rolling his mighty lats and delts, so that the cloth of his shirt popped. It was how he thought, Karp knew, and waited.

"Waley obviously does not want to go into this one straight up," said Roland, "just like I guessed. Did I tell you we found the kid's prints on the earrings and the toolbox? Another nail. So I'm waiting for the plea, I'm figuring manslaughter on diminished capacity, but Waley starts up about clearly a psychiatric disorder, which is what you were saying, he's going to go not-guilty insanity, but, God! As soon as the word *insanity* pops out of his mouth, the old guy goes ballistic. 'No insanity in my family. Never never never.' And then he starts on about his distinguished ancestors, with Waley going, 'Mr. Warren, please, Mr. Warren, sir . . . ,' and then he goes off on, 'I'll tell you what this is, this is a conspiracy against us. My grandson did not kill his parents, that African did.' And then he goes off with some shit about the DA is corrupt and he wants an investigation, and he brings in Lucy and you. The meat of his legal theory is that you're giving Feydé a walk to curry favor with the colored voters, as witness the fact that you got Lucy to go to the jail and slip him inside info, and that Lucy knew all about the secret compartment in the desk all along, and you all rigged it to implicate dear Brian. And as for the attack in the park, he's prepared to swear that Brian was within his sight for the entire time."

"I like the currying the black voters part," said Karp. "This explains why we prosecute so few African-Americans. What did Waley say?"

"He was exquisitely polite and got out pretty gracefully, considering. 'Clearly I need to consult further with my client. Sorry to have wasted your time,' and so on. I think he was a little shook. I know *I* was."

"You think the old man is over the line?"

"He sure sounded like it when he was in the midst. His wattles were bright red and there were little sprays of spit in the air. Legally?" Roland rocked his hand, palm down. "If it were a regular person, I mean not a prominent millionaire, and we had a situation where a minor ward was charged with a felony and the legal guardian was non compos, we could have the guardian examined and so declared, and then petition for a guardian *ad litem* for the minor. Meanwhile, poor people are crazy, rich people are eccentric. We try anything like that, and he'll have four and twenty distinguished shrinks swearing he's a second Louis Brandeis." Hrcany stopped pacing and sank again onto the couch. "Any bright ideas?"

Karp tried not to show his amazement at this nearly unprecedented request. He thought for a moment and replied, "Well, I don't see where you've got much choice, Roland. I don't see it as a pass-along to family court."

A harsh laugh. "Yeah, because he killed them. The old joke. He could appeal to the court as an orphan."

"So you'll indict, and you'll try him straight up, you and the great Lionel T. head-to-head. It won't be a gimme, either. All you've got is the prints, on the gun and the desk and the shells; oh, yeah, and the toolbox and the earrings, and the kid had access to all of those in perfectly innocent ways. Plus the state first indicted another guy for the crime — that's practically reasonable doubt right there. And take it as given that Waley will oppose every piece of evidence, pick up every flaw in every warrant, every interaction with the defendant, and remember, it's not *you* versus Waley in that regard, it's *Pincus* versus Waley."

"Hey, be honest, now — don't just try to cheer me up."

"Yeah, right. Anyway, say you win at trial. Then there are the appeals, pressed to the fullest, unlimited resources there, and Waley is as great an appealmeister as he is a litigator, and say you win again. What's the ultimate outcome, the biggest possible win for the good guys? Brian Maxwell serves twenty-five and walks out of Elmira at age thirty-six, a multimillionaire in the prime of life, with an enormous hard-on for humanity and a wide range of criminal skills."

"The system works!"

"Alternatively . . . I'll tell you what. With your okay, I'll make a call, talk to Waley."

"What good would that do?" asked Roland, bridling.

"Probably none. I had a brief conversation with him once, though, about the right thing to do in certain strange cases. He was claiming insanity on behalf of his client, and I was saying the guy was sane, in legal terms. He said it was sad that two intelligent and civilized people couldn't sit down and come to a disposition that was fair and protective of social interests. Maybe he'll remember it, now that the shoe is on the other foot. I take it that given appropriate safeguards you wouldn't be averse to a diminished capacity, or even an insanity plea?"

"Hell, Butch, I know you think I'm Torquemada come back again, but believe me I don't look forward to trying a little kid as an adult for multiple homicide. If this brat isn't twisted, Mona Lisa's a man. Go, see what you can do, but it ain't Waley this time. It's his client."

"Okay. Now, what about Bustamente?"

Roland's eyes narrowed dangerously. "Oh, *that* was a switcheroo! What is it with you and Bustamente? Are you fucking her on the side? She's going down for it, Butch, like a million others. She did the crime, she's going to do the time. End of story."

"She's not getting proper counsel. When it comes out, you won't have a case to try."

"You *know* this?"

"Let's say it's been placed in my way," said Karp elliptically.

Roland popped up again and leaned his hands on Karp's desk. His face reddened. Good Roland had left the building, and Bad Roland was back in charge.

"Placed in your way, horseshit! You have been fucking with this case again, after Jack specifically told you not to."

"Okay, guilty. Are you going to run to Jack and snitch on me?"

"I might punch you in the nose," Roland snarled.

"You might, but then you wouldn't find out how I fucked your case. Sit down, Roland. Calm yourself."

Hrcany sputtered for a moment, but neither punched nor ran snitching; he fell back upon the couch and waited, his mighty arms folded across his chest. Karp told him the story of what he had learned and how he had learned it. Roland heard it out and, at its conclusion, snapped, "Fuck you, Karp!"

"Is that a 'Fuck you, you're full of shit,' or a 'Fuck you, you're correct and I'm forced against my will to acknowledge it'?"

Roland ignored the sally, but it was clearly the latter he had meant, because he said in his surly fashion, "So what's the next step, counselor? Do I have to kiss your ass in Macy's window?"

"I'm hosting a meeting here at around five, after the trial breaks up for the day. Me, Vasquez, Siegel, and Father Dugan. See if we can just clear this up by us all washing our shorts in public. You're welcome, of course."

"Well, that's mighty generous of you, Butch, but I think I'll pass," said Hrcany acidly. "I do want to attend when you explain all this to Jack, though. I wouldn't miss *that*."

He left. Karp buzzed Flynn and told her to set up an appointment with Lionel T. Waley in his office, as soon as possible. Then he called out to Murrow, who had been lurking in his cubby with the door open. Murrow emerged and Karp asked him, "What did you think of that?"

"For someone who's just been outmaneuvered, he took it very well. Do you think he'll go to the DA with it?"

"I doubt it. Roland needs me, and so does the DA, and neither of them want to be placed in a position where it's impossible to ignore the fact that I disobeyed a direct order."

"You seem pretty confident. If you're wrong, can I have your chair? Mine has a spring loose."

"Get a pillow. Let me explain, Murrow, since this seems to be confusing you. The men, like Mr. Keegan, who run Leviathan often wish things to occur without actually ordering them, and wish things not to occur that they are on public record as desiring. For one example, I never ordered you to set up that meeting with Jessica Siegel, did I? Yet the meeting took place. The classic example is murder in the cathedral. The king mutters, 'Who will rid me of that troublous priest?' and

the thugs take the hint. This here is the opposite case: in his heart of hearts, Jack does not
want to send this poor schmuck of a girl up for
life, and if it turns out he doesn't have to, he'll
be content with a light grumble, especially as I
intend for Ms. Siegel to be the fall guy."

"And Mr. Hrcany's heart? Similarly
panging?"

"Mr. Hrcany doesn't have a heart as such,
but he very badly wishes to be the next DA.
He would not want to be involved in a scandal
in which an ultrafeminist lawyer sacrifices a
Puerto Rican girl to make a point. It would
not be the same as winning fair and square. A
stink would linger. Notice, he declined to attend the meeting."

"I did notice. You'll want me there?"

"I insist upon it, Murrow," said Karp, smiling.

Marlene was out shopping for groceries, on
her tattered principle that a gorgeous meal
made up for days of familial neglect, and Lucy
took this opportunity to dial the memorized
Bridgeport number. After the usual surly que-
ries in Vietnamese, she got to Tran, who
greeted her in French and said, "You are not
imprisoned, I presume."

"No. A fine and suspended sentence.
Thank you for what you did."

"It was very little, I assure you. Clearly it was necessary for you to give up our mutual friend in Chinatown, and fortunately, I was able to put other business opportunities in his way. He understands and harbors no resentment. Besides that, you are well, and content?"

"Well enough, but not content. Every time I try to become normal, a regular kid, something happens. I have no friends. Oh, I mean there are people I can hang out with, and talk to, but Caitlin, that's all over, she's out of school now and her grandfather's so mad at me and us, and Caitlin won't return my calls, she's probably furious with me, too, and Mary, well, I love her and all, but there are things she can't deal with — I mean, if you can't express it in cosines or whatever, she doesn't get it. So I'm lonely. I miss you, which is weird in the first place. I mean, you're not going to take me to the prom, are you?"

"The *prom?*"

"A ball for students. I'm just being stupid, Uncle, don't mind me. I just don't know what to do. Maybe I'm just doomed, like those horrible prodigies that end up in loony bins. They can do math in their heads but can't cross the street by themselves."

"But your spiritual life — this must provide some comfort?"

"Oh, yes, it does, but . . . that life pulls you, I mean if that's *all* you have, it pulls you out of the world. I'm not ready to leave the world and I have no real talent for good works. I'm not St. Teresa and I'm not Mother Teresa either. I wish I was a chucklehead. I wish I could go see *Scream* with a bunch of girls. I wish I could get interested in clothes or Beastic Boys."

After a brief silence Tran said, "Hm. I wish I were an Oriental sage. Then I could utter just the correct saying to assuage your difficulty. But I am just an old criminal. You should talk to your mother, my dear."

"I *can't* talk to my mother. She's all guilty about neglecting me and putting me in danger all the time, and she hides it behind being witty. And she thinks sex will solve everything. Wait'll you get interested in b-o-y-s, yadda yadda. She doesn't take me seriously."

"Then take *her* seriously until she does. There, I believe that is sufficiently cryptic for the moment. I must go now, my dear. Be well."

"Good-bye, Uncle Tran, and God bless you."

"Unlikely, but I thank you," he said, chuckling, and hung up.

After mooching around with routine matter

for a few hours, Karp left his office and went to catch a piece of *People v. Bustamente.* Vasquez, looking formidable and vaguely European in a dark suit with a flounce of lace at the throat, had just called her last witness on the stand. This was Perez, the father and putative rapist, a chunkily handsome lady-killer of thirty-odd with a fancy pompadour and several gold rings. He was dressed in a sober blue suit that may not have been his ordinary choice of clothing. He seemed uncomfortable in it, shifting and rolling within the jacket, so that the collar lifted unattractively above his thick neck. As he took his seat, Lourdes Bustamente, demure in a starched white blouse, hung her head fetchingly.

Vasquez now brought him through the sexual relationship that had started this whole disaster. He had been drunk, he said, after a party and gone home to sleep it off. They lived with his mother-in-law at the time. His wife was at work; his sister-in-law, the defendant, had been in the apartment, cutting school. She had been wearing a sheer nightie, showing off her body. She had seduced, he had succumbed. After that, a few more times. He was ashamed of what he had done. He had no knowledge of her pregnancy — no one in the family had. Yes, he was under indictment for statutory rape, but he had not remembered she was underage. No, no promise of easier treatment had been tendered by the prosecution in return for this testimony. Your witness.

Up to this point Siegel had not cross-examined, except to bring out, from the medical examiner, that the baby had not died of its fall but from exposure during the night. She had also reserved her opening statement. But now she rose and laid into Emilio Perez. He was lying about not knowing how old she was. He had signed an ornate birthday card for the defendant's fifteenth birthday. The card was duly produced and offered in evidence. Objection from Vasquez. Mr. Perez was not on trial. Overruled by Judge Urey. Siegel pressed on: the fifteenth birthday was a big thing for a Hispanic girl, the *quinceana*. How could he have forgotten her age? An unimpressive denial. Karp saw the faces of the Hispanics on the jury harden up. Then, the date of the rape. Not a weekday at all, school records produced in evidence, Lourdes had not missed a day of school that year until after the intercourse described. Objection. Overruled. It went on. Hadn't Lourdes told him she was pregnant? Dates and times. He denied it. Why then had he called the Chelsea Women's Clinic? The clinic kept good caller ID records, for obvious reasons. Here was his work phone number. Records entered in evidence. Siegel was good, Karp had to admit. Vasquez tried to repair the damage on redirect, but Perez mumbled and hung his head and looked beaten. The jury was glaring at him as he came down off the stand.

Vasquez announced that this concluded the state's case-in-chief. The judge asked Siegel whether she wished to make her opening now or wait for the next day. It was three-fifty, and Urey was clearly leaning toward an early dismissal. Siegel did not take the hint.

She faced the jury. She had a carrying voice, a New York voice, with New York vowels. This, he knew, was a shade put-on, as she had not sounded like that during their earlier conversation. That was one contrast with Vasquez, who consciously elevated her diction. Siegel, a middle-class woman, was lowering hers. Another contrast: Siegel was not nearly as attractive physically as Vasquez, and she did not try to compete here. She was not exactly dowdy, more flashy actually, like a garment worker or waitress in her Sunday best. Most lawyers wore subdued colors; Siegel was wearing what looked like a low-end department-store suit the color of blood, over a print blouse. The image was feisty girl of the streets fighting for the oppressed underdog. Karp could see only her profile when she turned to address the right side of the jury box. A band of red was upon her cheekbone; not rouge, but hectic excitement.

She opened with a rhetorical question: What are juries for? They determined what is fact, of course, but not only that. Juries are about power, ultimately, and for a thousand years people have felt right to place the ultimate power of depriving a citizen of life or liberty in the hands of people just like you. Not legislatures; not judges; you. Then a capsule history of great jury feats: Magna Carta, then one about the Puritans in England making kissing a capital offense. Imagine that! Kiss your girl on the street and you risk hanging. But was anyone ever hanged for this offense during the twenty-two years it was on the books? No, nor ever found guilty. Why? Juries would not countenance it; they knew it was wrong, whatever the letter of the law. John Peter Zenger, in colonial New York, printed something the royal governor didn't like, was tried, and acquitted. Did he do it? Heck, yes. Was it against the law? Yes, again. But the jury thought that freedom of the press was more important than the letter of the law — they ruled on higher principle, and they were right. Fugitive slave law — New York juries again and again refused to condemn escaped slaves back to their chains. Were they really slaves? Of course they were, and the law said they had to be returned to their masters, but once again, juries did the right thing.

Now she turned to infanticide proper, and Karp, with rather a sinking feeling, recognized the references she used as coming from Murrow's research paper. She was good, he thought, damned good. The jury had the look that every lawyer liked to see on juries, rapt attention, their eyes following the eloquent movements of her hands. Judge Urey was frowning up on his presidium. He didn't like this at all, and several times Karp saw him begin to break in, but he did not. He was giving her plenty of rope. It is extremely rare for an opening statement to be interrupted, for an opening statement is not evidence. Karp could almost see him thinking of how, in his instructions, he would torpedo this codswallop.

Now Siegel described her witnesses to come: teachers, a priest, who would paint Lourdes Bustamente as a nice girl, a decent girl, before she was debauched by a monster in the bosom of her own family. She would call a gynecological specialist who would testify that Lourdes Bustamente had experienced no more than three acts of intercourse in her life, that obviously the fiend Perez had raped a virgin. Finally they would hear from

Lourdes herself. They would hear what really happened in that dance-hall bathroom and how Ms. Bustamente's newborn came to die. After that it would be up to them, and only them, to decide whether Lourdes Bustamente, aged sixteen, really deserved twenty-five to life in prison.

There was an audible sigh as she sat down. The jury was in love. Karp had seen it before, and he had also seen juries go against their emotional predilections to bring home a verdict. In fact, infanticide was not fugitive slaves or press freedom, and Karp thought that these twelve people clearly understood that. Judge Urey said the usual monitory words, and the court adjourned for the day. Karp cut through the crowd and went up to Jessica Siegel.

"That was quite a show, Jessica. I don't think I've ever seen anything quite like it."

Siegel gave him a lopsided smile. "Gosh, coming from you that means I should be worrying. Should I?"

"Not about your performance. If you don't mind, I'd like you to drop by my office before you go. Say fifteen minutes?"

"To discuss . . . ?"

"Oh, the various aspects of this case." He turned away before she could ask any more questions and moved over to the prosecution table, where he told Vasquez he would meet her outside the courtroom. When she emerged, he led her to the end of the hallway, where there was a little alcove under the tall window.

"What?" said Vasquez testily. She had not liked Karp talking to Siegel.

"We're going into the tank on this one, Vasquez," said Karp abruptly.

"What? Because of that crap she was spouting?"

"No, because we're going to win. You really *don't* think Lourdes Bustamente deserves twenty-five to life for what she did and neither do I. Neither does the jury, but if they nullify, which actually I doubt they will, Urey will go crazy, he'll threaten the jury with contempt, he may declare a mistrial. I want to avoid that, having to go through this whole goddamn thing yet again. We need to get Lola her spanking and move on."

"For God's sake, Butch, what the hell am I supposed to do about that?" Vasquez cried in frustration. "We offered man one and they spat in our faces."

"Not exactly," said Karp, and he told her what he had learned.

They were assembled in Karp's office, around his long oak table, Karp at the head, flanked by Father Dugan on one side and Vasquez on the other. Murrow was in his usual place in the corner. They waited, making tense small talk, Vasquez grumpy, Karp irritated, the priest his usual veiled self. Siegel entered, took in the group, startled slightly when she saw Father Dugan, and sat down at the foot of the table. She brought out a leather portfolio, smiled her wolf smile, and said, "This looks like a job interview."

Polite chuckles. Karp made the introduction. Siegel said, "I hope I haven't offended the Church."

Father Dugan said, smiling himself, "I'm sure you have. I do all the time. But for my part this is purely a pastoral matter."

Siegel looked inquiringly at Karp, who said, "What Father Dugan means is that in the course of his work he had a conversation with Carmen Bustamente, your client's mother. He heard some disturbing things, and he came to me about them."

Siegel's smile was gone. "Why you? Why didn't he come to me?"

"Because he knows me. My daughter and wife are parishoners of his. In any case, Jessica, it seems that you've neglected to inform your client's family about the possibility of a plea bargain. In fact, you seem to have pressed it upon them that your strategy of jury nullification is the only way to save Lourdes from a long term in prison."

"That's not true," said Siegel dismissively. "Mrs. Bustamente has a fourth-grade education and a limited command of English. She's often confused about the legal situation. But she's very firm in her belief that her daughter is being used as a scapegoat and has given me complete discretion to handle the case as I see fit."

"Do you speak Spanish, Ms. Siegel?" asked the priest.

"Only a little. Lourdes translates for me when we have to confer. Do you?"

"Actually, yes, I do. Fluently. And I'm afraid something must have been lost in translation. Mrs. Bustamente knows absolutely nothing about any plea bargain. She said you told her that Lourdes's only hope of avoiding jail was to do it your way. In fact, she also seems to have a mistaken notion of her daughter's right to counsel. She thinks that you're doing her a favor, and if she doesn't agree with you, you'll dump her and then she'll have to pay for a lawyer out of her own pocket."

"That's an interesting conversation for a priest to have, Father," said Siegel, smiling craftily. "Full of legal detail. Could it be that someone put you up to it? Oh, yes. Butch, you seem to be making a habit of ex parte by proxy. First the daughter, now the priest. Maybe I should move for a mistrial right now. And does the DA know about this?"

"You know, Jessica," said Karp with a sigh, "we could sit here and trade repartee about who violated what legal procedure, but my purpose in having this meeting was to see if a group of reasonable people could come to some reasonable disposition of this case. I should have done this earlier. I didn't because I got tangled in the bureaucracy around here, and I regret it. Now it's gotten a lot more tangled. You've violated the ethics of your profession —"

Siegel flared, "What! Look who's talking! I resent the implication that —"

Karp held up a hand and beat her back with his eyes. "Shh! You'll get your chance, Jessica. And you've used your client to make a political point, which you hope will get you into the legislature next fall. You're trying for a nullifying jury in a big public case. But Ben Urey isn't going to let that happen. If he thinks the jury's about to run away on him, he'll call every member into his chambers, browbeat them individually, and threaten them with contempt if they violate his definition of what their oath as jurors is."

"He can't do that. A jury has the power to

bring in a verdict in the teeth of both the law and the facts."

"Yes, Oliver Wendell Holmes, *Horning v. District of Columbia*. I know the law, but I also know Ben Urey, who is no Holmes. In any case, it's not going to come to that. We're prepared to offer man one, three years, minimum security. She'll serve fifteen months, finish her sophomore year in high school, and meanwhile she'll learn that it's not nice to throw babies out of windows. She'll express remorse. You'll have frightened the big bad DA into reducing the charge from murder, and getting your client the kind of sentence we usually give out for selling nickel bags. A win-win in my opinion. So — is it a deal?"

"No deal. That jury won't convict her on murder two."

"That's not the *point*, Jessica. How can I put this? We're not *maneuvering* now. We're trying to do the right thing."

"And *you* get to decide what the right thing is? Uh-uh. We're going for acquittal on this one."

"I see. Well, if that's your decision, I see no need to detain Father Dugan or Ms. Vasquez any longer. Thank you both." Everyone looked at him in surprise.

Then, without a word, Vasquez practically dashed from the room, her face hard. Dugan seemed reluctant to leave, perhaps, Karp thought, because he was really enjoying the moral theater. When he had at last gone, and Siegel was replacing her portfolio in her briefcase, Karp said, "Just between us, Jessica, what exactly is the driving force behind this farce? You want to make the world safe for infanticide?"

"You know the answer to that. The law stinks. It's just another way for men to go on beating up on women, demonizing them. If infanticide is murder two, next it'll be abortion is murder two. Infanticide is essentially a social protest against the exploitation of women. It's a strike against extorted motherhood."

"And you think that . . . position is worth sacrificing your client for?"

She shrugged. "At least this way she'll do some good in the world. What in hell has she got to look forward to anyway? She's not going to kill them all, so by the time she's twenty she'll have three brats and a little macho asshole kicking her butt around some stinking apartment. Besides, I could still win. You never can tell with juries." She gave him that smile again, but he did not smile in return.

"You know, Jessica, human beings are supposed to be ends, not means. Kant proposed that as the basis of morality."

"Yes, well, men are real good at proposing moral dictates while someone else washes the shit out of the diapers." She hoisted her briefcase and made to leave.

"I'll send you a transcript."

She stopped. "A transcript . . . ?"

"Yes. Of this meeting. It should make interesting reading at the bar association and in the Legal Aid Society boardroom."

She stared wildly around her, a flush reddening her face. "Oh, *tell* me you didn't have this place bugged! You must be out of your mind! I'll ruin you!"

"Bugged? You mean like Nixon? No, that would be wrong. But Murrow over there has been keeping a careful stenographic record of everything we've said. You're surprised? See, that's where you fall down as a feminist. You never expected to see a man taking shorthand."

She was good, Karp thought. Her face was perfectly neutral, although he imagined the wheels spinning behind it. She stared briefly at Murrow, met Karp's eyes again, and said, "There's the little matter of you arranging for the good padre to see my client. I don't guess that would go down too well with the powers that be."

"No, I guess not, but see, I don't care, Jessica, and you do. You know, ferociously ambitious people like you have a lot of advantages. You put most of your energy into moving ahead, and you do move ahead, even if you leave a lot of roadkill behind. On the other hand, if you put your heart into what you're doing, the thing itself, in this case the law, then the glory part somehow doesn't matter quite so much. I was getting fired from this job while you were still in elementary school, and strangely enough, popping right back in. One more time won't make much of a difference. So when it comes to a situation like this, a Mexican standoff, if that's not a politically incorrect phrase, then I believe the advantage is with people like me. You'll let me know what you decide, Jessica, before court convenes tomorrow morning."

She glared at him, swallowed hard, nodded curtly, and left.

Murrow whistled. "Hardball."

"Very hard, Murrow. I hope it won't besmirch my reputation as the house Boy Scout."

"Will she roll on it?"

"Oh, yeah, she'll go over like a top. The kamikaze approach always works with people like that. They're unhinged by the very idea that a corner office and a big title isn't worth your immortal soul." Karp rubbed his face vigorously and stood. "I'm going home,

Murrow." He put on his suit coat and took his raincoat off the rack.

"Did you actually send that priest to talk to the mom?"

"Not as such," said Karp. "You know, there's an old Jesuit saying my wife uses all the time. It goes, 'I never lie. Never. But the truth is not for everyone.' It was sort of like that."

20

That night, in bed, Karp turned to his wife and asked, "What was all that Lucy was saying about going down to Wilmington over spring break?"

"Out of nowhere. We were making dinner, and she was doing her dutiful-daughter routine, like she does when she's pissed off at something and deciding whether she can reasonably blame it on me, when she asked me whether she could spend time with me at the trial."

"Unusual."

"Very. So I thought — do I really want her around? I'll be working like crazy, I'll be tense, it's not as if we could be touring the historic sights of Delaware, but then I thought, Why not? And I said, Okay, providing there *is* a trial."

"Any further on that?"

"Really, it's up to the Goldfarbs now. I did speak to Mike Brewster about this guy they want to examine Sarah. It's what I thought."

"A ringer?"

"Yeah. Dr. Palmer Dash is apparently famous in the state for never finding any mental disease or defect at all. Son of Sam? Hey, what's a few demonic dog voices? Everyone has *some* demonic dog voices."

"He sounds like my kind of guy," said Karp. "So the state is setting her up. She gets examined by this Dash fellow, and he testifies that she knew what she was doing, she planned it all. If you don't let her be examined, that means you can't raise a mental-impairment defense at trial. Had you planned to?"

"Not really. Our position is that Sarah was literally unconscious during the time of the supposed crime, and further, since the baby couldn't have lived outside the womb anyway, that there was in fact no crime at all, aside from failure to notify of death and improper disposal of a corpse, which we would be perfectly willing to plead to."

"Sounds like they're playing chicken."

"You got it," Marlene agreed. "The murder charge is crazy on the evidence, but they're playing the old where-there's-smoke-there's-fire card. Why would they charge her with murder if there wasn't something behind it? And they hope that'll frighten the defendant enough to force her into a halfway face-saving plea. It's disgusting behavior. And they used the press unconscionably, but what they failed to consider was that it works both ways. They tolerated and encouraged a leaky environment, but then they couldn't shut it down when the leaks started to favor our side. They're really not all that smart, and they've got no serious experience with an aggressive defense. So . . ."

"They'll blink first?"

"Mm. That depends. Tell you the truth, Sarah's real shaky. The guilt's eating her up. She's the kind of kid who'd do ten years to protect her parents, just to end the tension. Selma asks me, can I *guarantee* a win? I tell her, Selma, I can't guarantee I won't get hit by a truck. Listen, rub my back, would you? It feels like there's an iron spike across my shoulders."

He did this for a while. She was silent except for groans and yelps, and brief directions toward the worst knots.

"Speaking of disgusting," he said, "I think I fixed Bustamente today." He told her what had happened.

She caught his tone and asked, "It sounds like you feel bad about it."

"I do. You know, Phil Garrahy used to tell us that we should act as if anything we did was going to show up on the front pages the next day, and we should be able to read it there without embarrassment. I don't feel that way

618

about what I pulled there, with Siegel."

"Oh, please! Murrow was right out there in the open, wasn't he? What did she think, he was writing his memoirs?"

"Still. And also getting Father Dugan involved. It's funny, I somehow thought that if a priest was in on the play, it would cast an ethical glow over the whole mess."

Marlene hooted. "And you picked Father *Dugan!* God, Butch, the man's a total criminal. In a good cause, of course. He's worse than I am, and compared to *you*, I'm Ms. Beelzebub. So, you pulled a Marlene. Congratulations. I'll tell you from experience that the moral pangs tend to fade with practice."

"You think I'm becoming more like you?"

"Definitely. They say that married couples tend to grow indistinguishable from each other with time."

"I thought that was dogs and masters."

"Dogs, too. The strange part is that I'm also getting more like you. More decent, less violent. Fighting it all the way, of course. It's pleasing Dugan no end."

"What did he do, by the way? His crime. He wouldn't tell me."

"Oh, no one knows. It was probably something like running a numbers racket in Trastevere and using the proceeds to buy guns for the Mayas. On the other hand, he's probably the only priest in the diocese who could stand to be my spiritual adviser. Not to mention Lucy. Do lower down. Actually, I absolutely adore him. I think he's one of the three most interesting men I've ever met."

"Oh? Let me guess that Tran is the second. Who's the third?"

"Oh, you, of course."

"Me? I always thought you thought I was dull."

"Yeah, right, I'm just hanging around for the meal ticket." She twisted around to face him. "That you don't think you're interesting is one of the more interesting things about you. Nothing's duller than a man who's always polishing his accomplishments."

"What are some other things?" Karp said, miming avidity.

Marlene laughed. "Oh, see, now I've created an egomaniacal monster. Seriously? Okay, the *most* interesting thing is that you're good. You have all the stoic virtues in full measure — justice, prudence, temperance, and fortitude."

"Good is interesting? I thought good was boring. It's the bad boys they make movies about."

"Yes, but I was talking about real life, which is not like the movies, in case you've never noticed. Which is why I'm here instead of with one of the innumerable bad boys who have lusted after me. Oh, also, even though you're good, you're not a wuss. You're a little scary, in fact, which I like."

"Good but not a wuss?" mused Karp. "This is rare?"

"Virtually unique, in my experience," said Marlene. "You may continue the massage on the front side, if you so desire."

Lionel T. Waley had his offices on Pine Street in the financial district, on the top floor of a venerable building faced with sooty red stone. As Karp ascended in the slow elevator, a stately ship of bronze and cherrywood, he was feeling better than he had in some time. As predicted, that morning Jessica Siegel had rolled. The plea that would settle Bustamente was moving through the system. And Keegan had rolled with it, much to Roland Hrcany's dismay. Upon consideration, Karp believed it was the priest who had made the difference. Jack Keegan had been knocked around by Jesuits at a tender age. A *renegade* Jesuit did not figure in his calculations. If a priest was involved, then the archdiocese was somehow complicit in the deal, covering the DA's right flank. He grumbled for form's sake when Karp told him the story, but acquiesced, as he had in this meeting with Waley. Keegan was here no different from his two subordinates: he did not relish a long, nasty trial with an eleven-year-old parricide as a defendant.

The first thing Karp noticed when he was shown into Waley's office was the fireplace. It had an actual fire in it. Waley caught his stare.

"You're admiring my fire. This is one of the few office buildings in Manhattan that still has them. It's mainly why I stay, although the place is in many ways unsuitable for a modern office. It needs to be rewired, for one thing. Still, it has a certain tone. Have a chair, Mr. Karp."

Waley indicated a brass-studded leather club chair of darkest green and spoke some words into an intercom placed on his desk. Karp looked about him. In his career, he had been much around high-powered lawyers and had concluded that the office of a man who could have any sort of office he wished was a good indication of that man's character. Waley's place was about half the size of a regulation basketball court, a corner location, of course, with tall, old-fashioned windows. An Oriental carpet on the floor showed threads in spots, and the furniture was of the best quality, but not showy antiques. On one of the two long oak refectory tables stood neat piles of documents, the other holding only a tray with stemmed glasses and a chrome water carafe, and a white ceramic vase full of cut flowers, artfully arranged. Two small paintings with museum lights attached hung on the diaper-paneled walnut walls. Karp knew little about painting, but he thought that one of these, a portrait of a bearded man in a frock coat, looked like a van Gogh, and the other was a hazy red bridge over a lily pond. He imagined that the combined value of the two paintings probably exceeded his net worth. Besides these, no diplomas nor awards nor photos of Waley with the great. No mementos on the spindle-legged cherry desk either, which was lightly cluttered with legal folders. The impression was very rich, very successful, but not ostentatious, no wish or need to overawe the guest, an old-fashioned, hardworking lawyer who just happened to be better than everyone else in the game.

Waley sat in a club chair opposite, across from a low drop-leaf table with an inlaid chessboard on it. He was a slight, neat man of middling height, with a plain, large-featured face, whose most remarkable characteristics were large, gray-blue, canny eyes, deep set beneath thick white brows, and a mane of thick, fleecy white hair, from which he derived his sobriquet, the White Shark. He was in shirt-sleeves, the shirt silk crisp and white, the sleeves adorned at the cuffs with worn gold links. His tie was a modest navy rep, and his gray suit pants were supported by an alligator belt with a gold monogram buckle, also worn. No colorful suspenders for Waley. They chatted about the weather, about the prospect of spring. A slim young woman came in with a tray on which was a silver coffee service, china cups, and a silver dish containing petits fours, deposited it on the table, and departed.

Waley poured and said, "I thought you would come by. I was happy when I heard you'd called."

"It's commonplace, I suppose, a case this prominent . . ."

"No, I meant you personally. I find you an interesting man. Have you noticed, most of the people in our profession are remarkably dull fellows? Or where not exactly dull, have adopted a sort of grotesque persona, coming to court in python cowboy boots, or whatever. Tedious, that type. And also, I suppose there is some unfinished business between us, from our last association."

"Yes, the Rohbling case," said Karp. "I've been thinking about that, too, recently. The associations with Maxwell, the issue of insanity. You turning up on Maxwell. Why do you think I'm interesting?"

Waley smiled. "Ah, the instinct for cross-examination, the question slipped in disarmingly! I do it, too. Do you find it a problem in your personal life? I did, when I had one. All three of my wives objected to it. My children rarely call."

Karp hesitated. He did not really care to discuss his personal life with Lionel Waley and did not much like what seemed to be an offer of greater intimacy. He said, "My wife is a lawyer, too. It's something of a problem to leave the office behind, but we try."

It was not quite a rebuff. Waley selected a cake, ate it, and dabbed at his lips with a tan linen napkin. "Leave the office behind," he said musingly. "You mean like a used-car salesman. Unwind with a beer in front of the TV, as they say. You don't *really* think that's possible, do you? I mean for people like *us*." He met Karp's eyes with an amused look, waiting.

Karp nodded. "No, I don't. It's not like selling cars. What's your point, Mr. Waley?"

"My point? I'm not sure I had one, except to demonstrate the extreme difficulty of plain speaking between people like us, who live our lives in a nexus of ever reaching for some subtle advantage over an opponent. What's he aiming at, you think, as I offer a personal observation. What's he doing *now*, as he pretends to understand my prior suspicions?" Waley grinned, showing costly dental technologies. "Wheels within wheels."

"Yes, but we're opponents here, aren't we? Not pals."

"Are we? Did you ever see a film called *Grand Illusion*? No? Erich von Stroheim plays the commandant of a POW camp in the First World War. He's a Prussian aristocrat, and he forms, or he thinks he's formed, a personal relationship with a French aristocrat, one of his prisoners, a man named de Boieldieu. They're both noble, they're both professional warriors, and von Stroheim expresses contempt for both the politicians who start the wars and the canaille who serve in the ranks. He proposes to de Boieldieu that they are both protectors of something sacred, something higher than the passing conflict, the notion of honor, of which neither politician nor common soldier has any idea. In the end, though, de Boieldieu betrays the commandant and sacrifices himself to allow some comrades of lower social rank to escape. It's one of my favorite films. The illusion of the title, of course, is that there is any such thing as honor in war. There's merely enmity and competition."

"Honor has a bad track record, Mr. Waley," said Karp. "It's what makes gang fights. The motto of the SS was 'my honor is my loyalty.' That's why we have rules, and sanctions, and laws, the same for high and low."

"A shade better for the high, surely," said Waley, and gestured to the appointments of his office.

"We're working on that. But let's say that we did have honor in the sense of that movie, that we trusted one another, as, if you'll excuse the expression, gentlemen, then what? I recall you saying to me, during the first days of the Rohbling business, that it was a pity that a couple of intelligent people couldn't sit down and figure out the most decent thing to do in a case like that."

"Yes, I recall that conversation very well. I also recall that you were not receptive to the notion."

"No, I wasn't. The system by which decent people sit in private rooms and decide what's to be done about a third party — that system also doesn't have much of a track record. Our Constitution is very clear in that area, as you know. But there are exceptions to every rule, and I'm prepared to believe that Brian Maxwell may be one of them. What do you make of him?"

"Brian? Brian is . . . inexplicable. I know you thought Jim Rohbling was faking it, but I believed then and I believe now that he was seriously deranged within the definition of the law. But Rohbling is as you or I compared to Brian Maxwell. Did you ever meet him?"

"No. My daughter knows him, though. She liked him, too."

"Yes, he's a likable child. Charming, talkative, intelligent. Chatters away quite freely about killing his parents. His father was going to send him to a military school, so Brian killed him. He really did *not* want to go to military school. His mother woke up with the shot and was very upset with him, so he killed her, too. Brian does *not* like it when people are upset with him. He tried to kill his sister because he thought his grandfather was going to like her better, after she became a famous dancer. Brian *likes* being the center of attention. He just loves all the attention he's getting now. They have him in a cottage all by himself, up in Spofford, under constant guard. He'd like to have his computer, but besides that, he's just fine. I've defended a good number of bad people in my time, but I would put Brian Maxwell at the very top of the list of people I would not want to be walking at large in society. He's somewhere out beyond psychopathy."

"So what do we do?"

"What, indeed? Mr. Warren, as I'm sure you'll have heard, is not rational on the subject. I had a great deal of trouble dissuading him that I would not sit by while he perjured up an alibi for his grandson. He wishes me to prove that Brian did not do it."

"Did you explain . . . ?"

"Oh, yes. I was speaking loosely. Of course, all I need do is demonstrate that you all have *not* proved it. I suppose I could do that. You'll not be taking the case yourself?"

"No. Roland Hrcany is eager for a chance at you. I suppose there's no way you could change Mr. Warren's mind? The state has no great desire to try a child for this, especially a child of Brian's particular . . . um . . . character. But, of course, we'll grind ahead with it, second-degree murder times two, plus attempted murder."

"Yes, I suppose you must. You have the luxury, I suppose you could call it, of serving the god Juggernaut. Rules, as you say. As for me . . . I could drop the case, of course. But I'm disinclined to do that." Waley smiled and held his hand up languidly, palm out. "My honor is my loyalty. I've actually never dropped a client, although I've threatened to a number of times. Do you suppose they know how to cure people like Brian? He's not exactly a human being, you know. Could they, could anyone, given limitless resources, try to *graft*, let us say, an actual human person onto that empty physical form?"

"I don't know," said Karp. "A saint could, maybe."

"Yes, a saint. Are you religious, by any chance?"

"If you mean do I think there's a God who watches over us and does miracles and things like that, then, no, I'm not."

"Hm. Neither am I. And I doubt saints are much in evidence in even the best mental institutions. It all seems to be a matter of chemicals nowadays. Perhaps they can adjust the soup in Brian's head. Or perhaps we're all somehow missing the point." Waley was silent, tapping a manicured nail against his china cup. On the mantelpiece a clock loudly ticked. Karp cleared his throat and asked, "So you'll push on with a straight defense?"

"Oh, yes. A very vigorous defense. It will drag on of course, who knows for how long? A year at least, probably two, maybe even three or four. As you know, I am not unskilled in these matters."

"The Duke of Delay."

Waley grinned like a schoolboy caught at some naughtiness. "That's me. Mr. Warren, you know, is seventy-eight. He was a smoker for a long time. He has a cough, and his blood pressure is not what it should be. I would be very much surprised if his grandson came to trial during his lifetime. In fact, I can almost guarantee that he will not. Brian's guardian-ship would in that case pass to the late mother's younger sister, a woman of unblemished rationality, as I have already determined. After a decent interval, therefore, a couple of decent men will sit in a private room and determine what's best for the boy, which I don't doubt will be to vanish forever into some comfortable spot, there to be worked on by the high priests of the psyche. What do you think of that, Mr. Karp?"

"Not much, sir. Technically, I suppose it's a violation of legal ethics. I could report you to the bar. Or your client."

"Yes, you could, but you won't. Because though you hate it, and properly so, you know it's the right thing to do."

Karp thought of Jessica Siegel and what she had done and what he had done back to her. It was the same thing. Technically. That anti-septic word. The situations were entirely different, he told himself. Siegel was sacrificing a client to aggrandize herself and her cause, whereas Waley was simply thwarting the will of a half-senile old man and grasping a chance to save a monstrous child, while still protecting society. Or was he? Had the White Shark calculated that he would lose in a straight defense and was he now manipulating Karp so that Karp would not actively oppose the strategy of delay? Because Karp could. He could push to bring Brian Maxwell to trial as an adult. Or he could acquiesce and let the months spin by. The right thing to do. How did we know what it was? The law? Codes of ethics? It was like trying to wallpaper a running hog. He thought of his daughter, of her sure and certain sense of what was right, whatever the letter of the law. He hesitated to walk on the thin ice upon which she cavorted with such apparent confidence. Was it religion that made the difference? They called it gut feeling, but surely that was figurative only. Karp understood, of course, that some people in his profession steered closely around the buoys, who took pride in this, in fact, and who, if they could undermine the spirit while staying within the law's letter, thought it a fine day's work; and he understood that he himself was not one of these people. Was Waley?

Who was still looking at him, relaxed, waiting, confidently waiting.

"I suppose I do," said Karp, and read, to his great surprise, a profound relief in Waley's eyes and body language. He was frightened, thought Karp. The signs were unmistakable under the bland lawyer's mask. Of what? he wondered. Not that I wouldn't go along, or that I'd turn him in, but that I wouldn't *engage* him as a person, that I'd treat him like another scumbag manipulator. It was some kind of test.

"Good. I hoped you would feel that way. Well, that's settled." Waley leaned back in his chair and looked around the office. In a distant room a telephone rang, but Karp was sure that no call would be transferred into this sanctum. Waley was not the sort of man to take calls while he had a guest. Now he said, "Tell me, Butch, have you ever thought of going private?"

Now it was "Butch." "Well, actually, Lionel, I did go private once, a tort firm down the street. I made a lot of money and didn't much like it."

"I meant criminal defense."

"Not really. I'm pretty happy where I am."

"What about when Jack Keegan gets the federal judgeship he's been wangling for lo these many years?"

"Then I'll have to see. Why do you ask?"

"Oh, just thinking. I'm sixty-eight. This is a one-man firm. I'd like to take it a little easier."

There was a long pause. Then Karp snorted and, grinning, asked, "Lionel, are you offering me a *job?*"

"Not really. Not now. Just planting a seed." Waley smiled mildly.

Karp felt a laugh bubbling up from deep

within and let it out. Waley chuckled along with him.

"Lionel, you're perfect."

"I try to be." Waley rose and dropped his napkin on the tray. "Come, I'll show you out."

Marlene drove back to Wilmington through a damp Jersey just beginning to show the green dust of spring. Mulcahey had, at her request, arranged a furnished suite in a development off I-95 north of the city, the sort of place that corporations stash their Southwestern branch managers for the annual sales conference. She drove there and checked in. It was a modest tower in a kind of ersatz park, attached to a small shopping center called, oddly, Blueball Plaza. It was clean, largely beige and gray, equipped with a large bath, a tiny kitchenette, a fax machine, and a terrace the size of a card table, from which one could see the interstate and perhaps 80 percent of Delaware. Marlene arranged for an additional bed to be delivered and left for Mulcahey's office.

"How was Blueball?" that person asked when she arrived.

"Divine. If I ever want to commit suicide, I know where to come. Seriously, thanks, it's just right. My daughter will be down later.

She wants to see Mom do a trial, so the suite works out well."

A faint look of disappointment crossed Mulcahey's face, which Marlene caught, but ignored. Clearly he thought there might be long, relaxing, liquid-fueled evenings at Blueball, talking over the day in court. Sorry, Kevin, not to be.

"We get the focus-group reports yet?" she asked.

"Yeah, the other day. Somewhat depressing reading." Marlene had thought this expense a waste of what little money they had — to pay a firm to run various combinations of testimony in front of local citizens representative of the probable jury pool and charting their reactions — but both Mulcahey and Brewster had insisted. It was the done thing now. She had also resisted hiring a jury consultant and had won on that one. If she couldn't pick a jury herself, she thought, she was in the wrong business.

"Hit me with it."

"Bottom line? They feel sorry for Sarah, but it's hard for them to believe that she didn't know she was pregnant — this is especially women with kids — and it's hard for them to believe they didn't go to the motel to have the baby. The men — they don't really buy the story that she was afraid to tell her mother. And *nobody* likes that the baby went into the Dumpster. When the kids saw what was happening, why didn't they dial 911? Why didn't they leave the baby in a basket by the emergency room? Basically, they want someone to pay for the baby in the Dumpster. So it doesn't look that good, I'm afraid."

"No, not that thrilling," said Marlene. "Have we told the Goldfarbs about this yet?"

"No, we thought you'd want to break it to them."

"Of course. Thank you. I'm so popular with them already, this'll be the whipped cream on the shit pie. Any other bad news?"

"Some good news, as a matter of fact. Shearing ruled on the polygraph motion. It's in only if Sarah submits to the state's lie-test expert."

Marlene raised her eyes and clasped her hands. "Thank you, Jesus. Any idea who the state's expert is?"

"No, but our guy taught the Delaware State Police and Newkirk PD's lie-test officers. We'll know real soon, but read the decision. He bought our argument about improvements in technology, especially utilization and reliance by the FBI and other government agencies and major corporations. And the papers have been giving it a play. I have the clips. That woman who wrote that awful

Newsweek piece about soulless teenagers did one called 'Rush to Judgment' admitting that she might have been too hasty."

"You could say that, the bitch. It makes some sense, then. The good judge may be running a little scared. He's been ruling against us all along, and he figures he'll throw us a bone at the end so as not to look like the prejudiced bastard he is. Tell me, did the focus group have the polygraph results?"

"No, because we only gave them stuff we were sure we could present. You think it'll make a difference?"

"Maybe. I sure hope so. But it's clear that we need to provide someone for the jury to punish and have it not be Sarah."

"That leaves the boyfriend."

"That leaves him. What about the boyfriend's girlfriend?"

"Willa Shields? I interviewed her up in Chambersburg. She's reluctant and embarrassed, but she'll make an okay witness, I think, if all we want from her is that she called Peter several times on the night of the event to make arrangements to meet later, and did meet him later."

"Good," said Marlene. "That counters the state's position that the messages on Peter's machine were Sarah's machinations. It'll also interest the jury that the night after Jorgensen dumped his baby in the Dumpster, he was dallying with another woman. It speaks to his character." Marlene clapped her hands briskly and looked around the cluttered office. Piles of files were on every horizontal surface. "Okay! We're rolling now. Let's get this brothel organized. First, witness lists, theirs and ours, in probable order. For theirs, probable testimony and notes for cross-examination, a file for each. For ours, a list of questions, lists of exhibits, in order. We need a schedule for witness prep — work with Brewster on transportation. After we get that down, I need to put some time in on my opening."

"Will you want me to handle any of the courtroom work?" Mulcahey asked this tentatively, and Marlene felt momentarily bad for him. He was at the stage of his career where a court appearance in a high-profile case like this would lift him to a new level in the profession.

"Yes," she said. "As we proceed with the prep, you'll let me know what you feel comfortable with, and we'll discuss it. You know that it's important for the jury to identify with lead counsel, so I'll have to take the lion's share."

"No problem, Marlene," said Mulcahey, understanding.

With that, they turned to the colossal labor of trial preparation. Here Marlene thought she had an advantage over the people doing the same thing across the street in the state's attorney's office. They had more troops, but she had more experience in preparing trials and had been trained in a far harder school than anyone on Abt's staff, including Abt himself.

They knocked off at seven that evening, among a litter of fast-food wrappers and coffee cups. Marlene spruced herself up in the ladies' and drove out to Mt. Holly. Mr. Goldfarb let her in. He looked as if he had lost fifteen pounds and had the pallid, waxy look of a fresh corpse. Mumbling a greeting, he led her through the house to the living room, where Selma Goldfarb and her daughter sat. The dad sat, Marlene sat. They all looked at her expectantly out of sad brown eyes that were all smudged underneath with the circles of despair. It was like addressing a family of raccoons. She gave them the good news first, about the polygraph decision, which it turned out they already knew, from news reports. Then she described the results of the focus group. When the import of what Marlene was saying sank in, Selma let out a little cry.

"That's it! That's final! We are *not* going to trial. We have to make a deal."

Marlene kept her voice calm as she said, "Selma, listen to me now! The state has offered first-degree manslaughter as a plea —"

"How many years is that?" Mrs. Goldfarb demanded.

"Between ten and twenty years."

"So? That's better than life. It's better than *execution!*"

"Yes, but Selma, listen. That deal is contingent upon a psychiatric finding, by a state-employed psychiatrist, that Sarah was not in her right mind at the time of the alleged crime. That's what manslaughter is, why it's not murder. The defendant was in such extreme emotional distress that she didn't know what she was doing and someone ended up dead. The law wants to distinguish between that kind of homicide and the kind where someone got killed to get the insurance money or because some Mafia don ordered it — in cold blood, that is."

"Right, and that's Sarah, not in her right mind, having convulsions. The doctors all said."

"Yeah, Selma, *our* doctors said. But, look — the state's whole theory of the case rests on the opposite argument, that Sarah masterminded this whole thing, that she was in control, that she ordered the disposal of the baby. Their deal with Jorgensen rests on that premise. So given that, what is their psychiatrist going to find when he examines Sarah? That she was a cold-blooded calculator throughout, that she's lying about being out of it? I'd bet that way."

Selma looked stunned. "But . . . but he's a *doctor*."

"Yes, and we've determined that he's a doctor who has never once, in any testimony, declared that a defendant was not entirely in control during the commission of the charged offense. So once they have that examination, they can say, 'Wait a minute, she wasn't in extreme emotional distress, there's no deal,' and they have an expert witness who will testify to that effect, damagingly, at the trial."

Selma was shaking her head slowly, from side to side, like the pendulum of a large clock. Her husband and daughter were watching her as if mesmerized by the motion.

Marlene continued, trying to break through, "Selma, believe me, we can't let them do this. They're desperate. They have *nothing* to offer, except an incompetent autopsy medical examination, and the uncorroborated testimony of a coconspirator to whom they have offered a sweetheart deal. Their investigation is a botch. I will tear it to shreds. They *need* something else to paint the color of truth onto Peter's testimony, and this corrupt shrink is —"

"No," Selma interrupted, "no, no, we can't take the risk. The risk . . . it's my baby. You don't understand, it's her whole life. My husband will die, she'll be in jail, I'll *die,* she'll be in jail."

"Selma, I understand your concern, but —"

Selma turned to Marlene with a look of impotent fury on her face. "You *don't* understand. All you care about is your trial, your trial, you don't *care* about my *baby!*"

This last word was shrieked, and in the shocked silence that followed, Sarah said in a calm voice, "Mom, I'm not a baby."

Selma stared at her daughter. "What are you then?" she shouted. "A grown-up? A grown-up does what you did with that bum? A grown-up ruins her life, kills her parents? You don't understand anything, *anything,* you and your shiksa lawyer. *You're murdering your parents!*"

After this, pure hysterics. Mr. Goldfarb ran off and came back with a pharmacy vial and a glass of water and urged pills on his wife, who gobbled two down. He led her off, weeping.

Sarah did not move while this was going on. She sat limp in her chair, like a wounded animal.

Marlene said, "I'm sorry. I was just trying . . ."

Sarah cleared her throat. "I know. It's not

your fault. This, what just happened, is all the time now, every day. I don't know if I can take it anymore."

"Trial's next week, Sarah. It'll be all over soon, either way."

"I want it to be over, God, you can't imagine how bad. Do you know what I did? I was in the garage the other day, all alone in the house, my folks were at the doctor's, and my dad's car was in there, and I thought, Oh, I'll just sit in it and turn on the engine and that'll be it, no more problems. I actually sat in the car for a while."

"That's not a good way to think, Sarah."

"No? It's not as operatic as jumping off the castle walls, I guess. But I don't feel operatic. I feel like a worm on the sidewalk that somebody smooshed, and the together part is still twitching. Do we have any chance at all?"

Marlene gave this the consideration it deserved. It was not the moment for a cheap pep talk. "Yeah, we have a chance. They do have a weak case. If I can break Peter, we have a very good chance. But if we let their shrink in, I think we're screwed. You want odds? I'd say it's sixty-forty, ours, right now. I think it'll improve during trial, but an acquittal's still a long shot. Like the focus group said, they don't like the baby in the Dumpster. On the other hand, this is a political case. The AG has to face the voters this fall. She wants to face the voters with a success, or failing that, she wants there to be a decent interval for amnesia to set in before the election. If we make a strong enough showing, if we make them look like the fools they are, if it looks like they've got no chance to convict, I don't think they'll risk even a hung jury, which would mean they'd have to set up another trial right in the middle of primary season. I think in that case they'd come crawling to us with at least the same deal they gave Jorgensen. It'd mean prison time for you, though. And you'd have to stand up before God and everybody else and admit you'd been an irresponsible jerk."

"I *was* an irresponsible jerk, Marlene. And prison would be a relief."

21

Marlene met Lucy at the Wilmington Am-trak station on Friday afternoon. April showers were descending. Lucy was wearing her nurse's cloak, a dark beret, a black jumper, black stockings, and clunky lace-up boots. She carried her khaki musette bag and a small, worn thrift-shop leather suitcase, the refugee look again. Marlene sighed as the girl walked toward the car. Ordinarily she did not mind her daughter's eccentricity, the pot ought not to call the kettle black, but just now she could have used a little cheerful normality. Lucy climbed into the car and kissed Marlene formally on the cheek. Marlene said, "I'm glad you're here — the Nazis are everywhere."

"Really?"

"I meant your outfit," said Marlene, driving away. "The local ones seem quiescent, although DeWayne Westerman is suing me for two point one million dollars. The name doesn't ring a bell? That's the guy whose face I busted up."

"Is it serious?"

"Who can tell? It's Delaware. Meanwhile, I'm not worrying about it. Worse comes to worst, I hear Venezuela has some very nice neighborhoods. You'll visit."

"I'll bring from Zabar's," said Lucy. "How's the trial going?"

"We finished jury selection today. Four men, eight women, two of them alternates. Two black, one Asian, the rest whiteys."

"Is that good?"

"You got me there, kid. The only thing they all have in common is that they're all liars, because they all swore they hadn't heard much about the trial, and believe me, there are crabbers on tiny sand spits out in Delaware Bay, where they still speak Elizabethan English, who know as much about this case as I do. Your dad and I agree that a little too much is made nowadays about jury selection. They say defense juries should have a few singletons on them, like my Asian, and there's one kid who's younger than anyone else on the panel, the idea being that they'll tend more to resist a majority stampede to convict, but I don't know. Obviously, you challenge for cause, when you've got somone who's obviously prejudiced, like a guy with a shaved skull and a swastika tattooed on his forehead, and you get a black defendant, maybe you want to avoid an all-white jury, but beyond that? Most people, most of the time, will do the right thing, given a decent presentation. We'll see."

Marlene steered the Volvo across the Brandywine and north on Concord Pike. "This is pretty," said Lucy. "Where are we going?"

"To our lovely bachelorette apartment at, don't laugh, Blueball Plaza."

Lucy laughed.

"There we will get you settled and I will work on my opening statement. Then we're going to have dinner at Shanahan's in Sherwood. She's got a daughter about your age. You might want to stay over — you're invited — because I still have a ton of stuff to do."

"I have stuff to do, too," said Lucy coolly. "Will we spend any time together?"

"As much as I can spare, but it's going to be intense. You may have to amuse yourself a little."

Lucy said, "Uh-huh," and removed from her bag a Walkman and a thick manual entitled *An Ka Bamanankan Kalan*. The manual had a big stamp on it that said BUTLER LIBRARY — FOR LIBRARY USE ONLY, but, clearly, thought Marlene, language-library regulations did not apply to her daughter, no more than it would have occurred to a Princeton librarian to stop Einstein from slipping out the back with a copy of *Physical Review Letters.* Lucy put on the headset and started the tape, thumbing through the manual as Bambara sounded in her ears. They drove the rest of the way in silence.

Shanahan proved that evening to be a good plain cook: leg of lamb, new potatoes, salad, chocolate cake; hearty fare, and they all dug in, except Marlene, who had been faintly nauseated since the beginning of the trial. Maureen's boy, David, was home from college, a lanky, humorous kid who seemed to have repressed the worst aspects of his father's personality. Lucy, Marlene was glad to observe, was in charming mode. No one mentioned the few subjects on which she was a lunatic. From time to time Marlene caught David casting interested glances Lucy's way. Oh, great, I *will* have grandchildren, thought Marlene.

David wanted to know all about the trial, and Marlene was prevailed upon to stand up after the dishes were cleared and declaim her opening statement. The audience was assembled, and Marlene stood with her back to the hearth, declaiming thus:

"Ladies and gentlemen of the jury, it pains me to inform you that you and I are involved in a farce. It is a farce because, as you've just heard, in order to convict my client, Sarah

Louise Goldfarb, of intentional murder, the state must prove beyond a reasonable doubt that on the night of November 11 into the early morning hours of November 12, last year, she planned to murder, and did in fact murder, the infant known as Baby Boy Jorgensen. Beyond a reasonable doubt. That legal phrase, ladies and gentlemen, is far too slender to support the huge, the absolutely convincing mass of testimony and evidence that we will place before you, evidence that demonstrates the absolute contrary of all that the state must prove. You will learn that, first, far from intending the murder of her infant son, Sarah Goldfarb did not even know she was about to deliver a baby. She had, in fact, been informed by competent medical authority that, as of the first week of July, she was not pregnant, believed, in fact, when she went to that motel room, that she was having a five-month miscarriage. Second, you will learn that for nearly the entire duration of her stay in that motel room, Sarah Goldfarb was suffering from severe eclampsia of pregnancy, so severe that she was virtually comatose during that period, and in fact nearly lost her life. And finally, you will learn — and this is perhaps the most farcical aspect of all — there was no murder at all. The supposed victim in this case, the infant boy, was so severely malformed in the womb, and suffered so badly from the disease of its mother in the hours before birth, that it could not have lived for more than a few minutes. It could not have lived if it had been born in the intensive care ward of the finest hospital in the country. Ladies and gentlemen, no one killed Baby Boy Jorgensen; it died of its birth. We will bring forward witnesses of unimpeachable professional credentials, and you will learn from them exactly what was wrong with this poor infant, and what was wrong with his mother, my client, Sarah Goldfarb, as she struggled to give birth. You will further learn of the incompetence of the state's medical examination, that mistakenly attributed this death to homicide, and you will learn that the skull of this infant was crushed after it died, not before, crushed by heavy objects being placed on its corpse as it lay in the Dumpster where it was placed by its father. Let me say this, too, ladies and gentlemen: we are all repelled by the idea of a human being, a baby, being tossed away like garbage, and no one feels that more keenly than Sarah Goldfarb. But, as you will learn, Sarah Goldfarb had absolutely nothing to do with placing that baby in the Dumpster, and you will hear testimony, from medical personnel, that Sarah Goldfarb had no idea, no idea she had delivered a full-term baby until she emerged from her coma more than twenty-four hours after the birth in the motel. She never saw her baby, she didn't know it had been born, she didn't know it had died. And finally, ladies and gentlemen, you will hear the entire story of this tragedy from Sarah's own lips. Only two people in the whole world know what happened in room number ten of the Hospitality Inn on the night of November 12. The state intends to call one of them as a witness, Peter Jorgensen. The defense, you know, has no requirement to offer up the defendant as a witness. She has every right to remain completely silent. She is under no obligation to prove her innocence. The state must prove her guilt, beyond, as I said, a reasonable doubt. But Sarah wants to speak to you, to tell you her story. Now, we have scientific proof that this story is true; you will hear experts testify to that effect. But in the end, it is you the jury who are the ultimate judge of the facts. And I feel confident that when you have seen and heard the over-whelming mass of evidence the defense will present, you will conclude that far, far beyond there being merely reasonable doubt as to Sarah's guilt, there is indisputable proof that she is in fact innocent of all charges that have been brought against her, and that therefore you will find her innocent in your verdict.

Thank you, and excuse me while I throw up."

Vigorous applause and laughter. Marlene flapped her arms. "God, I'm sweating like a pig, even in the living room."

"You'll do great, Champ," said Shanahan admiringly, tinged with envious regret. "Abt will poop in his pants."

Lucy said, "Really, Mom, I'm impressed. How do you keep all that stuff in your head?"

"Oh, look who's talking! What's the Thai word for toilet paper?"

"Kràdàat cham-rá," answered Lucy without apparent thought, "but that's not the same thing. I have a Broca's area the size of Utah. It's like breathing to me. But I could never just, like, think up a speech and say it, especially not in front of people and a judge."

Marlene cried, "Lucy! I'm so glad you're proud of me at last."

Here Lucy gave her, instead of the expected badinage, a peculiar sad smile.

After that, fun: liar's poker, popcorn, and for the adults the flowing bowl, flowing in such measure that, at twelve, Marlene announced that she was not about to risk a DWI offense in the First State during trial and would Shanahan give her and Lucy a bed?

The next morning Marlene woke early, her head remarkably clear, considering. She even remembered to step over the mastiff. Leaving brief notes stuck to the fridge for her daughter and her hostess, she drove back to Wilmington and worked all day with Mulcahey in his office. Then she drove back to Sherwood. There she found Lucy among a gaggle of girls, listening to Beck and A. Morissette, and then some local boys came over, and they all had a cookout. During this, Marlene found herself momentarily alone with her daughter, the two of them clutching loaded paper plates, and she said, "Well, what do you think of America?"

"You mean normal life? I could grow to like it. Shannon's neat. She likes Fra Angelico, too."

"Is that a new band?"

"Mom . . ."

"Do you feel deprived? Have I ruined your childhood?"

Once again, instead of quipping back, Lucy regarded her for a long moment. Marlene felt peculiar under this stare. It was something new, and disconcerting. Lucy said, "I'm supposed to take you seriously."

"Supposed . . . ?"

"Yeah, Tran said. I was whining to him about my hard life and he said that, so I am. You're a serious person, so it's not hard, except when you do your guilty-mom routine, with the one-liners. What do you expect me to say to something like 'Have I ruined your childhood?' All this" — here Lucy gestured with her hamburger — "it's great, it's incredibly safe-feeling and relaxing. I mean talking about movies and who's cute. It's like hamburgers: fine, love 'em, but do I want to eat them all the time? No, sometimes I want *soon dubu jigae,* and Senegalese goat couscous, and *fuhnjáau.* And sometimes today, I felt like I was in a museum, like in the Museum of Natural History, where they have these dioramas, Indian toolmaking, Congo village, and I was looking in through the glass at native customs. So would I have liked to be more like this? I can't tell now, all that's so *gone* for me. I used to be angry about that, why aren't I normal and all, and I did blame you, but that was stupid. I mean, maybe if you'd brought me up in the whole suburban trip I'd be such a geek that I'd be drugged out or suicidal by now, or maybe I'd be a cheerleader and thinking a lot about hair, big deal. There's no point in thinking about that. Maybe we should make a deal. I won't do resentful daughter if you won't do guilty mom."

Marlene said, "I think I have to sit down. I'm having a progeny-maturity attack."

"Seriously, Mom."

"Seriously? Seriously, I guess you may have noticed I'm not a very nice person. I'm sneaky, mendacious, violent, vengeful, and angry. The great terror of my life is that you'd turn out that way, one, or that you'd be the opposite and hate me. So since I'm sneaky, I tend to hunker down behind all the, like you say, one-liners. It's a way of asking for forgiveness, I guess, backhandedly, of course, since it's me."

"*Ego te absolvo,* okay?" said Lucy around a mouthful of burger. "Now could we at least be *regular,* as Giancarlo says."

"I'll try. I get bitchy when I'm nervous, that doesn't help."

"Yeah, your trial. It must be scary. I'd die."

"It also doesn't help that I'm carrying that whole family on my back, it feels like. It's like *Night of the Living Dead* over there. I wouldn't mind so much except Sarah's got to sit there all day, and she radiates doom. I'm just hoping the jury doesn't read it as guilt."

"I'd like to meet her."

"Oh, you will. I wish I knew what to make of her. I thought I had her read pretty good, but she's been through a lot of changes the last couple of weeks." Meeting her daughter's copper eyes, Marlene lifted her plate. "She's not hamburger, not anymore."

Marlene got no more than two hours of sleep the night before the trial proper started, but to her delighted surprise, the minute she stood up before the jury and began to speak, it all came back to her, like riding a bike, and beyond that, she discovered that the preternatural coolness that came upon her during armed combat also served her in the metaphoric variety. The nervousness had gone; she could hardly recall it now. She rose, she spoke, she sat, she objected, as if it were all happening to someone else, this last only lightly, since from the first it appeared that Jason Abt needed little help in getting into trouble. Marlene knew he was not much of a litigator, but even she was surprised by how bad he was. He stood wrong, his angle to the jury was wrong as he questioned witnesses, he stood too close to the witness, he lost his place, he repeated questions that had been answered, he said *um* a lot. Or maybe it was his case.

The Newkirk cops were experienced enough in the average, straight-up suburban case, where they were going against a harassed public defender. They were simply not up to the kind of grilling a prepared and intelligent and merciless defense lawyer could give them on cross. Lieutenant Ray Hill's voice got ever tighter and lower as he tried to defend his obviously rehearsed story of the investigation and of the second interview in which Jorgensen had completely changed his motel-room story. Detective Yeager stuck to his tall tale about all the various things he had done on the night of, and how he had learned all the things that later proved to be figments. Yeager was learning that lying to a magistrate and lying at a hearing were far different from lying in front of a jury, with the press on hand in force. For one thing, the jury could laugh at you, and this jury did.

But not as much as they laughed at Officer Claiborne, as he described how he found a baby stuck under a fifty-pound exhaust fan without actually climbing into the Dumpster. Judge Shearing had to gavel them into silence several times. And then came Maryanne Bollinger, the Delaware medical examiner.

Bollinger was a stocky woman of about forty, with a chubby-pretty face, and white-blond hair that fringed her forehead in bangs and fell down her back in a ponytail. She had big blue eyes circled by thick, colorless lashes. Abt took her quickly through her credentials and her testimony — how she had done her autopsy, and why she believed that Baby Boy Jorgensen had lived outside the womb and been killed by shaking and skull fracture. Marlene listened to the testimony in growing disbelief. Abt was not going to touch on the second autopsy at all, or the sectioning of the baby's brain. Did he think she was going to *forget* it?

Marlene's turn.

"Doctor, how many neonate autopsies have you done besides this one?"

"Two."

"Hm. Only two. Either of them violent deaths?"

"No."

"Hm. You testified that you found evidence of crushing of the skull, and that you assumed it was the cause of death, correct?"

"Yes."

"At the time you informed Mr. Abt's office that the death was due to blunt trauma to the head, at that time you had not sectioned the brain, had you?"

"No."

"So you didn't know that there was no blood present in the skull fracture lines?"

Objection from Abt: no evidence presented to indicate that fact. Sustained.

Okay, that was their plan, ignore the second autopsy and the sections, protect Bollinger. New tack then.

"Dr. Bollinger, as a forensic pathologist, can you tell the jury what is the result of a skull fracture of the type you said this baby endured?"

Bollinger described how the brain bleeds,

how clots form, how pressure builds up so that blood cannot reach brain tissues, how the brain dies as a result.

"Thank you, Doctor. So you must have found lots of blood clots in this baby's brain, yes?"

A long pause. Oh, yes, now she did it, she *looked* at Abt, and the jury saw it.

"Oh, don't look at Mr. Abt, Doctor, Mr. Abt is not a forensic pathologist. You're not either actually, are you, not a diplomate of the American Board of Pathology?"

"No."

"So you're not board certified by the American Board of Pathology in any special field of pathology?"

"No, I'm not, but —"

"Thank you, that's enough. Now, could you answer my previous question: Did you or did you not find blood in the baby's brain?"

"Not on the outside, no."

"And you neglected to look on the inside, didn't you? You didn't section the baby's brain, did you?"

"No, it's not standard procedure in —"

"A plain *no* is fine, Doctor."

And so on, working the negatives, Bollinger hadn't observed this, she hadn't noticed that, she considered the baby normal in all respects, she thought the lung-float test was an adequate indication of a live birth. Did it ever occur to you that the fractures occurred postmortem? Objection, speculative. "Your Honor, may we approach the bench?" Marlene asked.

Shearing beckoned, Abt and Marlene went forward. Marlene said, "Your Honor, the state has presented this person as an expert in pathology. Her analytic process is a vital part of her expertise. That's what medical experts *do.*"

"Your Honor," said Abt, "in direct, I asked Dr. Bollinger the cause of death and she answered that it was the fracturing of the skull, obviously premortem. Asking her to speculate in contradiction to her testimony is out of order."

Shearing considered this. Marlene felt that this was a critical moment, because whatever his prejudice, Shearing was a judge, and he did not like what he was seeing in his courtroom, and he did not want to be associated too closely with what was turning out to be, in Marlene's own words, a farce. "I'll allow it." Marlene thought the look on Abt's face was worth a month's pay.

Marlene asked the question again. The answer was no.

"Why not, Doctor?"

"There was no indication that the body had been abused postmortem."

"Weren't you told that the baby had been found in a Dumpster under a load of junk?"

"No, I was told that the baby had been found in a motel room." Startled murmurs from the jury. An angry gavel. Nothing further.

Maryanne Bollinger stepped off the stand. Abt declined redirect. It didn't matter. Cyrus Wohler and Samuel Chapin would tear her testimony to shreds. Chapin himself had done over four hundred neonate autopsies, and Wohler had been president of the American Board of Pathology. Maryanne Bolliger would have to wear a paper bag over her head.

That was the day in court. Afterward, Mike Brewster and several of the large persons in his employ ushered the Goldfarb family, their two attorneys, and one attorney's daughter, through the gibbering horde of journalists that surrounded the Wilmington courthouse and spilled out onto Rodney Square. (Judge Shearing's gag order was still in effect, although the jury was sequestered, and the press was desperate for commentary; they were talking to courthouse janitors and second cousins of the principals.) Brewster had acquired a big van with smoked windows, and in this they drove back to Mt. Holly, all except Marlene, who took daughter and dog in her Volvo.

At the Goldfarbs' home there was a marked contrast between the mood of the legal team, which was elation, and that of their clients, which remained low. Marlene introduced Sarah to Lucy, who tried to engage her in conversation, but only got weak smiles and short answers. It was hard to judge how much of the senior Goldfarbs' lassitude was due to the medication they were taking, but Sarah herself was clearly depressed. The hostess part of Selma's brain still functioned, and there were coffee and pastries, but the mood was that of a failed dinner party. Marlene felt her mood turning to irritation. She seized upon an opportunity to get Sarah alone in the kitchen, where she had gone to refill a coffee urn.

"We need to talk, kid," said Marlene. The kitchen in which they stood reflected the prevailing mood of the house. It was no longer the spotless shrine she had seen on her first visit. Sticky stains were on the floor in front of the refrigerator, and the stove had not been wiped down in a while. Sarah stood with her two hands on the edge of the sink, leaning, head hanging, as if she were thinking about going down the Disposal.

"About what?"

"You. About what's going on. What *is* going on? I explained to you we had a great day in court today. I knew their case was weak, but in my wildest dreams I never thought they'd show so badly. Abt is a patzer. Shearing sees which way the wind is blowing. He knows the tide has turned in the press. You're not a monster anymore. If anything, you're a tragic figure. Their case is dead, and when I get Peter J. on the stand tomorrow, it'll be another nail in the coffin. And we're not even up to bat, yet. We have a medical team that'll make Maryanne look like someone who just failed the Girl Scout first-aid course. But you can't sit in court like a walking corpse. Every time something dramatic happens on the stand, the whole jury looks at you, to see how you're taking it. But when I was tearing up Bollinger, you looked like you were going to burst into tears. So what's wrong?"

Shrug. "I'm sorry," in a whispery voice. "I'm just tired."

"*Everyone's* tired, Sarah," said Marlene, trying to keep the irritation from her voice. "But this is the home stretch. A couple more days and this'll be over and you can sleep for a month. I know *I* will."

This sally brought no response. Marlene resisted the urge to shake her. The girl bumbled around the kitchen like a somnambulist. A cup fell to the floor and shattered. Sarah sagged against the refrigerator and closed her eyes, from which slow, fat tears leaked.

At that moment, Lucy entered. "What happened?"

"Sarah broke a cup," said Marlene, and placed a hand on her client's shoulder. "Sarah, it's all right. We're doing great. Perk up!"

Lucy grabbed a sponge and a paper towel and swept up the broken crockery. When she had dumped it in the trash, she said to Sarah, "Let's go to your room and talk."

Sarah stared at her for a moment. Then she smiled and said, "Okay," and the two girls walked off, leaving Marlene dumbfounded. Upon instant reflection, however, she understood. Sarah, who had been an intensely social creature, a club member, a volunteer, a cheerleader, had been cut off from the company of her peers for over a year, except, of course, for the despicable Peter, and the subject of intense and often hostile attention by the adult world. The chance to talk with a normal (ha!) teenager must have seemed like a cold compress on a fevered brow. Marlene wondered what they would find to talk about.

At first, not much. Mutual acquaintances were nonexistent, of course, and the usual topics discussed by the young seemed absurdly trivial given the circumstances. The only thing they had in common, besides approximate age and their sex, was Marlene, so they discussed her, at some length, sitting on the bed, among the stuffed toys. Lucy provided a number of anecdotes about her parent's past behavior that made her listener goggle, gasp, and eventually, laugh.

"It must be great having a mother like that," Sarah said. "I never met anyone like her before. She's like . . . someone in a movie. Bigger than regular people."

"Well, it's sure *interesting* being her kid," said Lucy, "but it's also a full-time job. Sometimes I feel like I'm *her* mother."

"I never felt like that with mine," said Sarah with an almost wistful air. "My mom was always, like, *gigantic* to me. God and my mom were in charge, except maybe my mom knew a little more. If *she'd* made the world, there wouldn't be so many messy parts. And while I was, you know, pregnant, every day I waited for my mom to sit down with me and say, 'Okay, I know you're pregnant, here's what you have to do.' I really waited for that. But it didn't happen. Toothpaste back in the tube."

"Come again?"

"Oh, an expression. When I was around six, I squeezed all the toothpaste out of a fresh tube into the sink, and I got scared my mom would yell at me, so I tried to put it all back in with a teaspoon. My one recorded act of naughtiness. It became an expression around here for something that couldn't be fixed. Cute. But I was thinking about how I was, I mean back when this all happened. How can I ever squeeze myself back into that tube? I think, oh my God! In court today, when they were describing what I did, I was thinking, God, I actually *did* do that! I got pregnant, and I wouldn't go to the doctor, I was afraid my mother would find out. Eighteen, and I was afraid my mother would find out! And that person's dead, that me, and it's killing my parents, because that's the person they want, little Sarah sweet and mild, they don't want *me*. Whoever I am."

"They still love you."

"Yeah, I guess. Whatever love is. Peter said he loved me, too. My friends. You know, nobody's called me, ever. It was like I dropped off the earth, like I didn't exist. My mom wants me to confess to something I didn't do, manslaughter, just to get this over with. 'It's just words, Sarah, say the words, and it'll be over, and you can get back to normal life.' That's what she says. She can't understand why I can't. I mean, there's no me left except that, what really happened, the truth. She wants me to make that into nothing, too, so that . . . I don't know, we can go back to how it was, she planning everything for me, buying my clothes, taking me to the doctor. Tooth-paste back in the tube. And your mother wants me to perk up." Sarah threw herself facedown on her bed and pulled a pillow over her head.

Lucy said, "In general, we must not wish for the disappearance of any of our troubles, but for grace to transform them."

There was a pause, and then Sarah rolled over and asked, "What?"

Lucy repeated what she had said, and Sarah asked, "What does that mean?"

"Oh, it's advice on what to pray for. Simone Weil said it, not me." Lucy felt a blush arrive on her cheek. "It's a religious thing. If you're afflicted, like if you're really sick, you're not supposed to pray for the relief of the affliction, you're supposed to pray for the grace to turn the suffering into greater openness to God. That's the *point* of earthly life, and the point of suffering."

"You're religious?" A tint of amazement here, as in, *You have two belly buttons?*

"Extremely. Boringly. Are you?"

"I used to be." Sarah laughed bitterly. "I wrote a letter to God. They presented it today as evidence that I was planning to get rid of my baby. I said, 'Please, God, help me stop this from happening.' But He didn't, so . . . I don't know anymore."

"The vending-machine model of God. I'll be good, I'll do anything You want, God, just let me pass math. Just let this boy fall in love with me. Just don't let my dad die. It doesn't work so you kick the machine and move on to the next one. Or none. Or it does work, and then you become a nut. Simone Weil says, though, that God sends affliction without distinction to the wicked and the good, just as He sends the rain and the sunlight. Let me think how the rest of it goes. Oh, yeah, He did not reserve the cross for Christ. He enters into contact with a human individual as such only through spiritual grace, which responds to the gaze turned toward Him, which is to say, to the exact extent that the individual ceases to be an individual. No event is a favor on the part of God, only grace is that."

"Who's Simone Weil?"

"A French Jew. She escaped from the Nazis but she died because she didn't want to eat anything more than the Nazis were feeding their slave laborers. So she starved."

"God! But she became a Christian?"

"No, she never did. She didn't think she should join the church because she thought her spiritual work lay outside it. They called her the apostle to the atheists. I have her book with me if you want to read it."

"I'd rather hear it from you. What else did

she say about suffering?"

"A lot. It's a long story, really."

"That's okay," said Sarah. "I have a lot of time."

Downstairs, the phone rang. Only desultory conversation was going on in the living room, and they all stopped and waited for the machine to pick up and for the caller to announce his business. It had been a long, long time since a call was picked up unscreened at the Goldfarbs'. It was a woman, who announced herself as Jason Abt's secretary, and could Ms. Goldfarb or her attorney call back as soon . . .

Selma picked up the phone then and handed it to Marlene, who spoke into it for a minute or so and then hung up. "Abt wants to see me now, the pig."

"They want a deal," said Mulcahey jubilantly. "Are we going?"

"I said I'd get right back to them. Let them sweat a little for a change."

"It has to be better than they gave him," said Mrs. Goldfarb, now forgetting that she had demanded Marlene agree to one very much worse.

"Oh, it has to be a lot better than that, Selma, now that they've taken their best shot and the whole world has seen it's a cream puff. I want a dismissal."

"Really?" asked Selma, a little spark of hope glimmering in her eye. "Do you think that's possible?"

"I think it's likely. I think it's all over but the shouting, folks." Marlene picked up the phone and dialed.

The state's attorney's office was nearly deserted when Marlene and Mulcahey arrived, the press gone, only a few scattered employees in the halls, who looked at her curiously as she went by. Yes, she was famous in Wilmington, her girlhood dream.

Abt was waiting for her with one of his assistants, a plain young woman in a kelly-green suit and a depressed, sulky look. Abt was on the phone when they walked in, and he gestured to chairs as he talked or, rather, listened mostly. He was grave as he hung up and faced them.

"Let's not beat around the bush, Ms. Ciampi. I've been authorized to modify the terms of the offer we made to you some weeks ago."

Marlene stared at him, saying nothing. He returned the stare for a long moment. She had to give him credit — the arrogant prick was playing it well for someone who had hardly any cards. He was, she saw, far more comfortable making deals than standing up in court. Abt continued, "We're prepared now to offer the same plea bargain given to Peter Jorgensen. Negligent homicide, twenty-six weeks in minimum security, time served to count against."

"You're serious?"

"Yes. We think that's fair, given the current situation."

"No, it might have been fair a year and a half ago. It might even have been fair when you cut that deal with Peter Jorgensen. Now, however, it's absurd, because 'the current situation,' as you so delicately put it, is that I'm about to cream your ass in open court. You haven't even demonstrated the underlying crime. There was in fact no homicide."

"I beg to differ. The infant died as a result of your client's negligence in not seeking medical care."

"Oh, that's an interesting take, Mr. Abt. You know, in some other states they've taken to defining crimes in writing. I think they call them laws. I guess Delaware hasn't gotten around to that yet, which is peculiar, because, as you so often advertise, you're the First State. What are you going to do, lock up all the Christian Scientists? All the people who don't like doctors and deliver at home?"

"You're offensive, Ms. Ciampi."

"Oh, no, I was being nice. This is offensive: you miserable, cruel, irresponsible man! You stupid, incompetent nincompoop! Have you any idea how much pain and suffering you've caused to a perfectly decent kid and her family? You've known for months that Sarah Goldfarb was not a murderess. You've known for months that you couldn't possibly prevail in court, and yet you persisted, in the face of the evidence, in the face of all human decency and honor. And why? Because your office wanted some petty political advantage. Because you sold your public trust for . . . what? To be in the state senate of Delaware? To be the next attorney fucking general of this miserable slab of sand? Those skinheads I beat up at least have an excuse — they're uneducated morons, but you, for Christ's sake, have a law school diploma hanging on your wall. You obscene toad! You're a disgrace and a shame to every decent public prosecutor in the country."

Marlene said this in a conversational tone, without histrionics, but despite this, or perhaps because of it, her words had a devastating effect. Abt had gone white around the lips; his eyes were bulging even more than they usually did, and his hands were clenched in knotty fists on his desk. No one had ever spoken to him like this before, although the attorney general had been fairly vivid earlier on the phone.

Marlene rose in the shocked silence. "Take your deal and shove it, sir. Come on, Kevin. See you in court, counselor."

They were nearly at the door before Abt said, "Wait!" in a choked voice.

"What?" said Marlene, still facing the door.

"I've, ah, been authorized to accept any . . . whatever. Whatever you want. She, the attorney general, she wants to stop the trial."

Marlene turned. "You want to stop the trial, sir, you can dismiss the charges."

"I can't do that. There has to be a plea. Sixty days, minimum security, youthful offender status, record to be expunged at age twenty-one."

Marlene walked out without another word, with Mulcahey behind her. When the door had closed, in the deserted hallway, she leaped into the air, clicked her heels, and planted on Mulcahey's mouth a chaste, but not too chaste, kiss.

She was still elated when she marched into the Goldfarbs' living room a little later, holding both arms above her head, V-fingered like Nixon, grinning like a maniac.

"What happened?" cried Selma Goldfarb.

"Victory!" yelled Marlene. "The bad guys

crumpled. Abt was practically on his knees begging for a deal."

"What did he say? What did he say?" demanded Mr. Goldfarb, color appearing in his cheeks for the first time in weeks.

Marlene told the story, waiting for applause as she repeated her excoriation of the state's attorney, and getting it from everyone, except, oddly, Sarah herself, who sat between her parents, silent, listening.

"Oh, thank God! Thank God!" said Selma, tears flowing, as she embraced her daughter. "It's over, baby. No more trial. Sixty days is nothing! And no criminal record!" And to Marlene: "You said we'd take it? Is that it, or do we have to sign something?"

The smile froze on Marlene's face. "Um, Selma, maybe I wasn't clear. We don't have to deal with him at all. We're going for acquittal. Sarah is going to walk out of that courtroom a free woman. Zero days."

"You turned that down?" Selma shouted. "Are you crazy? My daughter is on trial for her *life* and you turned down sixty days?"

Marlene faked looking wildly around her. "Excuse me, is there something wrong with the acoustics here? I just explained that a deal like that *means* they have no hope of conviction at all. None. It was all a bluff and we called it and now they're just trying to save a little face. Do you want to give those bastards that comfort after what they did to your daughter? Or do you want to sit back and watch me dance on their heads? Don't you want to see Peter Jorgensen exposed as a liar and a son of a bitch?"

There was a silence then, into which Sarah Goldfarb dropped a single word.

"No."

Marlene stared at her. The girl looked somehow different than she had earlier. She was sitting up straighter. There seemed to be more bone in her face, and in her eyes there was more pain, but less fear.

"No? Sarah, what are you talking, no?"

"I mean no, there's no reason to drag this out anymore. I'm not interested in punishing Peter or Abt or anyone else. And I'm not . . . I mean it's not right that I should walk away from this like I had nothing to do with any of it. I'm not guilty of murder like they said, but I'm not innocent, either. God placed a human life in my care and I let it die because I was afraid to go to a doctor . . ."

"Sarah, come on," said Marlene, "you can't tell if that's true."

"Let me finish, Marlene! The fact is, I was afraid. I was a moral coward. I could have said, 'No, I can't have a baby now,' and gotten an abortion when it was hardly anything

675

at all, and taken whatever guilt is connected to that, or I could have gone and gotten treatment and then the baby might've been all right, but I'll never know that, I was too chicken to do either one. And I brought all this horrible stuff down on my family, all this suffering."

"It's not your fault," said Marlene. "The state had no business —"

"Please! Yes, they were wrong, but I let them . . . I gave them the occasion. So whether it's a crime or not, it's a sin of omission. Today in court, when they were talking about the medical stuff, the autopsy and all, it hit me for the first time that he was a human being, my child, not just a *problem* for me and Peter, he was a human being, just like I am. And, to go on with my life, after this, and, you know, I can't ever be like I was back then, there has to be *something*, an expiation. It wasn't just *littering*, my son ending up in a trash can. I have to stand up in court and say, 'Yes, I was negligent,' and suffer the consequences, and go through penitence." Sarah cleared her throat and looked directly at Marlene and said, "So, Marlene, I'm directing you, as my attorney, to accept the plea bargain Mr. Abt just offered."

Marlene looked around at all the faces in turn — the Goldfarb family, Brewster, his big boys, Mulcahey, Lucy. They all looked moved. They were nodding their heads. They all looked mildly surprised, too. All except Lucy.

Later, driving back with Lucy in the Volvo, Marlene realigned her deranged emotions and took stock. She was somewhat pleased with herself that she had not done anything unforgivably awful at the Goldfarbs'. She thought she had exercised lawyerly self-control. She had not punched out her client. This was a moral advance. Perhaps some of her fury had been dissipated in Abt's office, where it belonged. Perhaps she was successfully making the transition from actual to metaphorical combat. Still, something rankled, something about the language Sarah had used. Sin of omission. Expiation. Penitence. Marlene doubted that these concepts had figured in Sarah's former vocabulary. Someone had given the girl a quick course in moral calculus, and there was only one likely suspect.

Lucy reached into her bag and brought out a Steiff stuffed tiger. "Sarah gave me this as a memento. Her dad gave it to her when she got out of jail. Symbolic of something, I guess."

"I guess. What did you give *her*, Lucy?"

"Give . . . ?"

"Yeah. That Frankenstein scene back there, where the little mouse tells me to shove it. I've been building up the kid to stand up to her mom all these weeks, and then she turns on me. What, did you convert her in two hours?"

"I just gave her some language, Mom. She was sad and groping. She had the feelings but no semantic boxes to put them in. Whatever you think about the Church, you can't deny it's been developing analytic moral language for two thousand years. We just talked about good and evil and suffering, and we read some Simone Weil. And she had an epiphany. It happens. Are you mad at me?"

"Aside from a single moment of blinding murderous rage? No, I'm not. I just have to remember to keep out of your way when I'm planning to exercise my numerous vices."

Back at Blueball Plaza, Lucy said to her mother, "Look at this. Moussa gave it to me just before I got on the train."

It was a small ebony box. Inside, set on a lining of green leather, was a miniature desk in Louis XV style, like furniture for a doll's house, but a doll's house in heaven, exquisitely crafted, with working drawers and drop front, and actual tiny marquetry panels.

"It's gorgeous!" exclaimed Marlene. "Did he make this?"

"Yes, but a while ago. It was for his daughter, but he gave it to me. He's a nice man. He reminds me a little of Tran, but peaceful, not violent. He has the same calm. Maybe Tran would've been like that if it hadn't been for the war."

"Maybe. Well, another memento of your goodness. It'll have a place next to the stuffed tiger when they build your shrine."

"Mom . . ."

"Sorry. My flourishing hidden tree is not so hidden anymore. You know I love you."

They embraced warmly, and Marlene discovered with something of a shock that her girl was nearly two inches taller than she herself was.

"I have to call your father," said Marlene.

"Give him my love."

"I will." Marlene dialed.

He answered, picking up after she spoke into the answering machine. "How are you? The news said the trial went pretty much your way. Way to go, babe!"

"I'm okay, I guess. There is further news, however." She told him of the evening's events.

" 'Obscene toad' is good," said Karp. "I'll

679

have to remember that. You don't sound like you're celebrating."

"Oh, I wanted to *win*, Butch! I wanted to hear the foreman say, 'We find the defendant, Sarah Louise Goldfarb, not guilty.' I wanted to be the star. And I wanted to crush them, grind their faces in it. Don't you feel that way?"

"Mm. Maybe a little less than formerly. Maybe it's the bad influence of our daughter. This Bustamente case — the same issues, really, and maybe even Maxwell. The right thing to do doesn't always coincide with the classic win-lose. And even though I *know* that, it still rankles. It's my training and the movies — crime, chase, apprehension, punishment, and usually the really bad villains get offed by the heroes in single combat, no boring trials and appeals. It's all over in two hours and highly satisfying, which is why we all hate defense attorneys like you, clouding our simple brains with ambiguities and technicalities."

"Except when we defend the innocent, which I, for one, always intend to do, ha ha. How're the boys?"

"Terrific. Posie came back."

"What!"

"Yeah, last night, with a big shiner and two plastic trash bags full of stuff. Still with the long *schmatte*, though. Apparently, she didn't

understand some of the finer points of traditional Arab family life, such as that she's the
slave of the mother-in-law and gets beaten
when she doesn't do right. The short version
is she got beat, she coldcocked the old lady,
and Walid pounded her. So the *shiddach* is
off. The twins were peeing in their pants they
were so happy."

"Gosh, what news! It looks like I no longer
have an excuse not to do law."

"Gulp."

"What? Oh, you mean, if I practice criminal
law in Manhattan, I might tromp on your
darling little piggies?"

"The thought had occurred."

"I could go back to . . ."

"Yeah, and I could study to be a Jesuit
priest and . . ."

"All right, it's a deal — God, the heavens
would have to be forever realigned."

"You know, Marlene, that might not be
such a bad idea."

The employees of Thorndike Press hope you have enjoyed this Large Print book. All our Large Print titles are designed for easy reading, and all our books are made to last. Other Thorndike Press Large Print books are available at your library, through selected bookstores, or directly from the publishers.

For more information about titles, please call:

(800) 223-1244
(800) 223-6121

To share your comments, please write:

Publisher
Thorndike Press
P.O. Box 159
Thorndike, Maine 04986